Fiona Pardington, *Uncanny Tui/Kakahu*, 2008

BLACK MARKS ON THE WHITE PAGE

EDITED BY

WITI IHIMAERA & TINA MAKERETI

VINTAGE

VINTAGE

UK | USA | Canada | Ireland | Australia
India | New Zealand | South Africa | China

Vintage is an imprint of the Penguin Random House group of companies, whose addresses
can be found at global.penguinrandomhouse.com.

Penguin
Random House
New Zealand

First published by Penguin Random House New Zealand, 2017

3 5 7 9 10 8 6 4

Design by Kate Barraclough © Penguin Random House New Zealand
Cover art by James Ormsby
Prepress by Image Centre Group
Printed and bound in China by RR Donnelley Asia Printing Solutions Ltd

A catalogue record for this book is available from the National Library of New Zealand.

ISBN 978-0-14377-029-9
eISBN 978-0-14377-030-5

The assistance of Creative New Zealand towards the production of this book is
gratefully acknowledged by the editors and publisher. Our grateful thanks also
to the Tautai Trust and the Tautai Fetu Ta'i patrons for support to the Pasifika
visual artists whose work appears in the anthology.

penguin.co.nz

For all who walk, carve, talk, dance, chant,
paint and sing the Pacific into the future

A talanoa awaits you

Welcome — join the kōrero

CONTENTS

INTRODUCTION

STONES MOVE, WHALE BONES rise out of the ground like cities, a man figures out how to raise seven daughters alone. Sometimes gods speak, sometimes we find ourselves in a not-too-distant future. Here are the glorious, painful, sharp and funny stories of Māori and Pasifika writers from all over the world, and one guest Aboriginal writer whose presence asks us to rethink the boundaries we have set up between ourselves and our neighbours, literal and figurative. The editors collected this work from their location in Aotearoa New Zealand, but this is an Oceanic collection. It crosses the borders that have been constructed between nations, genres, languages and between ways of seeing. By making these Black Marks on the White Page, we redraw the map, rewrite the histories, connect lines across globes that were constructed in the last century, or the one before.

We admire the writers collected here for their work as artists and their individual points of view as fiction writers. Some of them we know not just as writers but also as essayists, teachers of creative writing, reviewers, commentators and opinion makers; not only do they talk the talk, they walk it. Consciously or unconsciously, their work embodies the disruptive act that Māori, Pasifika and Aboriginal writing constitutes in the worldwide literary landscape — still the page is white, and still the marks we make upon it are radical acts of transgression, of forcing others to see us in all our complexity and wonder.

WE BRING OUR DIVERSE range of writers together as a talanoa, a conversation, and we are grateful that most were able to accept our invitation. The talanoa is a place that one of our contributors, Jione Havea, would characterise as existing in many dimensions, not just in space but in time. We particularly honour Patricia Grace, Albert Wendt, Alexis Wright and Déwé Gorodé at our gathering. They are our elders who, together, represent different communities. Patricia Grace has given us a previously unpublished short story; Déwé Gorodé's extract from *The Wreck* is translated from the original French; Alexis Wright has offered a chapter from her new novel; and Albert Wendt is represented by an extract from his verse novel *The Adventures of Vela,* which won a Commonwealth Writers' Prize for Best Book in 2010. We are moved that their writing continues to celebrate the survival of the alternate imagination.

Along with Albert Wendt and Witi Ihimaera, we have assembled other Commonwealth Writers: Sia Figiel, who won the South East Asia and South Pacific Prize for *Where We Once Belonged* in 1997; Mary Rokonadravu, who won the Pacific regional Short Story Prize for 'Famished Eels' in 2015; and Tina Makereti, who won that same prize for 'Black Milk' in 2016.

We welcome new and vibrant voices to the talanoa, like Nic Low, and Gina Cole, whose anthology of short stories was published in 2016. Present also are the evocative voices and talents coming out of creative writing classes — writers like Anahera Gildea and Kelly Joseph. Our youngest writer is Anya Ngawhare, whose exploration of youthful male sexuality is an extract from a soon-to-be-completed novel. Dramatists like Victor Rodger and David Geary bring a different formal background to fiction that invigorates and charges it.

WHAT WE HOPED FOR, and what our writers delivered, was to go beyond the edges of what is expected from Oceanic writing. First boundary: where we live. Māori are a Pacific people, but when we talk about Pasifika writing this does not generally include Māori writing. Aotearoa is a group of islands in the Pacific, but we usually don't think of ourselves as islanders. For too long we have all been thinking within boxes constructed by old theoretical maps. In *Black Marks on the White Page* we have taken a more inclusive approach: we wanted to remember our kinship in the wider Pacific.

Black Marks on the White Page creates a new star map, a new navigator's chart. It draws its original template from the Pacific Ocean as our continent, as remembered in Epeli Hau'ofa's 'The Ocean in Us', Albert Wendt's 'Towards A New Oceania', and Alice Te Punga Somerville's *Once Were Pacific*. Our commonalities are more stimulating than our differences; we find ourselves in the same waka when it comes to literature. So *Black Marks* contains work from all over the Pacific: as far north as Canada, as far west as Australia, as far south as New Zealand, with Hawai'i, Fiji, Samoa, New Caledonia and Tuvalu at the centre.

Some of the main beneficiaries will be the contributors to the talanoa. We need not live in a Māori or Pasifika or Aboriginal bubble. In greeting each other — we belong to the same community — we can use our synergy to create new ways of looking and working.

OUR SECOND BOUNDARY: what we write. All writers are subject to preconceived ideas regarding who we write *like*, but for Māori writers, writers from the Pacific, Indigenous writers and writers of colour, the preconceptions can become widely held stereotypes. Even though we sometimes bemoan the scarcity of an Oceanic fiction that looks like us, smells like us, walks like us and therefore must *be* us, none of us should be constrained by any sense of what we're supposed to look or sound like. Creativity doesn't live there. There must be no compulsion to write in any particular way about any particular topics, outside of the writer's own creative project. So, whether our work is motivated by whakapapa or by European form, in this volume we can be confident that what our writers write about is endlessly diverse, crossing not only boundaries, but subjects, genres and approaches.

We head into the political arena in the work of David Geary, Déwé Gorodé, Nic Low and Michael Puleloa, and it is revealing how often political thought is associated with the shifting of stone. Low also takes us into a dystopic future where Facebook is a thing of the past, and Bryan Kamaoli Kuwada takes us along a Kānaka Maoli-Steampunk alternate timeline. We would have been very happy to see more experiments with Indigenous imaginings of the future. On the other side of the same coin, mythology and history inform the work of many writers such as Alexis Wright and Mary Rokonadravu, perhaps giving rise to the notion that the Oceanic present is infused with both the past and the future.

Some of our most beautiful, subversive and shocking work arises when we write about sex and sexuality, as do Sia Figiel, Anya Ngawhare, Victor Rodger, Tusiata Avia and Albert Wendt. The shock is not that we write about such things so frankly, but that such work still constitutes subversive writing, and that our stories about sex and sexuality still contain experiences of sometimes violent sanction.

Perhaps at the other end of this scale is work that slips quietly under our noses simply by presenting the lives of ordinary people, at the same time challenging our understandings about the way things are. We're excited to include a new story by Patricia Grace, the pioneer of this 'radical ordinariness', exemplified also in the work of Kelly Ana Morey and Kelly Joseph. These narratives get under our skin with as much tenacity as their flashy brothers who experiment with form.

OUR THIRD BOUNDARY: *how* we write. Experiments in voice abound in the work of Cassandra Barnett, or Anahera Gildea, who establishes a successful collective first person narrative. This is an approach that students of creative writing often express an interest in. Reading work from Jione Havea, Serie Barford, Paula Morris and Witi Ihimaera, we might ask: is it fiction or non-fiction? Does it matter? Or, at least, how much are they one and the same? We suspect that the collisions and intersections of contemporary Oceanic lives with literary techniques are enabling our writers to go into rooms hitherto unexplored. There, some interesting encounters allow genre to bend as in, say, Courtney Sina Meredith's work, or that of Albert Wendt and Selina Tusitala Marsh. Similarly, several writers sent us poetry even though we asked for fiction. When we asked Courtney Sina Meredith about the 'form' of one piece, she sent us virtual laughter: *I don't know,* she said, *I think it's in the va.* Perhaps the division between different forms — fiction, creative non-fiction and poetry — doesn't necessarily make sense to an Indigenous Oceanic world view. Words | stories | art | songs | dance | mythologies | ancestors | film | contemporary life | poetry — these may all exist in the same moment, in the same space, and none of it is untrue.

Simply put, *Black Marks on the White Page* demonstrates stylistic innovation that comes from the border crossings that many of our writers are making between literature and theatre (opera, dance, play, musical theatre), literature and film (television, feature film, short film, video installation, gaming), books and other literature platforms (blogs, Twitter, iPhones and other digital screens), the various genres of literature (poetry, non-fiction, essay, long-form story) and, in particular, between literature and visual art. In *Black Marks on the White Page* we therefore offer a portfolio of work by such artists as Fiona Pardington, whose work deeply influenced Tina Makereti's 'Black Milk'. Cassandra Barnett's piece references Alex Monteith's digital artwork and shows the kinds of experimentation that can take place when the art and writing worlds intersect. Witi Ihimaera's 'Whakapapa of a Wallpaper: A chimerical fiction' comes from the catalogue for Lisa Reihana's Venice Biennale show *Emissaries*. James Ormsby's remarkable cover illustration exemplifies the kaupapa of our volume in visual language that draws from our complex, diverse and rich histories and cultures.

At the talanoa, the stories do the talking. This work comes from the ten-year window since 2007, and we hope the juxtaposition of the stories within excites you. These are stories that expand our world aesthetically, politically, linguistically and culturally. At the 2016 Te Hā Māori Writers Hui we talked about writing ourselves into existence. We talked about how writing has always been a subversive act for us, from the moment each one of us learnt about the power of the pen. Sometimes there have been black marks against us for our writing. This book provides only a taste of the abundance offered up by Te Moananui-a-Kiwa — our great Pacific. It is up to us — it has always been up to us — to keep carrying this medium that we have loved from the first moment it landed in Aotearoa and elsewhere, and to make it our own. To make our own Black Marks on the White Page.

A NOTE ON IMAGES

THE FIRST TIME I saw Pati Solomona Tyrell's work was at Fresh Gallery in Otara last year. The image was like a portal to another world, its colours saturated by night and desire and the youthful swagger of its subjects, whose eyes issued a challenge and invitation. They were the Fafswag Collective, creators of the legendary Fafswag Ball. I walked around the gallery, seeing a lot of exciting work, but Tyrell's image called me back to it.

I can remember the first times I encountered all the artists in this volume: Fiona Pardington's black and white visions in books at high school — we were all obsessed with her images — then in 2015 at City Gallery in Wellington. Yuki Kihara's extraordinary imagery in *Landfall* journal, and many places since. Lisa Reihana's astonishing *in Pursuit of Venus [infected]* online, but also the earlier iconic gateway at Te Papa. Robert Jahnke's 3D dexterous manipulations of word and symbol, first in metal at Massey University in the 1990s, then in fluorescent tube lights at Pataka Gallery, Porirua 2016. Shane Hansen's clever graphics on greeting cards in a gift shop. James Ormsby's delicate linework at Pataka again. Rosanna Raymond's exquisite tableaus in various publications. Cerisse Palalagi's playful *poly*phonics on Tautai's website. Each of these encounters was marked by searing recognition, a gut-kick of wonder, the curling back of mystery. We are drawn to revisit these images because they represent fresh and significant ways of seeing ourselves.

This is also what we see in the stories presented in this anthology.

Witi and I were keen that this collection should recognise the many ways narrative is expressed in the Pacific, to establish our collection of stories within the context of a wider conversation. We're keen also to acknowledge the deep relationship between visual and literary storytelling forms. We are only able to present a very small sample of visual works here, but the juxtaposition of Oceanic art and writing is so exciting we hope that, like us, you will continue to seek out these portals to other worlds inside our own.

TINA MAKERETI

Pati Solomona Tyrell, *FA'AAFA*, 2015, still from video work

CICADA CINGULATA: THE BIRD OF REHUA

ANAHERA GILDEA

WE HATE BLOWFLIES. THEIR fat glossy eyes, green and blue, come to drone through the summer of our houses. Mean and heavy. Make noise like the tarakihi instead, girl; train your ear to their clacking applause, singing with voices like the roaring rain, we say, calling for mates from between the leaves.

We see the dog. We see him come round the back of the house. We see him. Lolling panting hound wolf. Hound of god. Nah that old kurī been here for donkeys, we say. Mangy beast. Bloody dog animal. We don't like your dog, girl. Dangerous teeth. Hazard. Bloody hazard. Our kōtiro chooses tāne like dogs. Wild boy men. Pretend heart. Savage.

Our girl loves church. That Jesus. Her best tāne, all the kuia say. Rubbish. Rubbish, say the koro. Rubbish, say the whaea. Leave all those kurī behind. Sing your big song, girl. Listen to the cicada; make your voice loud, girl, loud.

Jesus didn't put that pēpe in there. Get off your knees.

SHE LEFT HIM. KAWHENA with her rolling gait and massive puku, walked away from her ahi kā and her tāne and her kāinga. For herself she could do nothing, but for her baby she could raze heaven.

Make noise, Kawhena, whisper the kuia. Pātere start small. The drumming? Safe. We say. Safe Pēpe. She's going to change the world, this girl.

She carried us inside, from the flanks of Ruapehu up to Tāmaki-makaurau on the overnight flyer. Her phone lit up, over and over, the whole way so that she barely slept. She thought about hiffing it out the window but there was no money for a new one. Her parents, Nick, her friends, all calling and calling. The bus stopped under the Sky Tower and she had nowhere to go. In the toilets she washed her face. She had a month or so before the baby would come and that meant she had to find a place to stay. Her duffel bag was heavy. She put it on to balance out the weight of her stomach, and turned toward K'road. It was going to be a hot one. The few trees she passed were already alive with the tympani of cicadas. At home she used to lie on her bed and listen to them through the open window. Make noise, Kawhena, they'd say.

HE HAD SEDUCED HER. Or she had seduced him. Or both. In Korea. Nick was there teaching English too. From her home town. Turned out it was common to go overseas and meet someone from right where you left. K'road reminded her of Itaewon. Dirty streets perfumed with a strange combination of seaweed and steak. Vendors in their dozens, hawking and disdainful because here in the American quarter you were probably associated with GIs, and everyone hates someone.

She would wander like a kite whose string was uncertain and if pulled tight may not hold. She could hide here but still make noise, throw her voice like the ventriloquist cicada. Throwing her voice so no one could tell where she was standing, where she rubbed her legs together from, nor her wings. She felt stupidly free.

She walked in the wet heat with a singlet on, and an umbrella. She liked the feeling of a moist tongue on her skin, the way lovers feel from sweating after sex. Like that. Rise up, Kawhena, she heard. Sing. The smell was cos of the heat. Cos of rotting cabbage. And people. And smoke. And the clinging tang of alcohol.

The prostitutes in Itaewon looked like they were straight out of a movie; hanging on the door jambs of their rooms in narrow crooked streets, eyeing each passer-by for the hint of cash and the fuck-eye — music and incense eking out — as if either of those snake charms would entice the lonely. Those things are really for the ashamed and the secretive. The lonely don't care.

She took Nick's hands and led him into the night. Everything comes out at night. Creatures from behind their screens, critters, like the roaches that infested her building, come out to eat, to find a glass of soju, and she had come out with them. Twenty-three years she'd been underground. Longer than most. She came out to be with others, to smell their feral smells, to sweat with them. Everyone lost things here: their wallets, their dignity, their hearts.

The leaves underneath them were damp and soft beneath her bare knees and then her naked back. As though she was being massaged. As though she was being loved from the ground up. From the earth up. Even on the driest of summer days she could detect the wet beneath her. She could smell moisture. You are the rain, Kawhena, she heard. They said. When a tree shed a leaf she could smell moisture leaving it. The wind and sun taking its life second by second. Sending it back to te pō.

Her rhythm when on top of him was slow and uncomplicated; maybe it was the heat, or the liquor, or love. It can take a year for a single leaf to pass. We keep vigil for our girl, whisper the whaea. Broken tiny. Pieces, tiny bones. We watch. Shhh. Sometimes when she had sex she felt used up like those leaves. Fallen. Threads of memory where the flesh of the plant had disintegrated and nothing but the whispery skeleton remained. Women are low to the ground, her mother had told her. Hine-ahu-one. They hug it and sniff it, beating their chests and letting their blood run out of them in their monthly grief. Better that than babies, she said. Not better than babies, we say.

Afterwards, she lay talking with him. They were both passionate about the Treaty. About poverty. About changing the world. When they got back to New Zealand they would make a difference. They would clatter and clamour. They would smack their wings against the branches of trees. Under that foreign liquid sky, everything was possible; a noiseless, colourless space, so massive it felt like anyone could start again.

THE CHURCH ROSE UP in front of her as if it were a beacon. That Jesus, we say. She loves him. Years of wooden pews and rosary beads flooded her memory. The stained glass windows of her childhood were repeated here, throwing a kaleidoscope of colours and feelings onto the floor. It had been too long since she'd prayed, to anyone. To anything. She dipped her fingers in the font, crossed herself as she'd been taught, and sat down.

Perhaps if she hadn't spent the summer singing. Perhaps if she'd kept her legs closed. Impossible, we say. Find your voice. Find your song. He might not have felt trapped. She might not have felt trapped. They didn't even like each other. There were only odd jobs and no money. She wouldn't repeat the cycle. She meant what she said in Korea about doing it differently. About change.

She looked up into the blue eyes of the crucified man on the wall. He looked like Nick. Or Nick looked like him. Dangerous, mutter the koro. Put that dog down. His emaciated body and bleeding hands were supposed to give her comfort. She would sleep here at the foot of this white man for as long as she could. She had no choice.

OUR GIRL PLANNED A water birth. Make noise, Kawhena, we say. Karakia, e koro. Even at eight days overdue she was still hoping for that. Her waters broke first. It doesn't always happen that way. The labour was so long she thought we would never come out. After the first twelve hours she was numb with fighting but still we didn't come. No drugs she had told everyone. No intervention. Listen, we whisper. Hear the koro chant.

Nick-kurī stood guard like a sentry, his eye immediately drawn to anything that looked medical. It was something for him to do instead of watch our mother cry and call out. Where are her women, the whaea growl. The koro are making drums. Bring forth your tāne, Hine-te-iwaiwa. When he came to her she was at a backpackers. Some church set her up. Gave her a food parcel and put her in a box. She rung him and he came.

Kawhena needs to have a caesarean, the doctors said, crowding and measuring and timing. Our kurī father questioned and grilled them. That baby is struggling to come out, they shouted at him. There will be consequences. Come, tāne, come, the koro are loud now. He asked what that meant and would the baby die and what about Kawhena. Haere mai, child. Into the light. He made the decision to not have the caesar and to just continue. They threatened him then. Told him that they would do the operation if the baby was not born in the next hour. They said that the baby was in distress. We are in distress. The doctor looked angry. His beard wobbled even when he wasn't speaking because he was grinding his jaw. They looked similar in that respect — our matua and the doctor — the latter an older whiter version of our father's anger, the both of them warring while our Kawhena moaned and sweated.

Kurī-Nick decided; the hospital and all the doctors were not for us. Sing koro. A breath, e tāne. It was discrimination. He told mum and the midwife they were leaving and even when the midwife protested and told him to calm down he yelled that she could fuck off back to her institution too. Manawa mai, take heart, one breath.

Anxious koro. Loud koro. Make noise, Kawhena, say the kuia. He grabbed mum's suitcase and walked her out with her arm over his shoulder, rescuing her. Big man, shout the whaea.

They made it down the long corridor, wide enough for all the other patients to stop and watch the spectacle — momentarily relieved from their own concerns — as our loyal kurī urged our mother on. We can do this by ourselves, he half yelled, half cried, almost carrying Kawhena by now. He was sweating as if he were the one having labour pains and then, on the lino before the door, our girl fell to her knees and called out for the midwife who had been trailing along behind talking to the muscled back of Nick. She too was crying and afraid.

Nick-kurī father bared his teeth. Cornered hound. Lost dog. His face contorted and he urged our mother again to get up. I'm sorry, he kept saying, let's go back. We can go back, babe. You can make it. But we were somewhere else by then. And Kawhena refused to move. Access your life, e tama. Break forth. The koro turn. Change, the koro chant.

Change, we scream to Kawhena. Now we come. Kawhena hears. Kawhena will have her voice. Several of the doctors including the angry bearded man come to tell the midwife that she needs to move my mother out of the hall and our mother stands up. Back, she roars at them. I don't need any of you. Back. And there on the blue lino, white knuckles holding the perfectly placed handrail, the koro making the blood thrum in her ears, through excruciating push by push, this woman, this whānau, is born.

WE WERE DELIVERED INTO our girl's arms and onto her belly and at her breast. We opened our eyes to the horrible brightness, to tears from Kurī-Nick, and to Kawhena's glazed smile. In the hall they brought blankets and warmed us and gave us a few minutes. Then they brought a wheelchair and wheeled us back into the birthing room before the placenta had even been delivered. And it wasn't until after the placenta came that they looked and found a girl.

Our father spoke like a different man, a whimper voice we had never heard. Hello, my little one, he said. When the iho stopped pulsing he cut it. Now this child is born, say the koro. Now the voice is found, say the kuia. Our mother laughed and Nick-kurī smiled back not minding because all that anger of before had passed.

When the midwife checked us over she didn't find anything wrong, we were already suckling like we'd been doing it forever. Everyone in that room was glowing and exhausted. We felt that. It had nothing to do with our death. If they could've, they would have sensed our smile too.

The midwife could never have known that there was something wrong with our lungs, and then our heart. In the moment before it stopped our girl had handed us over to Nick-kurī and he was nuzzling us and calling us his little one. He was the most gentle man he had ever been in those minutes as he lifted us up and put our cheek to his chest. The koro began again. The winds of change. So that the sound of our kurī's heartbeat could carry us back into the dark.

AT THE GATE, THE eyes of the tekoteko bore down from atop wide arms. The rain came, slashing and ripping the world apart. Here Kawhena would bury the tiny box. Here she would bury everything. She stood in borrowed blacks with Nick at her side. They would carry this child home. This was his tūrangawaewae. Would her dead gather behind her, cluster around, watchful and slightly dangerous, taiaha raised, warriors with one foot cocked back, ready? We are here, we say. Would thick-bodied women blockade the path with song that becomes karanga and tears at you, as if the dead they are calling on exist within you and the whaea are pulling them out tendon by tendon? We will, we say. Would her dead walk towards her with heavy ankles, as though shackles dragged behind them, as though they were the slow prisoners of an army, forced forward to take up their own front line, chins high. We do, we are, we have.

THE MAIHI WELCOME HER. Into the bones we go. Into the womb of Papatūānuku where we do what Māui was unable to. We become immortal. We are not crushed between frightened thighs.

She is not crushed. The rain softens the ground for all the noisy creatures to emerge.

KAWHENA IS ANGRY SO that the muscles in her stomach tense into strands of ropey distress. Her rage has thew but she stands with her dead on the verandah, maihi holding the house up above her. She has changed since Korea. She has changed since every single thing that went before this moment. She does not invite you in. She does not welcome your dead to come and mingle with hers. She is no longer the friendly native.

OUR GIRL LINES UP, we line up, the women and her, along the porch with linked arms. We line up with them, her, our dead. Those who died in birth. Those who died defending us in the world. We stand shoulder to shoulder, adorned in kahu-kurī. Where once the tekoteko kept all at bay, demanded they wait at the gate, commanded respect, now it is just us; the women whose children have died, the men whose children have died, caught with their foot perpetually raised behind. This is the front line. You may no longer come in.

You, our girl wails, you must listen. Hear the roar of the cicada, we say. Sing girl, sing. Her toes are dug into the flesh of Papatūānuku. You, rise up, she calls. Make noise. Get off your knees and make noise.

MATARIKI ALL-STARS

PATRICIA GRACE

WATSON HAD SEVEN DAUGHTERS who were all stars. 'There they are,' he told Annie one night when he was sitting on a box by the clothesline, looking out into the northeastern skies. 'Our awesome daughters, all on stage.'

The actual daughters, inside watching television, ranged in age from three to thirteen. The eldest was Lainey. The twins, Pattie and Trinny, were eleven months younger than their older sister, and at next birthday, for a month, all three would be thirteen. Of the remaining stars, Poppy was nine, Maddie seven, Rosie five and Dixie three.

In regard to his teen and soon-to-be teen daughters, Watson had been stressing out about 'women's stuff' and 'facts of life' — how to divulge, transmit, what to say to his girls, what to do. 'Women's stuff' had already begun, had taken him by surprise three months back.

'I have to do better, Annie.'

When Lainey told him about the blood, had *shown* it to him on the bed sheet, he'd felt sick and rushed her to the doctor. The doctor patted his arm and sent them in to see the nurse. However, he didn't go in to the nurse's room with Lainey because the other daughters were waiting in the van for him. He went out and used his phone to let the teachers know the girls were going to be late for school.

More to come.

More than just monthlies, and for the first time in three years Watson thought of contacting his sister. Going through his mind were words she'd yelled at him the morning he'd gone and taken Dixie from her.

'What do you know about girls?'

Sister Zelda had come and helped him when this youngest girl was born and Annie was dying. His sister thought they were irresponsible having all these kids, all these girls, and didn't mind who was witness to her saying so. 'Idiotic if you ask me.' Watson hadn't asked her to come, knowing what she was like, but it was true he needed her at the time, couldn't have managed without.

Irresponsible?

He would've stopped at five kids, even four, but Annie kept telling him he needed a son, which wasn't true. 'Girls make me happy,' he told her.

'One more try,' she said three times.

The last pregnancy and her illness were both discovered at the same time. Because of the pregnancy she refused treatment for the illness.

'Don't worry, Wattie,' she said, 'I'll stick around. Can't get rid of me that easy.'

It wasn't what the doctors were saying.

Watson wanted her to have the chemotherapy even though it meant the baby wouldn't survive. Annie couldn't do it, and after she realised all hope of her own survival was gone, told him she had no regrets.

'You'll manage, Wattie,' she said.

One month after Dixie's birth, she died.

Sister Zelda stayed on, ruling their lives, demanding that they all stop crying because what good would that do? They were worse than the baby. It was true Baby never cried. Passed from hand to hand, fed, changed and talked to, Dixie was a reprieve, a little blink during the dark days.

'I gotta get back to the farm,' Zelda said when Dixie was twelve weeks old. 'I'll take Maddie, Rosie and Dixie with me. You get yourself back to work. Get after-school care for the older ones. Get someone in to do a bit of housework.'

'I'm not going back to work,' Watson said. 'The kids need me.'

'You can't manage on your own,' she said.

'I can manage. I will. The babies aren't going anywhere.'

It was the only time in his life he'd ever stood up to Zelda. His daughters supported him by screaming.

'All right. All right. Shut up. You girls are as silly as your father. Shut up or you'll have CYFs knocking on your door thinking someone's being murdered.'

ZELDA WAS FOUR YEARS older than Watson, and she'd looked after him when he was a kid, scratched for food, washed their clothes, stood over him while he scrubbed himself — all so that the Social Welfare wouldn't get them. Only a kid herself, he realised now, she'd get in to their mother's handbag or go through her pockets for money and, if she found any, run off to the shops for bread or milk. Stole. Jar of Marmite in her pocket. They'd have Marmite on toast for breakfast and Marmite sandwiches to take to school for lunch. If you didn't take lunch to school, the Welfare got you, according to Zelda.

IT WASN'T UNTIL NEXT morning, when Watson returned from walking Maddie to kōhanga, that he realised his sister hadn't completely abandoned her plan to relieve him of at least the youngest child. He had Rosie in her stroller and was turning onto his front path when Zelda came backing down the drive in her car with Dixie behind her, strapped into her baby seat. He left Rosie and ran across, calling, 'Whatcha doing?'

She stopped and opened the window. 'Don't panic. Only for a month 'til you find your feet. Look at you. Total disaster. Bring her back in a month.'

He ran after her as she continued backing out, but she zipped around at the bottom of the drive and shot away. He wheeled Rosie to the back of the house and sat on the step, head between his knees, eyes leaking.

'I'll get her back,' he promised Annie. Thin figure of his wife in the white bed, teeth and eyes breaking out of her face. Dozing, waking. Little Dixie tucked in beside her sleeping and snuffling.

'You'll manage, Wattie.' A whisper.

'No worries, my love.' A promise.

He'd brought mother and baby home from hospital and Zelda had arrived. Girls on the sofa having turns holding Dixie, a distraction from DHB coming and going with their drips and jabs.

Rosie was calling him. 'We got to get her back, Rosie,' he said, unstrapping his daughter from the buggy.

THE OLDER GIRLS HIT the roof when they came home, but he had calmed down by then and decided to wait out the month. There wasn't much else he could do without a proper vehicle. He had a work van, which his mate, Tai, had helped him fit out with shelving and security bracing to take his paint and plaster gear and his ladder. Only enough seats for three in front.

Each morning he dragged himself, sleepless, out of the pit, dizzy, fat-eyed. Kids crying. Had turns, or did it all together. Who could blame them? He made breakfast and school lunches while Lainey dressed Rosie, washed her face and hands and helped her with her Weet-Bix. She'd decided this was her role now. After breakfast Lainey followed her sisters off to brush their teeth while Watson began washing dishes.

He saw Lainey, Pattie, Trinny and Poppy away to school and set out in the opposite direction, with Rosie in her stroller, to walk Maddie to kōhanga reo.

At home again he finished tidying the kitchen with Rosie playing on the floor around him, ignoring toys, getting into the pot cupboard, or climbing. Climbing was what she most wanted to do, but she liked the fridge photos too, which he had put down low for her to see.

'Mummy?'

'Yes.' He wondered how much Rosie remembered. By that time of day his insides were collapsing — inside his face, inside his head, inside his stomach. Legs going bandy. Arms, heavy as tyres hanging out the washing, carrying Rosie, bringing the wash basket. Flashbacks. Eyes dripping. Had to get his head down.

'Change your bum and we go moe,' he said to Rosie. 'Go ni-nighs.' He changed her nappy and prepared her morning bottle, lay her down on the big bed and crashed out beside her. Dead sleep. Best sleep. The only sleep.

If Rosie woke before he did, she would jump on him, sit on his face — which was just as well because he didn't know what she might get up to if he slept on. Climb? Fall? Squeeze the toothpaste out of the tube, take off along the street never to be seen again? Rosie gone. That is, if he forgot to lock the doors. Maddie not collected from kōhanga. That is, if he forgot to set his phone alarm as back-up.

Getting off the bed he'd go to the bathroom, cup his hands under the cold tap, give his face and hair a soaking, glimpse the wreck of himself in the mirror. All this splashing and gasping amused Rosie. Her mother's round eyes. When he was done she would grab hold of his leg and he'd walk with her clinging.

'Thank God for you, Rosie,' he'd say as he opened the fridge.

SOMETIMES WHEN WATSON AND ZELDA were kids their mother

would wake in time to see them off to school. She would make a cup of tea and ask, but not in a really interested way, if they had everything and if they'd done their homework. Her hair would be poking out in all directions. Watson would answer 'Yes' to both questions, but Zelda would either not reply or, before walking out the door, say something smart like, 'What's it to you?'

'Don't be like that, Zee,' their mother would call, and she'd turn to him and say, 'Givus a hug, Wattie,' so he would do that before going out to catch up with Zelda, wishing he was sick so he could stay home with his mother until she went to her job at the hospital later in the morning.

After school he and Zelda would look on the windowsill to see if their mother had left them any money. If she had, they'd go and buy a bumper burger, which they would share, sometimes a can of coke. On other nights they'd have bread and Marmite, saving the rest of the loaf for the next day. Or they'd eat it all.

Zelda would go through his bag, slap his reading book and his maths homework on the table and see if he had any school notices. He'd read his book to her, she'd do his maths homework for him if he couldn't do it or if he was too slow, then take out her own books.

Their mother would return, sometimes with milk and saveloys, at around seven o'clock.

By eight o'clock she'd be showered and ready to go out again, all done up, telling them not to stay up late.

'You have to sign our homework notebooks,' Zelda would say. Sometimes there was money needed — two dollars for a puppet show, or twenty dollars for a school trip. Permission slips had to be signed. Their mother would sign the notebooks and the permissions. She'd leave two dollars, or even five, but if more was needed there'd be a row.

'Where'm I supposed to get twenty bucks from?'

'You work, don't you?' was Zelda's reply. 'You get paid. You get paid *money*.'

'There's rent you know. You want us to get kicked out? There's petrol. There's the electricity.'

'There's the pokies.'

'Don't get smart, Zelda. It's nothing.'

'Stay home then, if it's nothing.'

Their mother would walk out, calling back, 'Go and ask your father.'

They had once gone, after school, to the garage where he worked. Walking along the motorway, because it was quicker, they hoped they wouldn't get picked up by the cops. Their father wasn't happy to see them or to hear why they had come.

'I'm already paying through my back teeth for you lot,' he said. 'What does she expect? I got a wife and kids you know. Now I'm supposed to subsidise her habits? No way.' He gave them two dollars each and told them to catch a bus home. It was getting dark. They didn't go there again.

But there were times, sometimes months on end, when their mother would stay home at night. She'd shop and cook. They'd stay up late watching television together. After a while it would start all over again. The rows would make him feel like running away.

He did run away once but Zelda found him at the mall sitting with his bag, swinging his legs. She came up behind him, grabbed a fistful of his shirt and shoved him along in front of her, bad-mouthing.

Stopped when she realised people were staring.

WHEN WATSON ARRIVED AT kōhanga wheeling Rosie, Maddie was sitting on the grass with her bag beside her, looking out through the enclosure, as though she'd been waiting there all day. She leapt up at him and he carried her against his shoulder for a while, pushing the stroller with his other hand. He was working out how he was going to manage all of this once Dixie came home. He could withdraw Maddie from preschool, but he didn't want to do that. Could get a double stroller, or a car. Well, couldn't afford a car at the moment but he could clear his gear out of the van, remove the shelving and get another seat put in. He decided to go and talk to Tai. They could work on it over the Easter break.

THE MONTH WAS UP and he hadn't heard from his sister. That night he rang Zelda and asked her when she was bringing Dixie home.

'Never mind about Dixie,' she said. 'You've got enough on your plate and Dixie's all right here, better off.'

'Not without her sisters. You said . . .'

'I changed my mind.'

'Look here, Zee . . .'

'When she's older, going to school. You get back to work. Get babysitters, daycare and after-school programmes.'

Watson put the phone down with a soft hand, planning how he was going to go and get Dixie. *You can do it, Wattie.* The girls had their eyes on him, knew what was going on.

'Aunty Zelda's a pig,' Lainey said, tears springing out of her face.

'Don't talk like that about your aunty,' he said.

'But, like, she is. She is,' Pattie said. 'Like . . .'

'We're going to get Dixie, going to get little sister.'

WHEN ZELDA WAS FOURTEEN and he was ten, his sister found part-time work in the takeaway part of a fish restaurant — Friday nights and all day Sunday. He'd go there and hang out in the street or help where he could — wiping down, sweeping, putting out rubbish.

'Don't talk about me to anyone,' Zelda said, 'I'm sixteen, don't forget. Don't tell them nothing.' He saw a different side to his sister as she took orders and money, gave change, salted and wrapped the hot bundles and handed them over. Have a great weekend, a great rest of the day, a good evening. A different face. Big eyes, smiles and makeup.

Though he didn't get paid for his help, there was always a meal for him at the end of the day. Zelda gave him two dollars every week to put in his pocket and bought butter and luncheon to go on their bread. She said she would save and he could go to school camp with his friends the following year, but he didn't want to go to school camp, didn't have special friends.

'Well, it's all stupid anyway,' she said. 'Who wants to sleep in a tent?'

WHEN THE GIRLS WERE in bed Watson went out to the garage and began removing shelves from his van. He'd already taken the paint gear out, knowing he had to give up on the notion that he would get back to his paint business. He'd been in business on his own for three years after working under a boss for ten. He and Tai had modified the van, he'd bought his gear and built up custom, and Annie kept the books. He and Annie, their own business. Even Zelda had been impressed. Three years out on his own when Annie died. Didn't finish the last job, couldn't remember much about it. The only use he had for the van now was when he and Rosie went to the supermarket.

The next morning, he strapped Rosie into her car seat and went to see Tai at the wrecker's yard. He told Tai of his predicament and said he needed to make the van into an eight-seater so he and the girls could go and get Dixie.

'All do-able,' Tai said. 'We look around for seats. We work on it, but . . . takes too long. Look at you, stressed to the max. You got to go and get Dixie now or y'not going to stop crying. Tomorrow. Saturday. Take Lainey. Me and the missus'll have the girls. Up there in the morning, back in the afternoon. All good. We do the van later, not a problem.'

After he left Tai he went into town and bought a baby seat for the van, bottles, milk formula and a pack of nappies.

Early next morning, Tai and his wife came in two cars to get the girls, and Watson, with Lainey beside him, started up the van.

'Hit the road,' Tai said, 'and don't take "no" for an answer.' Tai knew Zelda. 'Pick up Bubba and go.' Which was what Watson intended doing — leaving everything and taking off, no clothes, no bags, no nothing. There was a drawer full of baby stuff at home anyway.

When they arrived at the farmhouse he saw his sister out in the yard pegging little garments on the clothesline. It made him swallow. He told Lainey to wait in the van, and on his way into the house called out to Zelda that he had come for Dixie. He went through to the bedroom and took the sleeping baby from her cot.

Zelda came screeching, 'What's got in to you? Leave her alone, she's sleeping. You think you can manage on your own?' He brushed past her.

'Kids crying every day,' he said.

She followed as he hurried out to the driveway. 'Because they miss their mother, you fool . . .'

He opened the van door and strapped Dixie into her cocoon on the middle seat, words slicing from behind.

' . . . who shouldn't have smoked in the first place. Her choice not to have chemo.'

'Shut your ugly mouth,' Lainey shouted from the window.

'Don't talk like that to your aunty,' he said as he got in, turned the key and wound up Lainey's window.

'She's a cow.'

'Don't talk like that . . .'

'There's better cows than her running round the paddock.'

As Watson turned and started down the drive his sister banged on the window shouting, 'Okay, okay, wait. I'll get her things,' and went toward the house.

So, he stopped. 'And anyway, look,' he said to Lainey. 'Little sister. Little fatty, eh?'

Lainey sniffed onto her sleeve, dried her face and peered at her sister. 'Our room, Dad. Her cot. Me, Trinny, Rosie, Dixie.'

'When she's older,' he said. 'Keep her by me 'til she's older.'

He thought he should go and help Zee, but he'd had enough of her hammering on. When he saw her coming he got out, opened the boot door and took the bags from her without speaking.

'What do you know about girls?' she shouted as he drove off. He glimpsed her in the rear-vision mirror, standing in the driveway, stiff as a ladder, watching them go.

WATSON HAD KEPT OUT of Zelda's way since then, hadn't contacted her for over three years, though she had texted him a few times asking him to come and visit during school holidays. He'd replied that he was working and left it at that. But now, what to do? Lainey needed a bra. Couldn't go to the doctor for that.

And different clothes. Stuff. He'd dropped Lainey, Pattie and Trinny off to the end-of-term disco and noticed other girls of their age all dressed up in outfits and costumes, glow and glitter, coloured shoes, earrings, hair decorations and makeup.

Phones. What did he know?

Facts of life. How could he?

Anyway, it was time he visited. Couldn't stay away from Zelda forever, though there was little time for visiting now that he was working again. The landlord had come to see him about painting the house. 'She can do with a lick of paint,' he'd said. 'Hourly rate, in lieu of rent. Take as long as you like.'

'No worries,' Watson said.

Maddie was at school now, Dixie off to kōhanga, which gave him four or five hours a day on the job. If he had to take time off for school things, doctor visits, or if kids were home sick, he could.

'Outside first,' the landlord said, 'then we might think about the inside. Inside could do with a lick.' Watson wondered if the landlord was doing the place up for sale. 'Take your time. She won't run away. And not selling her, if that's what you're thinking. Just looking after my investment. You and the girls got a roof over your heads as long as you want.'

'No worries.'

'At least until I kark, and not planning on doing that any time soon.'

Watson enjoyed the work, making something old and shabby new again, and for the first time he had savings. When he and Annie first started out they'd had debts to pay off for the van and gear. They'd only just cleared those when he'd had to pack it all in.

ZELDA LEFT SCHOOL WHEN she was fifteen, to work full time in the fish restaurant. A year later he began his secondary schooling in a uniform sourced by Zelda from Savermart, which was where she outfitted herself too, in excellent style. She bought him new shoes and school books. During that year their mother died.

She came out from the bathroom one morning and asked Zelda for money again.

'No way, José,' Zelda said.

'A loan, Zee. 'Til tomorrow — pay you back tomorrow.'

'The tomorrow that never comes, you mean?'

'Don't be like that, Zee.'

'Like what?'

'Until tomorrow, otherwise . . .'

'Get lost.'

'A bit behind, that's all. Repayments. It has to be today . . .'

'Drop dead,' Zelda said, and walked out.

That night there was a phone call to say that their mother had collapsed at the casino and been taken to hospital by ambulance. They found out later that she had died on the way there.

Despite his own sadness, what Watson remembered of the days that followed was Zelda's constant tears. Zelda's sorrow. He had thought she'd be glad.

Three people, their mother's sister, a cousin and an uncle, who they had never met before, came from the South Island to get her. All three looked like their mother. They were kind, like her, and when everything was over wanted him and Zelda to stay, come and live close by. There was family property, they said, where perhaps they would like to build a house one day.

Zelda wouldn't agree to it. She had recovered from tears and said she had to get back to work, and that he, Wattie, had to get back to school, his mates, his rugby. She made things up. He didn't have mates, didn't play rugby. There were their mother's clothes and things to deal with, she said, which was true. There were debts to pay, she could've added.

Zelda left the fish restaurant for better-paid work at an appliance store where she could get discounts on electrical goods and technology, and where she was soon winning prizes for salesperson of the week — a hairdrier, a telephone, a television set. She saved for a computer, went on a course, read the manual and became a skilled operator. She bought him screen games and a Nintendo, told him he wasn't to hang out at the video parlours or he'd get picked up, and that he should bring his mates home after school instead. He didn't want to go to the arcade and kept telling her he didn't have mates — which was true during those junior years — but she didn't seem to believe him.

It wasn't as though he was friendless. Kids in his class liked him all right, thought he was a crack-up the things he came out with sometimes, but he didn't hang out with them. He went to school. He came home, did enough homework to keep him out of trouble then watched television or played the games.

Once a week he waited around town for Zelda to finish work and they did their grocery shopping, or he'd go into the store and check out the latest technology, check out this other Zelda — smart, sharp and trusted, cheerful and heading for management positions.

During his last two years at school there was a group of four, including Tai and Annie, who attached him to themselves. They dragged him off to their sports on Saturdays, where he wore the scarves and found that he enjoyed himself, especially enjoyed the netball — all those legs.

'Bring them home,' Zelda urged him. 'There's nothing wrong with the house, nothing to be ashamed of. There's food in the fridge. What's up with you?'

But he couldn't get used to the idea.

'You think I'm going to jump on their necks or something?'

He wondered about Zelda's own friends, or if she had any. He'd only heard her complaining about some of the idiots at work.

'THERE'S MONEY,' HE TOLD Lainey, Pattie and Trinny, 'from the painting job, so you can have new clothes.' He was wiping down the table and stove, and the girls were at the sink doing dishes. They switched to face him and began jumping about and clapping like Americans on sitcoms, so excited that he felt sorry for them.

'From the shop?'

'Awesome, Dad.'

'Aunty Zelda will help you,' he said.

That stopped them.

'Nah. Nah, Dad.'

'Not Aunty Zelda.'

'We can, like, buy our own clothes.'

'It's not just the clothes,' he said. 'Other things. Things for you to know. Grown-up things. What do I know about girls?'

'I already told them, like, about their periods,' Lainey said.

'Yes, she did. Gross. And bras,' said Pattie.

'Yeah, gross. I don't want, like, periods and boobs,' said Trinny.

'I don't too,' said Pattie.

'Der. Like you got a choice,' said Lainey. 'Anyway, I done the research. Farmers. You go to Farmers. The bra specialist lady, like, measures you, finds the right size and gets you to try them on.'

'You went there? Farmers?'

'Julie told me.'

'You should've said. Why . . .?'

'Cost heaps. Rip-off.'

'But you . . . and I just thought . . .'

'God no, not Aunty. Old school.'

They turned back to the bench, listing the things they imagined themselves wearing if they went shopping with Zelda — skirts down to their ankles, tops with frills, button-up cardies, men's pants, policeman's shoes, flares. They were laughing, clowning, funny, pretty, like their mother. He moved the chairs to sweep under the table. So, shopping with his sister wasn't a good idea. But.

'Facts of life,' he said, when he could get a word in.

'What's that?' they wanted to know.

'Girls growing up, what you have to know.'

'Sex education,' they said. 'Dad, we have all that at school.'

And his daughters came out with all this vocabulary that was difficult for him to listen to, goofing about in the kitchen — pubic hair, body changes, sexuality, sexual orientation, condoms, safe sex, relationships. And — what were the schools thinking? — erections, wet dreams. He felt like going down and having a go at them at that school. These were only little girls.

'Imagine Aunty.' Well, no, he couldn't, another bad idea.

'Like, she'd probably make us go out and watch the horses.'

'Doing it.'

'Go tomorrow,' he said. 'Farmers, or wherever. Get what you need. Something for the little ones too.'

'Doing what?' asked Poppy, coming in from the bathroom with Maddie.

'Get your socks on,' said Lainey. 'Did you let the water out? Did you wipe round the bath?'

'What horses? Doing what?'

'We're getting you and Maddie some cool-as slippers tomorrow, from Farmers. Did you hang up your towels?'

'Dixie dropped mine in the bath. Rosie and Dixie wouldn't get out the bathroom. Like, we called out. Why didn't you come and get Rosie and Dixie out the bathroom?'

'Go and turn TV on. Charlie and the Chocolate Factory's on soon.'

'Slippers?'

Watson went into the bathroom to run water for Rosie and Dixie and left them playing in the water while he put a load of washing into the machine. Returning to the bathroom, he soaped the two little girls and swished them up and down the length of the bath, in turn, a head resting on the palm of his hand. They kept him at it until the water had cooled right down.

If only they could remain this age.

He lifted the girls out, wrapped them in towels and sent them ahead of him into the sitting room where the heater was on. He helped them into their pyjamas, put jerseys and socks on them and sat them together in one of the big chairs.

Out in the kitchen Lainey and Pattie were making chocolate crackles. Next thing it would be boyfriends. Nah. No, no. Get that thought right out of the way.

He picked up a big painted star that Rosie had made at school. She'd given it to him and wished him Happy Matariki, which he found amusing. Dixie had brought home a Matariki calendar — June to May, or he should say Pipiri to Haratua, with information about Māori New Year. Fallow ground, earth's preparation for new growth, the appearance in the sky of the cluster of stars known as the Matariki, which all signified a time of change. New beginnings.

He should ring Zee.

ZELDA WOULDN'T LET HIM leave school until he had something to go to, something with a future. Told him he couldn't stay working in the fish shop all his life. She had decided on a trade apprenticeship for him and had gone about town in her lunchtimes making enquiries of builders, mechanics and plumbers. There were no positions available anywhere so she rang their father.

'Nothing here,' he said, but gave her the name of a friend, Mack, who was a painter and paperhanger.

'Givus a look at him,' Mack said.

Watson left school but kept in contact with Annie and Tai, attended their rugby and netball games. Sometimes, if he was working nearby, they'd visit him, watch what he was doing, chat for a while and make arrangements to meet. He liked having a job. It was good having mates. Had a thing for Annie — her dark, round eyes, teeth like a fall of rocks filling her mouth and pushing the bottom of her face out, bushy ponytail, the best legs — shortish, big muscles, skinny ankles, like the old coke bottles upside down. Better than bottles, flicking and flying about the netball courts.

Something else he enjoyed was going to Tai's place and spending whole Sundays with Tai and his father fixing cars or motor mowers brought there by their neighbours and relatives.

HE STOOD FOR A moment at the lounge doorway. The paper cases from the chocolate crackles were on a plate on the floor, the two little ones were asleep and the others had their eyes fixed on chocolate rivers.

'You girls make me happy,' he gasped into the room. 'I'm going out to look at the stars.'

WATSON CAME HOME ONE day and told Zelda that he wanted to bring Annie home, to live. He was nineteen, had completed his hours as an apprentice and Mack had kept him on as an employee.

He thought his sister would blow her top, slam him with twenty reasons why he wasn't ready for responsibilities, most of them to do with money, his immaturity and his ignorance. Instead, she was silent for longer than he'd ever known her to be, pacing up and down the lounge rattling car keys.

'Is she pregnant?' she asked after a long while.

'Not that I know of,' he said.

'Get married,' she said. 'Don't have kids. Or not 'til you're thirty.'

Zelda did more pacing. 'You can live here,' she said, 'pay the rent. I'm going off to marry a farmer,' and walked out the door as though to an immediate wedding.

Later, when he asked her about the farmer, she said she hadn't met him yet but she'd done the research. According to Zelda there were plenty of farmers with lots of money needing wives and business partners.

Zelda found her farmer. Watson didn't ask where or how. Cattle farmer, Grant, was ten years older than she was, had a ten-year-old son who lived with him and an eight-year-old daughter who lived elsewhere. Zelda never had children of her own. Watson didn't know whether this was by choice or not.

THE LANDLORD WAS IMPRESSED with the paint job and said he'd give Watson work on his other rentals if he wanted it. Cash jobs — fences, decks, exteriors, bathrooms, kitchens all needing a lick. And he would pass Watson's name on, give him a thumbs-up to others needing work done.

He decided he'd put the extra money into a holiday account. They'd take a trip down south, look up relatives, and he'd show the girls where their grandmother was buried. Zelda had kept in touch with some of the cousins, who had visited her at the farm. One of them lived on family property where there were campsites and camping gear available for rellies wanting to stay. After Christmas? Or perhaps the following year. He and Annie had never had a holiday.

He went to the bedroom for his jacket and jandals and out into a night already frosting over. The sharp air blew his mind, expanded him. He sat on a box by the clothesline looking up into the pitching sky, the prickling stars, and out towards the horizon where he found the constellation of seven, newly risen. The eyes of the ariki, plucked and flung there in a fit of rage. Or seven sisters, or a flock of doves.

'They can be whatever to whoever,' he said to Annie, 'but to you and me they are our wonderful daughters.' Untouchable, unreachable, he wanted to add, but couldn't.

Watson thought of going inside and bringing the girls out to look at themselves, but then decided he'd keep the moment to himself and Annie. There'd be other nights, or early mornings — the best times for audiences — before the performers took their bows and danced off stage for another year.

'All our brilliant and beautiful daughters,' he said. 'All dancing. All stars.'

He watched until theme music, coming from inside, told him the movie had come to an end.

He went in, carried Rosie and Dixie to their beds and decided he'd ring Zelda, just to say hello.

RUSH
NIC
LOW

THERE ARE FIVE OF them crammed into a white council ute, speeding through the waking city. Jackhammers and shovels rattle in the tray. The young guys in the back are knee to knee in work pants and steel-capped boots. One of them slugs at a Farmers Union iced coffee. It's a Monday morning in Melbourne and just past dawn. The sun ripples bronze across the highrises, licks out from laneways like a golden tongue.

Big Toff's driving. He's a reassuring bulk up there in the front, not even forty but big and dark and weathered. His massive shoulders protrude from either side of his seat. Next to him, Archie looks tiny. The old man's barely five foot and all sinew, wired tight like an old-time bantamweight boxer. He riffles the paperwork with tattooed hands, one last time. His scowl is cast-iron with concentration.

Relax, Uncle, Toff says. He speaks with the sharp, tumbling cadences of the Western Desert. You can't beat 'em?

Archie looks up and cracks a grin, and puts the papers back in the glovebox.

Past the CBD, Toff swings the ute off St Kilda Road into the cool green of Kings Domain. They crawl along the triumphal avenue with hazard lights winking, and on up to the Shrine of Remembrance. The blunt stone monument squats above the city like a misplaced Greek temple.

Toff parks on the forecourt next to three other council utes. One's got a small excavator on the back. The shrine's grey stone is a bright confusion of workers in high-vis vests. They're setting up a safety perimeter. A hard-case woman in mirror shades hammers a white planning sign into the lawn.

Archie climbs down from the cab and jams a foreman's hard hat over his wiry grey hair. He looks out across the glass spires of the city skyline, as if appraising their value. Then he looks up at the shrine.

All right, you mob, Archie calls. Let's get to work!

BY THE TIME THE police arrive the paved forecourt and wide granite steps are a mess of smashed rock. The excavator has piled the debris to one side, where a team of workers sift the dirt with wire-mesh pans. A small crowd of onlookers has gathered at the safety perimeter.

A police cruiser pulls in beside the utes. Archie's shoulders hunch tight. Toff drops his sledgehammer and walks quickly over.

Let me, he says.

A sergeant and a constable step from the car. They look like they're at the tail end of a long night shift, their faces creased and tired.

You with the council? the sergeant shouts. The percussion of jackhammers is relentless.

Yeah, Toff yells.

You the boss?

I'm the spokesman.

The policeman cups a hand to his ear. What?

I'm the spokesman!

Huh?

You got a nice tan! Hang on. Toff signals the others to stop work, and soon a dusty silence falls over the Domain. What's the problem?

We had reports of someone vandalising the shrine. But you're council, right?

Right, Toff says.

What're you doing? Maintenance?

Not quite. Here. Toff points to the planning sign, then folds his thick arms across his chest. He waits with a half smile.

The sergeant leans down and reads. His weary, businesslike expression ruptures with surprise. He looks at Toff. You serious?

Serious.

Mineral Exploration Licence?

You got it. G-two-eighty. Eight weeks, eighty metres down, mining lease if we hit pay dirt.

Pay dirt? You mean you're digging for—

Gold, Toff says.

THE SERGEANT RUNS A hand along his stubbled jaw. Right, he says. Gold. This is kind of unusual. You got any paperwork?

Sure, Toff says. I got a twenty-seven-F, all the back checks, an ECB and two double-oh fours. You want them all?

The sergeant shrugs. Toff ducks his bulk under the safety tape and retrieves the papers from the ute. The sergeant reads in silence.

Hang on a minute, he says. *Land* Council? You're from the *Aboriginal Land* Council? He looks sharply at Toff and the work gang at his back. Is this some kind of stunt?

A small, mostly elderly crowd has drifted closer to listen. An unusually tall old man in a blue blazer, a red poppy pinned to his lapel, hovers behind the sergeant. He radiates distress like an old-fashioned bar heater. Activists, the man moans. They're activists.

Toff's black eyes are trenched deep in his fleshy face, but they're shining. He's been waiting for this. He laughs. *Were* activists, he says. Now we're the Aboriginal Land Council — of *Minerals*.

The sergeant shakes his head. What's your point? he says. What are your demands?

No demands, Toff says. This isn't a protest action. You know what they say — if you can't beat 'em? He smiles and shrugs. Now we're a real-deal mining company.

The sergeant stares at him and, for the first time in his life, Toff feels the sweet righteousness of bureaucracy rising up in him. This is totally legit, he says. Call the Department of Crown Lands. The number's on the forms.

The sergeant looks sceptical, but he pulls out his phone and dials the number anyway. He is put on hold. After a long wait, a bored operator comes on the line. The sergeant paces while he talks, one hand shading his eyes from the glare.

Who the hell signed off on — okay. Sorry. Sure, the paperwork. Twenty-seven-F? Yep. Two double-oh fours? Two of them, got it. Yes. What? How much to look it up? Jesus! And where'd they get that kind of money? No, it's not a set of GPS coordinates, it's the Shrine of bloody Remembrance. No, that is not fascinating. It's — *what*? A typo? It's a fucking typo? The what? Online complaint form? Wait—

The sergeant glares at his phone in frustration.

See, Archie calls, a challenge in his voice. The old man approaches, the high-vis vest around his shoulders like a modern possum-skin cloak. All paid up, he says. We've got a *permit* to do this. Your laws, mate, so you're with us on this one.

Permits can be revoked, the sergeant says. Who are you?

Archie Ryan. I'm the CEO.

Wait a minute, the sergeant says. I know you. You're a serial protester. You're at everything. Any cause that'll have you.

Toff puts a restraining hand on Archie's shoulder, and when the old man speaks his voice is weary and tight.

We're done with protesting, he says. No one gives a shit about land rights in this country anymore. This is a commercial mining operation. You need an injunction to stop it. C-two-forty, federal, with underwritten DCBs. Takes weeks to get and easy as piss to overturn. While you're waiting you could keep that mob under control. They've been threatening my crew.

Damn right we have, the tall old man says. He steps forward and grips the thin safety cordon. His anger seems equal to that of Archie. Why do you have to dig here? he says. Men fought and died for this country. Why the bloody hell would you mine this?

Mate, Archie says with a sour grin, we're hardly going to fuck with our own land.

THE CITY EXPLODES. News crews and photographers and lawyers scramble. The airwaves burn with confused outrage. Conservative blogs are spotted plagiarising Wilderness Society press releases, and vice-versa. Rio Tinto and Fortescue come out in support of the dig, and the internet is soon awash with rumours of a joint venture to open-cut mine the MCG. Only Tony Abbott distinguishes himself, giving an apparently incoherent yet tactically brilliant speech wherein he coins the slogan 'Support all the Diggers, all the time, whatever they're digging.'

At Kings Domain the crowd swells throughout the afternoon. The workers douse the Sacred Flame with a Kmart fire extinguisher. From behind the police line Toff and Archie watch gleaming charter buses disgorge a flow of pensioners, ferried in from suburban RSL clubs. The protesters carry hand-scrawled placards, bags of knitting and Gladwrapped sandwiches. They surge up the hill in a blue-rinsed wave.

Mixed with the elderly crowd is a steady stream of sympathetic locals, students and activists. Away to the east, the youth wing of Socialist Alliance is digging a solidarity hole in the lawn.

A nuggety man with tattooed arms pushes to the front of the crowd. He's wearing a sticker-covered hard hat and carries an enormous red flag. Orrite, lads, he calls in a broad Scottish accent. We come to show solidarity. This is a bloody good action.

Piss off, mate, Archie says. This isn't an action.

Ha, the man says. Tha's a good line. That'll confuse the hell out the bosses.

I'm serious, you little cunt, Archie says. This is a commercial mining operation. You can't coopt this. Piss off.

The man's face darkens. We took a vote, he says. The rank and file unanimously voted t' support your action. Why'd you turn that down?

Sorry, mate, Toff says. Us bosses got a press conference to do.

The news crews have been allowed inside the cordon. A big PA has been set up so the crowd can hear. Toff gives Archie the thumbs up.

Go for it, Uncle, he says. Stick to the script, don't lose your cool, eh?

Archie nods. All right, you bastards, he mutters. Let's do this.

After years of speaking to polite but indifferent crowds at other people's rallies, the old man's restless, wary features take on a cast of authority. He seats himself before the bank of cameras. He takes out his notes and pulls the microphone close. Over the gunfire rattle of jackhammers, his amplified voice echoes across the Domain.

Afternoon. I'm Archie Ryan. I'm a Wurundjeri man, and CEO of the Aboriginal Land Council — of Minerals. Today is the first day of work at the Kings Domain mine. We have every confidence this mine will yield significant quantities of gold.

There are cries of *Shame!* Signs reading HANDS OFF HALLOWED GROUND bob above the crowd. The tall elderly veteran has made it past the police line, claiming he is feeling faint. He sits against Toff's ute as if resting, then reaches a bony arm under the chassis and handcuffs himself to the vehicle. There are angry shouts and he is swarmed by police.

It is clear, Archie continues, that local people will support this mine, because it brings jobs and money to the local economy. Stand back a minute, would you.

The work crew has chipped out the base of the cenotaph with a jackhammer, as if notching a tree for felling. There is a cry of *Timberrr!* and the twelve-metre-high stone spear tips slowly forward, then thunders to the ground. The now-huge crowd shrinks back in fright. *You're dead! You're fucking dead*, screams a voice from in the crush.

Now, Archie says, we understand that there are concerns from old soldiers. We have consulted and listened to their concerns. Watching TV and visiting RSLs has taught me the fundamental value of respect for veterans. Listen.

A pre-recorded clip of an RSL consultation meeting booms across the Domain. Over the insane chirping of pokies comes a scrum of angry voices, the thump and squeal of feedback as someone tries to grab the mic. There is shouting, and the terrible splintering sound of dentures crushed underfoot.

I deeply respect old soldiers, Archie continues. There is no ripping-off here. The more time I spend with them, the more I consider myself their true friend. We recognise they have a long history and a rich culture.

The police line tightens as the crowd surges forward in anger. The superintendent watches the mob's every move, his radio at the ready. Archie pushes on. He's enjoying himself now.

We recognise veterans have a long history, but the sad reality is that this memorial was built to commemorate soldiers who are all dead. None of them actually use the shrine. It is a dying culture, and this mine will help to preserve it. Once we have dynamited the structure, we will donate fragments of rock to the museum. We will plant two large shrubs to commemorate the diggers' sacrifice, all at our own expense. Most important of all, we will offer work in the mine to any able-bodied veteran. As we have learned, it is better to work for, rather than against, the mining industry.

The crowd roars its disapproval over the grunt and wheeze of the excavator. Archie's crew works on in the background. From time to time one of them rises from the fast-expanding mineshaft, nervously scans the crowd, then bobs back out of sight.

Archie's nasal voice booms out over the PA. We also offer

compensation to veterans. We offer point-zero-six per cent of turnover, shared among all veterans who can prove an unbroken link to this hillock since seventeen eighty-eight. This will be about six dollars each, and will rise even further once gold is found. We hope this generous offer will be looked upon with gratitude.

This time the bellow of anger from the crowd is a physical force. The police have drawn their batons and fixed their visors. The light is fading, and shadows pool in the shaft where the workers tunnel beneath the shrine. Up the front a TV technician switches on a bank of halogens. Archie's tense form is a sudden island of light among the seething mass of protesters. He begins to wind up his speech.

We look forward to working with the old soldiers of Victoria, contributing to the wealth of the nation, and making a meaningful living for ourselves, like you've always wanted. Thanks and if you don't mind me saying, go fuck yourselves.

The crowd erupts. The noise is catastrophic. The police line stumbles back under the onslaught. Two dozen police horses thunder into action, charging the crowd from either side. There are screams as pensioners go down beneath the hoofs.

Toff moves to Archie's side and it is just the two of them standing in the light, the focus of the crowd's rage.

Shit, Toff says. We have to call this off. Look.

To their right a mass of burly men with crewcuts shoulder-charge the police line. They look like off-duty soldiers. Old-timers beat the police back with their crutches and walking frames. A catheter bag slices the air above Toff's head.

Toff looks back, afraid for the work gang's safety. They have emerged from the mouth of the diggings in a tight high-vis huddle and are shouting to him. He can't hear them over the noise. They move slowly towards Toff and Archie and the brilliant halogen lights.

From the opposite direction the soldiers lead the charge, bellowing and pushing at the cops. Somewhere in the back a furious martial drumming starts up. The police line disintegrates. The crowd is upon them.

They all reach the spotlight at the same instant. As the work gang enters the light, the halogens' fierce rays catch their vests as if reflecting off a huge mirror-ball, and the enraged crowd rears back.

Toff realises the workers are moving in a phalanx because they are carrying something enormous. They lower it carefully to the ground at Archie's feet, then peel away. There is a hot, sharp intake of breath: first from the old man, then the cops, soldiers and pensioners, and those watching live on TV across the country.

It is a gleaming slab of crystalline white quartz, prised from the earth beneath the shrine. And running through it, like a bolt of lightning frozen into the rock, is a seam of gold, as thick as Toff's enormous thigh. Half a million bucks' worth, at least.

For one brief moment the crowd stands in silent awe, and in that glittering pause, a microsecond before the Melbourne Rush begins, each of them feels the ripe slink of blood in their veins, and something else too, something huge and fierce, welling up inside.

I DREAM OF MIKE TYSON
From an untitled novel
TUSIATA AVIA

EVERYBODY HATES FALE — they don't say it out loud like that, but they hate her.

'Oh, Fale,' they say, 'she's a hard woman.' They laugh like they're glad it isn't them that has to live with her. Even the men are afraid of her.

On Fale's wall there is a big picture; it is a picture of Jesus. Someone has cut a great big hole in Jesus's chest and his heart is sticking out. His heart is just sitting there, like a hunk of red meat. Whoever cut that hole in Jesus's chest has also tied a piece of barbed wire around his red, meaty heart.

It's not fair, but Jesus just looks at you like he's saying: 'Look what they did.' He looks so beautiful, with his yellow hair like a girl and his sad blue eyes. His fingers point at his heart, like he's a taupou, a virgin-princess with beautiful dance-hands. Sometimes when I'm by myself, I just go and look at the picture and I feel so sorry for him. I wonder why his father hasn't gone to look for the person that did all that stuff to him. I wish I could take that barbed wire off. It makes me feel sore.

'E, ki'o, you shit, you not go anywhere after da school.' Fale's voice comes out of the quiet. 'Just school and home and do da weeding, uai loa, OK?'

Sometimes I can sneak out the front door without her seeing me. Not today though.

'Ia, you know your name, a? Ki'o. Ki'o-kae-shit.' And she laughs, 'I fink dat's be your new name now, OK? Ea, ea? I can't hear you. What's your name?'

'Ki'o, shit.' I say to the floor.

'No, dat's not right. I said, Ki'o-kae-shit. Das your really true name, suga, that's what your name it's mean. Ia, what's your name?'

'Ki'o-kae-shit,' I say to the floor.

'Ia, good.' She nods. 'Ki'o-kae-shit, you better come back after da school and don't hanging around with those bloody fa'afafine, uai loa, OK?'

'Yes, Aunty.'

When I first got here I tried to figure out how to make her happy, tried to figure out how to not make her angry. But now I think there is no way of making her happy — it pisses her off if you try to make her happy. I peel taro.

'E, pa'umuku, slut, what you fink you doing? Who told you to do da taro, a? Kaukalaikiki kele oe, you are da very cheeky one. An now you waste those bloody taro. You fink someone pay me to feed your big bloody mouth?'

I'm supposed to get the food ready when I get home from school, she never tells me what she wants, I should've peeled the yam, but probably the same thing would happen if I peeled bananas or made rice. I think she likes being pissed off. These days I just try and keep my head down.

I WAS CRAZY, I can see that now, I was really crazy.

I wait till she falls asleep, after hours and hours of massaging her big, ugly legs, and then I creep outside and turn on the shower and after a few minutes I run down the road and swap my lavalava for my 'out' clothes hidden under a bush. I meet my friends Whitney and Tina under the pulu tree. Those aren't their real names, but that's what we named ourselves — Whitney, for Whitney Houston and Tina, for Tina Turner. I am Madonna.

Whitney had done it, she'd been doing it since she was about twelve, she'd done it with just about everyone. She was proud of herself too and would always have a new story about some guy that she'd done it with — the head boy or the caretaker at school or the minister's son, or the minister — but she always had her eyes open for a Palagi, a white man. A real Palagi, that's what she wanted.

Tina did it too, but she probably talked about it more than she actually did it.

They were both pretty. Whitney's skin was kind of light, kind of half-caste colour, kind of orangey and she had blonde hair — well, actually, it looked more like orange than blonde from the dye. It kind of matched her face. Tina was dark, so we called her Nelson Mandela and meauli black all the time and she would get angry and call us dogshit and pig's balls and stuff like that. I reckon she was actually prettier than Whitney but you didn't notice it, because Whitney was so loud and so funny and such a big flirt that everyone always noticed her.

Both of them were skinny and their feet were massive. Theirs were even bigger than mine but they just kept squeezing their great big fa'afafine banana-boat feet into my shoes and stretching them out all over the place.

'E, pa'u, slut!' Whitney screeches at me as soon as I come into sight. 'We been waiting all night for you, bloody aikae, shit-eater! Se, hurry up, someone gonna take my man before we even get there!'

'Don't worry, suga, your man's probly got no polos, anyway!' Tina laughs back.

Whitney pusi-eyes me, 'E, I like your top, ka'i e sexy, lemme try.'

'What am I gonna wear?' I don't really want to hand over my halter neck.

'You wear my ofu.'

'I can't fit that!'

'Sista, you can, look it sooooo stretchy.' Whitney pulls her top out from her like bubble gum. I look like a sausage in that top, a big pink sausage, squeezing all over, that's going to pop out of its skin. I can smell her on me — man-sweat, mildew, Impulse — I'm a big stinky sausage.

Whitney puts on my top like a mini-dress and she looks great. We practically run all the way to Seabreeze, where I buy a lei from one of the kids outside the club, I hope the frangipani will hide my Whitney smell.

'Sailors!' Whitney gets a crazed look in her eyes. 'You gonna rock my boat tonight!' she yells into the crowd.

We clear a space in the middle of the dance floor and Whitney is pole dancing, disco dancing, lap dancing, Samoan dancing, dirty dancing, she is doing every kind of dance in the world. She is dancing on the stage, with the band, she is looking at the bar, but the barman crosses his arms and shakes his head at her. She licks her lips at him and laughs and then she is in the arms of one sailor and then in the arms of another.

'Come and lick my pipi, Palagi sea-man!'

We dance and dance. Kool and the Gang, Lionel Richie, Michael Jackson. Whitney is bumping and humping and singing my ears out, 'Fuck my boat, don't fuck my boat baby, fuck my boat, don't tip my boat over . . .' and laughing her head off. We are looking at the sailors, we are brushing up against them, we are shaking our bodies. I don't care about my sausage body anymore, I am twirling and twirling on the dance floor, I am shining and shining, I am smiling and laughing and the sailors are smiling and laughing to me.

A slow dance comes on and a Samoan man, kind of old like my dad, wearing an ie lavalava and jandals, comes and bows to me. I shake my head, but he keeps bowing and smiling and bowing and smiling. I'm really shame, but I get up and dance with him. He is a really good dancer, he swirls me round and round the floor, my skirt swirls round and round my legs, I shut my eyes and everything swirls round and round with me in the middle.

All three of us girls, with three sailors and a crate, go to Mulinu'u in a taxi. We always go there after the clubs, everyone does, piled into cars and pick-ups with bottles of Vailima beer. We drive up and down Mulinu'u until Whitney says, 'It's bloody too crowded here, we go to Taumeasina — come on, polos!' She laughs at the sailors like it's the funniest thing in the world. We know they will pay for the taxi.

Taumeasina is like you think Paradise is going to be, a tiny little island in the middle of the sea and when the tide is out you can walk up to your knees out there. It's blue sea, white sand, coconut trees, and someone has even made a seat underneath the trees for bad girls like us and their sponsors. The six of us drink our bottles of Vailima and laugh at Whitney's rude jokes. She sits in her sailor's lap and jiggles up and down, 'Come on horsey, come on!' She opens her mouth and I think she is going to swallow the whole bottle this time. Tina opens her mouth like a bird swallowing a big, big fish. Then all the sailors try to do better. I laugh — they will never beat Whitney and Tina, never!

Whitney and Tina disappear with their boys, and here I am with mine. His name is Jarrod — I think of Carrot. I can hear the guy with Whitney moaning like he's got a bad stomach ache. Carrot is wriggling and drinking and looking at me.

I laugh and yell out to Whitney, 'Suga, tell your boyfriend to go and have a ki'o in the bush, he must have a sore magava!'

'What does that mean?' asks Carrot.

'Just checking the time.' Carrot must be dumb, cos he just nods his head and keeps drinking. I'm not like Whitney and Tina — I don't like to make the first move, just in case he doesn't really like me, just in case he pushes me away. They never do, but I'm still like that.

Carrot's hands are in my hair, pulling out the pins. 'Wow, it's right down to your bum!' He is stroking me like you stroke a dog. I close my eyes. It's nice.

'You're pretty, you know, for a big girl. You should leave your hair down.' He pulls a squashed frangipani from my lei and tucks it behind my ear. 'See, you look just like a hula-girl now.' He tries to pull my top over my head; I have to help him cos it's so bloody tight.

And then my back is in the sand, Carrot has stopped talking and is breathing so hard like his face is going to burst. I look at his arms, I put my face against them, they smell hot. I run my fingers over his tattoos: things from the sea, hooks, a beautiful woman joined to a fish. I think of Tila, just for a second I have that drowning feeling, but then it goes away. I look up at the stars and listen to Carrot's slowing breathing, feel his arms around me and pretend that it will be like this forever.

Whitney and Tina don't know I am waiting for one of these polos to love me. Every weekend I look as happy as they do, but they don't know that I am waiting. Maybe the sailors don't go for me because I'm fat. Maybe it's because I'm a real girl. Maybe it's because I don't do all those sex things Whitney and Tina keep talking about. I don't want to put a guy's thing in my mouth. Whitney and Tina go on and on like it's the greatest thing in the world, like they really, really love it. Makes me feel like pua'i-ing, vomiting. But, if one of those polos would stay, just one of them, I would probably do it. Even though I hate it, I would probably do it.

Afterwards I wash in the sea, say bye to Carrot and run home before daylight to start the saka before Aunty wakes. I have been getting away with this for ages.

BUT THIS TIME WHEN I come in through the window, Fale is waiting.

'Sau i.' Her voice comes out of the dark and I nearly jump out of my body. 'Come here.'

I look around the room but I still can't see her.

'Sau i.' Her voice is friendly.

Cold, cold water runs down inside my backbone and underneath my scalp.

I see a black shape low to the floor. Fale is lying on a mat underneath the window. I don't even move. I am right in front of her, it's amazing I didn't step on her. Slowly, I crouch down in front of her.

She doesn't say anything for ages, she acts like she's gone back to sleep, but I know she hasn't, my whole body has rushed into my head. 'You had a good time?'

I say nothing.

'You had a good time, suga?'

There are rocks in my throat, I am trying to swallow them.

'You do somefing nice tonight, a, suga? Ia, I'm hope you do somefing very, very nice tonight. I'm hope you have da very good time tonight. Poor fing, must be so tired.'

She doesn't say anything again for ages, all I can hear is my head thumping.

'You just like da so special girl, you go out to da kalapu, club, and drink da beer an make da fuck with maybe da twenty mens and maybe da dog too, a? Ia, very good. Ua lelei. You better go to bed now.'

I look at her.

'Hurry up, you go to bed, you must be so tired.'

I get up very, very slowly, waiting for her foot or her elbow or her fist. I walk to the bedroom and stand just inside the door, I put my hand up to the doorframe and steady myself.

Her voice floats out of the dark. 'Suga, aumai le ipu vai, bring a glass of water.'

I walk to the kitchen and fill her a glass of water.

Her voice comes again. 'And bring da scissor.'

I walk back to her in the dark with the water and the scissors.

Fale is sitting up now, cross-legged. I hand her the water, she drinks it. 'You know what we do to da pa'umuku, slut, in da fa'asamoa, suga?' Her voice is steady. 'We make da sign so all da peoples know dat dis girl is da pa'umuku girl. Dese day, even da afa kasi, half-caste girl dey come from New Zealan and dey fink dey better than anybody else, dey fink dey can do anyfing dey want. Dey fink dey can act like da dog or da pig and no body gonna stop dem. You know what we do to the pa'umuku girl? A, suga?'

I nod.

'Come on, special girl, tell me.'

I hear my voice say, 'Cut off their ears.'

THAT NIGHT I DREAM. Mike Tyson and David Tua and The Rock all at Mulinu'u beach dancing. I am dancing too, with my hair flowing down my back, flowers in my hair. I am doing a slow hula and they are dancing round me, clapping their hands and slapping their chests and banging the floor. I dance faster, shaking my hips to the beat of their hands and their chests and the floor. I am shaking till I am a blur. They pick me up like a taupou-princess, they hold me above their heads, I sit on their hands, a throne made of my own glossy brown hair.

And then they are throwing me down, down, down to the ground. I fall on the ground and they body-slam me, WHAM, first David Tua, BAM, then Mike Tyson, SLAM, then The Rock. The Rock picks me up by the hair and Mike Tyson goes LEFT RIGHT LEFT, David Tua goes JAB JAB UPPERCUT. Mike grabs me by the face and bites me, he is biting and biting and the floor is covered in hair and bits of ear.

I DON'T EVEN LEAVE the house for weeks, not for school or church or anything. Aunty doesn't stop me, but I don't want to go anywhere.

I want to wait till my hair is long enough to cover my ears.

FAMISHED EELS
MARY ROKONADRAVU

I

AFTER ONE HUNDRED YEARS, this is what I have: a daguerreotype of her in bridal finery; a few stories told and retold in plantations, kitchens, hospitals, airport lounges. Scattered recollections argued over expensive telephone conversations across centuries and continents by half-asleep men and women in pyjamas. Arguments over mango pickle recipes on email and private messages on Facebook. A copper cooking pot at the Fiji Museum. Immigration passes at the National Archives of Fiji. It is 2011.

Fiji, with Guyana, Suriname and Trinidad and Tobago, had just registered the 'Records of the Indian Indentured Labourers' into the UNESCO Memory of the World Register, when my father, the keeper and teller of stories, suffered a stroke. Fate rendered his tongue silent. He cannot read or write — he first set foot in a classroom at fifteen, and was told by a nun he was too old. He ignores my journalist and doctor siblings to select me, the marine biologist, to finish his task. I am off the coast of Lifou in New Caledonia counting sea urchins when the call is relayed.

He hates me for not becoming a journalist, I say to myself.

I will be on the Thursday flight, I tell my older sister.

SHE MEETS ME AT the airport and drives me down to Suva. It is past midnight. We pass eleven trucks overloaded with mahogany logs between Nadi and Sigatoka. A DHL courier truck. A quiet ambulance. She smokes at the wheel, flicking ash into the cold highway wind. We pass a dim lamp-lit wooden shack before Navua. Someone is frying fish. We both know it is fresh cod. We remain silent as we are flung into the kitchen of our childhood at Brown Street in Toorak. We stop to sip sweet black tea from enamel pialas in Navua.

Come on, tell me, she blurts. Who you seeing now? Is it a dark-skinned Kanak? Is that what's keeping you in Lifou? Do you speak French now?

Screw you, I say from the back seat.

He wants you to do this because you won't lie to him, she says. The rest of us may. Just to make him happy. Just give him what he wants to hear. But you won't. You will find out and you will tell him.

Screw you, I say again, more to myself than her.

All his life, my father has sought one thing only — to know the woman in the photograph. To know the name of her city or town in India. To know that at some juncture in history, there was a piece of earth he could call his own. All he had had was a lifetime of being told he was boci. Baku. Taga vesu. Uncircumcised.

A hundred years was not enough. Another five hundred would not be either. In a land where the first peoples arrived a couple of thousand years before the first white man, the descendants of indenture would forever remain weeds on a forsaken landscape. A blight.

He had stubbornly remained in Fiji through three military coups and one civilian takeover. Everyone had left. He remained the one who rented out flats until his brothers' houses were sold. He supervised brush-cutting boys on hot Saturday mornings. He was the one to call the plumber to change faucets in grimy, unscrubbed shower recesses. He was the one who kept receipts for oil-based butternut paint, bolts and drill bits; photocopied them faithfully at the municipal library and mailed them to Australia, Canada or New Zealand. Each envelope had a paper-clipped note: OK. It was the only word he learned to write. I received Christmas cards from him saying the same thing: OK. The handwriting on the envelope changed depending on who the postmaster was at the time.

His younger brothers send out family newsletters by email. There is only one photograph of my father they use, a blurred profile of him holding a beer. They use the same caption — 'Still refuses to use email.' I wish to click Reply All and say 'fuck you' but there is a distant niece in Saskatchewan on the list — she writes me regularly for shark postcards and she knows the scientific names of eleven types of nudibranch. She recorded herself reciting it like bad poetry and put it on YouTube. I am the only one who knows this. She insists I use real handwriting, real stamps. She hates pancakes, frogs, flatlands. Her handwriting yearns for water. Salt water. Sea. In her milk-tooth grin I see the next storyteller — the one to replace the man who has gone silent. She is ten and wants three pet octopi.

I was born to be a bridge. All I see are connections. I bridge between time, people and places. I study migratory species. Tuna fish stocks. Whales. Sea urchins in between. Cephalopods. I was nine when I picked up my first cuttlefish bones on a tidal flat in Pacific Harbour. For years I thought it was a whistle. I wrote out the names of the world's oceans, seas, currents and fish in longhand, unaware the lead scrawlings were placing miles between my father and me. He watched me from across the kitchen table. My mother had died bringing me into the world. He washed okra with patient fingers. Boiled rice. Warned me he was going to slice red onions.

Make sure you buy land, he whispers. When you grow up, buy a small piece of land. Build a house just for you. Promise me.

Promise. But my eyes were already on the Kuroshio Current. I was already reading the voyage of Captain James Cook and the transit of the planet Venus. Hearing the howl of winds at Tierra del Fuego. No one told me that as recently as one hundred years before, ships had cut through the rough straits with people carrying the makings of my teeth in their genes. They almost never happened. Almost.

Keep writing, he says in our old kitchen. As long as someone remembers, we live.

My sister drops me off at the Colonial War Memorial Hospital.

I won't come in now, she says. I still smell of cigarettes.

My father is asleep when I reach out to hold his hand.

II

FOR YEARS THE STORY in my family was that she boarded a ship in Calcutta. After all, it was the holy city of pilgrimage. It was nice to believe I descended from the loins of a young devotee travelling north to immerse in the sacred Ganges. She was then kidnapped and sent to labour in the hot sugarcane regions of Fiji. She had hair the sheen of sea-washed rocks at dusk. The story was that she met Narayana on the ship, the son of a turmeric merchant. They were to have eleven children of which only two survived, one of them my father's father, Venkat.

I grew up imagining the digging of little graves at the edge of sugarcane. In rain. It was always night rain, as if miscarriages or infant deaths only occurred in rain-drenched darkness. In childhood, I added details from Bollywood films to it: night wailing, tug-of-wars over linen-swaddled baby corpses. Murder. Narayana strangles his own children. He uses an old cotton sari. There was no photograph of him so in my mind he wore the face of the Bollywood villain Amjad Khan. Rewind a few years to the port of Calcutta and the ship that crossed the kala pani, the black waters, and he is Amitabh Bachchan. He was the designated toilet-water carrier on the ship to Fiji — this much was whispered behind hushed curtains at home. At celebrations he is remembered as an astrologer, squinting his face at the heavens, reading palms on a heaving sea. He reads prosperity into suicidal hands, keeps men and women breathing until landfall. He has not created life yet. Nor ended any.

There is no photograph of him. But there is the one photograph of her. She is sitting rigid under a cascade of jewellery. For years, no one asked what a virgin devotee was doing with so much gold or with a nose ring that could collar a grown cat.

Now it comes to me.

III

MY FATHER'S HOUSE, THE new one, is by the banks of the Rewa River, directly opposite the township of Nausori, a rice-growing region of wetland and rain. He has a concrete house on a slight knoll. A sprawling pumpkin out back. He can see the old bridge from his kitchen sink. He has seen at least six women leap to their deaths from that bridge. The last one dropped two toddlers and a baby first. The Nausori Police Station knows his telephone number. A cleaning-woman comes in twice a week. I am told all this by his neighbour, a buxom Fijian woman who leads her children in loud, charismatic prayers before dawn. She sells pineapple and custard pies outside MH Supermarket and sings soprano at the New Spring Church Choir.

I put my bags in the living room. It is full of books and newspapers. There are boxes of printed emails, audio cassette recordings, photographs and signed copies of diasporic books by names such as Brij Lal, Mohit Prasad, Sudesh Mishra and Subramani. My father has been attending numerous poetry readings and lecture series at the universities. There was an invitation to a film premiere in Ba and a wedding in Labasa. He has been listening to ghazals I bought as a Christmas gift for him on Amazon. He was chopping tomatoes when he collapsed. Jagji and Chitra Singh were still singing when my sister walked in with a pot of duck curry.

He is so happy you're here, she says in the hospital corridor. I told him you're going to look at his boxes of research. I know he is happy.

My sister has showered and washed out the smell of cigarettes from her mouth. She watches the rain pouring out of the hospital's clogged guttering.

Do you think you can tell him about the photograph? Let him know who we are?

IV

MY EARLIEST MEMORY OF a story is my father's about eels. He is the oldest among his brothers. The only one not in school. He loves books, particularly books without pictures. He loves the smell of wood and dried binding glue in books. He loves cloth-bound books. More than anything, he loves the swirl and fixed width of ink, of typefaces, of fonts readers decipher like enigmatic mysteries. His youngest brother, Mohandas, now a retired pot-bellied plumber in Brisbane, Australia, is seven the year my father discovers eels.

My father grows and harvests rice. He keeps ducks that feed on tadpoles, fry and elvers. My father traps eels to eat the year the rice crop is destroyed by two cyclones. He makes a deal with Mohandas. He gives his share of eel cutlets to Mohandas in exchange for books being read to him.

My father goes without meat for about a year. Then a spell of dry weather sets in. The sky is cloudless. The sun, scorching. The rice paddies dry up into little pools of muck. On a routine walk around the fields he encounters his first writhing frenzy of eels. They have congregated into diminishing pools of water. He watches the large eels kill and eat the smaller ones. He empathises with the small eels. He learns to clean and roast eels on an open fire. He trusses them with a guava twig from mouth to tail. He fills his belly and takes home enough to go around twice. It turns out to be a good year.

He tells us we are like eels in a decreasing pool of rain. That we must work hard to buy land in another country.

What does it matter? I remember saying. We will always be the ones who arrived later.

You will be a new, young eel, he says. You will not feel as much pain for a world you have yet to love. You will be the famished eel. Hungry until death. I pray you find a black cloud to give you rain.

That's a horrible story, I say.

His laughter fills the orange-lit afternoon.

Yet now, here he lies silent. I place my fingers on his wrist. I feel my father's floating and hollow pulse, what the Chinese call the scallion stalk pulse. It is said to grace the wrists of those who have suffered massive bleeding. My father has bled all his life. I know the scallion stalk pulse has been a long time coming.

I do what I have not done in years.

I talk to God.

V

I KNEW YEARS AGO that my father knew I found out about the woman in the photograph, our elusive ancestor. He knows I am the researcher he taught me to be. He knows the path of relentless questions he first placed me upon. He knew this from the days of vegetable cleaning and fish chopping in the little kitchen in Toorak. He knew I knew when I stopped coming home. As a fellow traveller, he respected my path and my stance. I followed whale pods across the Tonga Trench the first Christmas away.

You will grow into your road, he tells me when I am a child. And I have.

The archives tell me she arrived in Fiji on the SS *Jumna* at thirteen. Her name is Vellamma. She is treated for a sexually transmitted infection off the coast of Africa. She is the cause of four brawls on board the SS *Jumna*, during one of which three coolies fall overboard, unable to be rescued. Coolies — that's what the records called them.

She has liaisons with more than ten men before she is put into the lines at Rarawai. She kills the first eight of her children. There are inconclusive police and court records. She keeps a daughter alive. The one daughter is taken in by the Methodist Church in Toorak the year Vellamma is imprisoned for the brutal murder of a Muslim man by the name of Talat Mahmoud.

By the time I have uncovered this story, I have sat through hours adding up to days and nights, weeks and months at the National Archives, hunched over both public and private records. I make copies of numerous photographs of her. I make copies of the only photograph of her daughter, at about eleven years old, acting Mother of Jesus at the Dudley Orphanage Christmas play. She has my father's eyes. She will bear him more than a decade down the line. She will fall in love with a Madrasi pot-seller who will drown on a clear blue day in a clear blue lagoon. For now, she looks alarmed at the camera.

VI

I AM FIVE THE year my father tells me how to tell a story.

Always make room for uncertainty, he says. Don't say someone said this or said that. Don't ever be sure. Just walking from this kitchen to the backyard you will lose what I have just told you. Make room for that.

My father teaches me the accountability of self-questioning reported speech. I have always made room. We all make room in different ways. My father edits his stories according to who is listening.

I leave for fear of telling the truth. I leave for fear of telling untruths. I leave for fear of not providing enough room in the parentheses I place at the juncture of words and stories. My story is not mine alone. It is the story of multitudes and it will become a thread in the stories of multitudes to come.

If according to my father I can lose truth between the kitchen and the backyard, imagine the chasms of separation demarcated by clocks and geographies, between oceans and sleeps. Between lives eating grilled okra at one table. A cat laying his fur on a warm stone. My sister calling him for a fish-head treat. My playing this very scene in my head eighteen years later on a reef in New Caledonia when I receive the news that my father wishes to see me.

VII

MY SISTER FIGHTS THE afternoon traffic to pick me up from my father's house in Nausori. I have a folder of papers and photographs in a satchel. I will tell my father about Vellamma and Narayana. I have reprints of photographs of Madras under the British Raj. I have photographs of the SS *Jumna*. I have reprints of immigration passes. I have death certificates. I have the photograph of a copper cooking pot.

But more importantly, I have three handwritten letters from the distant niece growing among the wheatfields of Saskatchewan. Today, I wish him to meet her. A new storyteller who is yet to grow into her road, which will bring her to the edge of British Columbia, to the Pacific coast of Canada. Today, I watched her recite nudibranch names on YouTube. I closed my eyes on the fifth rerun. This girl is coming home.

I listen to her growing hunger. This eel will find the great expanse of Saskatchewan too small for her. Her hunger will bring her home to the sea. The Pacific will be her black cloud.

At the roundabout in Nakasi my sister stops to refuel. I walk into the Hot Bread Kitchen to buy two cream buns. My sister and I will eat these as we head into Laucala Beach Estate, before the turn-off into Vatuwaqa and Flagstaff. I realise I have missed family. My sister licks her thumb and asks for a tissue. She has sugar grains on her nose.

At the hospital, my father is behind pea-green hospital curtains. The nurses have covered him. His body is growing cold. My sister has held him tightly to herself for me. She has not wept. She has not called his brothers. She has made me pack my stories into a satchel just as when we were children. She will hold my hand as we walk outside.

You do realise, she will say, it is you who keep these stories after Daddy?

She eases the car into the hospital parking lot. I see the sun caught in a wisp of her hair. We are two eels. Famished. Our black cloud awaits.

I have yet to find out as I hand her the tissue for the sugar on her nose.

Shane Hansen, *I AM MIXED MEDIA*, 2008

MY FATHER
DREAM NEW
ZEALAND
WITI IHIMAERA

my father dream new zealand.

'blue sky, green country, people very good peoples,' he says, 'many sheep, maori do haka, go the all blacks.'

no escape from civil war, people must flee syria.

father say, 'go with uncle and family, brother take you. me your mother doctors here, follow soon. go new zealand, no war.'

cross border to turkey, thousands in camps.

'must keep moving,' uncle say.

go with brother and uncle family by bus to izmir on aegean sea. take clothings, not much. uncle and brother keep money safe but sew some in my trouser cuffs, not much.

i take storybook too, pictures torn, about maori boy, favourite.

entire country on run stopped by sea, wish waves to open.

uncle must give many dollars to ship captain for family, brother and me. 'can only take what you are wearing and a few personal items,' captain say.

maori boy look just like me, i look just like him, twins. 'quick,'

i say to him, 'hide in here,' and I find safe place in my shirt.
ferry very crowded. cross sea to greece, rough.
'boat sinking,' woman cries.
jump in water orange life jackets, many drown, small boy drifting.

uncle, family, brother me at lesbos, greek islands, flee from soldiers.
'they take to refugee camps, not good,' uncle says.
arrive athens, thousands starving in streets.
uncle insistent, 'must keep moving.'
we head for macedonian border. i open book and talk to maori
boy, matiu, 'will you be my friend?' when i arrive new zealand
maybe i become maori boy too, not just kiwi boy.
go by foot long way long. at gevgelija, peoples fight guards,
armed. through wire, running running.
'don't let go,' brother says, holds my hand.

thousands on train, crowded, cross at tabanovce, then exodus serbia
long way long.
arrive hungary border, police water hoses to stop us gas make
eyes cry.
brother, uncle and family go over and have good fortune. uncle
finds man takes peoples in truck in dark truck dark. must use last
money in trouser cuffs to pay.
'get in, quick, get in,' uncle says. 'make no noise, be quiet as
mouse.'
truck motor starts.
door locks. soon we will be safe in austria.

truck stops.

very very tired.
will work very hard, save money. brother take me, go new
zealand, mother father follow soon.

'when is soon?' i ask brother.

he holds my hand. 'soon is soon.'

blue sky, green country, no war. people very good peoples. many sheep, maori do haka, go the all blacks. be good kiwi.

'go fishing eels with you, matiu,' i whisper, 'i meet your family, you meet mine, we not just syria family or kiwi family, eh bro. sit with you on marae, eat from hangi, poke out tongue, laugh together, laugh and laugh and laugh.'

all this, when the door opens.

'WE MOBS GOT TO START ACTING LOCALLY. SHOW WHOSE GOT THE DREAMING. THE LAAAW.'

from *Carpentaria*

ALEXIS WRIGHT

WILL HAD ALWAYS HALF expected that if he had been captured, the mining company bosses would queue up to have a look at the kind of person who would destroy a mine. The very same newsreader had called this kind of person the most feared of the North. But the red-faced Graham Spilling he had once seen on the television was not the kind of man who would be coming posthaste to the hangar in the light of day. The irony was, men like Spilling did not kill other men. Only the person, perhaps inebriated enough to turn into another kind of human being, like Frankenstein, could temporarily find courage to instruct the cold bloodedness of killing. Wasn't it in the dead of night when good people go about their dark deeds?

One becomes more confident when one's not alone, and somehow, this was how Will felt. An odd sensation that made no sense, yet it would not leave him alone. There was no rationale in the stupidity of thinking others — what others? — would come to help him. Even though he had not heard any movement, he was convinced the Fishman and enough men were outside, waiting for his signal. Now he saw a different perspective on his arrival at the hangar when he was thrown from the helicopter. The Fishman's two thieves were lying flat in the grass next to the shed when the helicopter had taken off. Through the dust he had seen them raise their heads from the grass. Hands signalled, questioning what had happened. Then when his eyes followed the flight of the kingfisher, now retracing its movement, taking notice of the whole panorama of spinifex to the foothills, he saw the subtle movement of other men from the convoy stationed in the distant hills on the other side of the fence. They were back-up for the thieves scouting the hangars for an overnight operation. Will knew if they were still around, then the rest of the convoy would be down at the lagoon. What was new? They were short of fuel.

Will looked for the kingfisher but it was now nowhere in sight. He kept an ear on the radio in the background, listened as the weatherman read the weather report. A cyclonic build-up in the Arafura Sea. Will grew interested, remembering an earlier report of a cyclone sitting off the opposite coastline, east of Cape York Peninsula. He could hear the words — *low-pressure system building into a depression heading in a southeasterly direction along the Arafura Sea*. This surprised him. What had happened to the cyclone off the Cape? Nothing. The weather report ended. It must have been in his dreams.

The day he had left old Midnight and taken his boat to sea he had heard the report of a cyclone hanging south-southeast of Cape York, somewhere in the Coral Sea. What happened to that? The weatherman ended with a short statement about a tidal surge due to the cyclone activity in the region. Will closed his eyes and saw the tremendous fury of the winds gathering up the seas, and clouds carrying the enormous bodies of spiritual beings belonging to other worlds. Country people, old people, said it was the sound of the great spiritual ancestors roaring out of the dusty, polluted sea all of the time nowadays. Will believed this. Everyone clearly saw what the spirits saw. The country looked dirty from mining, shipping, barges spilling ore and waste. Something had to run a rake across the lot. 'You really got to watch your step now,' old man Joseph Midnight warned when Will had taken the boat out. His voice had crawled over the water to Will. 'Last couple of years, there was one every few weeks, another cyclone jumping around. Whoever heard of that before?'

Jesus Christ! There was water piling up in the skies. Then nothing. The weather report was over. Stuck in an empty hangar a couple of hundred kilometres from the sea, Will imagined all the satellite activity hovering over the Gulf. Spies of the world zoomed in onto a pimple on your nose, or knew what you were saying in the privacy of your own home. Was anyone looking at Gurfurritt? If someone spied on the weather, why not provide more information about what was going on? Rich men paid for foreign cargo ships from the four corners of the globe to anchor in the Gulf to transport ore.

It was high tide. Will knew how the tides worked simply by looking at the movement of a tree, or where the moon crossed the sky, the light of day, or the appearance of the sea. He carried the tide in his body. Even way out in the desert, when he was on the Fishman's convoy, a thousand miles away from the sea, he felt its rhythms.

This feeling for the sea had been inherited from Norm, and Will began to think of his father on his journey with Elias. *I hope you make it to the old world.* But of course he would make it. Will scowled at his weak sentimentality over his father who never bore his children's burden. A saltwater man who insisted he belonged to the sea like fish. *I'll weather the storm.* So said the veteran of the mother of all storms, invading the hangar out of the blue, to this wasted luxury of his son, reminiscing what was once upon a time: *If the natural forces get me in the end, it will be on the flippen land. Never the sea. I bet my life on it.*

Puzzled, irritated by the commonsense madness of his father's hick-town philosophy, Will twisted about on the chair, muttering to himself: 'If you're dead, you're dead, no need to bet on that.' But the memories of his father were not done with Will's thoughts, even in this moment of crisis. Norm Phantom was keen to show his son, whom he had not spoken to in years, something else from the past. The little list. The list, boy! Did you remember to bring the list? How a man could come back to collect his winnings, if he did not keep his little list of fools in his back pocket: who owed him money, so forth.

'What's the matter with him?' The Fishman's men had been trying to attract Will's attention.

'Dunno. Throw a stone and see.'

Someone hit Will on the leg with a small stone to bring some sense into his head. Now he saw two men from the convoy standing by the door smiling at him. Then the mobile phone rang.

'Chuck,' the yellow-haired man spat his name into the mobile. He had come out of the kitchenette and was standing somewhere to the back of Will in the hangar.

'What? A fire. You got to be joking . . . Alright, I'm on my way.'

'What's up?'

'Graham said there's a fire over this way. Stay here, watch him, Cookie. I'll look around.'

The next moment Chuck returned, running to grab the fire extinguisher, and ordering his mate to get the other fire extinguisher on the wall next to the doorway. Ignoring Will, both quickly disappeared.

The Fishman's men had come prepared. Knives were produced to cut Will free from the chair. Within seconds they were outside the shed again and, looking back, sensed that Will was of two minds about going with them. 'You mad, Will?' They had only moments to get out of the place, and Will was holding them up.

'Give me a knife,' Will ordered, but no one listened to him. 'Fuck you! Give me a knife or I'll kill you. They killed Hope and my boy. I am going nowhere, I swear to God, until I kill them. So give me the fucken knife.'

Moving around the benches, Will saw a tyre lever, grabbed it, and headed out the door. The two lads felt blood draining from their faces: this was supposed to be easy. They looked at the fire down at the last hangar. The flames were arching out like waves and black smoke billowed into the atmosphere.

'Look, man, I know how you feel! But those arseholes are dead already. They're gone, man, I swear it, because as true as God I am standing here, this whole place is going to blow, as soon as the fire reaches the pits. Come on, we got to take you with us, fuck you, or we are going to die in this mongrel place. Look up there and see the friggen fire for yourself, man. Come on, man, or we will kill you ourselves.'

The two young men, no more than eighteen apiece, dressed in grey shorts, baseball caps, with Bob Marley staring from their Rasta-coloured T-shirts, worked simply to the letter of the Fishman's orders. They were still wearing workingmen boots supplied by the mine. A lot of the young men in the Fishman's convoy had done their stint in the mine, looked around, seen how it all worked, then walked off with their mining helmets and boots as souvenirs. Both still had their cigarettes hanging from the sides of their mouths, while they used the iron-fisted grit of their fathers to persuade Will to get the hell out of there.

The fire spread quickly across the grasslands, throwing long red tongues down to the south. Will looked at the black smoke billowing into the sky. He tried to see through the wall of smoke to locate the two mine men with their fire extinguishers, but could not penetrate the curtain of blackness. The only thing that was clear was flames reaching up into the sky at the far hangars. It looked like a giant candle, a millennium flame. A wind of intense heat forced Will and the two Bob Marley faces to flee.

'Come on, Will, get a fucking move on,' one of the lads said, maintaining a firm grip on Will's arm. The second lad did the same on the other side and they ran dragging Will along with them. They kept looking back over their shoulders as they ran, stumbling along through the spinifex and grass and gravel, seeing if anyone was coming from the mine, or if they were seen. Looking ahead at the distance to reach the fenceline, each knew, until they were over the fence and into the scrub land and hills, they would be in full view of the mine men when they turned up in their vehicles.

'Let's hope the bloody lot goes up in their bloody faces,' one lad said to the other as they ran, knowing it might be their only chance, if the bloody lot went up. But when they looked back again, the yellow-haired one and his mate were running after them.

'Split up,' Will said. 'Take the left and right, and I will take the centre, go low.'

'Do you know where the opening is, Will? Head to the left, one hundred metres. Remember that.'

'Get going. I know where it is, get going.'

The three peeled off in their different directions. The two young lads were looking around. Where was the backup? The whole operation had begun with several dozen men who had slipped in earlier, spreading themselves all over the mine site, to do 'a good job'. It was to have been a pilfering exercise on a grand scale, pure and simple. Then they got word: Fishman had changed his mind. The teams had come in the previous night. They moved on the fuel tanks, syphoning petrol into jerry cans which had to be carried over to the fenceline and into the bush on the other side towards a waiting vehicle. They had spread around. 'Have yourself a shopping spree, tools and equipment — for the road.' Freezer raid, the Fishman had ordered. Usual thing. Raid everything.

'Man! Where in the fuck are they?' one lad screamed across to his mate. 'Where's the bloody backup, mannn? Jesus!'

Guns were being fired. The two lads heard the strange sound for the first time in their lives as the bullets whistled by, inches past their ears, and both yelled, 'Duck, man, they are shooting at us.' Both ran faster, bolting for their lives like jackrabbits, and Will, where was he? They had seen him disappear into the ground like he was made out of thin air. And they did duck, unbelievingly, as they ran, seeking cover behind every clump of spinifex, as though dead spinifex could shield anyone against bullets. But that was what they did, and kept doing, with no backup at all, not even looking back to see that glorious fire tonguing down to the underground storage tanks, nor knowing there were only moments to go, and they would be all feeling what it was like to be blown sky-high, if they did not make it out over the fence and into the hills.

Fate and precious moments are tied up together, and as the saying goes, What goes around comes around: the yellow-haired man tripped. Instantly, his head was split open at the temple by a rock that had, up to that moment, lain on the ground, embedded in soil that was thousands of seasons old, untouched by humankind since the ancestor had placed it in this spot, as if it had planned to do this incredible thing.

Rock and roll, it was unbelievable to have seen what happened. Will had been so close, waiting to take what rightfully he claimed, and the man was running straight for him, and only Will saw what was about to happen, saw the rock was ready, waiting for this moment. Instantaneously, it was as natural a reaction as you would expect, but he felt cheated, you know. He had even thrown himself towards the man to try to break his fall. It was too late, a snap, how quickly a driven man could be defeated. Will had no idea a rock could rob him of his revenge. He stood, arched over the dead man in a moment of foreboding, watching the blood pouring out of the man's head all over the ground, the glorious yellow hair now tainted red and covered with dust, wishing he had the power to bring the dead man back to life. Where was the justice in this? The murderer struck dead, died instantly without pain, and went on to eternity with the look of peace on his broken face. And there was the stone, still there, unmoved.

'Will! What the fuck are you doing? Keep running,' one of the young blokes yelled back over his shoulder. 'Jesus Christ!' he yelled, 'I never seen so much craziness in you, man.' Seeing Will standing there looking at the ground, the young man was certain he would end up going back for him, just to appease the Fishman, and shouted: 'You are going to get us all killed, fuck you.'

Will heard and ran. Out in the open he looked back for the red-haired Cookie, but he was nowhere in sight. Will had missed the moment that the backup men with rifles in the hills had witnessed. In full flight, lifted in midair, Cookie kept running after his prey before he heard the piece of lead explode in his chest. His eyes jumped to the left, then to the right, as though undecided which way to go to hell first, before he sunk down into the spinifex.

A dozen convoy men scrambling out of the hills, leaping down rocks, hands cut by spinifex, raced to the fenceline to open a hole in the wire. The fence was rolled back for Will and the two lads to run towards. It seemed as though the whole world cheered them, yelling: 'Come on, come on, hurry, you can do it.' Then, the cheering turned into a synchronised ballet of men risking their lives without thought for themselves. They ran out towards the lads, and finally, had the three snatched up by a sea of hands. Their lungs burnt with exhaustion. A human chain passed each of the three along up to the hills, until finally they were thrown down for shelter behind the boulders, in the fold of the ancestral spirit who governed the land.

THE FIRE BURNED LIKE hell over there at the hangars, and even in the hills the air was that hot, it burnt your skin. It felt like being in a furnace. Dust-dry hair turned into rust, stuck up straight and waved in the air, charged up to the hilt with electricity. Well! The moment came then, just how the Fishman said it had to be. And it would not have paid anyone to look back if they did not want to have their head blown off in 'the process'. They were the Fishman's favourite two words in those days.

The day, all action-packed like it was, was now all said and done. The men of Mozzie Fishman's dedicated convoy to one major Dreaming track stretching right across their stolen continent, were sitting up there on the side of the hill — like rock wallabies, looking down at what was left of Gurfurritt mine. Just looking, and turning the sunset crimson with their thoughts.

A day at the mine had turned into a modern legend about travelling with the Fishman, and civil morality . . .

What a turnout. Gee whiz! We were in really serious stuff now. We were burning the white man's very important places and wasting all his money. We must have forgotten our heads. We were really stupid people to just plumb forget like — because the white man was a very important person who was very precious about money. Well! He was the boss. We are not boss. He says he likes to be boss. He says he's got all the money. Well! We haven't got the money neither. And now, all it took was a simple flick. A flick, flick, here and there with a dirt-cheap cigarette lighter, and we could have left the rich white people who owned Gurfurritt mine, destitute and dispossessed of all they owned.

Straight out we should have been asking ourselves — Why are you not hanging your head in shame to the white man? We were supposed to say, Oh! No! You can't do things like that to the, umm, beg your pardon, please and thank you, to the arrr, em, WHITE MAN.

Somehow, though, everyone got carried along the humpteen

tide of events, like, we must have swallowed one too many sour pills that morning for breakfast. Now, we were looking at the world like it was something fresh and inviting to jump into and do what you jolly well liked. That was how our dormant emotions sitting down inside our poor old hearts got stirred up by the Fishman when we listened to him talking in that fetching, guru-type voice of his, saying we gotta change the world order. Change the world order? Mozzie Fishman! He is sure enough a crazy man. Oh! We said that. But he goes on in his satirical slinging voice about what happened ever since that mine came scraping around our land and our Native title! 'Well!' he says. Us? He wanted us to tell him what that turned out to be! We were a bit cross with Mozzie standing up there, Lord Almighty-like on top of that rust bucket of a Falcon station wagon of his. It and all its white crucifixes wiped all over the car through the stains of red mud.

'You know who we all hear about all the time now?' he asked us.

'International mining company. Look how we got to suit international mining people. Rich people. How we going to do that?' Now, even we, any old uneducated buggers, are talking globally. We got to help United Kingdom money. Netherlands lead air problems. Asia shipping. United States of America industry, and we don't even know German people. 'I says,' he says like he is singing, 'we mobs got to start acting locally. Show whose got the Dreaming. The Laaaw.' He liked to emphasise 'The Laaaw' whenever he was heating up around the ears on the subject of globalisation.

We whispered among ourselves. Ignore him. Clap your hands over your ears to put an end to his blasphemy. Don't listen to him. Still he was not finished with us. He went on ignoring our pleas, and in the end demanded, soft as silk, he knew who he was playing with. All satiny voice, he said it was time now to end our cowtailing after the white people. It was finale time. Hands up. Who we got to follow? The white man, or the Fishman? This was the ultimatum. Well! He made us that wild. Of course, we got no choice — we got to go with culture every time. We should have known he was leading up to all of this destruction. But we? We were like following dogs, and we were happy to do it, not think, because we were acting solely and simply on pure rage.

The soundwaves coming off the explosion in the aeroplane hangars at the biggest mine of its type in the world, Gurfurritt, were just about as tremendous a sound you could ever expect to hear on this earth. Like guyfork night. Booom! Booom! Over and over. But one hundred times more louder than that. Ripped the lot. We were thinking, those of us lying on the ground up in the hills smelling ash — what if our ears exploded? What would deafness sound like? We should have thought of that first.

Sometime during our precious time on earth we could have asked a deaf person what it was like to not hear the sounds anymore, before we go around deliberately destroying our own good hearing on wildness. Oh! But there was no going back because no one was going to reverse where the rotten hand of fate was heading. So, even though we were shaking in our old work boots, thinking we got busted eardrums, we watched the fire rage like a monster cut loose from another world. It might even have come from hell. Even the devil himself would have least expected us weak people to have opened the gates of hell. But we watched full of fascination at the fire's life, roaring like a fiery serpent, looking over to us with wild eyes, pausing, looking around, as if deciding what to do next. Then, we could hear it snarl in an ugly voice you would never want to hear again. *Alright, watch while I spread right through those hangars like they were nothing, hungry! hungry! Get out of my way.* It did that roaring along, exploding through walls and rooftops which looked like toadstools bursting open, then once those flames shot outside, going a million miles an hour up into the sky, sparks just landing wherever, like a rain shower, out in the grass somewhere around the back.

The fire spread out the back of the hangars in the dry grass, and then it came burning around to the front again, fanned by a gusting southeasterly wind. Then, the monster smelt the spilt fuel on the ground. It raced through that, quickly spreading itself over the ground weeds, until it found the fuel bowsers, then it paused, maybe the fire had thoughts of its own and could not believe its luck. The fire just sitting there was as awesome a moment as you could experience for our men waiting in the hills, sneaking a glance from over the boulders they were hiding behind, peering through the black smoke, thinking maybe their luck had run out and what next.

It looked as though the fire was going to peter out. The fire was just sitting, smouldering, not knowing where to go next because the wind was not blowing strong enough to fan it in the right direction. Our men looking from the hills continued staring at the little flame flickering there, fizzing out. What could they do? It looked like defeat was imminent. And that same old defeated look, two centuries full of it, began creeping back onto their faces. But, it was too late now, they had a taste of winning, so they projected their own sheer willpower right across that spinifex plain, calling out with no shame, *Come on, come on*, willing the little flame not to fizz, believing magic can happen even to poor buggers like themselves.

Somehow, someone started yelling, 'Look, look, it is starting to move.' The unbelievable miracle came flying by. A whirly wind, mind you nobody had seen one for days, just as a matter of fact sprung up from the hills themselves. It swirled straight through from behind those men, picking up their wish and plucking the baseball caps which came flying off their heads, together with all the loose balls of spinifex flying with the dust and the baseball caps, the whole lot moving towards the fire. When it passed over the open rubbish tipsters the mine had lined up along the side of the hangars, it picked up all the trash. All the cardboard boxes, newspapers lying about and oily rags, spirited the whole lot across the flat towards the line of hangars on fire.

It happened so fast when the fiery whirlwind shot into the

bowsers and momentarily lit them up like candles. Well! It might even have been the old Pizza Hut box someone had left on top of one of those bowsers that added that little bit of extra fuel, you never know, for the extra spark, or it would have happened anyway, but the wick was truly lit.

The finale was majestical. Dearo, dearie, the explosion was holy in its glory. All of it was gone. The whole mine, pride of the banana state, ended up looking like a big panorama of burnt chop suey. On a grand scale of course because our country is a very big story. Wonderment, was the ear on the ground listening to the great murmuring ancestor, and the earth shook the bodies of those ones lying flat on the ground in the hills. Then, it was dark with smoke and dust and everything turned silent for a long time.

'You think they heard it in Desperance?' some young lad whispered carefully through the settling dust, because he did not want to frighten anyone by making the first sound of this new beginning. It was so incomprehendingly silent he needed to speak to hear himself talk because he was thinking of his family and the noise of his memories of them was the only sound he could hear.

The sound of this young voice being the first sound was a relief for the others who had been thinking they were listening to the sound of their own deafness. However relieved and pacified they were to hear speech, everyone kept listening, listening for what else remained missing — Ah! It was the noise of the bush breathing, the wind whispering through the trees and flowing through rustling grasses. We needed to hear the birds chirping, the eaglehawk crying out something from the thermals high above, but the eerie silence lingered on. The birds were nowhere to be seen or heard, not even a singing willy-wagtail lightly flittering from rock to rock wherever anyone walked, or a mynah bird haggling at your feet. We looked into the dust and smoke-darkened skies and saw no twisting green cloud of budgerigars dancing away in thin air. The wind had dropped. Silent clouds passing overhead cast gloomy shadows over the peaceful trees, while grasses and spinifex stood stock-still as though the world had become something false, almost reminiscent of a theatre setting. We men floated somewhere between the surreal stillness, and the reality of the ants, lizards and beetles and other insects moving through the rocky ground as though nothing had happened. No one spoke or answered the boy, because we guessed the explosion must have been heard on the other side of the world, let alone in Desperance.

One will never know what really happened that day. Fishman never stopped smiling about it. He said his recipe was top secret. He was regarded with awe whenever he came into anyone's presence because it was a privilege to know the Fishman. He was respected for what he had inside of his head. Too right! Nobody could know the highly confidential material in case someone like Mozzie had to do it all over again some day. Ignorant people would always ask, *How did you stop the mine?* And he would look at them for a long time with his steady eye, like he was making up his mind whether they were worth letting in on the secret. Finally, he would say, *I have decided to give you the truth*, and the truth was the very same words he had always used about what he would do to the mine from the day it got set up on our traditional domain. 'I put broken glass bottles on the road to stop the buggers — that's what I did.' Somehow, this was the truth. Truth just needed to be interpreted by the believers who could find the answers themselves just like the Fishman had done. At the same time he offered another piece of advice, which was, a smiling man would live for a very long time. And he did.

A FRENZIED MEDIA FROM the bustling world of 'Down South' fuelled up, to fly back and forth over the mine in their helicopters like flies. Unlike any fly, the journalists saw the Gulf through virgin eyes. It was a place few Australians had been to, let alone those of any other country tied up with the Gulf of Carpentaria. It was a world apart from their own. Anything in this new world could be created, moulded, and placed on television like something to dream about, or a nightmare.

What stirred their souls was the pureness of silence and the intriguing sense of loneliness each had discovered on their arrival in single-engine charter planes at the aerodrome of Desperance. There, hours could go by, and the only thing happening was the sound of the weather funnel rattling against a steel pole — Twang, Twang! Twang! Under these circumstances, for the fascinated news people romancing the Gulf, no story became too big or too small, to give to the world.

Televised on-the-spot reports of the dead ore body, lying across the ground like a fallen hero, filled the TV screens across the nation. Splashed into every news broadcast was a badly composed identikit picture of Will Phantom which bore no resemblance to him. A lot of people in Desperance started asking questions. They wanted to know who that person was that they saw on television every night, who was running around calling himself Will Phantom. It was a good question, because mix-ups and things like that did not help, if Desperance people felt they were complete strangers to one another, and they could not understand the truth of television. For mind you, they were still recovering from the shock of the mine. There was a thin feeling in the air. A tension. It became as though anything could snap at any moment over the very idea of life itself. Anything could fall from a loose hinge into full-blown hysteria.

The multi-million-dollar mine, from infancy to its working prime, was probed, described and paraded to network viewers. Interviews and footage of scenery went jig-jogging along in soap opera intensity, before finally shifting to pan, and viewers were encouraged to dissect what had become of this showcase of the nation. They watched forensic scientists fully covered in white protective clothing, risking their lives, hunting through the rubble. Who could even breathe while watching these brave men and women slowly prod through each piece of debris in this solemn post mortem, carried out with the meticulous thoroughness of an ant? It became a televised spectacular, just like the death of an icon, woven with the interactiveness of Nintendo. Viewers could call up. They could hear their own voices via satellite and underground cable, coming back to them from the mine itself on television. Ordinary people living thousands of miles away, who had no former interest whatsoever in the mine or its location, joined the growing numbers of bereaved viewers gandering at the still untameable, northern hinterland.

The face of a scientist, speaking behind his glass-fronted mask with a muffled voice which had to be transcribed into English on the bottom of the television set, like the SBS channel, became the anchorman for the task that lay ahead. On the first day he reported that a fire had spread from the main transport hangars to the fuelling bowsers. It was lucky no one was killed. On day two, the wash-up at the end of the day was like at the beginning, this was a major explosion in the remote Gulf of Carpentaria at Gurfurritt, the biggest mine of its type in the world. The scientists viewed viewing what lay on the ground were trying to discover what caused the explosion. There had been no fatal casualties. And so on. After a week of the hooded scientist, another bald, Mars-faced scientist appeared on the television screen. He was at home with a sad expression on his face which popped out of fawn-coloured clothes. He gave the scientific explanation on the news: 'The fire at Gurfurritt mine initiated from a grassfire. Spinifex exploded and the intensity of the fire it created quickly spread to the bowsers. (Pause.) This caused a major explosion to the underground fuel tanks. I understand that this explosion spread through the underground fuel pipes up to the mine. This action quickly reached the main fuel tanks, which caused another major explosion, causing major damage to the mine and machinery.

'The fuel line to the mine operations connected to the main fuel tanks caused further major damage to occur. The intense heat rising into the atmosphere from the initial explosions generated a chain reaction of explosions throughout the mine. (Footage to air of mass destruction.) An incidental fuel leakage running throughout the 300-kilometre pipeline to the coast caused it to be extensively damaged. (Pause.) This damage was caused by an explosion throughout the buried pipeline which was only running at a third of its capacity at the time of the incident. The force from this simultaneous explosion uncovered the entire pipeline and pieces were found many kilometres from their original site. (Pan shot: bits of pipeline sticking out of the ground and throughout the surrounding bushland like an exhibition of postmodern sculpture outside the Australian National Gallery or Tate Modern in London on the Thames.) At the end of the pipeline, there was extensive damage at the dewatering plant where storage tanks were destroyed.'

WHEN THE EXPLOSIONS STOPPED, the Fishman's men picked themselves up from the ground. They agreed that only the greatness of the mighty ancestor had saved them. It was a miracle they were still alive after the earth shook so violently underneath them, they had thought it would go on forever. A heavy red fog of dust and smoke hung in the air as they moved away, their visibility limited to just a few metres. The fine dust fell slowly, and when it settled on those men who were trying to regain a sense of the enormity of what had happened, they took on the appearance of the earth itself. One by one, camouflaged by dust, they began spiriting themselves away, quickly, carefully, as dust covered their tracks, back to the lagoon of the dancing spirits.

The ancestral trees at the lagoon danced wildly in the ash wind around the Fishman sitting on the ground staring red-eyed from weariness in the direction of the mine. He had been sitting in that position for hours visualising what was happening at the mine, waiting for his men to return. Their return seemed to be taking forever, and those extraordinary followers watching the master were making other rare discoveries. They were convinced that the Fishman had shrunk in front of their very eyes. They were sure he was growing smaller and smaller with every passing second of precious time. The chances were, if he continued to shrink, there would be nothing left of him by the time they would be compelled to flee. In this perilous locale, they nodded, he would become an obscure beetle left crawling around the edge of the lagoon.

It was true, Mozzie Fishman did seek obscurity. His instinctive trait was to crawl away from adversity, at least metaphorically, into invisibility and nothingness. What caused this peculiarity of his tangled personality was something that went berserk in what he called his stupid brain, whenever he had anything to do with white people. It seemed it was white people who could tug on his conscience, making him degrade himself like this. The truth was, Mozzie Fishman was shrinking, waiting for his men, *Oh! Great spirits of God, let there be no casualties*, he longed, moaning to himself. He was so full of the anxiety and, shrinking up into a beetle, he could not see the young men who ran through the bush hoping to evade capture, jumping for cover as skilfully as hares.

Yet, on the other side of his mind, he fought like a rabid dog to maintain an octopus vision of himself, where all arms led to great glory and success. In this view of the world, there was no room for doubts to interfere with the great spirits of destiny whose permanent home was etched into the land itself, in this place. No one tampered with these arms of destiny which belonged only to Mozzie, as though he had put out a single hand to catch a true stone after it was fired from a shanghai. His general mood was downhearted somewhat and forlorn, yet in spite of the world of calamity he had created, he felt calmly sated as he sat alone in contemplation.

BLACK ICE

GINA COLE

PASSANG TOUCHED HIS NUMB cheek as he left the dental surgery. He felt no connection with his own skin, as if his hand floated on the cold surface of someone else's flesh. Passang's name in Sherpa meant 'Friday'. He was born on Friday, same as his older brother, Passang, and his younger sister, also Passang.

A taxi swerved in to the kerb next to him. A startling manoeuvre, but since the car was a taxi he was unsurprised. The passenger door flew open, and alcohol fumes wafted out from the dank interior of the vehicle. A drunk white man with dishevelled red hair and ratty teeth slurred and cursed at the driver, a man of indeterminate racial heritage, maybe North Indian, western Turkish, northern Chinese or Croatian. He sat impassive, his tweed cheese-cutter meeting the edge of black horn-rimmed glasses.

'You are a Muslim prick,' said the passenger.

'Why?' said the taxi driver.

'Because you come over here and . . . why don't you just fuck off back to where you came from?'

'The camera is recording you.'

'Don't you threaten me, you prick!'

'I'm just saying there's a camera in here recording you.'

'You just blither out crap . . . you Islam filth.'

'Okay.'

'Are you from New Zealand?'

'I told you. I'm not from here.'

'So you're here to infiltrate our country.'

The taxi driver's tone remained gentle, exasperated. 'Seven dollars. If you want to pay me now it's good. Okay?'

'Why can't you just fuck off and go back to where you came from?'

'I will go. But first pay me, okay?'

'I'll pay you seven bucks when you tell me that you'll piss off back to the country you came from. You shouldn't be in New Zealand in the first place. We don't require your Muslim bullshit.'

Passang saw the passenger pull a hunting knife from his jacket and wave it at the driver. The driver left the engine running and ran onto the footpath next to Passang. The drunk passenger fell out of the cab and onto his own knife, stabbing himself in the chest.

Passang forgot his anaesthetised face and rushed to the man, much as he'd reached out two days ago to the woman who'd tripped over her crampon ties and cartwheeled her arms trying to right herself on the ice. In mid-flight she'd spun her elbow into Passang's face and broken his front tooth clean in half. Passang fell to his knees next to the man and held his hands on each side of the knife to stop the bleeding. Deep red blood pulsed over his splayed fingers, spattering the gold letters on the knife handle: 'Helico Hydraulics'.

'What's your name?' Passang asked him.

'Malcolm Buttworth,' he said, and passed out.

Passang kept the pressure around the knife wound until the ambulance arrived.

The taxi driver was Bilal Dareshak from Pakistan. Bilal showed the police the camera footage of Mr Buttworth's abusive tirade in the taxi, followed by his fall onto the knife, followed by Passang saving his life.

'He should get a medal,' said Bilal, jabbing his finger at Passang.

THE FOLLOWING MORNING PASSANG drove out of Queenstown on State Highway 6 towards Fox Glacier Township. He slowed down on the dark road through the Kawarau Gorge. Traffic signs emblazoned with the words '*BLACK ICE*' shone iridescent orange in the car's headlights. Passang knew to concentrate on the road ahead and not get distracted by the turquoise river glowing in the gorge below. This stretch of road had seen many vehicles slide out of control, smash through the barriers and plummet over the bank into the icy water. He peered at the road for any glossy sheen of black ice. Approaching the end of the gorge, he spotted a change in the asphalt. The tar smoothed out, and tiny shadows disappeared. He felt the car pull into a spin, and turned the wheels into the skid. The car fishtailed and slid back on course.

As he drove into Fox Glacier Township, shadowy mountains rose above him. He steered the car straight to the office of Blue Glacier Tours.

'HEY DADDY SHERPA, YOU'RE famous!' said Bernard Galway. 'Good to have you back. We've got a full book today.'

Passang was always respectful of the owner's youngest son. 'Not such a great day for it, Bernard.'

Outside the rain had started to fall, and clouds had settled over the summits of Mount Tasman and Mount Cook. The guides in the boot room busied themselves preparing for the first group of the day. Andrea was at the counter putting the sock bins out. As Passang bounced into the room, she straightened her lean, tall frame and tossed her brown hair to one side with a laugh.

'Hey, hero Sherpa. We saw you on TV saving that jerk's life. How's the tooth?'

'All fixed.'

Passang flashed a smile, showing his new crown. The guides gathered round, laughing and ribbing him about Malcolm Buttworth, about the tooth, about his star appearance on television.

ANDREA DROVE THE BUS up to the glacier. The tourists were split into two groups of six so that each group had at least two guides. She took one group into the carpark with Passang for a safety talk, and Bernard, Hans and Gunter took the other six to a large information sign for their safety talk. The two groups came back together, and Andrea led everyone on the track up to the ice. She wore a wide-brimmed leather hat that left her ears uncovered. When they arrived at the ice, she listened for rocks, water, cracking ice: any indication of a safety risk to their charges for the day.

On the glacier, the two groups split once more. Bernard walked ahead with his group of tourists and guides. Andrea led her group, with Passang following close behind her. She stopped occasionally to survey the ice, reading the signs for hidden crevasses and scouting for holes. Passang pointed out secure routes to the icefall and spotted ice caves and a pool of milky blue water surrounded by ice columns, photo opportunities for the tourists.

Bernard appeared on the ice face above Passang and Andrea. He hurled schist rocks into the pool, making loud splashing noises.

'What was that?' said one of the tourists in a Geordie accent.

'It's Bernard. Must be a boy thing,' said Andrea, and led the tourists to the next sight, a blue ice cave.

As the end of the tour drew near, the separate groups headed by Bernard and Andrea converged at the foot of the icefall and crossed behind a large schist boulder the size of an armoured tank. Bernard held his ice axe in one hand as he approached Andrea. The sharp metal ends were the same browny orange colour as the old algae-covered rocks in the valley. She edged past him.

'You've got mushrooms,' she said, eyeing the pick.

Passang laughed behind her, the group of six tourists following in a line behind him. Bernard's eyes changed from blue to dark grey. 'If I put this axe into your head it wouldn't make any difference,' he said, looking at Passang.

'Sherpa skull is pretty strong,' said Passang.

Everyone laughed except Andrea, who looked uncomfortable. The Geordie tourist asked Passang, 'Is that her boyfriend?'

'Yep. Boyfriend and girlfriend.'

A grey cloud lifted off the ice as they walked down the glacier.

Bernard's voice stuttered on Andrea's walkie-talkie. 'Where's Daddy Sherpa?'

'He's here with me,' said Andrea. There was silence on the other end.

IN THE BOOT ROOM that evening, the tourists removed their packs, raincoats, rainpants, socks and boots and left them in wet piles in blue plastic bins. Their faces were bright and energised as they thanked the guides and trickled out of the building into a dim evening. Passang helped Andrea put socks into the washing machine and hang boots up on the racks.

'We should go to the pub tonight,' she said.

'Yes, we toast the Sherpa hero,' said Hans in his thick German accent. Gunter, his countryman, agreed with him, and they spoke emphatic German to each other.

'Yeah, let's go and watch the game,' said Passang.

Bernard emerged from the office with a cordless phone. 'TV3 again,' he said, handing the phone to Passang.

It was a producer from the newsroom. The taxi camera footage had gone viral.

'We'd like to interview you,' she said.

'What for?'

'People are interested in how a Nepalese Sherpa feels about saving the life of a drunken racist ranter.'

'Oh?'

All Black supporters filled the pub, with a few Springbok followers huddled in small groups. The Geordie tourist sat hunched over a large glass of beer. Black bunting and silver fern All Black flags dangled over the bar, and large New Zealand flags hung on either side of the television. The crowd applauded Passang as he entered the room.

Andrea took Passang's arm and they were ushered, with Bernard, Hans and Gunter, to a table laden with handles of beer. People shook Passang's hand. One old man grabbed his shoulder and said, 'That bloody Invercargill bastard made me ashamed to be a Kiwi the way he talked to that taxi driver bloke. Not like you, mate. You are a top-shelf Kiwi Sherpa.'

'Ah, it was nothing,' said Passang.

When the All Blacks scored the match-winning try, Passang jumped up and punched the air. Andrea jumped with him, and then placed her hands on his chest and kissed him. He guessed she'd acted out of impulse in the heat of the moment. But her eyes had lingered on him far too long, and Bernard was watching them. Passang turned away from her and walked to the bar.

He could see Bernard and Andrea locked in stern conversation.

Hans joined him at the bar, shaking his head.

'They arguing over there,' said Hans.

'I'm going home,' said Passang.

'Me too,' said Hans.

As Hans and Passang walked through the carpark, Bernard ran out, grabbed Passang by the shoulder and spun him around.

'Hey, what are you doing?' said Passang.

Bernard jutted his chin out and shouted at Passang. 'You don't know what she's like.'

'I wasn't doing anything with your missus,' said Passang. Bernard punched him in the face.

Passang's head jerked backwards. The new crown flew out of

his mouth. He stumbled against a car door and collapsed onto the gravel. As he lay on the ground he saw people spilling down the steps from the pub. Andrea ran to his side and helped him up.

'My tooth,' he said, holding his mouth.

Andrea scrabbled about in the gravel and found the white ceramic crown.

'Come with me, Sherpa,' she said, holding his arm. Passang tried to bat her away, but she fussed over him.

'You're hurt,' she said, watching Hans shuffling Bernard to the office.

PASSANG SAT AT THE kitchen table in Andrea's flat, holding his jaw. 'Does it hurt much?' she asked.

'Just a bit bruised. I'll have to go back to the dentist,' he said, moving his jaw from side to side.

'This will help.' She dabbed arnica on his bruised face.

He winced in pain. 'Look, I don't want to get in between you and Bernard.'

'We broke up while you were away in Queenstown. We've been growing apart for a while.'

'I didn't know.'

'Bernard didn't want to tell anyone.'

'So why did he punch me?'

Andrea put her hand on Passang's leg. 'If we didn't tell anyone then I guess he could pretend we weren't breaking up.'

'Why did you kiss me?' he said.

'Why do you think?' she said, laughing.

'I love my job, Andrea. He could fire me.'

'His father does all the hiring and firing. He won't fire you, his best guide, his famous Sherpa.'

'I better go home.'

'Don't go,' she said, and kissed him again.

THE NEXT DAY AT Blue Glacier Tours, the guides scattered into various corners of the building. Bernard burrowed himself away in the office. Passang hid in the back of the boot room with Hans and Gunter, nursing a large purple bruise on his cheek.

'That's ugly,' said Hans.

'What happened to them while I was in Queenstown?' said Passang, trying to hide his broken tooth.

'What do you mean?' said Hans.

'She told me they broke up.'

'Not as far as I know.'

Tourists arriving for the first booking forced Bernard out of the office. He mumbled a grudging apology to Passang, offered to pay for the crown and blamed the drink. Over the next few days the pressure between them settled down. But Passang dreaded the close confines of the boot-room gatherings, and was relieved to get away into Queenstown to visit the dentist. On his return, he kept to himself.

'Why are you avoiding me?' Andrea asked him.

'Why did you lie to me about breaking up with Bernard?' he asked in return.

'I didn't lie.'

'Don't you know Sherpas mate for life?' he said, half joking, but half not.

DESPITE HIS BETTER JUDGEMENT, he began to look forward to Andrea's banter. He noticed a shift around the region of his heart, some movement inside, although he didn't want to lose control. He saw her whispering in the office with Bernard and tried to put it out of his head, but it was all wrong.

With the continuous effort of trying to rein in his emotions, he'd forgotten about the incident with Malcolm Buttworth. Then one day after a tour, when the tourists were leaving the boot room, saying their goodbyes and taking photos and buying souvenirs,

Passang looked up from a bin of jackets and saw a man with shaggy red hair.

'Are you Passang Phurba?'

'Yep, that's me.'

'I'm Malcolm Buttworth.'

He'd lost weight. His face looked haggard, and there were dark rings under his eyes.

'I didn't recognise you,' said Passang.

'I'm sober now.'

'I won't invite you for a beer at the pub, then,' said Passang, laughing.

Malcolm glanced around the room. Gunter averted his eyes. Bernard stood at the counter in front of the boot racks, sucking in his cheeks. Andrea and Hans sorted socks in the corner.

'How's your chest?'

'I still have more surgery to go. I just wanted to say thank you,' said Malcolm.

He looked uneasily at the other guides in the room and then down at his feet, rocking from side to side.

'I've been hounded by everyone. We've lost business. I tried to apologise to Mr Dareshak, but he won't talk to me.'

'Well, we all make mistakes we're ashamed of,' said Passang.

He looked over at Bernard, who was leaning on his forearms on the counter and peering up from under his hair. Passang turned back to Malcolm and placed a hand on his arm. Malcom flinched.

'Let's go next door and have a cup of tea,' said Passang.

'Sure,' said Malcolm, arranging his arm on Passang's shoulders. A camera flashed somewhere, and Passang felt the weight of Malcolm's arm lift off his body.

'Look. I just wanted to thank you. I have to go now,' said Malcolm.

He shuffled out of the boot room and into the waning evening light.

'Good riddance,' said Andrea.

'At least he's sorry,' said Bernard, glaring at her.

'Only because he got caught,' she said.

Passang followed Malcolm into the carpark to a white four-wheel-drive truck with 'Helico Hydraulics' in gold lettering on the side. The lights switched on one by one in the pub next door. Malcolm heaved himself into the cab of the truck and wound the window down to look at Passang. Another man appeared from the direction of the boot room and climbed into the other side of the truck.

'Got the pics, boss?' said Malcolm.

'Yep,' said the man.

'Where are you heading?' said Passang.

'Back to Queenstown.'

'Take care on those roads.'

Passang waved farewell as Malcolm started the engine. Malcolm did not return the wave.

'Bloody bungas. They're even here in the snow.'

Malcolm's words reverberated in Passang's ears as he drove away. Andrea walked up to Passang in the carpark as the light went out of the sky. He stared after the speeding truck. She cuddled into him and pulled her jacket tight.

'It's so cold tonight,' she said. Passang kissed Andrea's head.

A quiet misty rain was falling, smudging the edges of the streetlights. He put his arm around her and led her back to the office.

'I don't know how you could even speak to him. I'm not surprised Bilal refuses to have anything to do with him,' she said.

Passang hadn't seen Bilal since they'd appeared together on TV3 News. He'd rung him a few times to check how he was, though. Bilal had stopped driving taxis. The anxiety attacks were too much for him. He'd found a new job working from home analysing online surveys for a research company.

'Bernard wants the fuel taken up to the helipad tonight,' said Andrea.

'I'll run it up now,' said Passang.

'Thanks. See you when you get back, Sherpa.'

Andrea handed him the truck keys and ran into the boot room.

He pulled the hood of his jacket over his head as he walked to the truck. On the glacier tour that morning he'd decided that he wouldn't carry on the charade with her anymore. But he knew he might feel differently in the morning.

He fumbled with the keys, and dropped them on the icy gravel. As he bent over to pick them up a light came on in the office. Must be Bernard working late with the books, he thought. He drove to the petrol bowser and filled three cans. When he drove back past the carpark, he glanced at the Blue Glacier Tours building. Two people stood silhouetted in the office window. They merged into an embrace.

Passang drove out towards the helipad. He had his foot on the accelerator, and was too distracted to feel the slight tug of the back wheels beginning to slide out as he drove around a gentle curve in the road. When the truck started to spin he realised he was on black ice, and overcorrected the steering wheel. The vehicle swerved out of control. He tried to right the wheels, wrestle them back in line, but it was too late.

The truck flipped over into a ditch and smashed into a tree, exploding in a ball of fire.

The rain fell softly on the people running from the pub, from the restaurant, from the store, from the motel, from the carpark, from the boot room, from the office.

#WATCHLIST
DAVID
GEARY

1. #ENTRA5FLAG999995-124141cv—SURV—Mobile

—Let's rehearse. You need to create reasonable doubt.

—It's entrapment.

—Explain.

—They were led into something they could never come up with themselves. My clients were sick, addicts: they don't think and act like us. They were brain-damaged from years of prolonged drug use. Yes, they talked about **planting a bomb at the XXXXXX XXX celebrations in XXXXXXX**; but they would never have acted on this. The 'Arab businessman' who encouraged them was undercover RCMP — a Mountie.

—They were lost children.

—They were lost children. He gave them cash. They bought more drugs. It became a tragic dependent relationship. And when my clients expressed doubts, he distorted the scripture to justify their acts. He could have pointed them to other real scripture, words that would have led them to a peaceful path.

—And **the explosives were fake.**

—**The explosives were fake.** The Mountie supplied the plan and the **pressure cooker bombs that weren't bombs.** My clients committed no crime.

—That's your Press Secretary for the White House moment. Hammer that again and again. Now tear down the cops.

—They were just sick kids. Manipulated by cops who had failed to detect the XXXXXXX **pipe bomber heading** to Seattle and then LAX. Failed to detect the 1985 **Air India bombs at YVR**, failed to nail **XXXXXX XXXXXXX** for all the Downtown Eastside missing women in Vancouver. The cops needed a win. They're what Canada's known for — our poster boys: Mounties and Maple Syrup!

—Yes, build the picture of a desperate police force, with a string of failures behind them, who will do anything for a win. And these sick kids are **soft targets they can turn into terrorists**, not the real deal.

—Can we meet to go over this?

—No. I've got enough people who hate me already.

2. #NEWAR456-89Flag22-1 ENCRYPTED DARKNET BLOG POST

I tell tourists 'traditional' stories. A girl 'on the verge of womanhood' is warned of the Wild Woman of the Woods. Her parents tell her that this female **monster is a cannibal**. The girl goes down to the river by herself. Sure enough, the Wild Woman appears, old and wrinkly and wild hair. She invites the girl back to her house.

The girl is sick of her parents being on her case all the time and she's not afraid of any crazy old lady, so she follows. The house is deep in the woods, a total dump to look at but when the girl goes inside she's amazed to find it full of riches. The girl stares at all the food and tools and furs and treasures crammed inside. The old witch comes up behind the girl, strokes her hair.

'Oooohhhh, you have beautiful hair. Ooooohhhh, I wish I had hair like you.'

Which freaks the girl out totally, so she says she's late for salmon supper and bolts. The old lady cries out, 'Oooohhhh, come back, let me stroke your hair—' The girl doesn't hear the rest as she's running, running for her life. But she's lost . . . panics . . . then hears the friendly river, runs to it, and finds her way home. Her parents have been worried sick. The girl confesses she met the

Wild Woman of the Woods, went to her house.

The girls' parents are pissed. The Wild Woman eats children! No one has ever seen inside her house and lived to tell the tale! The father makes the girl take him to the Wild Woman's house. He brings his big canoe-carving chisel. First they can't find the house, but then they hear the old lady wailing — 'Oooooohhhhh I want young girl hair.' FYI she was always making that weird Ooooohhhh sound before she said anything, like old people make when they try to stand up after sitting down for too long, and complain about their bones . . . and their joints . . . and teeth . . . and their constipation . . . and everything . . . except worse with this Wild Woman. Like the sound of wild wind through rotting trees.

They follow the 'Oooohhhhhh' to the Wild Woman's house. The father knocks on the door, then stands in the shadows. The Wild Woman comes out, smiles through broken rocks for teeth at the girl, then suddenly reaches out to grab her. But the father jumps out and hammers the chisel into the neck of the Wild Woman. **Cuts her head right off** . . . And that, folks, is how we get the Wild Woman of the Woods mask. See it here on the wall of the Sweetgrass Cultural Centre. Be sure to buy your genuine local Aboriginal Indigenous First Peoples handcrafted souvenirs before you finish the cruise.

But first, back to the story, what does it mean? Any ideas, folks? . . . And all I get back from the tourists are these blank bannock-brain looks. LOL. But I keep at them.

'What does this story teach us?'

'Um . . . Listen to your parents.'

'Right on! But our Elders also say the Wild Woman deserves to have her head chopped off because she has a house full of riches but doesn't share them.' Then I stare at the old ladies with lots of bling just a little bit too long — that always gets me good tips. 'But that's not all,' I say. 'The old witch also deserves to have her head cut off because she's old but wants the young girl's hair. She wants to be young again. She's vain. She can't accept that we all grow old and die. So she kills young people and eats them.' And that's when I try not to look at the old ladies with dye jobs, facelifts, boob jobs and botox, but I do . . . for just a little too long. Then I smile, my sweet smile, because really I'm a pretty Pocahontas telling traditional stories between the salsa lessons and meeting the Norwegian fishing-boat-trained captain for a photo op — Captain Stig Stinkfist, who still smells fishy no matter how much Calvin Klein cologne he drowns himself in.

It's the same sweet smile I give the dumb white girl who wears the 'Party with Pocahontas the Sexy Squaw' costume to our Halloween party. The blonde bimbo who also adds a fake bullet hole to her head. I want to tell her about the real hole I saw in the back of my friend's head, but I think — she'll keep . . . They'll all keep.

3. #VETER347--67-21FLAG—MILITARY PYSCH-ASSESSMENT

3 guys — big guys — beards — running holding **bottles acid acid ACID**

3 of us — 1 me — stays — the 2 others herd the girls — 1 in front — 1 in back

we r used to this — we plan — it's our job: get the girls to the school — take a different route each day cos **Taliban** are waiting — watching

me i turn — i can't shoot — that's not what we do — peacekeeping — they know that

i hear the other 2 soldiers run — the girls run

the 3 bearded guys throw the acid at me — my hand is on fire — i guess i put up my hand

i punch one — we train bare-fist fighting — we're used to punching heads — but the beards give them some buffer — more acid — i duck — my hair my head my uniform burning — think this is the day i die — they punch — i kick — they kick me — i'm down on

the ground — burning — my jaw slack — broken — more acid
— i will die here — in this dusty shithole street — more acid —
still getting kicked — stomped — arm cracks — resigned — fuck
of a way to die — more acid — lots more acid — but strange not
burning — roll — blood eye sees shopkeepers come out to throw
water on me — clean me — while i'm still fighting — roll — kick
1 beard in nuts — he figured i was a goner — i'm back in that biker
bar off-duty — itching for a brawl — the boys send me in plain
clothes — civvies off duty to pick a fight — so then all the rest of
the boys can pile in and it's all on — frowned on — not in the
manual — but happens — more often than you want to know —
keeps us fighting fit — throwing haymakers left and right — one
eye acid blind — spit 1 tooth out — swallow 1 — scrapes all the
way down — go ape — til 1 soldier comes back — takes 1 beard
out — 2 beards run — shopkeepers throw more water — burning
— cleaning — 1 soldier radios — more water — washing in street,
stripping off naked to get acid off — probably not going to die
today after all — going to Rammstein first class — then . . . home
that's what we're doing there — taking girls to school — what you
do every day and never think about — i'm not a hero

4. #NEWAR66363YX-FLag19-ENCRYPTED DARKWEB BLOG POST

Fave place to hang on Alaskan cruises is the hot tubs on top of the
ship. Go there middle of the night, do a big **bomb** in the pool, then
chill in the tub and watch the Northern Lights — Aurora Borealis
— Arsaniit. Some old stories warn against whistling. That the lights
are the Spirit of the Ancestors dancing and if you disturb them
they'll come down and **cut your head off** . . . I whistle. Sometimes
the lights crackle back — angry electricity — but no one's **chopped
my head off** . . . yet. LOL.
Security cams everywhere. They watch me from the bridge. See me
in the hot tub. Don't give a shit. Told them it's 'A Native Thing — I

need to listen to the Ancestors.'

I got **50 pounds of gelignite** off some survivalist ecoterrorist type in Juneau hidden in my cabin. My roomate is Filipino. She never asks questions. They're very polite.

Q. Do you think it would be more impressive for a cruise ship to blow up and take out XXXXXXXX Bridge while going under it? Or for the bridge to blow up and take out the ship below?

📖 Just jamming. LOL. PS: And that would be spectacular but so what? What difference would it really make? Pipelines are the new Frontlines #Dakotameansfriend #StopKinderMorgan

5. #FRYER674-23-3Flag5-FACEBOOK POST
Why is everyone so **afraid of bombs?** The **Universe is a bomb.** It should have been called **THE BIG BOMB THEORY.**

6. #ALGOR45678-23Flag47890—GOOGLE SEARCH
'*The events of* **9/11 were the greatest work of art** *imaginable for the whole cosmos. Minds achieving something in an act that we couldn't even dream of in music, people rehearsing like mad for ten years, preparing fanatically for a concert, and then dying; just imagine what happened there. You have people who are that focused on a performance and then 5,000 people are dispatched to the afterlife, in a single moment. I couldn't do that. By comparison, we composers are nothing.*'

—Karlheinz Stockhausen

7. #NEWAR78834-flag7-ENCRYPTED DARKWED BLOG POST
I wait til the end of the Halloween Party for Blondie, for when she is drunk. By then I know she's a smoker — Marlboro. Follow her outside, ask for a light. She's still wearing her Halloween Party with Pocahontas dress but the bullet hole on her forehead is lifting

a little from the sweat. She sees me coming, gets the guilts, and scrapes the bullet hole off. I pretend not to notice.

'Sorry, but do you have a spare cigarette?'

'Oh, sure . . . So you smoke?'

'Yeah, tobacco is traditional medicine for our people.'

Try to keep a straight face, but then crack up. She laughs, relaxes. Wind is blowing hard so I get in real close. We make a little tent to light up.

'See we made a teepee. We're BFFs now.'

'For sure.'

'Thing about this part of the ship is there's no cameras. A blindspot.'

'What? The wind is too loud! What did you say?'

'Go look out there,' I tell her, pointing into the dark, 'that's my home.'

'Where?'

'There.'

She looks out into the darkness, leans out a little, then I do my best UFC move — a Double-leg Takedown from behind. Lift her legs, drive, flip, and she's gone. **Bombs away. I am a bomb.** Come on, dare u to **defuse me.**

8. #ALGOR889967L- FLAG 2—TWEET

Sykes&Picot = original *Middle-East t*rrorists* carved up countries + Winston's Hiccup — https://en.wikipedia.org/wiki/Winston%27s_Hiccup

9. #ALGOR457 REC—2015-10-16 (transcript)—FLAG—AGENT-012 INTERVIEW

—We love your algorithm.

—Oh, thanks.

—You know the 'Friend Algorithm' from *The Big Bang Theory*?

—I have that T-shirt.

—I guessed that. How much do you think it's worth?

—What, the T-shirt?

—Funny. You know the **Chinese would just steal your algorithm** 🙂 but we have laws.

—Sorry, what's this new job you want to talk about?

—My colleague by the door and myself we wanted to chat, make an offer . . .

—Are you trying to headhunt me because . . .

—*Citizenfour* 🙂, you've seen it right?

—What?

—The documentary, it won an Oscar, about Edward Snowden — the whistleblower?

—Oh . . . yes.

—And Naomi Wolf — I believe you discussed her at your Book Club — well, she said that the only way Big Brother really works is if you know you're being watched, right? No point in having a **#Watchlist** unless you know you're being watched, right? So maybe Snowden was allowed to walk . . .

—Look, I don't . . .

—You created an algorithm that can predict who will be next to leave a company . . . voluntarily. It works. You've made a small fortune because companies can significantly reduce the cost of losing an employee and hiring another one, right? If they can find these individuals soon enough, and turn them around, right?

—Right. Who do you represent?

—The CIA . . . (LAUGHS) Your face. Seriously, we want to identify who are the next Edward Snowdens, who has the whistleblower profile . . . **and blow the whistle** on them first. Two million bucks, that's what we valued your algorithm at in the private sector. But if you helped us adapt it for governments, well, who knows?

—What kind of clusterfuck nonsense are you talking?

—Um . . . language, we do record these conversations.

—Is this some kind of hidden-camera prank? I'm leaving.

—So your friend, Karlheinz Stockhausen, he said 9/11 was the greatest work of art ever, right? You agree? I mean we'd find that on your browser history, right? . . . Right? Why would you look that up?

—I like his music. Why . . .

—You call that music. I tried to listen to his 'masterpiece', *Kontakte*? You'd have to be seriously disturbed to call that music. I mean there's no beat, rhythm, melody, chorus . . . order. Do you know how many people work for Homeland Security?

—No.

—A lot. Do you know how many are fuck-ups? Criminals even? Cartel members? Too many. Homeland Security hired so many new people, new agents, new border guards, after 9/11, and we got the dregs, not to mention organised crime who saw an opportunity, and now . . . now we need to weed them out. And you can help us.

—Weed them out?

—Weed them out.

—What would you do to them?

—They'd be . . . managed, found another career. Not your problem.

—So you seriously work for the US Government?

—No. No. We are a private company who pitch projects globally to various governmental bodies. And we have a great hit rate. Get a lot of research grants. Sure, governments have people paid to do research for them but it's often bureaucratically cumbersome. There's all these checks and balances, and whistleblowers — Enemies Within — so it's easier to outsource. So . . . so tell me, what are the secret signs someone is thinking of leaving their company?

—Um . . . they update their *LinkedIn* profile.

—Right. I don't think that's really what we're looking for, but what about the books they've read? Movies they've seen? I see you watched *Captain Fantastic*, the movie with Viggo Mortensen. You like those off-the-grid, anti-establishment, let's celebrate Noam Chomsky Day types? I preferred him in *The Lord of the Rings.* Did you like it when

Viggo came out of his hippie bus, flopped out his junk and talked about how even animals have a penis? I mean, seriously, what kind of weirdo listens to Stockhausen? I mean my kids could . . .

—You know it ruined him.

—Who?

—Stockhausen, what he said about 9/11. It doesn't matter what a revolutionary he was in terms of musical composition and electronic experimentation, now that's all he'll be remembered for.

—Uh huh. And how would you like to be remembered? As the guy who turned down the deal that would make him a multi-millionaire, and make his lovely wife and two kids happy forever? Or the loser who got ripped off by some Chinese Dark Web hackers who stole all his secrets and left him with nothing? It's up to you. So what else? What else might be a sign someone is a whistleblower? I mean, trouble with intimacy? Intimate relationships with women, with men, children? Missing parents, messy divorce, reacting against authority, truancy at school, drug use, watching *Mr Robot* over and over? How would we measure that? Factor that all in? What about IQ? Are they frustrated smart people? Or angry stupid people? Is there a genetic predisposition to being a terrorist? A genome? And how can we really do 'extreme vetting' and 'ideological tests' when there's so many liars in the world. What's a true test of morals? And ethics?

—Isn't that somewhere near Sussex?

—Funny. You have a quirky sense of humour — a dark sense of humour? Would that be a factor? How could you measure that?

—I . . . I have no idea . . .

—That's okay. We'd ask for a whole swag of R&D money, based on your past success. And you university types, you're pretty good at writing proposals for research grants. Money for nothing. Then we'd pitch it — like a movie. Like *Minority Report* for real, for whistleblowers — future crimes. Terrible title for that movie, by the way. They could have done a whole lot better. I mean it's not about minorities. But, speaking of which, you'd have to factor that in, right: ethnic/racial/religious status as predictor? So, what do you say?

—I say . . . you'd need access to all the data on past successful, and failed, whistleblowers. That's the only way you could develop a new algorithm.

—But for you to have access to all that you'd have to be screened further. I mean we threw our algorithm at you — browser history, phone records, bank payments — relax, you did good, but we'd have to go a whole lot deeper, down to the bone, suck out the marrow . . . of you.

—And I'd need to discuss this with . . .

—You can't tell anyone.

—But . . .

—You can keep your business, oversee, delegate, but our deadline is to pitch to clients on February 14th for Valentines Day: Love your country, buy this algorithm.

—That's . . . terrible.

—So join us and make it better.

—I can't just . . .

—We know. We'll visit again soon. But, seriously, that Twitter account? — Delete it. That 'Sykes and Picot plus Winston Churchill's hiccup' sort of tweet — that Amateur Hour stuff won't wash with our clients. And watch what you Google. And this conversation didn't happen.

#ALGOR-ENDS SEC#457 REC—(transcript) FLAG— ORANGE (Time 3:12)

10. #NEWAR66777983-68999t34-flag17—ENCRYPTED BLOG POST

Fuck *The Walking Dead*! Native People already live post-apocalypse. We already had the Evil Alien Invasion, the brain-eating Zombies —Land! Land! Must have more land!

11. #VETER982114- PTSD Help Line Message Board

i'm not a hero — i can defuse an **IED — Improvised Explosive Device . . . and i can make one** — but no girls need me to take them to school anymore — they asked me to speak at schools back home here — but kids just stare — make jokes about my purple butt face — and it's a pain for everyone to have to wait for the bus to drop down and all move back to get my chair on — so mostly i stay home and watch movies — watch porn — because what girl is ever going to look at me now? They said they'd pay for me to study a new career — IT is always looking for people — everyone wants to help vets — i don't want to go back to school — 2 dumb to go back 2 school — U need more people on these phonelines — 2nd time i've rung and spoken to a machine — don't like speaking 2 machines.

12. #NEWAR345kkk9 -- flag 23- ENCRYPTED DARKWEB BLOG POST

Night. No more photo ops. We head out to open ocean to dump the black water from the cruise ship so it doesn't foul the coast. The swell gets up. Ship dips and rolls. I got my sea legs now. Just a big canoe to me. Heavy-Breathing-Asthma Guy is waiting. Waiting in the blindspot. He was at my Wild Woman of the Woods talk earlier. Stuck around like a bad smell. Lingered.

'Can I buy you a drink later? I'd love to hear more of your traditional stories.'

It happens. Sad old guys, and wolf-feature young dudes, and middle-aged saggy guys. It happens all the time.

'I'm sorry, crew aren't allowed to socialise with passengers. Come along tomorrow to my talk on native plants with healing properties. You can learn about the Medicine Wheel.'

'I'll pay extra — for extra. A happy ending? To a traditional story? Two hundred . . . five hundred?'

They need healing — We all need healing. I bumped him up to a grand. He gives me this wad but his pants are still bulging. I smile

Sexy Squaw, get in close and whisper.

'You seen that old movie, *Titanic*?'

'Sure.'

'Let's do it like that. Except you be Kate Winslet.'

'Huh?' he wheezes, 'how's that going to work?'

'Well, you lean out over the rail like she did at the front of the boat. I'll stand behind you like Leo. Then stick my finger up your butt, and reach around to . . .'

'Then we switch and I do you?'

'Sure, a grand buys a lot of Pocahontas.'

'I never met anyone like you.'

'No, you never did. Ooooooooh, you have beautiful . . .'

'Huh?'

I do my best Celine Dion in his ear — *Near, far . . .*

Reach around, unzip his pants. Then do my best UFC Ronda Rousey Hip Throw and he's **gone. Bombs away** 📖. I've been practising. Hit the bags in the gym. Spar with the Thai guys.

Every 6 months, on average, we can lose a passenger overboard. They can write it off as a suicide, drunken accident, death by misadventure. Any more than that and questions would get asked.

Aurora Borealis is out. I whistle. Ancestors dance. I dance with them on the deck while down there in the dark water he's choking on his own shit. I'm hungry.

Head back to the Midnight Chocolate buffet. There's always someone there who's feeling queasy but still has to stuff as much as they can down their throat cos they paid their fare and goddammit they're gonna get their money's worth! Same folks that are sloshed by 10 am.

It's the end of the season. We head to Hawai'i next. We'll park up by an active volcano, watch the lava erupt and flow while sipping cocktails that tinkle with pure Alaskan glacial ice. It's called our 'Fire & Ice Party'.

yours sincerely — Wild Woman of the Woods

WHITE ELEPHANT

KELLY JOSEPH

FOR THREE DAYS SLEEP was impossible — the nor'wester yowled through the valley and whined through gaps in windows, as people lay in bed imagining their roof peeled back by its raging fingers. In the morning they woke with dark-ringed eyes, feeling raw. They snapped at each other during breakfast, growled at their kids. And later when they flocked to the twilight school gala, the wind tormented them further — lifted skirts, blew grit into mouths, into hair, into glowering eyes.

Meanwhile, Hēni slept peacefully. When the wind rattled her corrugated roof it lulled the old woman into dreams and, beyond dreams, deep into nothingness. In the afternoon when she finally woke, she rose with unusual buoyancy. The cloud of black starlings that always flew inside her head had gone, for now.

She shucked off her nightie and pulled on a green frock, her gumboots and a possum-skin coat her papa had made a lifetime ago. Looking in the hallway mirror she donned a chipped pearl necklace, a present from a small boy who had once saved and saved his milk-delivery money. She stood back and smiled, revealing tea-stained teeth.

She petted the Jackalope that guarded the house, then slammed the salt-streaked door behind her and whistled for her mutt, who bounded from under the house, swathed in cobwebs. Her bungalow was perched on crumbling rock at the edge of a bay where large waves rolled in like silken sheets. Dolphins sometimes swam there and once, a barnacled whale. But it was a deceptive place where hidden undercurrents sucked and swallowed.

Walking up the hill towards the school, Hēni leaned against the wind. Her lips moved as she walked, her low mutterings accompanying the tune the wind played in the wires above, a mournful theremin. On the surrounding hills the bush rippled, each gust exposing the silver bellies of shivering leaves. Stands of mānuka creaked and cowered, shedding flowers like fragrant confetti. Low clouds were bullied towards the southern coast where the Cook Strait ferry heaved on whitecaps and waterspouts were conjured.

The old wooden school buildings were nestled in a stand of pōhutukawa. At the school gates Hēni stopped and looked around with pūkana eyes. She opened her mouth wide, let the rushing air expand her cheeks. Then with a sly smile she snapped her lips closed and took a great gulp. She held her breath. Her hair rose in greasy tendrils towards the pewter sky. She exhaled and giggled.

The adults heading to the gala tried not to stare at the apparition. Hēni the local bag lady. Mad but harmless, they whispered, gripping their kids' hands tighter. They had heard the rumours about the old woman — tales of dog-food consumption, hoards of junk, forts of yellowing newspapers and musty books, a mountain of rubbish bags filling the back garden and an inherited collection of creepy stuffed animals. And then there was the disappearance of her son. Some said she went funny after that. Others said she was born with strangeness, that taxidermy chemicals had leached into her mama's blood, and were absorbed by her in the womb.

The kids at the gala gawked at Hēni openly. The older ones called her Stinky Seawitch because she smelt like piss and brine, and because after a king tide she prowled the beach lifting bull kelp with a stick, poked around rockpools searching for who knows what, chanting sad, watery songs to herself. But sometimes the younger ones offered gifts, an oblation of sorts. With their hearts thumpitythumping in their chests, they left at her gate knotted driftwood, weightless balls of pumice, baby pāua shells and other sea treasure. Sometimes they gave her wandering mutt a bite from their sandwich when he visited the school at lunchtimes. In return, Hēni made small sculptures on the front lawn from their presents and from pieces of her own junk. Once she fashioned a fleet of tiny ships from wood, shell, stone and china shards from broken teacups. She let them sail upon the high grass, among the dandelions. The younger ones peeped over her punga fence to admire them. See, they said. Magic.

Hēni felt those same small eyes on her as she ambled towards the school office. She pinched the heads off two marigolds growing in a garden, popped them in her maw and winked at a small girl sitting nearby. The girl's eyes and mouth sprung open, before her mother yanked her away. Hēni shrugged and walked on. She passed a cake sale, a plant stall and the quickfire raffle. She stopped to admire the children's craft table with painted pet rocks, and swans made from soap, facecloths and pipecleaners. The tombola tent billowed dangerously and two surly teenagers were told to hold down its flapping corners. She made her way towards the school field where the mini-train and talent stage were set up. Nearby lay a deflated bouncy castle, cast aside by worried parents who imagined it flying to Blenheim on air currents. Little ones hyped up on fizzy and lollies darted around the field in a blur, happy to be with their friends. Hēni drank in the sights and smells. She left her mutt to beg at the smoking sausage sizzle and walked on through the school.

When she arrived outside the hall a crowd was already assembled. A sign was taped next to the glass door — two words cut crudely from coloured paper, glued onto card and embellished with glitter: white elephant. Hēni craned her neck, hoping to get a glimpse of the goods laid out on tables inside. People were pressed against the doors, obscuring the view — mainly old biddies from the church with their pointy elbows ready to nudge competition out of the way, and local second-hand dealers with shifty eyes. More people were lining up behind her. She leaned over to look at another punter's watch: four minutes to go. The owner of the watch eyed her suspiciously. He was Māori, thirties with a fleshy puku, a beard and a shaved head. His gaze softened and he grinned at her. Hēni recognised those large brown eyes. She looked away. Fingered her pearls.

'Mrs Knight?'

'Mmm,' said Hēni.

'Don't know if you remember me—'

Hēni looked again into those dark eyes and thought, Course I remember. Little Matty. Sweet fatty. Big family, no money. Her gaze fell to the ground.

'Nah, sorry dear. I don't.'

'Matthew Kopu. I used to hang out with your son Jo. Years ago. Before I was sent off to live with my nana.'

Hēni grunted a small acknowledgment, felt her good mood trickling away. He bent towards her to give her a peck on the cheek. She stiffened and leaned away so only his whiskers brushed her face. Wiry whiskers like Papa's. And hungry breath. Matty, always a ravenous boy.

'Yeah, I remember those neat animals you had.'

Hēni rocked a little on the balls of her feet, scratched at her arm.

'You were always good to me. Let me stay over. Fed me. Man, I remember your muttonbird and watercress boil-ups. Mussel fritters. And creamed pāua.' He smacked his lips and his eyes unfocused, remembering those rich treats.

'I just moved back. Me and my missus. We've got a son. Think he's wandering around here somewhere. Probably in search of kai. Takes after me, eh.'

He let out a sharp snort. A few people looked their way. He rubbed his head self-consciously and moved closer to her.

Hēni looked up at the sky, smelt ozone. Thought she could see the wind currents up there swirling and changing. Threatening to bring back the cloud of birds to rush and dive in her mind. Her fingers reached again for the pearls. She knew what was coming.

'So what's Jo up to these days?'

She stepped away from Matthew then, with his bovine eyes and his questions and his hungry breath. Felt a familiar lightness in her head, a spreading ache in her chest. The school bell clanged suddenly, the doors opened and people surged forward, towards the bargains. Hēni let herself be taken by the crushing tide and soon lost sight of him.

She found herself in the corner of the hall near the stage. Leaning against an old exercise bike, she looked around for Matthew, let out a long sigh when she couldn't see him.

'Silly silly you,' she muttered. 'Forget it, Hēni Penny. Forget him.'

She plucked at black, feathery thoughts, trying to recall the reason why she'd come there. Ah yep yep, teacups. She needed more teacups. Hers were all smashed, always slipped from shaky hand to wooden floor.

She squeezed herself into a spot at the nearest table. On the table there was a SodaStream with a rusty gas canister. An assortment of Tupperware. Twisty candlesticks. Nothing Hēni wanted. Unable to move along because people were squashing themselves against the tables, she bent over to see what was in the boxes under the table.

Nested inside a large boxful of cake tins and frying pans was a smaller box. Hēni lifted it out and opened it. Inside were two heavy mugs, one a rich brown and the other an emerald green. Both were moulded in the shape of a tiki face, with whātero and fierce almond eyes. Hēni crooned to herself, delighted. They were the same ones Mama had in her china cabinet when she was small.

She placed them carefully back in the box and closed the lid. But a man beside her had seen the mugs and looked at the box with small, coveting eyes. He had a long neck and slicked-back hair — he was a mix of man and mustelid.

'Wharetana, those,' he said, licking his lips with a tiny pink tongue. 'Crown Lynn. Worth a few bob.'

'Mmm,' said Hēni.

'I'll buy them off you.'

She shook her head.

'Look, I'll give you a fair price,' he said, his voice becoming reedy.

'Nup, keeping these for meself.'

The man looked around with those feral eyes to see if anyone was watching. Then suddenly his paws were on the box, trying to tug it from her hands. Hēni had a good purchase on it, pulled the box towards her chest. No one was going to get her mama's mugs.

'Come on, you crazy cow. You don't need them,' he said.

He yanked the box. As he pulled it away, one of his fingers hooked on Hēni's pearls. The beads were torn from her neck. Cream orbs bounced and scattered on the wooden floor, rolled under the table and between feet. Low guttural noises burst from Hēni's mouth. The Mustelid slunk into the crowd with the box under his arm.

She searched around her for friendly eyes but there were only backs bent over tables. A tremble took hold of her hands, and soon her whole body shook. The bird cloud gathered in her mind.

HĒNI IS TEN. HER mama lies in an open coffin in the sitting room. She is still pretty, thinks Hēni. Her big brown aunties have come to take her mama's body back to the family urupā. Papa, a ginger-bearded Pom, is throwing a fit, begs them not to take her. When they do, he uses a broom handle to smash Mama's cabinet with her crockery inside, and the paper nautilus, the gull feathers and small blobs of ambergris she collected at the beach as a child. Then he storms into his workshop and smashes his own vials of metallic dust, his fossils and rocks, his kauri gum, his bell-jars, his glass eyes, his artificial teeth and beaks, and his clay forms waiting for their skin. Finally, he rips apart his best stuffed specimens.

Later, when he is calm, he sews them back together but not as they were. He makes a menagerie of hybrids — mermaids, skvaders, griffins and creatures invented from his own madness. They become Hēni's friends because she isn't allowed real friends now. She loves the creatures, especially the Jackalope. She dresses them in her clothes, reads them stories and drinks tea with them, but what she really wants is a live dog. These are lonely days.

Her papa becomes more and more like the animal skins he tans. A husk of a man with desiccated lips and parchment skin. She believes his heart is stuffed with sawdust. He hardly ever takes baths, or drinks water or tea. But he will drink a clear liquid from a bottle that he keeps in his workshop. His breath is acerbic and so are his moods. Inside him is a desert with furious, hot winds.

Later, when the aunties come back for Hēni, to take her to their warm homes brimming with kids and life, Papa shows them his loaded rifle. After they leave empty-handed, he takes her to the special corner of the small farm where she sometimes talks to the elements, because the wind and rain and sunlight are her friends too. It is dusk and starlings chirp loudly as they flock above the poplars in a great dark cloud. She is mesmerised by the way they collect in the sky, how they undulate like water, how they tumble as one fluttering creature. Her father aims the rifle skyward. Black feathers and broken bodies fall to the ground. He says between shots, 'You better not leave me, Hēni Penny.'

When she is older, braver, she does run away from his obsidian rage. Moves beside the sea with its breezes and mists, where she can watch the weather roll in. She finds a man who loves her, but he has his own shadows and flinty moods. He doesn't wait around to meet his son. When Joseph is born with his smiling heart she feels she had done something right, she has made magic.

And much later, the aunties ring her up. Your papa shot himself, they say. Go back, sort out his estate.

Grief and guilt nibble at the edges of her heart. She becomes the keeper of the animals. She brings her old friends home to meet Joseph. He loves them too.

WINGS WERE FLUTTERING IN her head. She bent down, intending to scrabble on the ground for the pearls, but her head felt light and her legs threatened to crumple under her. She grunted and growled at herself. Then she noticed a little one watching her. He moved towards the protection of his mother's legs. Hēni shut her eyes, covered them with her hands. She didn't want to see his frightened gaze.

'Mrs Knight? You alright?'

She lowered her hands and blinked. Warm brown eyes filled her vision.

Matthew led her away from the crowd, out a side door and down a ramp. It was almost dark outside and there was an eerie hush. The wind had finally moved on.

Her mutt was waiting for her. He licked her hand as she shambled past him. Matthew guided Hēni to a low brick wall and she flopped down. She gulped in the cool air, felt a little better. The sea sighed in the distance. The clouds had gone and in their place a crescent moon sat like a yellow grin on the horizon. The sky itself was the blue of lapis and Egyptian kings, the blue of deep watery graves.

'He's gone,' she said, barely a whisper.

'Who?' Matthew asked.

'Joseph.'

'Where?'

'He went for a swim. Never came back,' she said. 'I look for him sometimes but Tangaroa won't give him back to me.' Her hands reached to her bare throat, but the pearls were still gone.

'I tried to let him be a bit wild. Let him make friends. He was lonely after you left,' she said. 'Other kids stayed away. Teased him about me. It was 'cos of me he went swimming by himself.'

Matthew shook his head. 'Nah, Mrs Knight. He loved the water, eh. Nothing could keep him away from it.'

A stocky boy, ten or eleven, with Matthew's eyes appeared from the direction of the field. He sat by his dad and patted the mutt.

'Himi, say gidday to Mrs Knight.'

'Hi,' said Himi. He stood, gave Hēni a peck on the cheek. He pulled a small paper bag from his pocket, untwisted the top and offered her the contents. Inside were squares of coconut ice. Hēni took a piece. The sweetness burned her throat, but she took another when Himi offered her one. She nodded at the boy and grinned as the bird cloud inside her curled away, scattering.

They sat for a while, eating, watching people pass by. Across the field there were one or two kids crying. Overly tired because their own sugar buzz had worn off. Stalls were being packed away. The day's takings were being counted. People returned to their cars with arms laden with loot. They seemed more relaxed.

'It's gone quiet, eh, we must be in between fronts,' said Matthew.

Hēni cocked her head, listening. She nodded.

'Yep, southerly's on the way,' she said.

Rosanna Raymond, *Beaten*, 2004 (photographer: Kerry Brown)

PITTER PATTER, PAPATŪĀNUKU

Monologues of 3 Gods

CASSANDRA BARNETT

PAPATŪĀNUKU [PUKEONAKI]

Pitter patter pitter patter. In a hurry, many tiny hoof, putting many tiny footprint here   now here   now here. A few quicker, wiry one enter fray too, running to   fro to   fro, making racket. Impairing roaming pitter patter hoof; making pitter patter into quiet, taut form. Human tweet tweet, canine trot trot, pitter patter hoof trip trip in turn into new front, new front, new front. One pattern uniting to map my outer coat, occupy me from frame to frame, many hoof parking, conquering my ripe crop . . . making territory my many worn furrow. For why? Human tweet tweet. Canine torment ewe. Ewe troop into turf tract. For why? For I make nutrient offering yet.

Echo come to me, faraway time when former human, my nearer kin, put out on feet, pitter patter near here, pioneer, take home, make root. Te Kāhui Maunga, mountain human, come when my tree were many. Tokomaru canoe human, putting in at Tongaporutu. Kurahaupō canoe human, meeting Kāhui human to make new kin.

Rua Taranaki come, naming mountain, naming kin. More human come, making Te Āti Awa, Ngāti Tama, Ngāti Maru kin. Time after, Waikato, Ngāti Toa roam. Time after, Pākehā feet roam, pitter patter pitter patter pitter patter   pitter   patter . . . Many my infant. Weighty human. Army human. Cunning human. Time after, Te Whiti, Tohu put root, make nutrient home for Parihaka kin. Time after . . .

Remoter year, when my Ranginui more near, young Pukeonaki mountain pitter patter too. Poor Pukeonaki turn from Pīhanga mountain torment, take hurt heart, uproot, run out to water rim frontier near here — making furrow, making Whanganui waterway. Run out out out. Run up up up. Run no more. Pukeonaki, carrying memory, pitter patter roam to here, to pine, to cry, to petrify. I hear, I know — for I too cry, when torn apart from Ranginui. What more, him Tangaroa cry on too. We part, we cry. My Pukeonaki too you hunt new root, take new name, now Taranaki, make home anew.

Mountain hanker. Ewe hanker. Human hanker, hanker. Human in a hurry to make nutrient from me — my turf my muck my mire. To make territory from me. To roam me, foot me, print me, to pitter patter my worn out, fraying furrow. Hankering human, my poor tot. My heir, my many infant. How keen to eat, make hurt, make art, make home. To mark your pattern, conquer, make take, make take. You trip troop trot trek tramp, keep roaming   roaming roaming new route on my many yawning pore. My Taranaki turf now home for your farm, your art, your money, your camera eye . . . For human foot, for canine paw, for ewe hoof too.

TANGAROA [TE TAI O RĒHUA]

Ah, you, free young one! Here right now, hair whipping wet, pumping arm knee hip, parting my way to make your own way home. Here right now, rapt happy turf gawk, imparting happy human fun. Here now, attune to me, keen hoping, premonitoring rapture . . . You whiff my air, try my wit, note my wink, my hinting rhyming way. You tarry on my foam, await my interior to mutate . . .

Hate you I ought. Time yore, your Mama too know my wink, my rhyming way — yet Papatūānuku turn to him. Him, your haughty parent, him, him Ranginui! I can triumph, you know. I can tower too high for you, too quick. I can make cataract. Yet . . . what ripper nipper you are. You win my whim, my care, my amity, my treat. Carefree caperer, for now your temerity, your open heart, win my offer: my heroic temperate perfect rhyming way.

Yore when my water were more pure, you took to canoe, water warrior. Your itinerant community in your canoe Tainui part my foam. Your incanting oaring party, your Hoturoa captain tracking our water-turf rim — for I yet keep Papa near. Marking your weary way home, Tainui anchor not far from here. Mōkau, Waimimi, where my watery arm yet whiff her, wink her, warm her . . . He too, her white tyke Captain Cook, your turf creature kin, turn up in my water here. He too remark her potent Taranaki peak. He too note how fair how fine your Mama appear from my water here.

Ah now, crafty creature, happy creature, turf creature. Her peaty roe, naughty neonate — you humour me. You know me more, more intimate, in your fun time. I know you too. Know how in your euphoria you yet keep your mutant hierarchy, or try to. Know your Mama, your Papa, know how you came. Yet for now I content to nurture you. Here, take it — free trip in my rain, my wet, my fermenting moat, my titan main. For now, I cooperate. I quicken you quicken. I act you act. Moment to moment we interact. I hike up, you mount, you foray out on your narrow raft — you pour . . .

PAPATŪĀNUKU [TARANAKI]

To fro . . . To fro . . . Water mountain . . . water mountain . . . Te Tai o Rēhua to Parihaka to Taranaki to Parihaka to Te Tai o Rēhua. One more car. Tracking a furrow, furrowing a track.

Mountain name Pukeonaki make water furrow name Whanganui. Whanganui keep making furrow. Canoe Tainui make furrow too, on him, on Tangaroa. Canoe Aotea, Tokomaru furrow him too. My human Hoturoa, Cook furrow him too. Poor him, how my infant keep furrowing him.

Keep it for me my kin, furrow me more.

In my Parihaka corner my Te Whiti, Tohu make furrow furrow furrow furrow furrow. Parihaka men, women, working, furrowing my muck. Comfy furrow, meek furrow, caring furrow. Parihaka men, women turn Parihaka turf, preparing, harrowing my mire. Making nutrient, making harmony when incoming men make war. Putting root when troop uproot. Keeping me tight when my worrying white mite take take take. To, fro, furrow.

Now your terra canoe, your car make furrow. Now you, my new potpourri tot, make queer new furrow. My infant you come home to me — orienting pennant car to, fro. You, I, one more time we rhyme. We quake, infect, interpenetrate. I am terra, I am Parihaka, I am Mama, I am Taranaki, I am Papatūānuku. I am you. We come one. I am propane, I am tar, I am fume, I am pennant car. In unity we make our way. From my wet point to my high point, from my high point to my wet point. We make offering, keep Tangaroa tame, amp up up up to Ranginui. Come one, come more. Aurora fingertip make pennant quake. We quake. Heart quake. Pennant car not for coming parting, taking making, rooting uprooting.

Pennant car for homing, knowing. My young return, my memory wake.

RANGINUI [OHAKEA, MANAWATU]

Oh yeah? I hear you, my heir. Priming up, waking up, warming up, opening up, firing up . . . Tracking out in a mighty whirr, uprearing . . .

Coming here, entering my air, you take off. Purring, pouring, wafting raptor, I hear you caw. Rocketing higher, on you caw. You caw, you roar. You waft, you pour. To her eye now a pinprick mote, you hang a moment, note my infinite unhappy height. You hang, you pry, enquiring. Infant, my height not your to take. Keep near her, my Papa, a comfy furrow . . . Yet I know your want. You my infant, I want you too. Hanging a tapering interim more, you make known your momentum — fire out — young harrier on amphetamine — to meet me.

Up, up muppet, encore encore. You parry, feint, attack, retreat. You worry me, whip me, whack at me. Pick me up in your mirror eye, tip me, turn me, rotate me. Make pattern, run, make pattern run. Warp me in your repeating frame, paint me in your pretty puff, ink me in her murky hue, taunt me — oh her rare perfume . . . Not knowing how in our capering I pain.

Or I parry, feint, attack retreat, worry at you, whip you, whack at you. I hike your wing, paw at your prop, frighten you, trick you, mock you. I whoop, I warp, I frame, I fume. Unfetter my frippery, metamorph, turn you, form you, pattern you. Paint my firmament in you, write my far Papa in you. For our perpetuity, protect you.

Muppet, your forerunner try my air too you know. Crafting kite from tree, mimicking wing kin: raptor, hawk, tūī, harrier, huia. Many time your kite-eye contact Ranginui. Kite-tracking human roaming way, peeking her terra in panorama . . . Tree-kite wafting my Papa to me. A nip from her warm matter cutting her memory mint for me.

Or, when your human eye more open yet, Māui, Tāwhaki waft kite here too. Connecting to my premier crew — Tāne, Rongo, Rēhua, Tū. Mantic kite-eye awake, attune, penetrating my upper empyrean.

Ah — now I hear tact in your amour. I note fainting in your infatuating. Now you repair. You run home to port Papa, meek, nay, weak. You fine-tune your manner, turn mute, retiring, inert, outrun. Preferring to wane in her firm tight arm. Can I hear quiet terror in your feature? Who king, who queen now our infant? Our erratic mutt, our kooky imp, our nutty younger ruffian tot. Our one contact point in a yearning night. How keen to inherit it you are.

PAPATŪĀNUKU [TE TAU-IHU-O-TE-WAKA, WAIRAU, WAIAUTOA, MANIRAUHEA, OKUKU]

Tiny to, tiny fro, you make to rock me, rock me. No hurry in your rocking. You untiring, firm. In now moment, enormity in your roar near conquer my enormity — my eternity. Now, you no hurry, no hurry. Rock on. Me not terra firma tonight.

No pattern, no form in your rocking too. You tip me to, tip me fro on my yaw. Tip me fore, tip me aft. Yet it not new. For night after night I turn on my yaw. Year after year I tiptoe fore — for company ammonia, comet, Mercury, Moon, Titan, Neptune, meteor. Year after year time yore I entwine him whiffing winking Tangaroa; after him, entwine my honouring Ranginui more. After parting from

Ranginui, I rock me fore. No, not new. Not new.

Now infant you rock to fro in Ranginui. Wean off my Taranaki peak, waft up on raw arctic current, peer your home from far, wafting to Te Tau Ihu, on on you peer, to pure water, to eating track, to where Te Rauparaha came furrowing more.

Now now you know. Pitter pattering to fro to fro to fro to fro to fro to to fro to to to to . . . More fighting time, racket time, war time, pain time. More hit cut knock kick whack amputate time. Making harm, making hurt, making home time. Human you penetrate my murk my muck my peat, my carpet my canopy my crown. Hungry human, my mean infant, you hunt, fire, cook, eat, conquer. You enter, you take root.

What hype make you now? What cry you human? What make you rock me? What make you eye me, query me, peep me, peek me, art me, craft me, poke me, rake me, ferret me, root me, part me, hunt me, roam me? More wary, more finicky you are. More wearing in your worry. More ruffian you are. I am your home, your root, your kin! Yet, tiring termite, you irritate my pore. My temper come tight. My frown make hate. My fury taking root.

I turn rocky, weighty, mighty, more . . . I cry to moon, comet, meteor . . . I riff on pain, make track from tear, turn away from my Ranginui more. Cut anchor, rock wintry empty unitary more. Contrary now am I. To fro, to fro . . . Opening high peak, quaking, tremoring out warning now am I . . . You eat me part me eat me part me? I might eat too, might terminate.

Yet yet . . .

I wait.

More kin come, more kin to rock. More infant I want rhyming for. Creating warm power at my core. I wait for you, communing one. Heck, when your anointing feet furrow me — I rate it.

I rock, I rhyme on. Wanting more.

THE VANUA IS FO'OHAKE

JIONE HAVEA

THIS TALANOA, TELLING STORY, shoots out from three people having a talanoa (conversation), telling and sharing thoughts and imaginations. Three males to be precise, but their sex should not sanction nor hinder this talanoa (story). Nor should we imagine that this talanoa (telling) tells everything about their talanoa.

A talanoa ultimately fails to capture the talanoa it tells. Even if I argue that 'this is a true story', as storytellers are known to do, do not assume that I will tell everything from the talanoa of these three men from different generations, and different walks of life.

A talanoa must be shared, so that it tells. I therefore share this talanoa, hoping to also unmask romanticised views on the practices of oral and storytelling cultures. A talanoa can also pierce and transform, stretch and transcend, in addition to retelling and remembering (and sometime forgetting) memories.[1]

---

1   For the sake of ones who do not understand the lingo, 'talanoa' is a word used in several (but not all) of the native Pasifika languages; it refers to the (three in one) triad of *story*, *telling* and *conversation*.

   In the world of talanoa, *story* dies without *telling* and *conversation*; *telling* becomes an attempt to control when one does not respect the *story* or give room for *conversation*; and *conversation* is empty without *story* and *telling*. In talanoa cultures, there is no separation between story, telling and conversation. They interweave in talanoa.

BETWEEN MORNING AND LUNCH, one cool Fijian day, outside a meeting house where smart-talking people were gathered, welcomed and entertained, three persons — two Fijians and one Tongan — stood with their backs to huge unfinished woodcarvings. Withdrawn from the views and agenda shared among the gathered people, almost like a congregation, these three old men shared their talanoa within the hearing of logs, birds, trees, crawlers, rocks, and so forth, at a spot where most congregants would rather be.

The time was in-between, between the equalling darkness of the previous night and the next event in the programme, lunch, a meal, another congregating opportunity.

The place was outside of the meeting place, outside in terms of both location and ideology, but in the open in terms of space and creativity.

Woodchips littered the surroundings but as we say in Tongan, the fo'i toko-tolu (these three, this trinity) did not notice the reclining figures that the woodcarvers were trying to impress and express.

The atmosphere of the recalled talanoa was work in progress, unfinished carvings, anticipating, and fearing, the chiselling of carvers to give them more detail. The carvings reclined as if they refused to stand up, as if they would rather just lie there, resisting completion and the digging, engraving and gouging of the carvers.

The unfinished carvings are fo'ohake, they lie on their backside where they have been laid. Or should I say that they were dropped, dumped, where they now lie? They lie there, in the many senses of the term: there, they lie!

THE TOPIC OF THE talanoa was vanua, a Fijian word that can mean land, place, country, district or village. Vanua also refers to people, who are the lewe ni vanua (inner part of the land), and the flesh of the land.

The identities of indigenous Fijians (iTaukei) intertwine with vanua to the extent that without vanua the people are soulless. Vanua is the ground of belonging, the locus of being Fijian, the means of livelihood and the nurturer of life. Vanua is life. Without vanua, indigenous Fijians lose something significant of their Fijianness.

In our sea of islands, the words for land are basically the same — vanua (Fiji), hanua (PNG), fonua (Tonga), fanua (Samoa), fenua (Wallis and Futuna), whenua (Aotearoa) — and they carry similar meanings.

This talanoa on vanua started because one of the two Fijians is preparing for a PhD thesis that aims to transform the roles of the matanivanua, as herald for a chief and as spokesperson for the people, into a mata-ni-vanua hermeneutic, eyes and face (mata) of vanua, and he was seeking the wisdom of the senior Fijian on vanua.

The Tongan was listening in, eavesdropping, because he is aware and critical of, and sorry for, the assault Maʻafu and his men, from Tonga, committed upon the vanua o Viti, land and people and identity of Fiji and Fijians.

THIS TALANOA HAPPENED OUTSIDE and in-between, surrounded by incompletion and splinters of wood, and by splintering thoughts.

It started at the entry to a meeting place. And it shifted away from the meeting place, coming to rest, at this point, delayed, for now, at this talanoa that I am sharing.

This talanoa is therefore about shifts, movements, and splinters, fragments, that come to rest, that come together, as if to congregate, on this occasion, on their telling, upon the face of incompletion. This talanoa is therefore a meeting place.

THE TONGAN ASKED THE senior Fijian, 'Kerekere Pio, what do you think about when you hear people talk about vanua?'

Pio queried, in response, 'Na vanua?'

'Io, na vanua,' Joeli, the other Fijian interjected.

It is not unusual, or impolite, for islanders to jump into a talanoa; a talanoa is usually inviting, seductive, interactive and communal.

'Isa!' Pio then made a sound with his mouth similar to the sound one makes when she or he sucks on the mouth of a coconut or kisses the forehead of a grandchild.

The three men chuckled, like children again, appearing not to know what to say next.

Then there was silence.

Then more chuckling, this time, it feels, because of uncertainty. You know how those kinds of chuckles sound.

'Come, let's move over there and talk,' Pio requested.

The three moved away from the meeting place, toward the reclining unfinished woodcarvings.

One of the woodcarvers was there, holding a smoke in one hand and a stick in the other, and he greeted the three. They talked for a little while, and then the three returned to the reason why they were in motion.

'Why do you ask me this difficult question?' Pio enquired further.

Joeli interjected again. 'I know the common understanding of vanua, but we were wondering if you have other thoughts.'

Joeli was not ignorant of Fijian cultures. As we say in Tongan, ko e tangata naʻe ai hono kuonga, he is a man who had his era (which means that he knows something, he has been around).

Pio nonetheless went on to recall those common understandings, not in disrespect for Joeli but partly for the sake of the Tongan, partly in order to remind himself of what his culture says about vanua, and partly in order to find a gap, a fracture, an opening in those understandings through which he might locate a shift.

It got repetitive. But repetition is an essential part of talanoa. And patience is required when islanders get into the talanoa moods, because the talanoa may circle and ripple around, touching here and there, before landing anywhere.

More repetition and patience!

Suddenly, Pio's eyes sparkled. His face relaxed into a smile. He put the stuff that he was carrying on the ground, as if to touch the vanua, seeking permission to continue, then his hands stretched out, palms facing down, then back again, and again, almost like a Samoan dancer.

Silently at first, then he explained, 'The vanua is a figure lying down!'

There was silence. This time, it was the silence of awe, not knowing how to continue.

Pio continued, 'If you look at the way a Fijian village is structured, you can see its head, its body, its arms and legs. The head and body of the village will die if the legs don't go fishing, and if the arms don't turn the plantation. The hands and feet will be lost if the head separates from the body. The vanua is like that, and it is lying down.' Reclining. Relaxing. Resting.

There was silence! This time, it was the silence of respect for the insights of a wise turaga.

Questions rippled to Pio from several directions.

'When did the vanua sit up?'

'When did it stand up, so that Fijian societies became hierarchical?'

'What roles did western colonisation and Christianisation play in raising up, erecting, the vanua?'

'How do we get the vanua to lie down again?'

'Can we relax the vanua so that it lies back down again?'

'Should we keep the vanua standing, but encourage it to move?'

Again, Pio wisely replied, 'Come! Let's go eat. It's time for lunch!'

A TALANOA IS DIFFICULT to complete, or contain. It lives on, beyond each of its tellings. Actually, each telling gives it new life.

The next time I see Pio and Joeli I shall ask them:

Did the vanua lie down willingly?

Was the vanua lulled into lying down?

Seduced, maybe?

Was the vanua knocked down?

Suggesting that 'the vanua is fo'ohake', lying or fallen on its back, materialises these questions. That the vanua is lying down, is obvious. But why? And in whose interests?

What about the chips? And the unfinished woodcarvings?

As I await the next talanoa, may we remember that vanua refers to much more than land.

Vanua also has to do, among other things, in our sea of talanoa, with identity and belonging.

AFTER THE TSUNAMI

SERIE BARFORD

PENG IS A SECLUDED beach on a wondrous stretch of coastline that has been ground by the sea to fine grains of coral sand. Tropical palms, vines and wild flowers soften cliff faces broken by the jagged mouths of caves, where bodies were once buried foetal-like in baskets. Most of the sandalwood has been gutted from the forests but flame trees still hoist their arms to Christmas skies, entwining with frangipani and clusters of ripening lychee.

The beachfront has picturesque ruins. Trees and ferns sprout from stone houses abandoned by a community weakened by leprosy and a lack of fresh water. Sharpened sticks mounted by hollowed coconut halves denote taboo places. The clan never went back, and I am living with them four kilometres inland.

There are always those who relish solitude. At Peng it's an ex-military French artist and a woman whose forebears once lived there. They reside amid sculptures behind a palisade patrolled by dogs. Two days after Christmas their dogs rushed me. The trio was maddened by sea-lice and the spectacle of a stranger ripping lychee from their rubbery casements with unbrushed teeth.

I decided to ignore them, concentrating instead on the turquoise sea. Then one of them nipped my heels. 'Piss off,' I hissed as the artist appeared and called to the dogs. He seemed agitated. Almost distraught. All the while I was thinking, 'My dog would make mincemeat of these buggers. He's bigger, stroppier and goes for the jugular when threatened.'

Drinking water is scarce at Peng and I wondered if the artist was dehydrated. He was of medium height, with a square face and skin roughened by constant exposure to salty wind and waves. 'Have you heard the news?' he asked, pushing the dogs away from me. He held a length of sandpaper in one of his heavy hands and a shell engraved with a spiral in the other.

'What news?' I had a radio but the power kept cutting out, which in turn immobilised the water pump for hours on end. I'd given up on the outside world and occupied myself with domestic matters such as keeping chickens out of the house, washing clothes with cold water as I showered, killing as many mosquitoes as I could, and finding affordable food at the market or village stores.

'Tsunami!' he gasped.

'What?' I was alarmed. The island had been fatally struck in the 1950s. An earthquake at sea had triggered a wave that obliterated entire villages along a shoreline usually protected by coral reefs. I turned to flee.

'Wait!' he shouted. 'It's already happened!' and the Boxing Day tragedy spilled from him. He recounted descriptive news reports while I patted the now passive, scratching dogs, considering how the unexpected can strike you, even when you're living beyond beyond.

We cried for strangers and for friends and for paradise lost. He thought he'd escaped all earthly horrors when he'd settled at Peng. Now he wasn't sure that he could be safe anywhere.

'What about aftershocks?' I asked. 'Are we okay on this island?' Doves cooed behind us. 'It's so tranquil here.'

His eyes scanned the horizon. 'For now,' he replied.

TRIBE MY NATION

from *The Wreck*

DÉWÉ GORODÉ

translation Deborah Walker-Morrison
and Raylene Ramsay

AND THEY'RE ALL THERE, the bros, the pops and the grandpops, the sisters, the mamas and the grandmas, comrades, mates and relations making up the extended family. The years have brought with them spouses, partners and children, sharing the same hopes, the same unfailing determination. Welcomes are sung out to the beat of kanaka music over the loudspeakers as the protest marchers arrive in a steady flow. They come on foot, by car, bus and taxi. From downtown, from the four corners of the city, from the villages and tribes, they answer the call of the movement fighting against exploitation and domination in all its forms. Fighting for freedom, for justice, for dignity.

Brothers born of long years of common struggle, the organisers meet and greet each other, and begin discussing details of the demands to be made in the speeches. Some deliberate as to what protocol should be observed, the customary gestures that must be made to local clans before speaking, singing, or setting foot on their soil. Speaking the link to the land. Others organise the banners and distribute placards and marshals' badges. Others again keep a tally of who's there and who's not. The loudspeakers alternate marching instructions and music: Melanesian, Polynesian, Caribbean, African, in the original language or in English, Pidgin or French. They are setting the tone for the Big March on the tarseal of the town. The cops stop the traffic to allow the march to begin, as motorists look on and as TV cameras and news photographers prowl, on the lookout for the shot of the day or the shot of the century to sell later to the highest bidder.

The party leaders and elected representatives lead the march arm in arm under the Kanaky flag, taking up the whole road. A giant placard at the head of the march pays tribute to all the exploited peoples of the planet in their ongoing struggle for dignity and a better quality of life. This march is part of the continuous struggle to beat the odds of a system stacked against them. The oppressed of the world are blinded to the true nature of the global market vampire that bleeds them dry. It appeals to them like a sky stuffed full of gods offering false promises to the colonised.

The marchers stream past in a steady rhythm, picking up and chanting the slogans that are shouted out between songs from the loudspeakers, in a single resolute voice. The women follow on, laughing and swapping gossip as they march. Those who haven't seen each other in a while seize the opportunity to catch up with old friends, and their children, marching by their side, are happy to see their former classmates again. And so the long protest line advances slowly but surely through the streets of the town.

Tom meets up with brothers, cousins and female relations from his tribe up north in the mountains across the Central Divide who have come to Noumea specially for the march. Their presence takes him back to childhood — memories of the schoolyard, of diving off the rocks or fishing for shrimp, loach-fish and eels in the creek.

They talk about the mandarin season when, at dusk, they'd light the fire that warms body and soul at storytelling time in the Grande Case; or of the long silent walks through the bush when they would join the men hunting roussettes, notou pigeons, wild pig and deer. He thinks back to the smell of the forest, the taste of honey and roasted bancoule grubs dug out of tree trunks and fallen logs. He remembers the perfume of niaouli flowers and tabou wood and the unexpected beauty of wild orchids.

The rhythm of the march and the chanting of slogans remind the marchers of the first meetings of the movement back home in the village, organised by the young people of back then, one of whom is among the leaders in the front row today. They march with the same enthusiasm, the same dignity, the same determination; with the same clear, simple, convincing voice that won a few old stalwarts of the colonial status quo over to their cause; with the same commitment that led the people to stake their land claims and begin political action on the barricades during the 'Troubles', under the control of party cells working towards a common purpose. They think back to the first time the Kanaky flag was raised, by an old grandfather who had the same measured gestures as the present leader, whose voice carried the same unequivocal truth. It was Tom's own grandfather, in fact — an old clan chief who has always offered his crucial, unwavering support.

And then, inside of Tom, they are there. His mother and father. They are still with him and will always be there with him. Alive as ever in his memory. They blend into memories of the tribu, that small corner of earth where he took his first steps and where, one day, he will lie again. He is what he is through what they made of him. They took upon themselves everything that might have weighed him down. The burdens of life. The weight of existence. And took it all away when they left him, when they were killed in the accident. Tom left too, not long after, for the army.

After the leaders have presented their official list of demands to the authorities, the procession returns to its starting point and the march breaks up. The marchers head off in different directions through the town. As today is also a 'Saturday shopping fest', the city streets are decked out with garlands and banners. Everybody's on the lookout for the bargain of a lifetime, anything from a multi-coloured beach ball to a reconditioned old car. Kids with their faces painted to look like cats, dogs or owls run around lighting firecrackers and firing water-pistols at imaginary bandits. Teenagers are checking out T-shirts, jeans and sneakers. Young girls try on lipstick, mascara, nail polish. Women pore over the prices of pots and pans, crockery and household items. Mums are busy perusing potted orchids, Colombo plants and cordylines, while dads linger in front of lawnmowers, weedeaters, rotary-hoes. The stallholders unpack their wares — stacking, displaying, covering the pavement with anything and everything they can possibly sell. The customers think twice, counting their pennies. Everybody's calculating to the max.

Except, that is, for the ones among the crowd who couldn't give a hoot for all this showy display of merchandise. The dead-broke ones who have just come to look around, have a wander, check it out. They wait for mates with a few spare bucks to shout them a drink, a coffee or a meal or takeaways from one of the many foodstalls: spring rolls, meatballs, sandwiches, that they can sit on the grass and eat. Others have trouble finding a spot for themselves on the lawn between the bodies sitting or lying around in groups, talking, eating, and sleeping. But the constant movement of people passing by, coming and going continuously through the streets and gardens, seems to lead all and sundry off on some preset path, pounding the pavements in search of the ultimate object of desire. The narrow confines of the town centre are awash in the festive atmosphere that makes everyone want to move, mosey, go with the flow. The crowd mills around the town in a kind of magic merry-go-round, the hordes of noisy kids having a ball, oblivious to their parents. Everyday cares and woes dissolve away in the general euphoria; all the problems of the world appear to have been put aside by common consensus. And for those who are still having trouble keeping up or who can't chill out, even for a few hours, there'll always be plenty of good mates to get them drunk or stoned. For the regulars, this Saturday shopping fest means double the usual number of cans of beer and cartons of cheap red wine or free booze, taking them even higher, crazier, drunk beyond their wildest dreams.

Tom's cousin, who has become separated from him during the march, manages to catch up with Lena, the girl he's been dating, though somewhat chastely, for a number of weeks now. Lena abandons the two cousins who had joined her for the protest and goes off with him. She appreciates the young man's quiet manner; she's not long lost her mother and is not in the mood for casual relationships. He's in the middle of doing his army service and, since he's on guard duty later this evening, he has to be back at the barracks quite early. But he also wants to find Tom and introduce Lena to him. They have chow mein and fried rice at a little Vietnamese place and are about to sit down for a chat in a busy café when Tom comes in with a girlfriend who happens to know Lena and who introduces them. Dressed in his Hawaiian shirt and smiling, Tom offers a friendly handshake all round and sits down opposite Lena. They order a round of drinks, then launch into a conversation that Lena has trouble following at first, what with the noise of the pool tables and pinball machines, the laughter coming from the next table and the sharp humour of Tom's girlfriend, who has everyone in fits.

Next thing, Lena hears her saying:

—*It's a story about a fisherman grappling with a big catch on the end of his line, so big it pulls his canoe behind it for an entire night along the length of a wide bay. At dawn, shock number one! He finds himself back on the beach, sitting in front of the biggest fish he's ever caught. With his axe he hacks a doorway into its belly that he then explores with a torch. And then, shock number two! He's in the biggest coconut plantation he's ever seen, with an endless supply of coconut milk. He walks on cautiously, driven by a mixture of curiosity and fear. And then, shock number three! An enormous woman, with a skirt and hair made of coconut fronds, a coconut trunk for a body, with coconuts for breasts and eyes, is lying before him on a gigantic mat. 'Come and have a drink from my coconuts, little man,' she whispers and her voice is like the wind that blows him between her breasts. 'Come on, take hold of my two coconuts and have a drink. You know how. Go on, little man, don't be afraid. Two good coconuts, just like the ones you drink every day! Help yourself, little man!' He does as she says and suckles at her two coconuts as if she were his mother. He suckles and suckles and finally falls asleep like a baby between her two breasts. A long time after, as if at the end of a dream, he hears her voice, a whispering wind that says, 'Farewell, little man, you're a big boy now. You are truly a man.' And there he is, back on the beach, under the coconut palms, in the place where the big fish landed his canoe. And then, final shock! No fish. No woman . . . Gone!*

AT REGULAR INTERVALS, PEOPLE they know come in, say hello, sit down next to their table or move on. The hustle and bustle of people from the surrounding boutiques and shops winds its way into the café and out the other side again, back onto the street. With all this commotion, Lena can't really make out what anyone's saying except for Tom, who has conveniently opted to address her exclusively, since she's sitting opposite him. But from time to time, it's the girlfriend's voice that dominates. She has the gift of the gab and a whole repertoire of funny stories that are a perfect fit for a day such as this. As she tells one story after another, Tom and Lena are in tears, looking into each other's eyes. Between peals of laughter, unbeknownst to them all, something starts between the two of them; they turn away momentarily to look at the storyteller then back at each other while they listen to her tale:

—This one's about a man who boasts of owning a taro field containing every species of taro that exists. Ones for eating, ones for planting, medicinal ones and ones you exchange. Soon his taros produce so many shoots, sprouts and cuttings that he can't remember their names and ends up completely lost and confused. The mountain taro ends up in the place where the water taro should be and vice versa.
—What are you doing down there in the water, mountain-taro?
—I am drowning, water-taro.
—What are you doing up there on dry land, water-taro?
—I am dying, mountain-taro.
—And so, the collector's taros perish. In wanting to possess them all, the man ends up losing them all.

SHE CONTINUES LIKE THIS, captivating an audience that comes and goes, gathering around their small, round table topped with an ashtray that is steadily filling with butts and cigarette ash. An audience that has completely lost interest in the rowdy joyous spectacle that fills the rest of the room and the street outside.

Tom and Lena are drifting now, borne along by their friend's stories like two twigs, two wrecks drawn irresistibly together at the whim of the unfathomable current that binds them one to the other as they careen headlong towards some enchanted atoll, some tortured ocean. Each one floats, hopelessly adrift in the other's amused gaze, carried away by the magical spontaneity of laughter. Like two enchanted children at a puppet show. For each of them, the telling of the stories is an exploration of the contours of a face, the meaning of a smile, the depths of a gaze. For each, the narration follows the lobe of an ear, brushes against a cheek, lingers at the nape of a neck. In this way, the storyteller's tale, her humour and her entertainer's art, serve the dual purpose of exposing and concealing the signs of an irreversible intimacy: tying the inextricable threads that will weave the story of a new couple waiting in the wings, about to be born, unbeknownst to them all.

Towards mid afternoon, doubtless weary of amusing her audience with this kind of repertoire — a therapy as absurd as it was unnecessary, given the euphoric reality of the day itself — the storyteller finishes her act on a slightly more ironic note.

—It's the story of a little girl who got pinched during the night by a big crab. Ever since, she can't stop catching crabs down in the mangroves. And every time she eats one, she feels a sharp pain, in the place where the crab pinched her. To stop the pain, she resists the call of the crabs and decides to stop fishing for them in the mangroves. But that night, she hears them crawling up towards her, so she goes and stands by the hearth with her back to the fire, facing the door. The big crab arrives, comes in and makes straight for her. The moment he goes to grab her between his claws, she moves sideways and the big crab falls into the fire, pinching at the embers.

THEN THE STORYTELLER, LIKE some disillusioned diva or world-weary star who must fly off to some other, infinitely more important engagement, proclaims that, having still more sales and bargain-hunting to do, she must leave them. Nonetheless, and with no illusions as to the answer, she asks Tom what he's planning to do. He announces that he's staying, as if to say 'too late'.

He is older than both Lena and his cousin, so he takes the lead in organising the rest of the afternoon. He starts by taking them out of the café whose magic, now broken by the end of the funny stories and the laughter, had allowed him to see himself reflected in the gaze of the young girl whose serenity now reminds him of the calm preceding the storm. He takes the other two for a short walk, his stride adopting the continuous movement of the carnival crowd so that they have no trouble keeping up as he leads them on a kind of enchanted wander, weaving through streets that have thrown off their usual sleazy rags and put on their party clothes, the myriad patterns and shades of which multiply with every step they take. On this extraordinary walk, they each savour what captures their gaze and their fancy in the orgy of colours and manufactured goods. Made in Japan, China, Taiwan and all those other mythical places of origin, in factories making mass-produced goods, ready to take production straight offshore, where, from the weaving to the printing, they make the symbols of our identity: Kanaky flags by the hundreds, or whatever you care to order. In this joyous, whirling dance, a furtive glance from beneath a blue-shadowed eyelid, out from a mass of dreadlocks or finely braided extensions, sets off the wildest imaginings. The three friends allow themselves to be carried off toward other dreams, like those others who, only the day before or that same morning, at the first light of dawn, had laid down their protest demands on behalf of all those who are excluded from the money economy of the merchant town; written them out on banners carefully spread beneath the leafy branches of a false pepper tree, somewhere on the other side of the hills. Now that they've shifted their beggar's bag onto the other shoulder or hung it up in a shanty-town hut down by the mangroves, the protesters can let themselves go, be drawn into the delicious whirlwind of the day's festivities and live it up. Happily putting aside the militant fervour of the morning, they give themselves, body and soul, to the wave of light-hearted pleasure that carries them toward more carefree shores. In this magical journey into the beating heart of shopping land, into the pulsing lungs of the city's marketing economy, off they go, hearts on fire and bodies in a trance, toward other shores, other desires, other pleasures.

Tom is suddenly gripped by an amazing burst of activity, an incredible surge of energy: like some multi-hull helmsman or a street entertainer, he gleefully drags the young couple from pavement to pavement, avenue to avenue, from one square to another. He is overflowing with a vitality that is every bit as sudden as it is surprising, but which is perfectly in tune with the fever-hot atmosphere of the afternoon that leaves little room for introspection. But there, on a street corner, hanging on a rack on the pavement, a pleated grey mission dress with white flowers suddenly forces upon him a distant vision of his mother, back home in the village up in the hills, amidst the columnar pines and fern-covered slopes. He would have liked to have given it to her as a gift, as he often used to do. He can't resist, and buys it. The assistant hands him his parcel, gift-wrapped, decorated with a little crêpe-paper rosette of black petals surrounding a tiny red heart that he spontaneously removes and pins on Lena's dress. She is moved by this sudden gesture, but all three nonetheless find it quite natural, in accordance with custom. Then, brushing a surreptitious hand against the nape of her neck as he pushes the parcel into her hands, he continues to guide them forward through the crowd.

They pass groups of young men having a good time, groups of girls laughing and joking among themselves. They make way for elegant women dressed in silk mission dresses, chatting quietly as they stroke a scarf or hand a sweet to a chubby-cheeked child, unmindful of the hustle and bustle of the crowded streets around them. They pass ladies with bleached, straightened hair, lashes thick with mascara, powdered cheeks and bright lipstick, their hips swaying as they sashay past, some in shorts, others in jeans and boots or high-heels. There is a growing warmth and intensity in the gaze of each passer-by as the minutes and hours tick away on watches that no one looks at, the better to lose all notion of time. Time and notions: emotions that, in no time at all, a rapper in the town square brings back into focus, quick as a flash, in perfectly measured rhythms and flowing rhymes, standing in the middle of a circle where he is joined by two or three pirouetting hip-hop dancers and break-dancers, rapping out his words in a two-three beat.

*Brotha in struggle/ Kanak bro/ Caledo/ from Oceania/ Rasta/ Wearin'
dreads/ wearin' extensions/ Bob in yo' heart/ he singin'/ 'no woman/
no cry'/ Kana sista/ from Oceania/ Islanda/ don't ya cry now/ don't cry
Ma/ my rebel song/ won't last long/ like our sorrows/ no tomorrows/ for
our dead/ like I said/ mates in arms/ comrade brothas/ gotta be leaders/
gotta stand tall/ gotta fight see/ for our dignity/ for liberty/ justice
and equality/ trod down/ to the ground/ this global trip/ everywhere
you look/ global domination/ global uniformity/ by the bomb/ heavy
artillery/ got the net/ internet school now/ so I learn/ and I dance/ and
I sing/ sing my song/ sing my roots/ they so long/ rebel song/ sing for
dignity/ for liberty/ justice and equality/ on my Island/ Isle of Light/
Light me home/ Home my land/ Land my tribe/ Tribe my Nation/ my
Country/ Kanaky.*

LIKE SHINDERELLA

VICTOR RODGER

1

AFTER THEIR FIRST FUCK, the man took a thick silver ring off his almost-black finger and offered it to Robert.

'Take this as a symbol of my love.'

His Samoan accent was strong so his s's came out as sh's. *Thish. Ash. Shymbol.*

Robert, even though he'd never admit it, was inclined to dismiss him as just another hot Fob full of cheesy one-liners. But the ring — the ring was interesting, even if the sex had been unspectacular. (As Robert fucked the man, his moans had climbed higher and higher until they hit almost a feminine register. When he fucked, he liked his men to grunt in a basso profundo — never higher than an alto.)

Robert took the ring and held it in his hand. Heavy. Definitely not cheap. Robert slid it onto his just-olive wedding finger and admired it.

'Maybe one day, you and me, we get married?' *Tay. Ket.*

The man raised his eyebrows twice in quick succession.

Robert smiled.

If only he could remember the man's name.

'Thanks, man.'

For now, that would have to do.

2

AFTER THEIR SECOND FUCK (much better than the first, since the man kept his grunting low), the man opened the wardrobe in his small Manurewa bedroom and pulled out three boxes. He placed them on the bed.

'Have a look.' *Haff.*

Robert opened the first box: inside were two beautifully hand-stitched black leather shoes.

'They're beautiful,' he said, both surprised and excited. His heart began to race as he checked the size.

'Twelves.' The magical number.

The other boxes contained the exact same shoes in tan and chocolate.

'Take them,' the man said, looking at Robert fondly.

The shoes were beautiful — more beautiful than any Robert possessed. Certainly more beautiful than his tatty brown dress shoes which lay underneath his quickly discarded pants and t-shirt.

'You don't want them?'

The man shrugged. 'Too big.'

There was the question as to why the man had three identical pairs of expensive shoes that were too big for him — but Robert didn't care. Instead, he grabbed a sock from the floor, put it on his foot and began to slide his foot inside one of the shoes.

But no matter how hard he tried, his foot resisted. Robert silently cursed his Samoan father for the one thing he'd ever given him: wide feet.

The man stood there, naked and amused, as Robert desperately tried to get his foot inside the shoe.

'Like Cinderella,' the man said. *Shinderella.*

Robert grimaced. He had absolutely no intention of being an Ugly Sister. He pushed and pushed, willing his foot into the shoe. It was a battle he'd fought many times, around the world, with his wide, flat feet. Sometimes he'd won; sometimes he'd lost. But this time, he was determined to get his foot inside.

The man seemed confused by Robert's determination: 'Too small, uh?'

Robert's natural impulse was to glare at the man but instead he kept pushing. And pushing. And pushing, willing the leather to give a little more each time. Finally, when sweat was trickling down his temples, Robert's foot slid into the shoe. His foot felt like it had been placed into an ever-tightening vice — but it was in.

He grabbed another sock, forced the other shoe on and then stood naked, his little toes throbbing. He gingerly walked towards a full-length mirror.

'Sole — you sure they fit okay?'

The shoes were killing him. Every step was absolute agony. But Robert was determined his wide feet would eventually make the shoes succumb to his width. It would just take time: time and persistence.

Robert looked up at the man. Fuck. He still couldn't remember his name.

'Thanks, man.'

For a moment he wondered what the man might bestow on him if they fucked for a third time but he looked at his watch: it was time to go.

Robert got dressed and hobbled out of the man's house with the three shoeboxes under his arms.

The man looked at him, clearly concerned at the way he was walking.

'Sole — you sure you okay?'

Robert nodded and smiled.

'Sweet. For real.'

They drove in silence: the man had agreed to drop Robert at his friend Patsy's house.

The man rested one hand on Robert's thigh, slowly stroking it up and down as he drove down Weymouth Road. Among the people-movers sagging with sticky-fingered children and arguing parents, Robert was surprised that the man clearly held no fear about being seen being affectionate with another man.

Robert looked over at him. He had a strong profile. Impossibly smooth skin. Beautiful full lips. Fine jet-black hair. It was obvious why Robert had drunkenly made a beeline for him at the club last night. And for a fleeting moment he wondered how his mother had felt, meeting his father, fresh from Samoa, for the first time.

The man was about to pull into Patsy's driveway but Robert had no intention of being seen with him in public and instructed him to pull over to the side of the road.

Robert got out of the car, his feet pulsating as though each toe had been hit with a hammer.

The man winked at him. 'Vili mai.'

Robert frowned: his Samoan barely went beyond pleasantries and swearwords.

The man clarified: 'Call me.'

Robert noticed Patsy in the distance, watching with interest from the deck of her dilapidated house, her short, stout frame encased in a faded white bathrobe, her skin a dark chocolate against it.

'Fa,' he said, quickly.

'Ia, fa.'

Robert watched as the man drove away, then turned to face Patsy, who had one plucked, bemused eyebrow arched.

'O ai le la kama?'

Robert ran through the phrases he recognised in his head, trying to translate without having to ask: Kama — *man*. O ai. *Who?* She was asking who the man was?

'Just a friend.'

'A friennnnnnnnd?' The word in Patsy's mouth was thick with derision.

Her eyes looked at the new shoes and the shoeboxes under Robert's arms.

'You been shopping?'

'Kinda.'

Patsy's eyes narrowed in suspicion as she caught sight of the silver ring on Robert's wedding finger.

'Oi, we're a married man now, are we?' she said, her voice dripping with sarcasm. 'Malo, malo. What's Mr Lucky's name?'

Robert opened his mouth and briefly considered lying, then simply shrugged.

Patsy shook her head: 'Oi sole.'

It was not quite dusk. Inside the house Robert could hear Patsy's husband, Napz, reprimanding one of their children, and a child's stifled cries.

Robert took two geisha-girl steps towards the house, his little toes pulsating prisoners desperate to break free from their jail.

Patsy clicked her tongue against the roof of her mouth as she watched him: 'E, kalofa e si Little Mermaid.'

Robert was about to follow her inside when she looked down at his shoes. He knew she meant for him to take them off before entering the house.

'Come on, Pats. If you'd seen how long it took to get them on . . .'

Pats raised one eyebrow.

'But . . .'

Patsy raised the other eyebrow.

Robert sighed and then, with great effort and even greater reluctance, kicked his shoes off.

Ahhhhh, the sweet, sweet release . . .

He looked down at the other discarded shoes outside the front door: well-worn jandals, grubby sneakers, scuffed black church shoes.

'Are they safe out here?'

'Ki'o,' Patsy said as she moved inside.

Robert couldn't bear the thought of them being nicked. He balanced the three shoeboxes under one arm, then bent down to pick up his beautiful new shoes.

'I'll bring them inside. Just in case.'

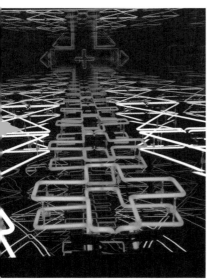
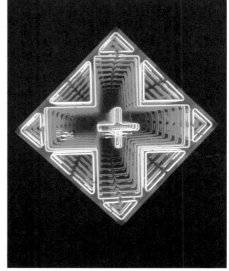

Robert Jahnke
Above: *Navarro tukutuku*, 2014–16
Below left: *Ata tuatahi*, 2016
Below right: *Ripeka whero*, 2015

BLACK MILK

TINA MAKERETI

THE BIRDWOMAN CAME INTO the world while no one was watching. It was her old people who sent her, the ones who hadn't chosen to make the transition, who stayed in their feathered forms, beaks sharp enough to make any girl do what her elders told her.

'It's time,' they said. 'They're ready.'

But was she?

There were things the people needed to know. But first she had to make her way into their world. She watched for a long time from her perch, trying to figure the way of them. They seemed so crude and clumsy to her — so slow with their lumbering bodies, their plain, unprotected flesh — no wonder they took plumage from her own kind, or made poor copies with their fibres. Their movements pained her — she would need to slow her own quickness, calm the flutter of wings, the darting of eyes that had protected and fed her all her wild life.

She saw what kind of woman she would be. She could keep some of her dignity if she held her head high, wore heavy skirts that fanned out and trained behind her, if she corseted in the unprotected flesh and upholstered it with good tailoring. A fine tall hat, or elaborately coiled hair beset with stones that caught the light. She had seen women such as this, glided past them on the wind. They saw her too, but didn't point and call out like the children. They saw and took note in silence, sometimes lifted their chins in acknowledgement. She saw spiralled markings on some of those chins, dark-haired women, and thought she could read meaning there. Though this was a rare sight, and though she needed to blend in, she decided she should mark herself this way too, so that the ones who needed to would recognise her.

So she came into the world when no one was watching, only just grown enough to be a birdwoman rather than a birdgirl. Then she moved through the forest to where the people lived. On the outskirts of the settlement, the men saw her first. They removed their hats and looked everywhere but into her eyes, for there was something piercing in her manner that made them uncomfortable. She walked past them towards streets lined with houses, alarmed that without wings the dust gathered itself to her and stayed. How did they stand it, the people with all their gravity and filth?

The women were less circumspect. They looked her up and down from their doorways, and made assumptions about where she came from and what kind of woman she was.

'Looking for someone, dear?' called Eloise, who had survived four stillbirths and adopted every stray child in town.

'Perhaps she's in the wrong place,' said Aroha to Eloise, loud enough for the Birdwoman to hear. 'Are you lost, dear?' Aroha was all right once you got to know her, but she was not an easy woman to get to know.

The Birdwoman thought about how to answer these questions, and the only answer that came to her was politely.

'I am fine thank you, but I am wondering if there might be a place for me to stay. Can you recommend a house?'

The women were disarmed by her directness.

'Mrs Randall takes in lodgers,' said Eloise. 'Aroha, take her to

Mrs Randall's, will you? I have this lot to account for. No knowing what might happen if I leave them to their own machinations.' Eloise was always using words that were too big for the meaning she intended.

Aroha's sullenness couldn't withstand the faint glow that emanated from the Birdwoman. Her hair seemed luminous and so marvellously soft that Aroha wanted to reach out but couldn't, for who knew what protection a woman such as this carried, seen or unseen? She'd never been so close to anyone quite so meticulous and, frankly, shiny. It was only moments before she found herself telling the stranger all the news of the town, including even her most delicious gossip.

There was a reason no one had been watching, the Birdwoman learnt, even though there were sentries on every hill. They were too busy watching each other and their firearms, too busy grappling with the ways of war, which, no matter how many times they went through it, could not be made intelligible. She knew they noticed her strangeness but no one had the energy to concern themselves about it.

Before now, she had only known them as the clumsy ones who took the small and fluttering bodies of her kin for food and feathers, even beaks and talons. And though it had sorrowed her, she knew there was a balance to it. The people called their greetings and gave their thanks, but they hunted. It was an old deal made right at the beginning: her line would be sacrificed to theirs. But the gods gave them two gifts to cope with the hurt — abundance, and a lack of other predators.

She got used to their ways. She helped. There were people to organise and mouths to feed. She kept her clothed dignity, but didn't mind rolling up her sleeves. And time passed. And the wars ended, but then even more people were hungry, and she didn't know if the old ones had been right after all — could she really do anything to help? Her sleeves remained rolled up, and she saw everything that had caused her family to send her to the ground — how they struggled, these landwalkers, her upright naked friends, how they hurt themselves like little children who had not yet learnt how to hold a knife safely or run without tripping.

SHE HAD BEEN SO busy with the people and their wars that she didn't notice until it was done. They never took her hunting, they'd seen her disapproval and didn't want to anger her. But one day they emerged from the forest with empty hands, nothing to offer their children.

'It's the rats,' a man said.

'It might be the cats,' Eloise nodded toward the friendly feral at her feet.

'It's the white man.' This was an old koro who was known to shake his stick and rant about the changing world. 'They take them for their museums. Put them under glass to stare at. I saw it when I went over there as a boy on the ships . . .'

'Āe, āe, koro,' the young ones rolled their eyes. They'd heard about the ships, the ships. But that was long ago. Before all the wars. The wars hardened them, and made them so tired.

'They trade in them. Take them by the hundreds.'

No one wanted to hear this part. No one wanted to believe it. But she heard.

'It doesn't matter what happened to them now. There's none left to take. Haven't seen a huia since I was a boy.'

Could it be that she had been gone so long? Could it be that she hadn't noticed the voices of her elders fading? Would she be stuck in this place with these fleshy fools forever? No. They weren't ready. How could they understand the gifts of her kind when they couldn't even restrain themselves or others? All that killing.

So she left, just as swiftly as she had come. She wandered between villages, her anger turned inwards, devoured by her grief. She forgot herself.

It was a dark place she got into. She no longer held her head high, no longer dreamed of the future. Despair sat on her shoulders where her wings should have been. Darkness consumed her, the quivering lip of a dying abalone, grease in the barrel of a gun. Sometimes she did not see or hear any birds for weeks.

Then, one day, she saw him, his great figure hunched so that he looked like one of hers, hair on his head shimmering in the way of the tūī. When he moved she thought she heard the whispered scrape of feather against feather. He came slowly, in a considered fashion, was heavy limbed, but when he turned a certain way — it was enough.

'Lady,' he said, and bowed.

He was a dark-feathered mountain. He was the shape of her nights. He was ink spilt in a pool of oil, volcanic rock, onyx eyes. The black enveloped them. There had been so many long days, she had seen so many things she didn't want to see. Lady, he said, and she liked the way the word curved around her and gave her a place to rest.

They had many children.

She had no time to remember herself then.

'Mother,' the children would call, 'we're hungry. Mother, we're cold. Help us.' Their mouths open with constant needs and demands. She was kept busy from the start of the day to the end.

They worked hard together to grow the children. It was easier for her to forget the guilt-ache and shame of where she had come from, how she had let it get so bad, how she didn't help her people. Better to let her children grow up in her husband's world, without the burden of her knowledge. She settled on this as the right path, though her husband would sometimes look sidelong at her, as if considering some puzzle he couldn't figure.

'Wife, sometimes you seem very far away,' he said one day.

'I am here, husband, look at me. I am always here.' But he was not convinced.

'Yes, your body is here, but I see when you leave. It is like you are up there somewhere.'

Even in a marriage, there is only so much you can hide. Or share.

'You can tell me about it, if you wish,' he said.

'Sometimes I miss my family, but then I think of the children.' That had been her answer. Focus on the children.

It was difficult, then, when one by one the children began to lose their way.

She watched them leave, sooner than she wished, on their own journeys of peril. But when her youngest son showed signs of following the same path, she took him aside.

'There's something I should have told you kids long ago.' Her son stooped so that she could whisper in his ear. She told him where she had come from, about her own kind, how there were so few left. Their gifts. The covenant they had had with his father's people. She told him how she had been sent a long time ago, and the telling was like an unravelling of all the things she had seen: the wars and despair, the museums and grief, the long, dark nights and the joy of making children.

'You were hope made real,' she told him. And she hoped it wasn't too late, hoped that the knowing would help him, hoped that the story would make him stronger than he knew how to be.

Her boy saw a world that was not what he thought it was. He saw many things that he hadn't known possible before. He only had one question.

'Why didn't you tell us? Why didn't you tell everyone?'

She thought how she should have opened her mouth when she kept it closed. How silence doesn't help anything. But would they have heard her? Maybe she didn't give them the chance.

'Perhaps I should have spoken sooner. Perhaps not. It is time when it is time,' she said, and placed her hand on her son's shoulder.

The unravelling of her story was an ending. The darkness came flooding back in. This time it wasn't bleak or hurtful, it was a flash of curved beak in velvet dark. Black milk. The depths of Te-Kore-the-place-before-night. More inviting, more liquid than you ever expected black to be. Darkness that holds all of light in it. Home, she thought, and she heard the movement of feathers through air.

THE
STONE

MICHAEL
PULELOA

1992

It's a big stone.

Five feet tall.

Cone-shaped. Upright.

It's smooth like skin.

The father says, It's time: The stone is ready. And they know it'll take all six of them to move it.

They've spent years and years and years with the stone. They've fed it and bathed it and watched it grow. Yes, the stone grows!

THE MULTI-PLATINUM, GRAMMY AWARD-WINNING rock musician sitting in front of Francis Palikiko doesn't look like he has money. He's unshaven, in a tattered T-shirt and torn, faded jeans.

The children, who had once been playing in the yard around the men, are now whispering to each other and when Francis hears one of them say the thin musician is kāpulu, he calls for Lei and asks his wife to take the children into the house. He knows, it's time. He can't stop the stone in his front yard anymore. He doesn't want to.

The only evidence of financial wealth — the only reason Francis is sitting with the rockstar right now — is the $60 million Gulfstream parked in front of the control tower and the open-field dirt parking lot at the Hoʻolehua Airport. He's never seen anything like the jet, and he joked with the rockstar the first time they shook hands that the rockstar must really be a god. (If there's one other reason Francis is still sitting right now, it's the rockstar's companion, Love. He hasn't made up his mind about her, either.)

They're sitting at a picnic table under a 20' x 20' E-Z Up in Francis's yard, less than two miles away from the airport. In a small yard in front of a small wooden house. There's a little garage with an old rusty car on blocks. Mango trees. An old forklift. An old mini-dozer. And the rest of it is overgrown bush and koa haole.

The rockstar has seen the stone, and though it's not as grand in appearance as he'd hoped, if it's what Francis Palikiko says it is, he's still very much interested in purchasing it. It's a beauty, the stone, and nothing like the ones he already owns, but there's no doubt it'll sit nicely with the renovations currently underway outside his Los Angeles home.

The rockstar has brought an archaeologist with him. He introduces her as Love, and she doesn't offer another name when she shakes Mr Palikiko's hand. She's here to substantiate the historical value of the stone and verify its authenticity. She's brought copies of sketched images taken by early European explorers and once stored in the archives of the British Museum. And now, under the tent, after she takes another sip from a bottle of water, she shows the photocopied sketches to the men. She points out how the details in the image correspond to details on the stone in the yard. 'It's a definite match,' Love says. 'This is the one.'

The rockstar slides the drawings of the stone toward him and lifts one of the copies to get a closer look. 'It appears that way,' he says. 'I'm almost afraid to ask what it's worth.'

Francis lets out a laugh. He knows the couple hasn't flown all this way to worry about cost. 'It's priceless,' he says. 'But you can make us one offer.'

The rockstar, of course, is happy. He's supposed to be in Italy right now, but the promise of obtaining one of the most storied stones in all of Hawai'i's history is too appealing to pass up. This moment makes Italy a stroll on the Venice Beach Boardwalk.

The rockstar looks over at Love.

Francis has seen it coming. He motions for the rockstar to take the photo over to the stone. He says, 'Go. Take one closer look. Think about it.'

The rockstar gets up and leaves the table. He heads for the stone. When he's there, he lifts the paper in his hand next to the stone so he has both the photocopied sketch and the stone in his view. Before long, the rockstar says, 'Any way we can get the original of this sketch from the museum, Love?'

He decides the whole thing is destiny. Not for the family, but for the stone. They're vessels, he thinks. It's the stone that's special. It's been confirmed. And his family agrees.

The stone heals them when they're sick:

Common colds, flus, fevers, pneumonia — no problem.

Headaches, backpain, depression — no problem.

Anxiety, hyperactivity, drug abuse — no problem.

LOVE TELLS FRANCIS SHE has a PhD in archeology but Francis has never heard of the school. She's been on assignment in Hawai'i before, to the northwestern Hawaiian Islands, she tells him, but her last real fieldwork was in Egypt, at El Hibeh. She's never been to Moloka'i but she says the view from the jet and the short ride from the airport have already piqued her interest in the island. 'Mr Palikiko,' she whispers. 'I'm hoping, really hoping, you're not going to sell it.'

Francis reaches for the remaining photocopies on the table. He's a little stunned. He's made up his mind, but he wants to hear what she has to say. 'You came Moloka'i to tell me *no* sell? Strange.'

Love smiles. 'This was a last-minute change of plans, Mr Palikiko.

We're supposed to be in Italy. We were going to look at art.'

'That's it, ah?' asks Francis. He keeps his eyes on the sketches. 'Real art.'

'It's quite a find. I'll give you that. But sell it? That doesn't seem like something a man like you . . .'

Francis looks at her. 'Huh, Ms Love? A man like me?' He keeps his eyes fixed on her. He puts the papers back down on the table. He continues his stare.

Love says, 'You've got something truly remarkable. I don't have to tell you that, but I will. You don't want something like this sitting outside a mansion somewhere in LA, do you? There are probably museums . . .'

'His yard, my yard. What's da difference? Look around. At least it'll have a nice view. Probably a pool.'

Love smiles again. She likes him. 'I can just tell him it isn't the stone, Mr Palikiko. Think about it,' she says. 'If you really want to sell it, at least consult with a few museums.'

'Why?' asks Francis. It's a question he's not really expecting her to answer. 'Because dey care? I tell you, if your boyfriend pay da price, he'll care.' He looks over at the rockstar, who is now leaning over with his face inches from the stone. 'Eh, rockstar,' he says. 'You be one stone star, too!' And he puts out another big laugh.

They use a twenty pound ʻōʻō and brand new shovels and dollies. They have machinery, heavy equipment, but they use their hands. It takes a full day.

They sweat.

They bleed.

They pray.

They cry.

And the stone cries, too. It sounds like singing birds, they say.

THE ROCKSTAR IS BACK at the park-bench table. He places the

photocopy of the stone onto a small pile of the others. He looks at Francis. 'Don't know these things like Love,' he says. He points to the stone. 'Good shape. How is that?'

'It's a stone,' Francis says, and they both laugh.

'I mean, what've you done? To keep it so beautiful?'

'We'll write things down,' Francis says.

Love looks over at the men and then reaches over for the photos on the table. She collects the photos of the stone, puts them into some kind of sequential order, and then places them neatly in a stack in front of her. 'It'll be quite a chore having to move it,' she says.

Francis keeps his attention on the rockstar. 'We get 'im on your plane,' he says. 'A'ole pilikia. No problem.'

When Love smiles, Francis knows she's just doing it to keep things civil, and as far as he's concerned, it's more than enough for him. She stands up with the stack of papers and says, 'I'm going for another look. I'll be there if you need me, boys.' And she makes sure the men watch her as she walks away.

The rockstar keeps his eyes on her until she's sitting on the lawn, right next to the stone. 'She's beautiful,' says the rockstar. 'Smart, too.' Then he continues, 'I know what she told you when I was over there. I understand. I'll take care of it, Mr Palikiko, the stone. You haven't changed your mind?'

Francis knows the stone. He believes the rockstar even though he also knows the rockstar himself doesn't completely believe his own words. 'Depends,' says Francis.

'I haven't toured in a while, Mr Palikiko. Not recording this year, too.'

'Then you're in the right place,' says Francis. He points toward the stone. 'There's your inspiration.'

The rockstar looks back at Love and the stone. He looks at them for about ten seconds. 'Five hundred?' he asks.

Francis smiles. He keeps looking at the rockstar.

'One?'

'Higher.'
'One-point-five?'
'Higher.'
'Two.'
'Close.'

The father doesn't care about what they've done. And he doesn't have to explain why they've done it, either. As far as he's concerned, he's listening to the stone.

They've lived years and years and years with it.

They've fed it and watched it grow.

The stone called to him in the first place. So why should he explain himself? No, he won't.

No. He's the one who heard it.

THEY ARE SITTING AT the table under the shade of the E-Z Up. The rockstar and Love are on one side, Francis and his eldest son on the other. In the middle of the table there's a large wooden bowl with a creamy, grey liquid that Francis tells them is 'awa.

'I know rockstars like their medicine,' he says. And then he smiles. 'No worry. Just try.' His son stirs the 'awa with a polished coconut shell, and Francis points, "Apu.'

The boy pours 'awa until the 'apu is brimming, and the three of them watch as he carefully stands up and steps away from the table. They turn to watch the boy when he walks toward the stone and kneels at its side. He holds the 'apu just above his head and then pours the 'awa at the base of the stone. Francis says, 'Ancestors first.' Then he smiles at the rockstar and says, 'Write that down.'

The four of them sit at the table, the boy serving them one at a time in the same way he served the stone. The rockstar and Love ask questions, first about the stone, and then about life in general. Francis answers until he feels they've heard enough. Every now and then, the boy offers another round, and they drink.

There's dirt all over their bodies and cramps in their arms, but they
don't quit. They can't. In order to move the stone, they tear up the lawn.
They uproot trees. The stone wants to move and they're doing it. Just
them. A family. For the stone. For the family.

FRANCIS IS NOW BESIDE Lei and his eldest son. They're in a circle
around the stone with the rockstar and Love. They're holding
hands. Still, the rockstar fidgets between Francis and Love.

'We happy you're here,' says Francis. 'Rockstar and Love. The
stone's happy, too.'

Everyone smiles. Francis bows his head, everyone does the same,
and Mrs Palikiko begins a prayer . . .

After a minute, Francis is the first to lift his head. He gives a
gentle squeeze to the rockstar's hand before he lets go. He places
one hand on the stone and then gestures with his other for the rest
of them to do the same. When they've all got their hands on the
stone he says what the rockstar believes is his own little prayer.

The stone has brought them strength, power:
　The father and mother — they never get weak, they never get tired.
　The sons and daughters — they see the future in their dreams.
　They know they have plenty to lose. They're willing to take that
chance. The stone has decided and the father knows it. They all know.
　They must keep at it, preparing the stone for the long journey to its
new home.

MRS PALIKIKO AND THE children are at one of the mango trees.
Love is beside them with a plastic grocery bag. The rockstar and
Francis are standing together beside the stone. The rockstar says,
'I'm glad plans changed, Mr Palikiko. This's been an experience.
For Love, too, I think.'

'With the stone, plans don't change,' says Francis. He's pleased so
he lets the space between them be consumed by their surroundings.

The warmth of the sun. The crisp wind. The sound of the children laughing. Birds singing in the trees. The stone.

'I'll stay in touch, Francis. I'll be back. And when you're ready, I'll fly you to LA for a weekend so you can see what I've done. Plan for that, too.'

Francis tells the rockstar he's never been outside Hawai'i.

'I've never had 'awa,' says the rockstar. 'And I'm sorry I hadn't.' He looks over at the children placing mangos in the plastic bag. He looks at Love. 'It'll be good for your family,' he says.

But Francis doesn't hear him, anymore. He's also looking in the distance, looking at his wife and children. Listening to the stone.

1999

ON AN OVERCAST MORNING somewhere in Los Angeles, the multi-platinum, Grammy Award-winning rock musician steps out onto the balcony of his palatial mansion. The grey clouds rolling in from the Pacific have already mixed with the haze drifting above the city, but he's not bothered by the fact that he can't clearly see the horizon. There are still empty wine and champagne glasses standing on the marble tabletops around him — ugly reminders of what was supposed to be an intimate gathering in celebration of the release of his latest album, *Chronicles of the Stone* — but they don't bother him, either. He's found himself again. He's been inspired to write and to play and to sing. To create. He has reignited his popularity, his fame.

His music is not the same anymore, and at first the critics were quite resistant. But in time, as the music started to sell, there was no denying the genius behind his new work. The critics retracted their earlier assessments, or they simply acted as if they hadn't written anything negative in the first place. It was all enough to make the rockstar laugh; one morning shortly after the success of his new album had been confirmed, he fell off his chair while reading the paper and enjoying a cup of espresso at his 16th-century table once owned by Henry VIII.

What does cause the rockstar some concern, even some panic, however, is the fact that as he stands there leaning on the cool aluminium railing at the edge of the balcony, he immediately sees that there is something very wrong about the courtyard. He knows what it is. He sees it, but he can hardly believe it. It seems impossible. He feels a warmth begin on the back of his neck before it shoots down his arms.

The stone in his courtyard, the one after which his most recent album is named, has fallen from its place. The tall, smooth stone is now on its side, lying on the immaculate, soft lawn.

The rockstar cannot determine what has happened. He is certain the stone was meticulously set, placed in position on a prominent spot in the courtyard specifically designed to prevent this. There was an architect. An engineer. They were both paid extra to ensure that the stone was properly secured. He had told them their only job was to keep the stone safe.

He thinks for a second (and finds himself instantly enraged) that someone has pushed it over. But this, he knows, is also impossible. The stone is just way too heavy.

He re-enters the mansion and turns on the television, looking for the news. He hops on his iMac, gets online, and also searches there. He's thinking perhaps there was an earthquake in the night.

The stone has fallen and he's quite shaken up, but also incredibly fascinated by the whole situation. There's absolutely no mention of any tremor, let alone earthquake, anywhere in the vicinity of California in the last twenty-four hours. And when the rockstar finally gets to the stone, he sees that it is still in perfect condition, even after the fall.

He places his hand on the stone. Rubs his hand across its smooth surface.

He decides not to call the architect. Or the engineer.

He returns to the mansion. He makes an espresso.

He walks back out to the courtyard and sits near what was once the base of the stone. He examines it for evidence of the fall.

Before he can finish the espresso, he feels a swirling wind cutting over the lawn. It's persistent. Leaves and flowers begin to fall from the shrubs — and then the trees — in the courtyard. He sits in the wind until it eventually calms.

He spills the rest of the espresso on the grass. White flowers of an orchid tree have lined themselves up on the lawn at the other end of the stone.

He stands up, looks down at the stone, then contemplates these things: the way the stone might've fallen to land in its new position, and the way the shape of the stone makes it appear that the white flowers have aligned themselves with the stone.

The rockstar turns and makes his way to one of the studies in the mansion.

Soon, there are blueprints of the property and maps of Los Angeles covering the desk and the floor. He cannot move without touching some kind of paper. He's surrounded by drawings, plans, layouts, symbols. He's looking for anything in line with the stone — something on his property, something underground, something in the city, a building, a home, a lot.

He finds nothing significant in any of the blueprints and maps. After nearly three hours, he's at a loss for what to do. There's someone he can call, but he doesn't want to do it. It might be his pride, but he also thinks the call would be premature. He's had the stone for years now, and this is not the first time something like this has happened. Only the first time the stone has moved.

There were times he'd awoken to find it was raining everywhere in LA except in the courtyard. And other times when the courtyard was the only place with rain.

There were times when the sky was dark for days, and the first rays of light came down to touch the stone.

He's chronicled these events.

He knows that he'll figure it out in time. He pulls out a drawer in the desk and finds a pen and a pad. After a minute, he opens other drawers in the desk. He pulls out two boxes and rummages through the first, taking out other precious stones he's collected from around the world. Then he opens the second box and slides out its contents: firm, clear plastic sheets with old postage stamps sealed in them. He scans the little stamps until he sees one in particular and then he looks back out the door.

He reaches for the pen and pad and begins to write, *It speaks again . . .*

That afternoon, he is out on the balcony. He looks up toward the horizon and sees a point where the clouds and the haze are parting, leaving a view of the blue sky behind them. He sees this point is perfectly in line with the stone. The tall stone, still on its side, is a line between him and the blue point in the sky.

2005

THEY THINK IT'S A simple two-man job so their plan is to the point: wait for Friday, down some beers, steal the stone, make the drop, done. By now, they really can't help themselves. It's not just the money. It's not just the drugs. They've driven past the old man's place since they were boys, thousands of times, and every time they have, they've found themselves — whether they've thought to or not — looking into his yard. They called the stone 'more beautiful than any girl we know' long before the old man and his family packed it up and shipped it to the rockstar. They heard the story. You can't keep something like that a secret on Moloka'i.

Now the stone has a new price tag, forty grand to the wharf. That's a small fraction of what they've heard it's worth, but it's also so much money they don't complain. They worry more about keeping the cash a secret than they do about the drop. They decide to go fifty–fifty even though they'll use the small one's truck. The big one, the powerlifter, he's the muscle, so he gets paid to get the stone in the bed of the truck and to shut people up if needed, after that.

They're brothers. And they don't think anything about stealing the stone. As far as they're concerned, the old man is doing them a favour. He deserves it for moving the stone in the first place. Besides, he's already got his cut. More than three million is what they've heard. They can't believe it (the old man, Francis, still lives the same way he did in '92), but if they're getting paid the way they are, it must be true.

The big one is not all muscle. He's got a heart. He doesn't tell the small one, but he plans to send most of his cut to their sister. She wants out of a bad marriage. He's told her just to come home, but she insists she'd sooner die than show up back on the island after all these years with nothing more than a suitcase full of designer clothes. He'll send her the money to get her started again, and he'll put the rest away. His girlfriend is having a baby. His brother doesn't know that either.

The small one is another story. If he had a good bone in his body, he'd probably sell it, too. Everything about him is *make that money*. And he's found over the years there's no faster way than with drugs. He's had fistfights with the big one a dozen times to defend this idea. And the fact he got his ass kicked every single time only helped to prove how adamant he was about this point. He plans to take his twenty grand and flip it five times in the next year. 'That's not a hundred grand,' he tells his brother, 'it's almost six and a half.' He'll be moving across the state.

IF THERE'S ONE THING that really gets them, it's the fact that the old man has put the stone right at the start of his driveway, less than five feet from the road. They've heard it's because he wants to let people have a look without having to drive onto his property. They've heard when the flatbed came to return the stone after the rockstar had it, the rear tires went flat and the straps holding down the stone slipped off right at that spot. They've even heard the old man says it was up to the stone. They've heard it all, but what they think is that the old man just wants to rub it in their faces.

They toss the empty beers into a chickenwire bin full of bottles in the garage. Then they roll out an old carpet in the bed of the Chevy, shut the hardtop, and jump in up front. It's a Friday night, but they don't expect any traffic on the road fronting the old man's house. It's 2 am and they know the old man and his wife have long since gone to sleep. Their children are all out of the house. The youngest is somewhere in California.

The small one starts up the truck and they each think for a second that they've overlooked the rumbling noise sputtering out of the muffler, but then the image of a fat stack of cash quickly erases their worries. The small one reaches for the door and rolls up the windows. Then he slips a CD into the deck beneath the dashboard and the cab fills with what the big one can only describe as fusion rock. 'What da hell,' the big one says.

The small one is bobbing his head front and back, laughing. 'Da chronicles,' he says.

'What?'

'*Chronicles of the Stone*. Da music. Da rockstah's music.' He raises a fist in the air.

The big one slaps at the deck until there is silence. The cab fills with swearwords and accusations regarding the small one's intelligence. 'I not playin' tonight,' the big one says.

The small one wants to say he's only adding to the mood, but he's not looking for another fistfight. He's got his mind on the money, and when it comes to money, he knows not to mess around.

The truck pulls out of the driveway and pretty soon it's making its way down Farrington Avenue. There are streetlamps every now and then, but for the most part it's pitch black and they can't see much beyond the headlights of the truck. There's a silence between them, and they're used to it, so they don't search for words to occupy the time until they reach the old man's home. Instead, they keep a lookout through the windows and the rearview mirrors.

They are pleased when they don't see another vehicle on the road.

When they reach the old man's house, the truck slows down and they look at the stone before passing by. They drive on for about another hundred yards and then make a U-turn right there on the two-lane street. When they approach the stone again, the small one cuts the lights and puts the truck in neutral. It rolls to the edge of the road until it reaches the old man's driveway and the stone is within feet of the bed. The doors open up and the big one immediately goes for the stone. His brother rushes to the bed, pops up the hardtop and drops the tailgate. The big one struggles to get the stone off of the ground — he wraps his right arm around it until it's up against his chest, then he pushes it over so he can get his left arm under it. He squats and lifts, and when he gets it off the ground, he easily lugs it over and rolls it onto the carpet in the bed.

They work together to shut the tailgate and the hardtop. The bed has dropped a few inches, but within a matter of seconds, the truck is at 35 mph and heading east down Farrington Avenue.

'Dat was smooth,' says the big one. He's already thinking about his sister. He felt the wad of cash in his pocket as soon as he realised he could pick up the stone.

'Time to get paid,' says the small one. He's smiling so hard he has to wipe his face.

They get to the intersection at the end of Farrington Avenue and make a right down Kalae Highway. There isn't another vehicle in sight. It's a beautiful, quiet night, they think.

The small one is about to joke that he's leaving the drug scene for good. He's thinking about the business of stones. He opens his mouth, but right as he does, the engine begins to knock and the truck begins to shudder. The brothers look at each other and the big one points to the side of the two-lane highway. He curses at the fact the truck should be able to handle the weight. It shouldn't be overheating. But when they look at the temperature gauge, it's perfectly fine, the dial exactly between the H and the C.

The truck veers off the highway and onto the grassy shoulder. The big one lets the back of his head fall against the headrest. 'Yo truck,' he says, so his brother jumps out to check under the hood.

The big one sits there in disgust as he hears the hood snap open and then sees the beam of a flashlight moving over the engine. He lets out a loud sigh. He's about to open his door and get out when he feels a rumbling behind him and then the bed of the truck spring up. The beam from the flashlight shoots through the cab and he squints for a moment before he opens his door. He goes to the back of the truck. He stops. He freezes.

The small one is soon standing beside him. He shuts off the flashlight. They stand there in the dark. The only thing they can do as they face the stone — now on the ground and upright, just as it was in the old man's yard — is curse their fate. There's a whole bunch of swearing.

'No can,' says the small one. 'No way.'

'You put da latch, ah?'

'Yah.'

The big one can't shake the eerie feeling running up his back, but he doesn't want to let on that he's scared. 'Go start da truck,' he says. 'Now!' He can't think of anything else to do but heave the stone back in the bed. He squats to wrap his arm around it and push it over but the stone won't move. It's so heavy he thinks it's stuck to the ground. He wraps both arms around it and heaves with all his might, but he can't move it. He feels a warmth on his chest emanating from the stone, so he jumps back.

The truck's ignition fires on and the hood slams shut.

They are standing side by side again. The big one points to the stone. 'Not moving,' he says. 'Stuck.'

But when the small one walks over and places his hand on the stone, it tilts over and falls to the ground. 'Pick 'im up. C'mon. Stop messin' aroun'.'

The big one leans over the stone, but he still can't move it, so the small one gets down to help him. The stone doesn't budge. They pull and push. They come at the stone from different angles, but after a couple of minutes it begins to rain, and they're forced to give up.

They decide the only thing to do is cover the stone with debris from the side of the two-lane highway. Go home, get a shovel, a dolly and some straps. It's their only hope. They haven't got much time. They jump in the truck and peel off back up the highway. The small one gets on his cell phone and makes a call to the wharf. It'll take them another hour, he says, no more. The big one lowers his window so he can get some fresh air. He hears a voice calling for him from the darkness. Then birds singing, even though it's night. The stone's got in his head, he thinks, there's no one out there.

When they finally pull into the driveway, there's a small sense of relief. The big one thinks for a second that he just might call it a night, go back in the middle of the day. He doesn't feel right. He'll tell his brother to call right back and say they don't want to damage the stone. They'll go back the next day and just park the truck on the shoulder of the highway to block it. They'll wait out any passing cars. But when his brother puts the truck in park, the big one doesn't get the chance. He starts to feel dizzy, drunk. Then his brother's head tilts back and hits the headrest — eyes and mouth wide open. And suddenly, the big one is stuck to the seat, paralysed.

The doors lock. The big one's window crawls up the track until it is shut. Tiny red and yellow lights on the deck of the stereo begin to flicker on and before long, he hears the beginnings of an ethereal, unforgettable song.

He closes his eyes.

He knows now that this isn't a simple two-man job, and in the morning, he won't be surprised when he wakes in the truck to find a message saying he wasn't supposed to just make the drop. He should've waited there at the wharf. He has until 8 am to get back and pick up his payment for the stone.

THE COCONUT KING

COURTNEY SINA MEREDITH

THE COCONUT KING SENDS me a text/ he wants to meet up and give me some coconut oil/ it isn't cold pressed/ his mother made it the traditional way in the sun/ he's from a different island where the women are in charge/ their men wait on them at home like wives in the west/ Helena says it's fine to have a holiday fling/ even if it's with the blackest guy on the island/ my aunty says to keep away from him/ he's a heart breaker/ she should know/ always getting caught on rusty men like rusty nails/ smartening up in a blue floral dress/ she puts on dangly earrings and does a twirl/ pretty as a picture/ I watch her leave the house smiling/ promise not to see the black animal/ lying through my teeth.

Helena's scooter works again/ hear it turn into my aunty's drive/ look down at myself in a pink mood singlet/ blushing into red at the end/ wipe passionfruit pulp off my shorts/ stop in the mirror/ turn my neck both ways/ clean and slender/ hair smelling like honey/ skin soft like butter/ take some deep breaths/ watch the black ants march across the bench/ Helena yells out over the spitting engine of the bike/ hurry up and lock the house.

We get to the markets while it's still light/ the coconut king is sitting in a circle with his boys/ they fish and hunt together/ bark at tourists in hotels/ wearing next to nothing/ stamp and wail about the gods/ pull white women up from the audience to dance and dance/ warriors for hire/ call it round the world but it's just round the room/ round and round the same island playing the same songs every Tuesday and Thursday/ he looks up/ sees my face/ jumps to his feet/ tells the boys to shut up/ does his best impression of a gentleman/ pats down the black curls of his chest/ creeping out from under his singlet/ wades towards me/ used to living underwater/ wades through an ocean of women staring/ saying dirty things behind his back/ looks at me like I'm the only girl at the market/ gives me a kiss on the cheek and two containers of white cake/ Helena's eyes go wide/ she grabs them out of my hands/ stalks off to a table with shade/ takes out her phone to text her papa'a boyfriend/ snaps a picture of the cake/ then a picture of her bust/ gleaming behind a sunburst knot.

I walk around the food stalls with the coconut king/ watch his leather skin glistening in the heat/ beads of sweat push their way through his temples/ I let him rest his fingers on my elbow/ let him hold my hand for a second before my steak roll is ready/ we walk to the back of the markets and cuddle by the toilets/ he melts in my arms.

The church took my grandmother's stove/ she signed the house over in her will/ I go to the flat land where she used to live and feel all the hairs on the back of my neck stand up/ she was a quiet woman/ always by the window lathering coconut oil into her hair/ combing until the white teeth turned red/ pleased when her scalp was raw/ my aunty says not to think about it/ the missionaries gave her something to believe in/ we drive to a garden on the other side of the island to pick frangipani for guests arriving from America/ more old white men to line the pockets of the island/ my aunty asks why I keep smiling/ tell her the truth/ I'm still drunk from the night before/ when we get to the house there's only babies rolling around on the deck and two dogs in chains/ the mum and dad aren't home/ we fill up a plastic bag with flowers and take off.

The darkest moments of the island unfurl in daylight/ geckos cluck/ fat with spirits/ in the car we talk about moves/ I want to inhabit his body/ how to move inside the coconut king like water moves inside the land/ Helena talks me through her wardrobe/ I can borrow whatever/ I'm going home in three days anyway/ her papa'a boyfriend thinks I can do better/ someone with a brain/ we smile at each other while my aunty drives/ his blond eyelashes shine/ Helena's riding shotgun and making a long list/ a shopping list/ a beautification list/ not that the coconut king will notice/ my aunty's given up/ I'm old enough/ girls my age make up their own minds/ their own beds/ their own faces with clouds of powder.

Studying the coconut king one night drinking cheap vodka/ dark and wide like a massive shadow with paws/ after the vodka he kisses my hand and leads me down the beach far away from Helena and her papa'a boyfriend/ closer to the edge of trees and rocks/ as clouds cover the moon/ the coconut king takes off his shirt/ lays it across the wet sand/ he takes off his pants/ kneels down on his crumpled clothes with both hands reaching out to me/ come and dance he says/ the waves are playing our song.

Sheets on the line hold their breath/ show off sharp ribs/ hold hands breathe out/ everything is moving on the island/ old faces reappear/ asking the same old questions/ why did they send you away/ were you a bad girl/ is that why your tongue is a dead fish/ did you kill your own tongue/ spitting city trash/ sitting unconscious in your own skin/ far away from your people/ sitting on the surface/ is it like being covered in plastic/ they ask over and over again/ flicking their dusty tongues between English and gibberish.

Helena lies in the sun/ waits for her glass to be filled/ I pour pinot noir/ her papa'a boyfriend has turned to gold/ he sits down on the grass beside us/ rolls a joint/ they've got a cat who likes to fight/ maybe they'll get married and stay on the rock/ teach the cat to love the heat/ Helena wants to study long distance/ do it on the internet in town once a week/ they've both gotten used to seeing the dead/ things go on here/ the elders are healing people by ending their lives/ moving their souls into animals/ that explains red-eyed roosters and goats looking for privacy/ why the wild pigs cry like boys/ they say that's what happened to my grandmother/ the church swapped her for a dog/ took all of her land/ sold all of her jewels/ Helena's papaʻa boyfriend jokes about me and the coconut king/ does he seem like a normal man/ how can I not feel what he is/ sleeping with a mountain ghost.

The coconut king turns up on his motorbike/ I kiss Helena on the forehead/ wave goodbye to her papaʻa boyfriend/ think about staying away for a while/ send my aunty a text that I won't be home tonight/ she replies with a smiley face.

We curve our way around the land/ climbing high above the sea/ pull up in front of a small house/ he says it belongs to him/ inside there's no electronics only coconut shells and soft fabrics/ a single bed neatly made/ boxes of beer and posters of wrestlers on the walls/ I hitch up my long skirt/ fan my face with a car magazine beside the bed.

The coconut king sits on the floor in front of me/ rests his hands in his lap/ goes soft around the mouth/ everyone wants me to stay/ goes soft around the eyes/ tells me to cancel my flights/ it's easy he knows the number/ his brother will answer/ my aunty will get a refund/ I can stay with him on the mountain/ my tongue won't be a dead fish/ he knows where they've taken my grandmother's stove/ we'll make them pay.

He says all of these things with the back of his head bleeding handfuls and handfuls of blood/ the room fills with small red waves/ staining the heavy flowers of my long skirt.

POOR MAN'S ORANGE

KELLY ANA MOREY

BECAUSE NONE OF US wore a watch we never knew what time it was once we disappeared into the rows to pick. Especially on surly days when the cloud cover blotted out the sun. So Jolene bought a clock and wedged it in a grapefruit tree right in the middle of the orchard. Every so often we would send one of the kids to find the clock, and that's how we marked the passage of the day.

It was the end of winter and I had heard about work at the orchard by word of mouth just in time for the first harvest and juicing. There would be a second in three months' time, for the fruit that had been left to sweeten on the trees. We worked six days a week in whatever conditions August threw at us. For a few days there, after a run of weather so gentle we thought spring had arrived, we had three days of snow showers driven in by a persistent southerly that had travelled up the country from Antarctica in a short, sharp, icy fury. Our fingers and lips turned blue and on we picked. It dropped to below freezing at night in the factory as we juiced, but at least we were out of the rain. In a funny way juicing was harder. When we picked we were moving constantly, but juicing meant standing on a concrete floor for six hours, either slicing the fruit in half, or pushing the sections onto the spinning juicing cones just enough to crush the golden liquid out of them but leave the bitter pith. I would go to bed sometime after midnight, the rhythm of the factory echoing through my shattered body like a stuck record. Too tired to sleep. Too tired to sleep. Too tired to sleep.

BUT THERE WAS GOOD stuff too. I loved the way the orchard smelled. It was organic so it didn't have the acrid reek of chemicals I had encountered at the other two orchards I'd worked at on previous holidays. Here my travels amongst the trees were scented with the sweet beckon of crushed flowers and the sharpness of citric oils from the fruit and leaves, which left your skin smelling and tasting like oranges. I also liked the quiet, because home usually wasn't. Yes, I did like that, how peaceful it was, for although we worked in teams of three or four, often all you could hear apart from the wind beating against the shelter belts was the continuous dull thud of the fruit hitting the tarpaulins we set up under the trees. There were no machines, not really, just people picking bin after bin of pale golden fruit. Not real grapefruit, but Poor Man's Orange, *Citrus paradisi*. The family who owned the orchard and fruit juice company were what made it so good too. They — Aden and Jen, and their three teenage daughters, Jolene, Alice and Mimi — picked and juiced alongside us, and made sure we were all well fed. I almost instantly became friends with Alice who was seventeen like me. She had horses and during our break in the afternoon, between picking and juicing, she would take me riding and we would canter for miles along a limestone track that led up into the hills of a neighbour's farm. The wind blowing and the rocking-horse motion of the mare beneath me as she dug deep to climb the hill sections. The slow trot home on the sweating horses. It was better than sleeping or crashing out in front of the television until work started again at 6 pm, which is what the others did.

AND THEN THERE WAS Cy.

Cy was the orchard manager who lived in the cottage near the factory. Married, rather happily I suspect. With three kids under five. But never mind. I wasn't the only one. We all loved him. Alice used to say how lucky I was to be living in the sleep-out in the garden at Cy's place, and would make up these long involved stories, usually containing murder, massacre or just plain bad luck, to get rid of the wife, who was actually very nice. I always said that I was more than happy to share, but Alice said there was no fun in that. Alice and the other girls would flirt with Cy, wolf-whistling when he took his shirt off on hot days as he picked alongside us. The only time I ever really looked at him was through the viewfinder of my camera, in case he could somehow see what was true, for me anyway. Because I'd always been afraid to look. You know, truly gaze into someone's eyes without irony or humour or some other agenda that skirts around the edge of everything in order to say absolutely nothing.

DAD HAD SENT ME the camera and a heap of film, mainly black and white, a few weeks before I started at the orchard. The camera wasn't new by any means, and it had none of the technology that cameras have these days, but it had a good lens and was more than up to the job required of it. Lorna was pretty scathing about the gift.

'When I married your father, my father said "He'll never have a bob to his name", and he was right,' she said when I showed her the camera. She had a point. Dad wasn't much more than a name on my birth certificate. It was an old hurt, but I hadn't wanted to hear it that day, so I had gone and sat in the band rotunda at King's Park even though it was raining, looking at the camera on my lap, knowing Mum was wrong. I stayed there for hours. Even after it got dark. It wasn't until a man in a raincoat walking a Yorkie came and sat beside me and tried to get me to touch him that I decided to go home. Lorna wasn't there. She'd gone out with her new boyfriend, the one with the *Miami Vice* suits who filled her up with Coruba and silly ideas, which she really didn't need any help with. They came home sometime after I'd gone to bed, waking me up by putting Led Zeppelin on the record player, because Lorna liked to fuck to *Stairway to Heaven*. Still, with the music up so loud at least it blotted out some of the noise coming through the walls from the bedroom next door. I wondered how long it would be before I'd have to listen to her begging him not to hurt her. My mother was the kind of woman who men hit. I didn't like him, the new boyfriend; I didn't like the way he looked at me.

THE NEXT DAY I went to the library and stole a book on black and white photography. I still have it. It taught me mostly everything I needed to know. I took lots of photos that long month when I took the job at the orchard. It was easy enough to get Mum to sign the note I'd written about nursing a sick relative, which got me out of school a week either side of the August holidays. So I packed my bag and caught the bus north, arriving at the orchard five hours later. Sitting beside Cy in the ute as he drove through the trees, heavy with first fruit and still bright with white blossom, to his place, tucked under a jacaranda, where I was staying for the next four weeks. The sleep-out wasn't anything special, but it was warm and dry and no one came scratching at my door at night. No wonder I fell in love.

One night, when the pick was almost all over, Alice kissed me. We were tired after a long week; pushing hard to get the last block done, we'd worked longer and longer hours. It was almost 3 am and a huge full moon was hanging in a mackerel sky. Alice and I were sitting side by side outside the factory, laughing at something lame and sharing a joint. I can't even remember it happening. One moment we were talking and the next I was drowning. We kissed for a long time, and I wondered if I too tasted of oranges. 'I'll miss you,' said Alice, when we came up for air. 'Come back for the pick in November. It's much more fun and a lot warmer.'

'I will,' I replied.

'Good. I'll tell Dad,' she said briskly, as if nothing had happened. 'Right, I'm off to bed.'

'Goodnight,' I said, watching her walk away across the orchard towards the family house. She had almost disappeared when I saw a lit cigarette parabola towards the ground from under the pear tree, and a figure step out from the shadows and into the moonlight to join Alice.

THREE DAYS LATER THE trees were bare. It was time to go home. Cy didn't say much as we drove into town so I could catch the bus. He waited with me until the bus pulled in, though I told him to go. As I was about to board he grabbed my hand, pulling me towards him.

'Look at me,' he said. And I did. Clear blue eyes, sandy close-cropped curls and crooked teeth. 'Keep yourself safe,' he continued. The instruction was urgent, like I needed to listen, take it to heart. 'I will,' I mumbled, dropping my gaze, not really understanding why he had said those words, wondering if he somehow understood something about me that even I couldn't wrap my head around yet.

When I got home Lorna was out, the fridge was empty and the power had been switched off. I found the unopened bill on the kitchen table and walked into town and paid it. That night, I sat eating fish and chips at the kitchen table in the dark, waiting for Lorna to come home.

'So you're back, then,' was all she said two days later when she walked in the door. She had a black eye. 'I fell over,' she said, though I hadn't even asked.

I had made a bit over $1400 in four weeks, which was a fair bit in those days. Minus the $100 for the power, and $5 for the fish and chips, I put the balance in the bank, keeping the account book in my locker at school so Lorna couldn't find it. On the inside door of my locker I kept a calendar and crossed off the days until November. I did my last exam and didn't hang around for prizegiving. Or to provide Lorna with too many details beyond a phone number and a general statement of intent.

ADEN WAS WAITING FOR me at the bus station. Not Alice or Cy, as I had spent three months imagining. Still, it was good to see him, and I was so absorbed in the absoluteness of my own anticipation, I barely noticed how quiet he was as we climbed into the truck. He'd never been much of a talker though anyway.

'How's Alice?' I asked.

'You'll see for yourself soon enough,' Aden replied dryly, as we drove over the railway crossing and headed out of town.

Alice was pregnant, and contentedly incubating her stolen baby. And Cy was gone. There wasn't much more than that to be said about the matter, so we pulled out the tarpaulins and ladders and began to pick the second half of the orchard. But something had changed. Although I had thought Alice was the centre of my world, she was so far removed from me now, sitting sleepily under the trees, clipping the stems and buttons off the fruit and piling it into bins, that I had begun to think I had imagined the kiss. And although Alice couldn't ride, she let me take her mare out, but it wasn't the same without her. Everything had changed, and time passed slowly. The clock seized after it was left out in the rain one night and I stopped following the transition of the sun across the sky. Time became about how much of the orchard was still emblazoned with the brightness of fruit, and how long it would take to strip that colour completely out of it. I stopped talking almost completely, and barely listened at all to the somnolent hum of tranquil conversation that meandered around, fading in and out of earshot. All anyone was talking about was the solar eclipse anyway.

We were on the homeward stretch when it happened. It was a partial, but rare enough, according to Aden, who said we wouldn't see another like this for, I don't know, something like 100 years, though it might be less. Aden had got hold of some welder's glass, and as the moon started to drift slowly across the sun, taking a bite out of it, we all lined up, passing the glass up and down the line so we could hold it across our eyes and stare into the sun. It didn't get all that dark, even when the moon was blotting out a fairly big chunk of the sun; it was like evening but without the boundary of night and day. The contrast had vanished, and the shadows darkened to a deep violet beneath the trees. But it wasn't eerie because the birds were still singing and there was a gentle northerly rustling the tops of the trees. And there was the smell of wood smoke all around from the smouldering gum stumps that Aden had fired earlier in the week.

I HAD ENOUGH MONEY when I left the orchard for a second time to set myself up in a shared flat in the city, and let Lorna know where I was. Eventually some mail turned up, forwarded by her, and I discovered I'd gotten into art school. I also got a part-time job in a black-and-white photo lab, behind the scenes in the darkrooms. The money was rubbish, but it was a good job. I was too ordinary to be a model, and too shy to take my clothes off, so mostly I was left alone to spend hours printing and washing down prints. It reminded me of juicing at the orchard. The slosh of hands in liquids and the steady trickle of water down the sink. The chemicals made the skin peel from my hands and my lovers complained that the smell and taste of them had permeated my skin.

I developed the films from the orchard and some of the photographs — the ones taken outside — were even quite good. The negatives have since disappeared and any prints I made have vanished into the ether of lost photographs. All except one. A black and white of Cy standing between the fruit-laden trees holding his three-year-old son Marco upside down by his legs and the two of them laughing and laughing. I keep it tucked inside the stolen library book; a reminder of winter fruit and something I cannot name.

I SAW ALICE ONE day, about two years later, on Victoria Street with her little girl. They were waiting for a bus. She lived in Swanson now, with her boyfriend. The orchard was, she said, exactly the same, but the horses were sold and gone. She looked exactly the same too. Except for the baby.

'What's her name?' I asked.

'Eclipse,' Alice replied, jiggling the toddler, who looked exactly like her father, on her hip.

'Just like the racehorse,' I said.

Alice laughed. 'Do you remember . . .?'

'Of course I do,' I replied. 'I remember all of it.' And I did too.

I waited until their bus arrived. 'Hey, don't be a stranger, Ruby,' she said, handing me Eclipse and collapsing the pushchair. 'Give us a bell, come out and meet Pete. We've got a cracking little place up in the bush. Not flash, but you know, nice.'

'I will,' I said, holding on to Eclipse for dear life, terrified that she would begin squirming and I'd drop her. Though all she did was hang in my arms and gurgle softly and look at her feet.

'That's it,' Alice said, straightening up and pushing her hair off her face. 'Look at you, you're a natural,' she said, taking Eclipse from me.

'Oh hurry up, love,' complained the bus driver. 'I haven't got all day.'

'Hold your horses,' Alice said cheerfully, climbing on board. I watched as she settled in a seat in the middle of the bus. 'Ring me,' she mouthed. And you know I always meant to. But nothing is ever exactly the same.

EXTRACT FROM *FREELOVE*

SIA FIGIEL

ENGLISH CLASS FORM 6 VOCABULARY LIST

Vehemently, Divulge, Brim, **Trimester**, **Forbidden**, Intently, **Hymen blood**, Retaliation, Scrutinize, **Conceal**, Monotony, Emphatic, Alacrity, Divergence, Contradiction, Exaltation, **Affair**, Conspiracy, Uncontaminated, Prejudices, Discriminate, Illuminate. Pulsate, **Penile erection**, Aesthetics, **Relationship**, Aeronautics, Retribution, Offender, **Apology**, Perpendicular, Contemplate, **Incestuous**, Splendiferous, Resolve, Critique, Nostalgia, **Subtle**, Lingers, Philosophical, Infinities, Opulent, Refulgent, Philosophical, Lustrous, Intimate, Opulent, Ecosystem, Suppressed, **Sinful**, Innuendo, Transparent, Symbiosis, Photosynthesis, Resemblance, **Reproduction**, Osmosis, Scintillating, Amaranthine, Nonchalantly, Cannibalistic, Resourceful, Alluring, Reasoning, Indulgent, Cacophony, Paradoxical, Irony, Instinct, Governed, Opulent, Wicked, Expanse, Beaut, Empiricism, **Illicit**, Humility, **Deflowering**, Bacteria, Spirituality, Omnipresence, Premonition, Stupendous, Prediction, **Semen**, **Sperm**, Traumatic, Recede, Gratification, Pleasure, Multitudinous, Precision, Manipulate, Determinant, Vehemently, Indulgence, Syllogism, Pavlovian, Inter-galactic, Nocturnal, Divulge, Interconnectedness, Rhetoric, Perpendicular, Theory of Relativity, Manifestation. Ceremonial.

SAMOAN–ENGLISH VOCABULARY LIST

Inosia. Despised. **Ino.** Excrements. **Sia**. pron. This. **Sia**. One passive termination, as motusia or inosia. **Alofatunoa/Alofafua**. To love unconditionally, to love freely.

Alofa. *s.* **1.** Love, compassion. *'O lona alofa.* **2.** A present, a gift. **Alofa.** *v.* **1.** To love, to be compassionate. **2.** To salute; as *Ta alofa*, contracted to *Talofa*, the ordinary salutation; *pl.* Alolofa; *pass.* Alofaina, alofagia; *recip.* Fealofani.

Fua. *Malay*, Buah, s. **1.** Fruit, flower. *I fua mai le nau ina utupupu ia.* *'O lona fua.* **2.** Seed. **3.** An egg. *Le fua lupe e tau tasi.* **4.** Spawn of fish. **5.** A good-looking child of a chief. *E le tauilo fua o ali'i.* **6.** A fleet of canoes. 7. A measure. Fua, a particle suffixed to the units, with *ga* as a connecting particle, in counting breadfruit, shellfish, & c., *e laufua, e tolugafua*; it is prefixed in counting tens, *e fualua*.

Fua. *adv.* **1.** Without cause. *Lau sala e fa'apua fua.* **2.** Without success. **3.** Uselessly, to no purpose. **Fua.** *v.* **1.** To produce fruit. **2.** To proceed from, to originate. *Fua mai lava.*

Fua. *s.* Jealousy; only of the sexes; *'O lona fua.* **Fua.** *v.* to be jealous. *pass.* Fuatia. **Fua.** *a.* Jealous. *'O le fafine fua.* **Afatasi.** *n.v.* Derived from the words afa and tasi. **Afa.** *v.* To be united in action; from afa, a mesh stick. *'Ua afa fa'atasi.* They all use one mesh-stick, and the meshes are equal.

'Afa. *s.i.* Sinnet, the cord plaited, from the fiber of the coconut, largely used instead of nails for house and boat building. *O la'u 'afa.* **2.** The name of a fish. **3.** An anchor. Syn. and more common term, taula. **Tasi.** a.i. **1.** One. **2.** Another; *O le tasi teine, po'o le tasi tamaloa.* The one girl or the one man.

Tasi. *v.* To be unprecedented, to be unique. *E tasi ae afe.* One in a thousand. **Tasi.** *adv.* Very. *E lelei tasi lava.* It is very good. **Afatasi.** *v. n.* **1.** To connect or unite in one action. **2.** To strengthen as one. **3.** n. One that is unique; the unprecedented one. *O tama'ita'i afatasi.* Plural. Unique women; unprecedented women. Women who come together to strengthen or to unite as one. Women who are anchored by one action or event.

AOGA MAUALUGA NU'UOLEMANUSA
NU'UOLEMANUSA HIGH SCHOOL
Ripoti Fa'ai'u o le Tausaga End of Year School Report
Itumalo Faleolela / Faleolela School District Malo Tuto'atasi o Samoa i Sisifo / The Independent State of Western Samoa **E fa'avae i le Atua Samoa / Samoa is founded on God** Tesema 20, 1985 / 20 December 1985

IGOA / NAME: **INOSIA ALOFAFUA AFATASI** Vasega: 6 / Class: Form 6. Mata'upu: Vasega o le Fa'asaenisi / Subject: Science Amio: Maoa'e le Lelei. / Conduct: Excellent. Tulaga i le Vasega: Sili. Place in Class: 1st Place. Togi aofa'i: 100% / Total Points: 100%

Fa'amatalaga a le Faiaoga / Teacher's Comments:
Inosia is one of those rare gems of a student that a teacher is blessed with once in a lifetime. Intuitive and mature beyond her years, Sia is able to grasp the fundamental concepts of Science and is able to excite and share her knowledge, particularly with those fellow students who struggle with them.

She is not afraid to ask questions and I have had the privilege of witnessing her academic growth through this last year of high school. Diligent and hard working, I have great faith that whatever she decides to study and put her mind to, she will do so successfully.

It has been an honour to have been her teacher, although at times, she has taught me more than she'll ever know.

O ou mama na, Sia. / Go with my blessings, Sia. Mr Ioane Viliamu. Faiaoga/Teacher

TOP 20 BEST SONGS OF 1985 ON THE 2AP

1. *Like a Virgin* by MADONNA.
2. *E Pa'ia o le Alo o le Atua* by TAMA O LE TIAMA'A.
3. *Sosefina* by TAMA O LE TIAMA'A.
4. *Pule Aoao le Atua* by TAMA O LE TIAMA'A.
5. *Mo'omo'oga* by PUNIALAVA'A.
6. *I Want to Know What Love Is* by FOREIGNER.
7. *I Feel for You* by CHAKA KHAN.
8. *Take On Me* by A-HA.
9. *Malu A'e le Afiafi* by FETU LIMA.
10. *Everytime You Go Away* by PAUL YOUNG.
11. *Careless Whisper* by WHAM.
12. *Sa Ou Nofo ma Va'ava'ai i Fetu o le Lagi* by PENINA O TI'AFAU.
13. *Taualaga a Solomona* by PENINA O TI'AFAU.
14. *Cherish the Love* by KOOL & THE GANG.
15. *The Power of Love* by HUEY LEWIS AND THE NEWS.
16. *Sina Ea, Sau Se'i Fai Mai* by TAMA O LE TIAMA'A.
17. *Pele Moana* by THE GOLDEN ALI'I'S.
18. *Beyond the Reef* by THE YANDALL SISTERS.
19. *Tupe Siliva* by 'ELEVISI' 'ELVIS OF SAMOA' LAUOLEFISO TO'OMALATAI.
20. *Saving All My Love for You* by WHITNEY HOUSTON.

I LISTENED INTENTLY TO Mr Viliamu as the breeze caressed both our faces.

He was a walking encyclopedia who knew just about everything there was to know, and yet he always made whatever knowledge he was passing on seem like it was a gift from God. That he was merely the medium with whom such a gift was exchanged for those of us who needed to receive it.

Momentarily, I felt lucky and special that he stopped to pick me up. To share this knowledge with my ever curious and hungry mind that seemed to absorb everything he said.

A penny for your thoughts, girl, said Mr Viliamu, drawing me back into the conversation.

I didn't know what he meant.

English, I'm afraid to say, was not my best subject in school, which meant I paid more attention to it than any of the other classes I loved, like Science, Mathematics, Samoan, Social Studies and Health. I kept vocabulary notebooks and studied them and studied them and studied them until I knew meanings of words, but found that there were not too many people in Gu'usa who spoke it. Perhaps I secretly loved English. Perhaps I didn't. Perhaps I did and I didn't. That's how I felt about English. It was a moody language. At times void of meaning. Empty. Perhaps this feeling of the emptiness of English comes from the blatant fact that I really had no relation to it just as much as it had no relation to me. It wasn't like my geneaology could be traced through it. Or that the veins in my blood were to be found in its alphabet, the way it is found on my mother's tattooed thighs. Besides, I did not want to appear fiapoko, like I knew everything, especially before my classmates who struggled with it, as it was a language I too found hard to swallow, that got stuck always in the middle of my throat, especially when I pronounced words like beach, peach, pig, big, and porridge.

And before I could respond, Mr Viliamu asked me again.

Why are you so quiet? What are you thinking about? I'd like to know.

Does he really want to know what I'm thinking about or is he just being polite? Besides, why would the thoughts of a 17½-year-old girl be of interest to an old man? He's at least 10, 12 years older than me! Not to mention the fact that he's a walking encyclopedia who just happens to be our pastor's oldest son, which technically makes him my brother!

Nothing, Mr Viliamu, I said, not wanting to disappoint him with my lack of enthusiasm.

I'm not thinking about anything. Besides, it's what you're thinking of that I'd like to know. Boldly smiling at him, supposing I had said something that he might find intelligent and would be proud of because it originated from him.

But instead he responded quite differently, as if he hadn't heard what I had said, which disappointed me, and I showed my disappointment by avoiding eye contact with him and stared instead into the ocean, watching her give birth to waves, listening to them splash onto the lava rocks below the cliffs of Si'unu'u, which meant we were halfway to Apia.

Mr Viliamu's voice echoed suddenly from a far away place, only he was no less than six inches away from me.

You might be embarrassed if I tell you what I'm thinking, he said, rubbing his stomach with one hand as if he hadn't eaten breakfast as he steered the pick-up truck with his other hand.

What is he saying? Embarrassed? Why would I be embarrassed? Is he going to correct my English? Should I have said a cluster or a crowd instead of a school of birds? They're birds all the same, aren't they? But then Mr Viliamu said something else. Something he spoke through the language of his body movements. He started scratching his knee and my eyes followed his hand as it moved from his knee to his inner thigh so that his shorts shrunk upwards and I caught a glimpse of his pubic hair.

Immediately, my eyes darted out the window.

Not only was I embarrassed, frankly, I became offended, not to mention deeply ashamed.

A nervousness entered my body and I thought for a moment that I was going to cry. After all, I had never seen that part of a grown man's anatomy, and I suddenly found myself thinking about all the males in my family: my uncle Afatasi Fa'avevesi, who was my mother's brother and our 'aiga's main matai, lived with his wife Stella behind the fale where my mother Alofafua and her sister Aima'a, Gu'usa's traditional healer, and my grandmother Taeao (short for Taeao'oleaigalulusa) and Ala (short for Alailepuleoletautua), my grand-aunt who was deaf, lived with all the girls of our family and boys under 13, which included my 12-year-old brothers Aukilani (Au) and Ueligitone (Ue), identical twins who loved to play identity tricks on people. The older boys, which included our Uncle Fa'avevesi's sons Chris and Emau, as well as our adopted brothers and other taule'ale'a or untitled male relatives from either Savai'i, Manono or Apolima, who were all technically considered my brothers, lived in a house behind Uncle Fa'avevesi's house, closer to where the umukuka or kitchen was located.

With all these males around, you'd think I would have seen a full grown man's penis by now. And yet, the taboos that governed the movements of our brothers in relation to us, their sisters, known as the feagaiga, or the brother/sister covenant, were so strictly observed and highly scrutinised that it meant I'd only witnessed a penis once.

Well, twice actually. But they belonged to my twin brothers Ue and Au, who had been circumcised along with their friends, and were waddling out of the ocean after one of them was stung by a jellyfish.

It was the funniest sight.

Q and Cha and I teased them so badly that their only form of retaliation was in empty threats that further paralysed them by the state of affairs they were caught in.

Imagine the fastest boys of Gu'usa reduced to waddling turtles, calling out that they're going to 'get us' once their penises were healed. Because that's going to ever happen, ha! It was utterly hilarious and became a family and village joke recounted over and over by the women at suipi whenever they needed light entertainment to break the monotony of someone's winning streak.

I clung to the image of my brothers and their friends for safety as I was beginning to feel uneasy with Mr Viliamu.

I didn't know how I was to ever look into his eyes again with the same confidence he had originally instilled in me at school, now that I had seen something so intimate as his pubic hair.

Perhaps it was an accident, I told myself. He didn't mean to expose himself to me deliberately. But then again, wasn't he the very same person who told our class that there were no accidents or coincidences? That every action we make creates a ripple in the universe, which means that all actions are interconnected?

How then could I possibly unsee what I had just seen? Instantaneously, I told myself that this was a bad idea. I never should have accepted Mr Viliamu's offer in the first place. I would have wholeheartedly given up the six tala my mother had given me for busfare to sit next to an old man who hadn't showered in a week in a crowded bus with babies crying and old women smoking Samoan tobacco, and Cyndi Lauper's *Time after Time* playing over and over and over, not to see what I had just seen.

But it was too late, I suppose.

As my Aunty Aima'a always said, *Once a cup of water is spilled, it can never be retrieved.*

Suddenly Mr Viliamu said, You're quiet again. I can tell you're thinking about something because your forehead looks wrinkled.

Ha, I laughed, nervously, touching my forehead.

Really? You can do that? Know from my forehead what I'm thinking about? I asked rhetorically this time, not really expecting him to answer.

I looked out the window so that I could catch a glimpse of my forehead in the mirror to see what Mr Viliamu meant. But Mr Viliamu told me that there was a mirror right above me and reached across me to fold it down. His arm brushed lightly against my left breast and a tingling sensation surged through my body, from my head to my toes, which had never happened to me before.

Oopsy, said Mr Viliamu. He looked at me and smiled.

I'm sorry, love, as he returned his arm to his stomach, caressing it, moving it towards his inner thigh, circling his pubic hair, this time, looking directly into my eyes.

Perplexed, I tried to avoid his gaze and the piercing effect it had not only on my own eyes but on my entire body.

What is happening? I asked myself, as I closed my eyes and felt the sensation of Mr Viliamu's arm against my breast, not to mention his penis, which had increased immensely in size, bulging under his shorts, which I was trying desperately to avoid seeing.

Is this osmosis? Is this symbiosis? Is this reproduction? Is this metamorphosis? What is this? I could not find a single process in Science to name what was happening to my body and how it was responding to Mr Viliamu's.

Nor could I comprehend how Mr Viliamu's body was reacting to my own body.

What process was this? Really? Could I call it a chain reaction? Was it a voluntary or an involuntary muscular response? But to what, exactly?

I did not know. Suddenly everything became a great big blur and for a moment I was swimming in a grey ocean, an ocean where there were no waves. No birds. And no blue skies above it.

Despite the haziness I found myself in, one thing remained certain. That the language Mr Viliamu was speaking with his eyes and his hands was an ancient sacred language. A language that had undoubtedly been spoken by our ancestors before us and was older perhaps than the waves and the birds themselves, older even than the big blue sky.

It was a language Mr Viliamu appeared to know intimately and spoke with the utmost fluency. A language I had never spoken before, and yet, I found myself drawn to it mysteriously if not instinctively as if I had a natural propensity towards understanding its nuances and hidden meanings.

I want you to do something for me, said Mr Viliamu. Startled that he finally spoke, I eagerly responded. What is it, Mr—? Mr Viliamu looked at me again. This time, his gaze pierced something in me that was similar to the brush of his arm against my breast. Only this time, I found myself looking boldly back at him as he tried to steer the red pick-up truck while holding my gaze simultaneously.

I want you to stop calling me Mr Viliamu. *Why would you want me to do that?* I asked myself. But instead, I remained quiet. Then he spoke again. This time, his voice caused the same sensation his arm had caused earlier when it brushed against my breast and his piercing eyes when they looked directly into mine. Only this time, his voice was like a fisaga, a gentle wind that caressed me and caused me to shiver.

I want you to call me by my name, Sia, he said.

But I *am* calling you by your name, Mr Viliamu, I found myself whispering back at him.

No, Sia, he said, looking out the window as we sighted the town clock, the Burns Philp supermarket and the Nelson Public Library.

I want you to call me Ioage, he said.

Those were the last words he spoke before we went our separate ways, while the sun's rays danced on the glass of the NPF building windows, its reflection blinding me as I stepped into the street and made my way through the busy crowd, anxiously looking for a store that sold giant white threads, while thinking about seagulls and waves and other unspeakable things that made me grin, inwardly.

Cerisse Palalagi, HOLLA BAQ series
Above: *Eeh Ma Trikk!, VAGAHAU, SO SAVAGE LMAO!*, 2009
Centre: *SAARP G, JAAACK!!, GOT JKZ, SOWI BOUT U*, 2010
Below: *Txt u Dox, Lol Up To?, Shammit!, Wats Gud?, Nah yooh*, 2010

KING OF BONES AND HAZY HOMES

From Average Kids and Bigots

ANYA NGAWHARE

I DROP ONTO THE wooden bench beside my bag, head finding the brick wall behind me. My heavy arms hang by my sides, lifeless.

The changing rooms always have this nasty smell to them after a game, a weird mix of dirt and Deep Heat, strapping tape and sweaty unwashed balls. It's nasty as hell, but also really comforting. It's one of the few scents that can stop my mind racing.

It was a fuckin' hard game. Some kid twice my size rucked the top of my back, and my left hip is aching so bad I just know it's going to be purple in the morning.

'That forward nailed you, man,' Bryan laughs, voice raised to be heard over the angry complaints and hurt rants going on around us. He tugs his black-and-burgundy rugby jersey up over his head. 'I thought you were dead for a minute there.'

'*I* thought I was dead for a minute there.' I make my left hand move, force its fingers though the damp fringe in front of my eyes. Every muscle tightens when I shift on the spot. 'My body's on fire,' I huff.

He pulls his black shorts off with a weird snort, lips caught somewhere between amusement and sympathy. They pick their side when I give him the finger.

Bryan's a big guy, six foot four and nothing but tanned muscle. And he's not ugly, either. He's some sort of Polynesian, but he doesn't have a flat nose or overly big lips, and his eyes are a grey-blue, not brown like you'd expect.

I can see why all the underdressed stick figures are constantly batting their fake lashes in his direction.

I haven't quite figured out why he never seems to notice.

'Does that mean you're not going to Dean's party tonight?' he asks, hands on his hips. 'Assuming he's still up for it.'

'Shit no,' I exclaim. Something bursts inside me. It straightens my back, makes my head light. Weightless. 'The party will be even bigger now that we're losers. They'll go fuckin' nuts. They're definitely going to burn something tonight.' I lean forward, right knee bobbing on its own. 'I'm definitely going. You?'

He scratches the side of his nose. 'I have to babysit till eight, but I guess I could hang out after.'

'You haven't suddenly started drinking, have you?'

He shakes his head slowly. I suck my lips inwards when I feel them curl.

Bryan sighs. 'Fine then,' he says flatly. He hunches over to open his bag. 'I'll get your drunk ass home.'

I jump to my feet. 'Thanks, man.'

He waves me off. 'Yeah, yeah.'

I KNOW DAD'S IN the kitchen before I step through the lounge archway. The familiar *thunk-thunk-thunk* of him cutting vegetables on the marble bench is unmistakable. I pass the long beige sofa on my way to the L-shaped counter my father is stood at slicing mushrooms.

'Hey, Jake,' he says when he finally notices me, his deep voice low as always. He pushes the mushroom away, swapping it for a red onion. 'Dinner should be ready soon. Moira from work gave me a recipe for this eggplant, spinach lasagne thing she makes. It's really nice. I think you'll like it.'

'I'm on my way out, actually,' I tell him, eyes wandering to the splash of colour where his sleeves have been rolled up. Sky blue and turquoise, a hint of crimson. A tail I know belongs to a fierce-looking dragon.

'Oh.' His knife hesitates, stops mid-slice. 'Just me, then.'

I look away swiftly, a slight lump in my throat. I try to clear it. 'Where's Mum and Ari?'

'Ari's spending the night at Allie's.' His pointed nose wrinkles when he adds, 'And your mother went out with Valerie.'

I roll my eyes and put my palms on the countertop. The stone is freezing despite the heat from the large open fireplace just a few metres away. 'She digging for gold again?'

He chuckles, the sound so quiet I'm not sure I actually heard it at all. 'Moneybags put a ring on a nineteen-year-old instead of her,' he tells me, turning to check the cheesy mix in the oven.

'Poor Valerie,' I drawl. I pull a stool out, sit. Lean forward so my forearms can rest on the bench. 'On the bright side, her new tits will make it a little easier this time round. The guys will actually be able to see where she is.'

Dad draws an invisible arc with his hands. 'Husband hunt five.' He drops his voice an octave. 'Platinum card required.'

My laughter spills out and fills the open room we're in. Dad joins in, his laughter lifting the mood more than mine. He laughs so rarely that it tickles my insides.

When we settle ourselves, Dad clears his throat and says, 'You better get going.'

I scratch my head. 'Uh, I um, I might just stay for dinner. No one will notice I'm missing.'

Dad doesn't say anything, just bobs his head and continues

making the salad. I know he's pleased though. I can see it in the curl at the corners of his mouth.

'I CAN'T BELIEVE YOU fuckers,' Noah complains from the wooden deck chair beside mine. 'I looked like a fuckin' loner. You turn up an hour late and Bryan doesn't show at all.'

'He'll be here soon,' I say absently, tapping the glass bottle I'm holding.

'You fucking homos,' he rambles. 'Cunts.'

The garden we're in is really, really nice. Pretty, even. Stone planters line the edge of the patio we're on, and I can make out the spiky stems of roses from where I'm sitting. Quirky little solar lights are scattered among the flowers, dragonflies and gnomes and even a cat with big glowing eyes, and fairy lights have been coiled around the trunks and branches of the trees, the sail-shade posts too.

'I was here, man.'

The voice is nasal and a fraction higher than any of the ones I'm used to hearing, and I turn my head to see Josh slouched on the other side of Noah. He's an average, unmemorable kiss-ass who's only on the first XV because his dad played for Aussie like a million years ago.

I look away again, mouth clamped shut. If I was going to suck up to someone, it wouldn't be Noah Hastings.

'Seriously, asshole, you coulda text or something,' Noah spits before Josh can add anything else. 'I couldn't even hang with Gio because he brought the fag with him. Fuck knows why.'

I stare at the mouth of my bottle. 'They're twins.'

'And what?'

I skull half my drink.

'I wouldn't be caught dead hanging out with a faggot, brother or not. And if he was my brother I'd fuckin' smash him until he got the message.'

Matilda appears all of a sudden, her bare skeletal shoulders turned inwards. Her lap-dogs follow her up the slightly curved yard with a few of the boys. They've got so much skin exposed that I shiver.

'I thought him being gay was just a rumour,' Josh says.

When they come to a stop I notice the phone in Matilda's hand, but she soon looks over at me with a smile.

'Someone must have seen something or there wouldn't be rumours,' Noah returns swiftly.

I get to my feet. Noah looks straight at me, blue-green eyes thinning with each quick breath he takes. Josh pokes at one of his ten thousand moles like it's way more interesting than anything I'm doing.

'I have to piss.'

I walk away before Noah has a chance to bitch about me leaving him on his own again.

I wasn't wrong when I told Bryan that tonight was going to be crazy. The backyard is pretty much deserted, but in the house you can't breathe without bumping into someone else. It's as if the entire school showed up to mourn our loss.

When I don't find a free toilet, I find a nice tree out of sight.

My heart jerks my body forward when something touches my right shoulder in the darkness, and I spin around swiftly, dick still in hand. A hooded figure stands a metre or so away from me. They tilt their head a fraction and the little rays of moonlight spilling through the tree's top hits their face.

I recognise the straight-shouldered silhouette instantly.

I tuck myself away with huff. 'You scared the fuck out of me, Matty.'

The hood falls away and the familiar face becomes clear. Dark hair and round eyes, symmetrical lines. Matty's lips curl and I'm immediately reminded of Giovanni and the look he gave me when I arrived earlier.

'Not sorry.' He pulls a small baggie from his back pocket. 'Smoke?'

'Like you have to ask.'

He pulls the bag away from me, keeping it out of reach. 'It'll cost you.'

I snort. 'Doesn't it always.'

He doesn't say anything else, just walks towards the front of the house.

I follow after him.

We've just reached the bottom of the driveway when Bryan comes into view. He moves towards us so silently that he'd go unnoticed if he weren't so huge. He hesitates when he spots Matty by my side, inspects him with a heavy frown.

Matty pulls a pack of cigarettes out and slips one between his lips. He lights up, casts a glance my way.

'Thought you'd be drunk by now,' Bryan says. He crosses his arms over his broad chest, makes himself look even bigger.

'Oh, I'm just . . .' I nod towards Matty. 'He's got something for me.'

Bryan's eyes flick between us. 'Do you still need a ride home?'

Matty lifts a shoulder when I look his way, smoke billowing out of his mouth.

'He can take me,' I tell Bryan, 'but thanks, man.'

Bryan's eyes thin like he wants to say something, but he doesn't. He just bobs his head and makes his way towards the overcrowded house.

Matty clucks his tongue. 'What was that about?' he asks when he has my full attention. He nods in Bryan's direction. 'He wondering why you're with the school fag?'

I shove him playfully. 'He's probably trying to figure out why the richest kid in a school full of rich kids is dealing drugs.'

He shrugs, takes another drag. 'It's good business.' He laughs to himself. 'Daddy would be proud if he wasn't such a cunt.'

He exhales heavily, tosses half a cigarette on the ground by his feet. He doesn't bother to stomp it out.

'You're so wasteful.'

He gets his keys out with a cocky smirk. 'I can afford it.'

THE PARK HAS AN eeriness about it that sends a prickly shiver down my spine. The swings are completely still, the bark beneath them undisturbed. I take in the rustling trees that line the park edge with a laboured breath. My heart skips a beat when I imagine rotting corpses stumbling out of the untamed bush that lies just beyond them. Snarling zombies.

I need to stop letting Ari pick the movies we watch.

Matty moves for the playground like the dark, secluded area isn't the slightest bit creepy. He doesn't bother to follow the curved path, just stomps across the moist grass.

I slip my cold hands into my jean pockets and follow his lead.

Matty drops down on a wooden bench and starts rolling a joint. I sit beside him, watch his nimble fingers work. People always say that dealers shouldn't get high on their own supply, but he clearly doesn't follow that rule. He smokes so much weed that he can probably roll and light up with his eyes clamped shut, not a single crumb wasted.

Matty takes the first hit and I inch towards him, throat tight. He exhales in my direction and I breathe the musky smoke in eagerly. He takes another drag, longer than the last. I snap my fingers impatiently.

He shakes his head at me, holds the smoke out of reach. 'You get what you want when I do.'

He keeps his eyes on mine when he sucks on the smoke again. The burning tip glows and I lick my lips slowly. He leans forward, blows smoke into my face. I snatch at his hoodie, fingers twisting tightly in the fabric at his neck. I pull him towards me.

'Shithead,' I say, face inches from his.

'Faggot,' he returns drily.

I breathe in deeply, breathe out.

I close the slight gap between us, press my lips to his.

He tastes like sweet grass and sharp nicotine, bitter and awful. My fingers lose their grip and I lean into him. My mouth pulls at his desperately like I can lick away the residue of his habits, like I can take away the filth. I feel his fingertips on the nape of my neck, the touch so slight you could miss it.

He pulls away from me with a sharp breath, finally hands the joint over.

I watch him silently, smoke pinched between my fingertips. His eyes are on the sky above us, consumed by the stars. He stares like they know all of life's secrets, like if he's patient enough a beautiful weed angel is going to float down and whisper everything he's ever wanted to know.

'Can I stay tonight?' he asks, voice low enough to be a whisper.

I don't say anything, just kiss his cheek and take a drag.

MATTY HAS A JOURNAL that he takes pretty much everywhere, but he doesn't write his thoughts like most people do, he draws them. He lets me look at it whenever I please, but he rarely shows anyone else. And it stirs feelings in me that I can't really explain. It does something to my nervous system that makes me want to keep turning pages and look away at the same time.

The two of us have been in the same art class since year 9, and somehow, despite the fact we've been taught by the exact same people, our styles are polar opposites. I enjoy drawing animals in their natural environments. People, too. I draw life. Matty though, well, he's drawn to death. His journal is a dark place, full of lost and tortured souls.

I asked him about it once, when we were stoned and on the verge of sleep. I asked him why he was drawn to bones and suffering.

He just grunted at me and said, 'They'll eat my brain if I don't get them out.'

I laughed and went to sleep.

I STEP CAREFULLY, WADE through the sea of dirty washing and empty Red Bull cans that lead to Matty's black, perfectly made bed. I step up onto it and sit cross-legged in the centre, eyes on the poster-clad walls. Heavily tattooed men cover every inch of available space; some have expensive custom guitars, others have their mouths stretched wide next to microphones. Most are just huddled together with stern expressions on their perfect faces; their lined eyes narrowed, lips pressed into tight lines.

Matty moves towards the bed carelessly. His feet manage to miss every discarded item like he's following an invisible path, and he flops down on the bed beside me, half hanging off the right edge.

I stare down at him. 'Aren't you graceful.'

'Fuck off,' he grumbles. His lean arms curl around a plump pillow.

I uncross my legs to tangle an ankle with one of his. He doesn't seem to mind. In fact, if I stay quiet enough he's bound to fall asleep, surprising the famous men that surround us.

I'd let him if I weren't worried about his brothers catching us together. Or worse, his father. Gio introduced me to their grey-haired dad once, and that was more than enough for me. Something about the way he stared gave me the creeps. He's a scary fucker.

'Stay awake.' I tap Matty's lower back gently. 'Your family will be back soon.'

He groans into his pillow, punches it like it will make me shut up. 'Fuck off,' he says again.

I pull my hand back. 'Fine.'

Matty catches my wrist before I get far at all. He keeps me beside him. His fingers tighten their grip, their familiar calloused tips waking my insides, and when he turns his head, his amber eyes widen in a way only I can understand.

'Fine,' I repeat, defeated.

He tugs on my wrist and I go easily. I always do. I lie flat on my back so he can drape himself over me. I struggle to ignore the warm tickle of his slow, even breath on my neck, the way he nuzzles into me.

I look up, focus on the ceiling instead.

It looks just like the rest of the walls, every bit of white covered like he doesn't want anyone to see that beneath all the glossy muscles his room is just as plain as everyone else's. They surround him like a shield, famous faces he'll probably never meet. They stare from every angle, watch us like they're gods or something.

Matty shifts and I look away, bury my nose in his dark hair instead. I breathe in deeply. It stinks of styling wax and cigarettes, but somewhere beneath that I can just make out the sharp scent of tea tree.

My left hand rests on the arm he has stretched across my stomach. 'When did you swap my cheetah for some scrawny ginge dude?'

'Yesterday,' he mumbles, distant and dreary. 'I needed it.' He clears his throat. 'The empty spot was weirding me out.'

My fingers creep towards his elbow, rub tiny circles on the textured skin. 'What for?'

He exhales loudly and pulls away from me, blindly reaches for something on the floor beside him. He rustles around for a minute before he finally sits up and looks for what he wants.

I flinch when a hardcover book hits my gut. Matty curls into my side again as I pick the familiar thing up.

'I'm getting inked,' he tells me before I have a chance to open his journal.

'What?' I blurt out.

He nods against me with an absentminded hum.

I poke his cheek and he opens his eyes. He doesn't look all that thrilled, but I'm not either.

'Matteo,' I say firmly, demanding almost. 'What the fuck?'

'I hate it when you call me that,' he complains. He props himself up on his left elbow. He holds my gaze for a moment, dead silent. 'I thought you'd be happy.'

'Why?'

He doesn't say anything, just takes his journal and sits up

completely. I follow his lead. Our shoulders brush when I'm upright, but there's no pleased hum in my chest, no warm tickle. I watch him flip pages quickly, searching for the source of my assumed happiness, I guess.

He finally stops. 'Here.'

I hold my breath, unable to look away from the picture he's showing me.

'You cut it up,' I say at length, unsure if I'm horrified or awed by what he's done to the drawing I gave him. 'You—'

'Fuck no,' he says quickly. 'No, it's — I copied it first. I cut up the copy.'

Somehow I don't notice just how hard my heart is pounding until I hear his reassuring words. King cheetahs are his favourite animal in the world; he adores them more than the crash of cymbals and wail of guitars. I spent days getting that piece perfect for him. It's important to me, fucking special.

The portrait I drew a good year ago now has been cut straight down the middle. The left half is untouched, but the right has been redrawn from scratch, reborn in a way that's distinctly Matty. My cheetah morphs into a rotting corpse, all bone and torn flesh. He dies as your eyes cross the page.

Or maybe he doesn't. Maybe he starts out dead and comes back to life, resurrected.

'It's us,' he tells me.

'It's beautiful,' I admit.

He steals my full attention with, 'I'm getting it on my back. The whole thing.'

'Matty, no.' I shake my head rapidly. 'You can't. That's way too big. And what if, like, something happens and we don't . . .'

The softness his face shows when we're alone vanishes in a split second, his amber eyes darkening so fast I flinch. His jawline is hard, his soft lips as straight as his shoulders. Every muscle in his body has stiffened and he's suddenly wide awake.

This is the face the rest of the world is forced to see. This is the bitter resentment that protects him.

'It's my body,' he tells me, tongue sharp and deliberate. He snaps his book shut. 'I'll do what I want. You don't like it, don't look at it.'

'I do like it,' I insist, palms up defensively. 'I do, Matt. But I just — Your whole back? Seriously?'

He tilts his dark head, eyes locked on something other than me. He scratches his jaw.

Matty looks back at me with a smirk, forehead relaxed once again.

I lean back a fraction, uncertain. 'What?'

He licks his bottom lip slowly. 'I'll get a smaller tattoo if you get one too.'

I blink. 'You're out of your fucking mind,' I say bluntly.

Laughter knocks him backwards and he hits his bed with a soft thump. 'Don't act so surprised,' he says brightly. His eyes slip shut. 'And don't be such a pussy, either. It's just a little prick. You can take it. I do all the time.'

I purse my lips.

He's trying to get a reaction, wants to provoke me into saying something he can tease me about for the next month. But I can resist. I can ignore him. I will fight the urge to—

I'm on him in seconds, familiar warmth in my guts. I yank his shirt off. 'I'll show you a little prick, fucker.'

I IGNORE THE ANGRY insults and follow the soft strum of guitar strings instead. My feet stop outside Arielle's bedroom door and I push it open slowly. I spot her quickly, sat at the foot of her bed with an old acoustic balanced in her lap. She glances up at me, but her fingers don't stop their graceful movement.

'What is that?' I ask with a nod in her direction. 'It's . . . familiar.'

'Some old song from the radio,' she tells me, eyes neck of her guitar again. 'I can't get the melody out of my head.'

The sound stirs something in me. It fills my head with strange images of Dad smiling and laughing, his heavily tattooed arms exposed while his fingers dance across piano keys.

We've never owned a piano, and Dad never listens to music.

I sigh. 'How long they been at it?' I ask, feet shifting. I lean against her doorframe.

She lifts a shoulder. 'I dunno. An hour, maybe?'

'About?'

Ari stops strumming. 'Who the fuck knows.' She clucks her tongue, sky-blues taking me in properly. 'Where have you been, ditcher? School finished ages ago.'

'A friend's,' I lie. I swallow thickly, cross my arms over my chest. 'Have you eaten?' She shakes her head no and I jerk mine towards the hall. 'Come on, Dad won't mind if we take the car.'

'I'm poor,' she whines, a ridiculous pout on her face. Her bottom lip quivers when she rests the guitar on the bed beside her.

I shake my head at her. 'You're always poor, and I'm always paying.' I push myself off the doorframe. 'You need to stop buying so much band merch and shit. The stuff just sits in your closet anyway.'

She jumps up with a grin, pulls her too-tight jeans up when she's on her feet. She tugs the hem of her hoodie down, struggles to hide the bulge of her stomach.

'I'm saving for a new keyboard, actually.'

Of course she is.

Ari pushes past me, stepping into the noisy hallway. Mother's hateful tone attacks our ears. It's louder than it was a minute ago, more intense.

Ari looks over her shoulder at me. 'A good brother would help me convince our parents to chip in.'

I snort. 'Better find yourself a good brother, then.'

MATTY AND I HAVE been together over a year now, ever since his oldest brother Lucius threw him and Gio a surprise sixteenth.

And maybe to old people that's not significant or anything, but to people our age, we're practically married. Or would be, if people actually knew we were together. Point is, the longer we're together, the easier it is for him to talk me into doing stupid shit.

I figure that's why I'm where I am now: sitting in a tattoo shop after hours, watching some over-inked twig attack my boyfriend's ribs with a buzzing needle.

'Calm down, man,' he tells me, amber eyes focused on mine. He breathes in deeply, exhales. 'It's not that bad. You'll be fine.'

Matty hasn't flinched once since the tattooist started, but I know it's more painful than he's letting on. It has to be.

'Liar.' I wrap my arms around myself. 'You're a fucking robot.'

He laughs and the man working on him shakes his dark head. 'Don't make me fuck up,' he says, wiping Matty's ribs with a black-gloved hand. He sounds like he smokes a pack a day. Maybe two.

Matty sends a half-arsed glare my way. 'Sorry,' he mumbles.

I smile at him, try to think about the way he beamed when I agreed to do this and not about the agonising pain I know is coming my way.

The monotonous buzzing stops and the tattooist brushes Matty's skin again. His short fingers inspect their work. I bite my lip, try to ignore the way my heart beats a little faster.

I know it's his job, but every time he touches Matty's body I want to close the distance between us and break his fucking fingers.

His ugly eyes meet Matty's. 'It's looking really good.'

I could punch him in the back of the head right now. He'd never see it coming.

'You should seriously think about becoming a tattoo artist,' he adds. He rests his free hand on Matty's leg. 'I'd take you on as an apprentice for sure.'

My spine stiffens.

What the fuck?!

'I dunno, man.' Matty chuckles like some random dude's hand

isn't on his fucking thigh. 'I'm good with a pen, not a gun. I'd probably fuck up.'

The guy laughs like Matty's hilarious, and he pats my boyfriend's leg before he places his tool on the small wheeled table beside him.

I've mentally killed him at least three hundred times before he's on his feet.

The guy tugs each glove off, says, 'Piss break.'

Matty nods, shoulders slumping when a huge gust of air leaves his parted lips.

My eyes follow the sleazy fucker all the way to a staff door, fingers twisted into fists.

I snap my head in Matty's direction when he laughs again. His amber eyes are twinkling like one of Matilda's little minions. He puts his hands behind his head and his lips curl on one side.

'What?' I say, and the word sounds sharp to my own ears.

He tilts his head a fraction, eyes on my lap. 'Jealous much?'

My gaze drops, and I grit my teeth when I realise how white my knuckles are. I flex my fingers, let the blood flow back into them.

'How do you know this creep, anyway?'

'Customer,' he says with a shrug.

Fucking stoner.

He drops his arms, scratches the tip of his nose. 'He's got like a four-month waiting list or something, but I told him I'm going away tomorrow so he said tonight's cool. Well, as long as I bring him some weed.'

My lips purse. 'What else does he want in return?'

Matty shakes his head at me. 'A blowjob, obviously. A fuck if he does yours too.'

I know he's joking, but it doesn't take the tension from my muscles.

I'm pretty sure he's joking.

'Jake,' he sighs when I don't ease up. He gets to his feet, crosses the room in a few easy strides until he's stood right in front of me.

He takes my hands in his, shakes my newly formed fists loose. 'He's harmless, Jake.'

His fingers are freezing compared to how hot mine have suddenly become.

'I wouldn't cheat on you for a tattoo.' He pauses. 'Maybe for a big cat,' he says thoughtfully. His eyes drift. He nods. 'Yeah, I'd fuck him for a pet tiger or something.'

I squeeze his hands and he laughs again. He leans in until his mouth is barely an inch from mine. I can taste his last cigarette every time he breathes out.

'Don't be so paranoid, babe,' he says slowly.

'Don't call me babe,' I mutter back. 'I'm not a girl.'

'Sure act like one,' he returns quickly.

He kisses me before I have a chance to reply. His lips press to mine gently, barely. His day-old stubble makes my skin itch, but I like it. I love it. He's warm and familiar and mine. All mine.

A sudden bang makes me pull away from him. My head hits the back of the chair I'm sat in.

Matty doesn't move for a good minute or so, not until the tattooist has returned to his seat and asked if he's ready to finish. He doesn't say anything, just nods and crosses the room again.

The buzzing resumes and he doesn't take his eyes off me for a second. But I can't tell what he's thinking. He's shut me out the way he does sometimes, showing me the mask he insists on presenting to the rest of the world. It's like he doesn't want me to know what's going on in his head.

When it's finally my turn I feel like I can't get any air into my lungs. My heart's beating so hard that it's suffocating me, crashing into my ribcage over and over and over. I'm gripping my chair so tightly that my fingers could snap off at any second. It's my lifeline, and I can't focus on anything else. Not the angle of my leg or holding my underwear up high enough.

'It might be easier if you just take them off,' the tattooist says, his brown almond eyes on me.

'Easier for who?' I bite.

He grins, lips pulling into a crooked smile that exposes the black smoke spot on his two front teeth. 'You need to relax, kid. It'll hurt less if you relax.'

'Kid?' I breathe through my teeth. 'Who are you, my dad? You look twenty, dude. Twenty-two, tops.'

'I'm actually twenty-eight,' he says with a shrug. 'And married. With kids. So like, we have to get this started now.'

I look down at the outline on my left thigh. It's just like Matty's, only a fraction of the size. I can cover mine with a closed fist, but his would probably take both of my open hands. He says it'll be quicker than Matty's, an hour tops, but I don't think I can handle it. I won't handle it.

I shake my head quickly. 'Matty, I—'

Matty's behind me all of a sudden, his right hand on my shoulder, his left on the leg of my boxers so he can hold them up. He squeezes my shoulder. 'You'll be fine.'

The chatter in my head dies when I feel his thumb on my inner leg. Matty's calloused tip runs back and forth slowly and I quickly realise I have a whole other problem on my hands. What's worse: crying in front of a strange dude, or getting a boner in front of him?

I can't decide.

The tattooist makes his gun buzz a few times and I turn my head slowly, stomach in painful knots. 'You're eighteen, right?'

'Fifty bag says he is,' Matty tells him.

I shake my head rapidly. 'Sixteen,' I confess.

He makes a contemplative hum, forehead creased. My heart freezes. It waits for him to tell me to put my pants on and fuck off, waits for his fatherly conscience to kick in and stop me doing something so fucking stupid.

The guy shrugs. 'Close enough. Got my first when I was fifteen, so who am I to judge?'

My breath stutters when he starts his gun again.

I don't want to do this. I'm afraid, scared that if I watch the ink-covered needle make contact I might actually puke. Or worse, cry like a little bitch. I don't want to be one of his band boys and I definitely don't need more secrets. And seriously, as fucking painful as the thought is, what if we break up? What then?

I look up at Matty, stomach in mangled knots. His eyes are already focused on me.

'It's okay,' he says gently.

My heart slows like that's all I needed to hear. A little.

'I think— Holymotherfuck!' I yell as the needle finally hits my skin.

Matty and the guy both laugh.

I blink back tears, a jagged rock jammed in my throat. It traps the few wisps of air I managed to take in. I can't focus. On anything. The pain in my leg is hot and sharp and achy all at once, and I don't understand how people can do this willingly. How did Matty talk me into this? How the fuck did he hold a conversation during his?

I don't look down when familiar fingertips brush the back of my right hand; I look at their owner instead. My eyes find Matty's and the painful lump in my throat dissolves. He bobs his head, lips twitching upwards.

Maybe they don't matter, all my fears and concerns. We'll be together forever or we won't. We could live together when school finishes or, shit, we could be over by the end of the year. Next week. Tomorrow. Maybe I'll find the courage to tell people the truth about him and what he means to me. Who knows?

We don't say the words, but I know what this is. Our bond. It will never go away, tattoo or not. I'll carry him with me the rest of my life.

I breathe in deeply, breathe out.

I focus on him.

GREAT
LONG
STORY

PAULA
MORRIS

At the graveside of Robert Johnson, I was stung on the neck by a bee.

Before he died Robert Johnson was living in Greenwood, Mississippi. Greenwood still calls itself the Cotton Capital of the World, though nowadays Greenwood farmers prefer corn and soybeans and catfish. The Amtrak train called *City of New Orleans* stops there en route to Chicago. At Greenwood, two rivers — the Tallahatchie and the Yalobusha — become the Yazoo and run through Vicksburg to the Mississippi. Some people say that Yazoo is a Choctaw word for 'river of death'.

Nobody knows exactly where Robert Johnson died.

We drove along Johnson Street in Greenwood, looking for the place in Baptist Town where Robert Johnson may or may not have lived. Johnson Street is not named after Robert Johnson. We were looking for a building on the corner of Young and Pelican, where

Robert Johnson may or may not have died. There's no building there anymore, just a historic marker. Residents of Baptist Town were out in the street, eating barbeque. It was Saturday afternoon, Halloween. A local hospital had set up some kind of information tent. We read the marker without getting out of the car. The neighbourhood was like New Orleans, but smaller and shabbier. Some of the houses were falling down. People looked at us, sitting in our car. We looked at the historic marker.

Nobody knows exactly where Robert Johnson died. Some people say he died out at the Star of the West plantation, north of Greenwood. There is no plantation house out there anymore. Paige at the Greenwood Convention and Visitors Bureau thinks it fell down, or was torn down, many years ago.

The Star of the West plantation was named after a Union steamship captured by the Confederates and sunk in the Tallahatchie River. Some people say it was sunk to avoid recapture. Some say it was sunk to block a Union flotilla headed for Vicksburg.

Nobody knows anymore exactly where Robert Johnson is buried. His death certificate said he was buried at Zion Church. Someone erected a grave marker near Payne Chapel Missionary Baptist Church in Quito, south of Greenwood. Some people say that the last place he performed was at Three Forks in Quito.

Some people say that the Three Forks where Robert Johnson performed for the last time was a club west of Greenwood, not south. We drove to the intersection of Route 49 East and Route 82 where the juke joint once stood. It's very close to Wal-Mart. Some people say it wasn't called Three Forks. It was just a juke joint around the back of Schaeffer's Store and was probably destroyed, along with the store, by a storm in 1942.

In 1991 Columbia Records placed a marker at Mt Zion Missionary Baptist Church on the road between Quito and Morgan City. They thought this was the Zion Church listed on the death certificate. But nine years later an old woman named Rosie Eskridge said her husband was the person who dug Robert Johnson's grave. He was a field hand on the Star of the West plantation. She said he dug it under the pecan tree near the Little Zion Missionary Baptist Church. This cemetery is just north of Greenwood, across the Tallahatchie River.

At the graveside of Robert Johnson, I was stung on the neck by a bee.

Halloween. I stood reading the historic marker at the cemetery just north of Greenwood. On the other side of the road: a field of stubby cotton. The ground was muddy, waterlogged around the pecan tree. It had poured with rain the night before, when I was doing a book-signing in Oxford. I wore a long chain around my neck — silver, dangling a silver globe. Something touched my throat, something that wasn't the chain. I reached up with one hand to brush it away. A piece of fuzz, I thought, until I registered the pain of the sting. The red welt kept growing and throbbing. I was having an allergic reaction. We had to drive to Wal-Mart, on the west side of town, to get antihistamine cream. Robert Johnson sent a bee to sting you, said my husband. You stood too close to his grave.

Nobody knows anymore exactly where Robert Johnson is buried.

At Wal-Mart, a woman approached my husband and asked him the kind of question someone asks a pharmacist. He is a white man, like the pharmacist. At that moment, in the pharmacy section of Wal-Mart, he was the only white man anywhere in sight. She seemed to think he was the actual pharmacist. I wondered when the red welt on my neck would stop growing and itching and hurting. We had to drive to Jackson for another book-signing at four. The book I was signing is a ghost story. It was Halloween.

The gravestone at the cemetery just outside Greenwood may not mark the spot where Robert Johnson is buried. Even if he is buried in that cemetery, he may not be buried under the pecan tree. He may be buried near the historic marker where a bee stung me on the neck.

At Wal-Mart, my husband approached the pharmacist behind the counter and asked if we were buying the right kind of antihistamine cream. The pharmacist said that we could just buy meat tenderiser instead and make it into a paste. This would draw out the sting, and it would be cheaper. But we had lingered at the cemetery where Robert Johnson may or may not be buried, and then we'd driven around looking for a pharmacy. It was too late for the paste to work. We had waited too long.

Robert Johnson lay dying for three days.

Nobody knows exactly where Robert Johnson died. Some people say that he was carried from Three Forks to a house in Baptist Town and that he died there. Some people say that he was carried from Three Forks to a house on the Star of the West plantation and that he died there. Some people say that he was carried from Three Forks to the house in Baptist Town and later to a house on the Star of the West plantation. His death certificate reads: Greenwood (outside).

Robert Johnson lay dying for two or three or four days. He died on August 16, a Tuesday. Elvis Presley also died on August 16, a

Tuesday, thirty-nine years later. Like Robert Johnson, Elvis Presley was born in Mississippi. He was three years old when Robert Johnson died.

There is no birth certificate for Robert Johnson. His half-sister said he was born in 1911. The State of Mississippi was not required to keep birth or death certificates until 1912.

Robert Johnson was born in Hazlehurst, Mississippi. Hazlehurst is the county seat of Copiah County, once the Tomato Capital of America. Like Greenwood, it used to have an opera house. Without realising it, we have driven past his birth site many times. The house was moved to accommodate a ramp leading to I-55, on the east side of the highway. The house had to be moved in the 60s, when the highway was built. In 2009 it was moved again, into downtown Hazlehurst. The house was falling down. Trees and vines were growing in it. The roof had collapsed. Only two original rooms are left.

Things I wrote in my notebook at the graveside of Robert Johnson: Pale blue sky. Muddy hollow. Scattered graveyard. Puddles of water. Pine trees. Pecan tree, rusty leaves. Water in the grooved ridges of the field. It hurts to get stung in the neck by a bee.

Nobody knows exactly where Robert Johnson died. It was August. It was hot. He had to stop playing at the juke joint because he was violently ill. He'd drunk bootleg whiskey, the same as everyone else there. He wouldn't have been carried to the big house on the Star of the West plantation. He would have been taken to one of the shacks, where someone he knew lived. Some people say it was a shotgun house. Some people say the man living in the shack was known as Tush Hog.

The gravestone in the cemetery outside Greenwood quotes Robert Johnson's song 'From Four 'Till Late': *When I leave this town/ I'm gon' bid you fare, farewell/And when I return again/You'll have a great long story to tell.*

On the other side of the gravestone the engraver has reproduced the handwriting of Robert Johnson. These lines are not song lyrics. They are words Robert Johnson wrote down on a piece of paper 'shortly before his death'. They read: *Jesus of Nazareth King of/ Jerusalem. I know that my/Redeemer liveth and that/He will call me from the grave.* Some people say that the piece of paper was found in the shack where Tush Hog lived.

Paige at the Greenwood Convention and Visitors Bureau says Miss Rosie Eskridge's house is still there, on what used to be the Star of the West plantation. But nobody can go there anymore, because it's private land.

At the graveside of Robert Johnson, I was stung on the neck by a bee.

The road to the cemetery north of Greenwood is called Money Road. We passed a small white house on the edge of the cottonfields. A sign on the house read WABG 960 KH. We tuned the radio. The station was playing the blues.

Money, Mississippi is eight miles north of Greenwood. It used to be the Woodstock plantation. It still had a cotton mill in the 1950s, but now so few people live there it's not a town. Its official designation is Populated Place. In 1955 Emmett Till, a black teenager from Chicago, was there visiting his uncle. It was August. It was hot. At Bryant's Grocery he whistled or said something to a white woman. Several days later her husband and another man took

Emmett away from his uncle's house. They beat him up, fracturing his skull and his legs and his arms. They gouged out one of his eyes. They shot him. They used barbed wire to fasten a cotton-gin fan around his neck. They threw him into the Tallahatchie River. When his body was fished up three days later, Emmett Till could only be identified by the ring on his finger.

This was 1955 — not that long ago. My husband was a little boy. He was growing up in St Louis, further up the Mississippi River. His parents would have heard about Emmett Till on the TV news. They would have read about Emmett Till in the *St Louis Globe-Democrat*.

In 'Hellhound on My Trail', Robert Johnson sang: *I got to keep movin'/Blues fallin' down like hail.*

Nobody knows exactly how Robert Johnson died. Some people say it was strychnine poisoning. But strychnine is hard to disguise, and it wouldn't have taken days to kill him. The poison might have been made from boiled mothballs. It might have been made from arsenic. He was poisoned by a jealous lover, or — more likely — by the husband of a jealous lover. Maybe the husband didn't mean to kill him. He just wanted Robert Johnson to leave town.

Robert Johnson got sick at the juke joint. He had stomach cramps and then maybe he got pneumonia. Maybe he had some underlying condition that was triggered by the poison. Some people say that Robert Johnson had Marfan Syndrome, a genetic disorder. No cause is listed on his death certificate. The only thing written in that column is: *No Doctor.*

In 'Preachin' Blues', Robert Johnson sang: *The blues is a low-down achin' heart disease/Like consumption, killing me by degrees.*

At the graveside of Robert Johnson, I was stung on the neck by a bee. The bee flew onto my neck because it was attracted by the sun glinting off the silver chain. It stung me because I tried to brush it away.

Robert Johnson may have sent a bee to sting me on the neck because I stood too close to his grave.

Robert Johnson may have been called from his grave and transformed into a bee. When I brushed him away, he stung me, and then he died. I may have killed Robert Johnson.

During his lifetime, Robert Johnson was not diagnosed with Marfan Syndrome. Signs have been deduced by examining one of the three extant photographs. One of his eyelids seems to droop; his fingers are very long and thin. Another sign is joint flexibility. Maybe this is why his playing could sound like two performers, two guitars. Some people think that the violin virtuoso Paganini had Marfan Syndrome as well. It can result in aortic dissection. One of the symptoms of aortic dissection is severe, stabbing pain.

Nobody knows if Robert Johnson made a pact with the devil. People said that about him, because he played so well. The same thing was said of Paganini. The Archbishop of Nice wouldn't allow Paganini a church burial. Paganini's embalmed body lay in his house for several months before city officials insisted that it be moved. For a while the body was on public display. Paganini wasn't buried in Parma cemetery until 1876, thirty-six years after his death. Some people say Paganini was poisoned.

Some people say that Robert Johnson sold his soul to the devil at the crossroads of Highways 61 and 49 in Clarksdale, Mississippi.

Some people say that this intersection did not exist during Robert Johnson's lifetime. Some people say that the crossroads in question is in Rosedale, where Highways Eight and One meet, or further south on old Highway Eight, where it crosses Dockery Road, or somewhere south of Tunica, known as the cross-town road, or somewhere else in the old cottonfields outside Greenwood, or any number of other roads in the lush green Mississippi Delta.

The juke joint where Robert Johnson performed for the last time was on the crossroads of Route 49 East and Route 82. It's very close to Wal-Mart. In Greenwood these roads cross in more than one place. Even if you're at the right crossroads, the crossroads have changed. These are big roads now, highways. They're not the same as the roads in the 1930s. We pulled over and wandered the grass verge where the juke joint may or may not have stood.

Robert Johnson wrote a song called 'Cross Road Blues' but it does not mention selling his soul to the devil. Robert Johnson wrote a song called 'Me and the Devil Blues' but it does not mention a crossroads.

Some people say that the reason Robert Johnson is so desperate in 'Cross Road Blues' to flag a ride is that it was dangerous for a black man in Mississippi to be out alone at night.

Another Johnson, Tommy Johnson, born around 1896, claimed to have sold his soul to the devil in return for the ability to play any song. Another Johnson, Robert Johnson, born around 1582, wrote the music for a song in Shakespeare's play *The Tempest*. The song was 'Where the Bee Sucks'.

Crystal Springs, Mississippi is ten miles north of Hazlehurst. Crystal Springs was once known as the Tomato Capital of the World.

It is the home of the Robert Johnson Blues Museum, although Robert Johnson was from Hazlehurst, not Crystal Springs. Tommy Johnson, the blues musician who said he sold his soul to the devil, lived in Crystal Springs. He died in 1956. He is buried in a cemetery outside Crystal Springs, but nobody can go there anymore, because it's private land. He has no gravestone.

Robert Johnson had two known recording sessions, the first in San Antonio and the second in Dallas. Robert Johnson had two known marriages, the first to Virginia Travis and the second to Calletta Craft. There are two known photographs of Robert Johnson, one taken in a photo booth and the second in a studio. He may have made other recordings, an audition record. There may be another photo, of Robert Johnson and Johnny Shines. There may be three or four or five photos of Robert Johnson. There were many other women in Robert Johnson's life, but no more wives.

Even if Robert Johnson is buried in that cemetery, he may not be buried under the pecan tree. Rosie Eskridge was 85 or 86 years old when she told that story. It was 2000. Robert Johnson died in 1938. She says that Noah Wade, who owned the Star of the West plantation, told her husband to dig the grave. Rosie went to the cemetery to take her husband some water. She pointed out the spot in 2000, when she was 85 or 86 years old. She may have remembered the correct spot. She may have been confused.

I can't remember things that happened last year. I can't remember if we drove around Baptist Town before we went to Wal-Mart or afterwards. Maybe this was why we were too late to make a paste with the meat tenderiser. My husband had to remind me about the pharmacist suggesting meat tenderiser. I had forgotten this part completely. I didn't write it down in my notebook.

Things I wrote in my notebook at the graveside of Robert Johnson: empty whiskey bottles, crushed can of Red Bull, Howard County library card, condom packet, Mardi Gras beads, rain-soaked flattened straw hat.

In 'Me and the Devil Blues', Robert Johnson says: *Baby I don't care where you bury my body.*

Nobody knows exactly how Robert Johnson died. He was married twice, but he moved around a lot — Mississippi, Arkansas and Texas; Memphis and Chicago — and had liaisons with a lot of women. He may have been poisoned by a jealous husband. The night he was taken ill at the juke joint, the jealous husband was Ralph Davis, known as Snake. His wife, the one Robert Johnson was sleeping with, was named Bea.

Everything in this story is true, apart from the things that are wrong, and the things that are lies, and the things that are misremembered.

Halloween in Mississippi. Cemetery on the road to Money. Pale blue sky, stubby cottonfields. I lingered too long at the graveside of Robert Johnson, and Bea stung me on the neck. She didn't want to kill me. She wanted me to leave town.

POULIULI: A STORY OF DARKNESS IN 13 LINES

SELINA TUSITALA MARSH

'The Blacking Out of Pouliuli (1977)'

Al,
I've taken a black vivid marker
pressed it against your page
and letter by letter, word by phrase
inked across your lines
streaking pouliuli pathways
wending in and out of the Void

Al,
the black ink on black font crack open lines with lava
tracks that frack the land of your story, hijack meaning,
ransack intention, back-packing on your own invention,
hacking into, wise-cracking about the side-tracking and
bric a brac-ing of lines till back to back black on black
makes pouliuli on the night's page shoot stars that light up
windows of words through which we peer into pouliuli.

the

Void heard

'brave footsteps'

'Go away!' he said,
'I don't need you.'
The man insisted
'But you do

7

The

small problem

stored

the

small favour

and

scheming

lowered the fale blinds.

9

old

evil aitu.

whisper

an

exorcising

logic.   dominated by

listening

eyes,'

13

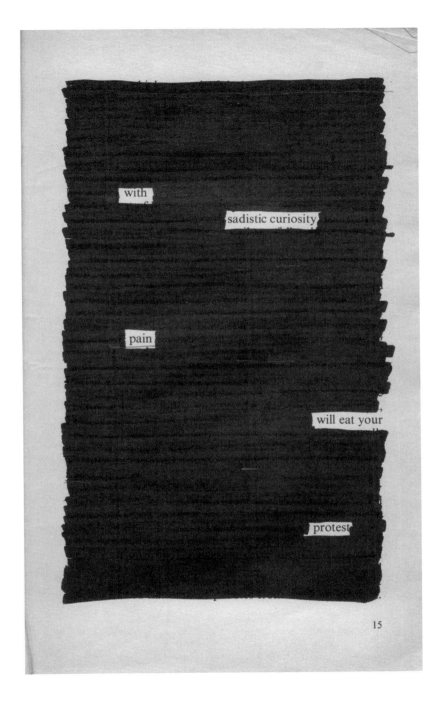

with

sadistic curiosity

pain

will eat your

protest

15

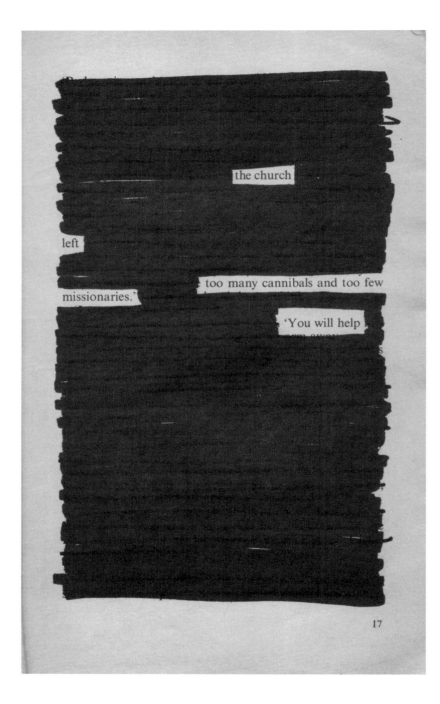

the church

left

too many cannibals and too few
missionaries.'

'You will help

17

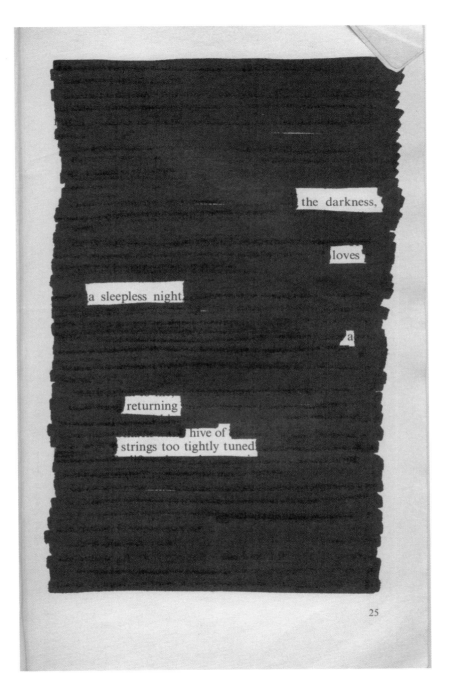

the darkness,

loves

a sleepless night.

a

returning

hive of

strings too tightly tuned

25

alofa

The only trustworthy

promise

39

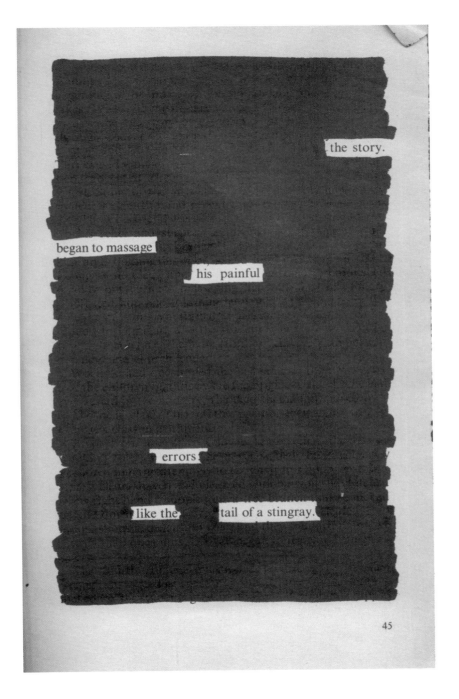

the story.

began to massage

his painful

errors

like the   tail of a stingray.

45

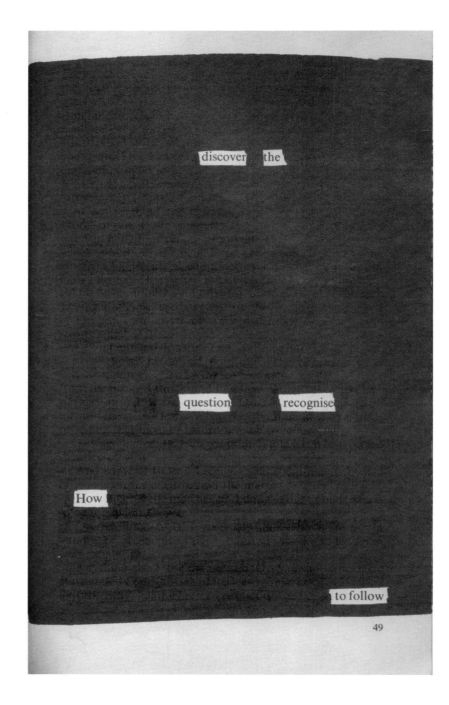

discover the

question recognise

How

to follow

49

SELINA TUSITALA MARSH

Chapter 5

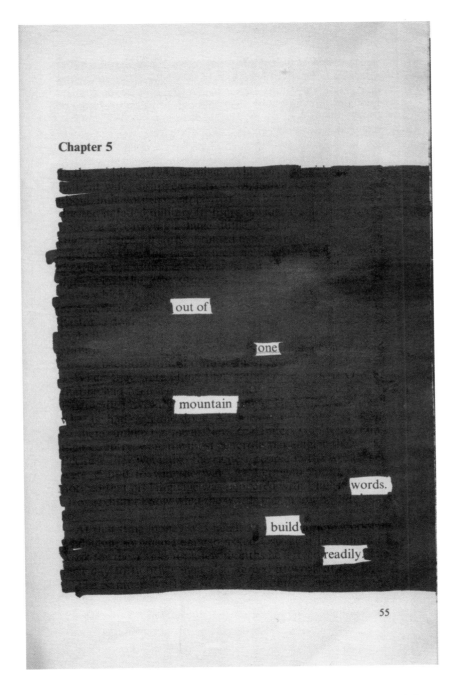

out of

one

mountain

words.

build

readily

55

black bastard   papalagi bastard,

delight

in

                    interpret

        ing

                    beer

57

deep   laughter

is

hypnotic dance.   so

beat   but the frantic rhythm,   before

death's

embrace.

61

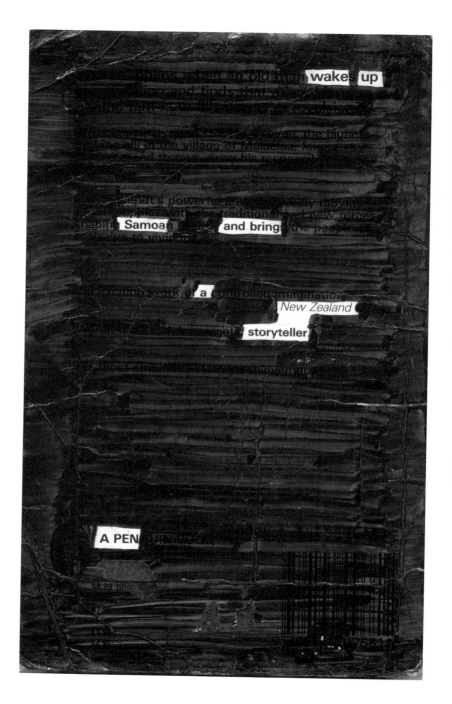

wakes up

Samoan **and brings** the people

a controlled imagination

New Zealand

storyteller

A PEN

KE KĀHEA: THE CALLING

A steampunk story

BRYAN KAMAOLI KUWADA

The Tutua

THEY ALWAYS COME ON the highest tides of the year.

When the pull of Hina is strongest, the leviathans lumber forth from the depths. Some look like armored whales with tree-trunk legs made for walking the land, others have great sprays of spines on their backs and light, speckled underbellies; they drag themselves forth with flukes and flippers, awkward and ungainly out of the water. More yet are living coral islands, vibrant with color, sidling from the sea, craggy backs carpeted in algae and ferns.

We call them Tutua.

Most of us have glimpsed the leviathans from afar. We watched from hilltops and distant valleys, our legs trembling with the desire to run. The Tutua have been coming for long enough that we know what to expect. They are drawn to our heiau and burial caves, the places where our chiefs' bones and carved god-images call out to them.

And the Tutua destroy them. They devour the black basalt stones of the temple walls and suck the burial crypts like marrow from caves. The leviathans leave nothing in their paths, not even dust or fragments of ancient bone. The same every time.

Moon. Tide. Tutua. Destruction.

The first handful of Tutua came ashore several years ago near Kekuanohu Fort in Honolulu. They were drawn to towering Kūkaʻōʻō, a heiau deep in the broad and fertile bowl of Mānoa Valley. Gun defences bristled from the fort's walls like the spines of its scorpionfish namesake, but the tutua shrugged off the fire from steam-powered chain guns and clockwork repeaters. They advanced in a slow and inexorable march, leaving a line of rubble and flames leading up to the terraced walls of the green valley.

The fort fell, the Tutua fed from the heiau. When they returned to the blue depths off Honolulu, an entire complement of soldiers lay among the rubble of the fort and hundreds of others in the Tutua's path had gone to join the soldiers in the sleep of ages. Steam from the gigantic boilers below the fort hissed quietly as if exhaling their last breath. Huge swathes of the nearby city had been crushed under foot and reduced to piles of coral blocks, broken wooden shards and shattered gearwork.

The missionaries who brought the Book to Hawaiʻi preached that the leviathans were the instrument of their God. He had sent them to punish us for our idolatrous and heathen ways. Most of our people felt this must be true, as the Tutua only began to appear after the missionaries' religion had gained a foothold.

But I was never a believer in the missionaries' talk. None in my family ever sat in a wooden pew listening to them or other foreigners calling us ignorant savages and mangling our language through their crank-powered voice amplifiers. And those who kept to the old ways, like my mother, and her mother before her, knew the truth anyway.

We who had hidden the bones and the carved god-images knew the real reason why the Tutua came. The great leviathans came to feed on the mana imbued in these objects, the strength of our ancestors.

Kuʻu makuahine, ke kahuna
My mother, the kahuna

THOSE WHO FOLLOWED THE old ways paid a high price.

Few openly held to the old gods and old religions anymore, and those who did were shunned and ostracised. No epithet was as shameful those days as 'kahuna', a title the people in my family had always worn with pride.

My mother was such a prophetess. She was a kind and wonderful woman, but damnably stubborn. Despite my remonstrances, she kept to her traditional beliefs and refused to observe the foreigners' Sabbath or the laws passed to ensure compliance with their commandments: no physical labor on Sundays, no loud noises to disturb prayer, not even a cookfire, whose smoke might obscure people's reflections on *their* one god. Even the soughing steam carriages did not run on Sundays. Yet for my mother, certain moons were better for performing our ritual ceremonies, or planting and gathering medicine, so if those moons called for that work to happen on a Sunday, then Sunday was when she was going to do it. She had nothing against the missionaries or their beliefs, but she had seen too much from her 400,000 gods to accept that there was only one.

On my ninth birthday I witnessed the consequences of insisting on tradition. My mother refused to allow me to attend the mission school, so I was never drawn to the missionaries' teachings, but I felt no real attraction to my mother's practices either. Although I was an inquisitive child and readily learned what she taught me, her world always seemed at odds with what I saw beyond the walls of our compound. There, I could enjoy all the books and clockwork gadgets that the foreign traders brought back from 'Amelika and Beretania. For my birthday, I pestered my mother for weeks about getting a bisque doll I had seen. She finally relented, even though we didn't really celebrate birthdays with gifts the way foreigners did.

I was in the happy oblivion of childhood as my mother and I went to purchase the porcelain-skinned doll. I practically skipped along, holding her hand as we walked down the packed dirt of the bustling King's Street, dodging muttering people and hissing steam carriages. I was in my play-stained frock and I was so proud of my mother. She was the most beautiful woman in the world, wrapped in her kīkepa made of barkcloth scented with ferns, the brown skin of her bare, tight-muscled shoulder drawing the eyes of everyone on the street.

I was so busy chattering away about how I would bathe the doll and teach her Hawaiian and show her which plants to pick for salves that I didn't notice how stiffly my mother was walking. I looked up at her silence and saw her jaw clenched, her nostrils flaring in anger.

I glanced around and noticed that all the men, both foreign and native, in their dark coats were giving her hard stares and turning their backs on her in the street. The women in their high-necked dresses were giving her pitying looks and calling out prayers for her soul. I didn't know what was happening and nearly fell back when an especially angry woman snarled, 'Kahuna!' and then spat on the street right in front of me. We never hid the fact that we were from a kahuna family, but the woman's look of disgust made me ashamed.

Even when we got to the store, Kamaka, the shopkeeper, whose infant son my mother had treated just a few weeks prior, pointedly ignored her. He threatened to call the constables when she spoke sternly to get his attention.

My mother led me out with her head held high, but her arms shook as she held my hand. After all, our family had advised the ruling family for generations, and that association had usually buffered my mother from this sort of treatment. But as the men of the Book grew in power and influence, she began to lose the ear of the king.

Things escalated after that incident. My mother was denounced from the pulpit. Angry sermons were delivered on the street corner through crank-powered amplifiers across from our house. Broadsides appeared around town mocking my mother; they were adorned with block prints of a witch doctor in a kīkepa dancing around a cauldron.

People even shouted at me while I was playing in the yard. I quietly asked my mother if she couldn't just try to be more like the people of the Book. Instead, she moved our whole family out to the countryside.

When the religion of the Crucified Man took hold our people moved away from worshipping the 400,000 akua who inhabited all aspects of the world; they turned their belief to the single foreign akua. Without the mana that we fed them with our worship and ceremonies, our gods began to weaken and disappear. Now, few whispered in awe at the majesty of Kānehekili, dozens of feet tall, with one side of his body tattooed completely black, representing the thunder and lightning that always attended him. Few spoke of giving tobacco to an old woman only to find out that they had been in the presence of the volcano goddess Pele. Few attribute those of wondrous birth to the powers of Haumea, who was reborn in every Hawaiian woman. Few told stories about the akua at all.

This was what summoned the Tutua.

They were not malevolent; they merely came to ensure the balance of mana in the world, absorbing what mana was in the sacred structures and ancient relics to keep it from dissipating.

Ke kau o Hoʻoilo
The season of Hoʻoilo

WHEN I WAS TEN my family moved out to the country, but things did not get much better, at least not for me. I begged my mother to let me go to the mission school nearby. She thought it was because I was lonely with no real playmates, but it was just that I was so hungry for knowledge about the outside world.

Like most families, we read the newspapers aloud to each other. My mother and the rest of the family loved all of the traditional stories and songs that were printed; sometimes we acted out particularly funny or risqué parts, like when Pahulu, the lecherous fisherman, was tricked into having sex with a stone, thinking it was a beautiful goddess. I tried unsuccessfully to cover both my eyes and my ears when Uncle Hoku started reenacting that part.

I would mostly sit quietly on the side when my family was gathered together and read to myself about what was happening in foreign countries. The civil war in ʻAmelika, telegraphs, the London Underground, Lister's use of carbolic acid in Beretania.

My mother finally gave in and let me go to the mission school, but it wasn't exactly what I was hoping for. I had access to more books and learned about world history and literature and natural science but, if anything, the pupils from the countryside looked down on me even more than the people in the capital had. And, as always, they would refer to our family's traditional standing, hissing 'kahuna' at me as they pulled my hair or yanked my satchel out of my hands.

My mother would spend time each morning making me a fragrant lei of pua kenikeni or pīkake or sometimes even maile to wear to school so I would look nice and smell pretty, but anything that stood out about me became fodder for bullying by my classmates, so I stomped home one day and told my mother that I didn't want to wear those foolish garlands anymore. She pressed her lips tightly together as if she were going to say something, but only nodded. From then on, I did my best to blend in, only answering if I was called on and trying not to show too much avidity about what I was learning.

I STAND THERE, BARE feet digging into the hot sand, rolling and unrolling the large sheaf of newsprint in my hands. The satchel with the clockwork device in it is heavy by my side. And damn it all if the collar of my dress isn't already sopping wet. Sweat drips into the hair curled at the back of my neck. I have put it up with a fine whaletooth comb my mother gave me, one of the few adornments I allow myself, but my hair is always so unruly, especially in this kind of weather.

It is the season of Hoʻoilo, the time the elders insist used to be the cool part of the year. But everyone knows now that the weather only cools after the Tutua come and eat their fill. The sun really has teeth today, this whole year in fact, but that's not what is making me sweat.

The elders in my family, normally gregarious and good-natured, had turned their backs on me quietly when I told them what I was to do today. They had always tolerated my attempts to get them to move back to the city and join the modern world. They even put up with me nattering on and on about the technology I had seen in London or the newest steam-powered marvels being deployed in Honolulu.

They were disappointed when I decided not to finish training as a kahuna under my mother and left instead to study the foreigner's medicine in Beretania. Nevertheless, they had been understanding and even kind, often writing me letters and sending clippings of traditional stories published in the newspaper — both extravagances of a sort, considering the cost of paper here. When I came home from London, heartbroken from a failed relationship, my mother gently but firmly pulled me out of my grief with liberal doses of hugs, backbreaking work on our land, and my favorite raw fish. And my uncles helped my recovery as well with their merciless teasing, gentle songs and boisterous laughter.

This morning is different. I had got up early and picked pua kenikeni to make a lei for my mother. My uncles filed in, chuckling and muttering, while I was clipping the blossoms before stringing them. Each smiled and came to press his nose against mine.

We gathered around the bowl of fragrant flowers and chatted idly. Uncle Kalae limped over to get some dried fish to snack on and rasped that these hot days felt so much cooler with the scent of flowers in our nostrils. Uncle Hoku, wearing only his malo, teased me that I always dressed like I was still in London and laughed that hissing laugh of his. Uncle Hali'a, who was the youngest, came over and put his rough hands on my shoulders and watched quietly as I strung the flowers.

My mother walked in with an armload of hō'i'o ferns that she had picked from near the river. 'Ho, Kahalalaulani! What, sleeping in today?' bellowed Uncle Hoku, but he knew she had been up working before all of us.

She flicked them a glance that made them fall silent instantly, put down the ferns and gave me a big hug, inhaling the scent of the pua kenikeni. They were her favorite, and she knew the lei I was making was for her, even though I hadn't said anything. My mother and her brothers chatted about what work had to be done today and which of their children would watch the grandchildren.

When a break in the conversation happened, I spoke quietly. 'I agreed to do what the king wanted.'

Uncle Hoku's shoulders tensed like he felt a cane spider on his back. All the uncles began to shake their heads. Hoku and Kalae exhaled audibly in disappointment, and Hali'a tried to stand up for me by declaring, 'No one refuses the king's summons!' Each of the men vowed that they would take the carriage into town and set Kalākaua straight, listing off all of the things our family had done for the monarchy.

My mother just stood there, silently regarding me. A single look from her was often enough to bring my boisterous uncles to heel, but this was different. There was no anger there. She could tell that the king had needed no compulsion to get me to do what he wanted.

'She wants to do it,' my mother said.

My uncles fell silent, and then started up again. Why would you agree to fight the Tutua? Why would you help those foreigners who spit at us on the street? How could you do this?

They didn't even wait for my answer. The three of them just left. I ran after them, telling them that it was for the best and that it would help our family get back into the king's good graces, but my pleas fell like pebbles from my lips, clattering to the floor, small and insignificant.

I stood quietly and put the lei around my mother's neck. She smiled wanly and reminded me of the prophecy made a hundred years ago.

'The land shall come from the sea,' she said.

Ke kāhea 'ana i ke kāhea
Summoning the lā'au kāhea

MOST PEOPLE, INCLUDING ME, felt the prophecy referred to the foreigners who had come on their ships from so far away, who had washed over us like the ocean and taken so much of our land. My family, however, had always insisted that the prophecy was yet to be fulfilled and that the true power over the land had yet to arrive from the sea. Everyone could clearly see how much influence the foreigners wielded, but my family, and my mother in particular, refused to believe that these missionaries-turned-businessmen were so powerful as to be the fulfilment of the prophecy.

I couldn't tell my mother that I was the one who had suggested the plan to Walter Murray Gibson, the king's science advisor. I felt such a stirring when I read those old stories my family sent me in London. They were reminders of how far Hawai'i had come since making contact with the foreigners. We were an independent nation among nations, and it was because we were not afraid to embrace change.

We couldn't just hold on to the past. The foreigners had so much to offer us. Knowledge. Technology. Business. We needed to show the rest of the world that Hawai'i belonged in this family of nations.

Large tracts of land near sacred sites remained unused. State-of-the-art steam machinery rusted away because investors had no guarantee that their money and effort would not end up as rubble when the high tide brought the Tutua. If I helped the king rid the land of the leviathans, maybe I could win back the king's favor. Maybe I could make a place for my family in our kingdom's future. Maybe I could even help shape that future.

The king's summons directed me to use my lāʻau kāhea with a clockwork device that Gibson had built. My family was skilled in many types of incantations, but we were most known for our lāʻau kāhea, the art of summoning the highest spiritual powers to heal with just our voices. Indeed, my mother had been among the last of those to know the chants and skilled enough to implement them in the appropriate ceremonial ways and she had been inducting me into the art, though I hadn't finished my training.

My mother hissed and sucked her teeth when I made the mistake of telling her I met with Gibson. 'Tsā! He is a usurper, giving poor counsel to the king. I don't trust that pirate with his devices and talk of progress. He is a plover nosing around other birds' nests.'

Kalākaua has always been interested in the latest technological advances, and Gibson had drawn the king's attention by crafting intricate spyglasses and ticking brass puzzles for him. As Gibson's influence at court had grown, so had his devices. He believed that every problem could be solved by the application of technology. One of the most recent machines he designed was a gigantic steam-driven furrower that could plow acres and acres of sugar fields in a single day.

And now he had made a device that would amplify my voice so that my lāʻau kāhea would have the sonic strength to overpower the Tutua. It was a burnished brass mask that covered the lower half of my face. An ornate grille adorned with stylised clouds and puffs of wind housed a mesh screen that let air in and out. Leather straps fitted the mask to my face.

'It is essentially a music box,' Gibson said.

He told me how he miniaturised the comb and tuned its one hundred teeth to play particular notes that were nearly outside the normal range of human hearing. 'But the cylinder! The cylinder is where the magic happens!' he crowed. 'Once the cylinder is wound, it will spin hundreds of revolutions per minute, repeating the melody over and over, too fast to even hear the individual notes.'

Gibson was convinced that the sonic distortion from his device would shape the words of my kāhea into a battle song of all songs.

My mother stopped me before I left, and we pressed our foreheads together to share our breath. She inhaled, and said:

'You know, don't you, that when you unleash the lā'au kāhea, you have no control over it. The kāhea will go where it will and do what it will. It may help you in your mission but then . . . it might help me in mine.'

What did my mother mean?

'What you're doing is wrong, but the time is right.'

No ke kai mai ka Tutua
The Tutua from the sea

I GLANCE OVER MY shoulder and see the king and his retinue lounging under their great canvas pavilion a hundred yards away. They are far from the booming winter surf crashing on the shore. Each wave comes closer, as if desperately trying to gain audience with the king. The court sits unaware, dressed in their finery, sipping iced juices, attendants cooling them in the salt air with large fans woven from hala leaves. King Kalākaua and Walter Murray Gibson, the science advisor, watch me intently.

I look away from them and scan the horizon.

A CROWD GATHERS AND waits for the tide change, though they keep a respectful distance from Kalākaua's tent. Foreigners with their light skin and dark suits stand out among the sea of brown faces. The richest are in the pavilion with the king, but everyone in the crowd, whether businessmen in tailored suits or plantation workers in roughspun, is looking at me.

I feel what they're thinking. They wait to see what a woman can do in the face of a Tutua.

This is my chance.

Waimea Bay is a gentle moon of white sand shoreline, with a small river drawing a lazy arc out from the terraces and loʻi of the valley to empty into the sea. The fertile joining of fresh water and salt attracts all manner of sea life, and it is a favorite place for my family to catch ʻōpelu. There, high up on the mountain above the deep blue waters of the bay, stands Puʻu o Mahuka heiau, one of the largest temples in the islands.

Many of the believers in the new religion speak only in whispers about the sour tang of pain that tinges the air there, blood-spattered pagan rites, living victims disemboweled and eaten, their blood and innards offered to the hungry akua. My lineage is one of healers, so we do not know all that the temple priests did, but I know enough to recognise how misinformed this belief is. Our gods did not want putrid flesh and rotting entrails. The mana rests in the bones. People were indeed offered up as sacrifices to our gods — but never living beings. Living offerings were too messy, and the necessary preparations for the bodies were too meticulous. Most were chiefs killed in battle or executed, the flesh cooked to strip away from their bones. The mana rests in the bones.

I am shaken out of my reverie as the air around me shifts and thickens.

It becomes harder to breathe, and an insistent buzz fills the air just below my hearing. Heat begins to roll off the thundering waves as they race towards the beach, each breaking set creeping closer to where we stand.

Everyone turns towards the sea, fans stop mid-stroke, glasses sweating with condensation pause halfway to lips.

A hundred breaths indrawn at the same time punctuate the appearance of a giant bony spine rising through the rhythmic ocean chop. A few people cry out in fear as a dark shape swells the ocean's surface and the Tutua's armored carapace rises into sight. But most stand in quiet awe.

What emerges from the roiling shorebreak looks like no sea creature anyone has ever seen, yet it is undeniably of the ocean. As it strides powerfully through the shallows onto the mounded sand at the shore, its sheer size overwhelms my mind. This one stands as tall as a mature koa tree, over a hundred feet tall.

The Tutua stands on four thickly muscled legs, each mottled and scaled like an 'o'opu. Its feet are reminiscent of fins, but end in a fringe of webbed spines. Waves of heat rise off the leviathan, distorting the air around the creature. Bony growths range across its broad, variegated, four-armed torso, while the black orbs of its eyes seem to devour light, never letting it escape. What I can not stop looking at, though, is its mouth. Though I quail at the sight of this most bestial of countenances, its mouth is different. The Tutua snuffles at the salt air, crinkling the leathery skin around its nostrils, and I catch a glimpse of its teeth. They are broad and flat, as if for grinding and crushing.

Truth be told, it is magnificent.

Now is the time for me to unleash the lā'au kāhea. I start to chant and my words, amplified, fill the space between earth and sky.

And then I see my mother, and she is also chanting the words. And I wonder . . . Although I have come here for one purpose, there may be another . . .

I remember the prophecy:

The land shall come from the sea.

Lisa Reihana, *in Pursuit of Venus [infected]*, 2015–17, still from video work

WHAKAPAPA OF A WALLPAPER

A chimerical fiction

WITI IHIMAERA

1.

> A hee mai te tua, e ia papama 'ehe
> No te tai a tau te Po . . .
> The sea rolled, the tides mounting
> For a period of nights . . .
> E po fanaura'a atua, o te po Mua Taia'aroa
> It was the God's birth night,
> The night of Mua Taia'aroa[1]

HERALDS IN THE HEAVENS often presage changes coming to earth.

Thus did our whakapapa begin when it became known that Venus would transit across the surface of the sun.

The announcement brought scientists rushing from their hemisphere in the north to set up observatories in the south; on their arrival the womb of the world enlarged. From their centre of power in Europa they came to ours in the azure Pacific where we held the tino rangatiratanga. Here, we kept the sovereign balance to their own domain.

One such scientist was James Cook who arrived in Tahiti to observe the transit on 3 June 1769. In the world that has gone before us, we were the iwi, the original settlers, with our own music in our southern spheres. Purotu, gift of the gods, was our *Garden of Eden*. The sky was above, Ranginui ē! The sea was below, Tangaroa ē! The islands were in between, ngā motu of Te Moana-nui-a-Kiwa ē!

Other voyagers, of a most marvellous kind, scattered to the Indies and South America. Quickened by the irritation, the pregnancy reached parturition, became swollen; it spat out and delivered of itself ships that were wondrous to look upon, carrying their own clouds above them. Aiming their telescopes to the infinite air, the star seekers saw Venus, moving in the heavens like a giant waka. There it sailed, with the star clusters of Alcyone, Elnath, Aldebaran and Alhena looking on. The canoe bucked in the fiery cyclones that burst across the blazing eye of the sun. Its timbers smouldered, and its sails burst into flame. Would the waka survive? Yes! There Kōpū was, making escape into the cool universe beyond.

No such escape awaited us. Having calibrated heaven, the strangers began to calibrate the earth. From marvellous they became mischievous; measuring, sketching, surveying, naming, they turned their telescopes on us.

2.

> Forêts paisibles,
> Jamais un vain désir ne trouble ici nos coeurs.
> Peaceful forests, never a vain desire
> Trouble here our hearts.
> Jouissons dans nos asiles
> Let's enjoy our refuges
> Jouissons des biens tranquilles
> Let's enjoy peaceful things![2]

IN OUR GESTURES ARE our genealogies. Our ritual movements convey the stories of the shimmering Pacific womb from which we were born.

Thirty-five years later, in 1804, we awoke to find that we had been transported to the Napoleonic Empire, Revolutionary Year XII. Our lashes parting, we discovered a new wonder:

We were figures in a wallpaper!

And we inhabited an extraordinary, vividly polychromatic, painted world of twenty paper drops, each 10 metres long. We asked ourselves, 'By what magic and which tohunga have we been brought to this place and time?'

Our creators were entrepreneurs Joseph Dufour and Jean-Gabriel Charvet.

'Over a thousand multiple woodblocks have gone into your production,' Monsieur Dufour told us, 'and careful hand-painting has given you the graduated gouache sky above you. We have named you *Les Sauvages de la Mer Pacifique*, The Native Peoples of the Pacific Ocean.'

Monsieur Dufour told us they had drawn inspiration for creating us mainly from the three voyages under Cook's command between 1768 and 1778.

'Other accounts by de la Pérouse and Louis de Bougainville have also assisted in your composition,' Monsieur Charvet added. 'Your world is a set of parkland entrées inspired by such botanists as Joseph Banks and Daniel Solander. Their journals and illustrations were re-worked as engravings by John Webber and William Hodges.'

'We researched the most popular illustrations,' Monsieur Dufour said. 'And for the wallpaper's final design we added our own neo-classical, Hellenistic and Pompeiian references and—' he opened his arms to embrace us, 'here you are, *belle et magnifique*.'

Indeed, we were beautiful and magnificent, and it thrilled us to see ourselves, we from Ra'iatea and Tahiti, so richly garbed and elegantly attired. Dufour and Charvet had visualised Tahiti as the birthplace of Aphrodite, and the splendid theatricality reflected Jean-Antoine Watteau's *L'Embarquement pour Cythère*.

We were both real and mythic living in exotic harmony.

Were we to blame that our creators had added Greek and Roman touches to our faces, physique, regalia and ornamentation? No! Now chimerical Arioi, bleached, without blemish or physical flaw, we engaged in decorous amorous play and danced a chaconne.

SUDDENLY, AS WE DANCED hand in hand, we tripped over a gouache rock and found ourselves tumbling from our 10-metre paper drop into the one next to us.

E hika! What was this? There were other Pacific peoples in the wallpaper!

We accordingly re-composed ourselves and formally made mihimihi to them: 'Where have you all come from?'

They told us that Cook and other captains, on other ships with clouds above them, had also visited them in their lands.

'We collected them for our wallpaper world too!' Monsieur Dufour exclaimed.

With great wonder we went from panel to panel as our brothers and sisters of the Pacific introduced themselves and showed us their own vignettes: Canadian Nootka Islanders, Islanders of Ha'apai, Tonga, Tanna, New Hebrides and Vanuatu, the Sandwich Islands, Māori of Aotearoa, Islanders of Sandwich Sound, Alaska, Rotterdam Island, New Caledonia, Tongatapu, the Marquesas, Easter Island and Palau.

Together we marvelled at the various picturesque tableaux-paysages. Each entrée was a pastoral arioso, unfolding a tale of exoticism amid leafy splendour, of amorous intercourse in a remote part of the globe. One entrée was discordant: Cook's death by Hawaiian hands on 14 February 1779, had merited only a small pictorial.

Too real, perhaps?

Certainement, the public preferred the fantasy of Pacific harmony. So did our creators glorify the ancient regime. By composing an artful, ethereal, exotic paper enchantment, they enabled the viewer to escape their reality.

We, however, could never escape ours.

3.

> E ngā iwi ē, e karanga e ngā iwi ē!
> We call to you, all the peoples of the world!
> Titiro mai ngā iwi me ngā mahi o ngā iwi
> Look at our works, look at us as we dance
> On the strand beside the sea
> Auē te aroha, te mamae i ahau ē![3]

OUR JOURNEYS THROUGH THE 19th century began.

We floated through Napoleonic France. The well-to-do delighted in our fabular *fêtes galantes* and the *curieux* lyric entertainment we provided.

They also saw themselves in *us*!

Just as the ballet heroïque *Les Indes Galantes* by Jean-Philippe Rameau was played every year on the King's Feast Day, so did they stage ballroom carnivals inspired by the wallpaper. They transformed their garden bowers into idyllic Pacific arboretums where they held their own *fêtes galantes*. At the outdoor entertainments the courtiers mimicked us, dressing in the accoutrements of Polynesia but enacting classical baroque scenes within a pristine wilderness.

When they weren't looking, *we* copied *them*, dipping and swaying and fluttering our eyelashes and handkerchiefs as we danced. Oh, it was so much fun!

WE BEGAN TO JOURNEY beyond France to the rest of Europe and across the Atlantic to the Americas.

Hundreds of copies of our wallpaper were produced. We were

cloned, and our Utopian landscapes were pasted on the walls
of castles and chateaux, palaces and pleasure domes. We were a
quasi-travel revelation. Visitors peered with nostalgic interest at
the symphonic spectacles of singing, dancing and courtly love.
We provided them with a vision of a Paradise that celebrated the
universality of human nature.

AUĒ, OUR PACIFIC HISTORY was no longer paradisiacal.

In reality the practice that Europe and the Americas exported to
the Pacific was exploitative.

Following Ferdinand Magellan who, in 1520, had renamed our
ocean without permission, the explorers were covetous. In our
sorrow, greatly troubled and smitten with fear, we saw the impact
of European discovery by such as Abel Tasman, James Cook, Jean-
François de la Pérouse, Samuel Wallis and Louis de Bougainville.
We wept at the subsequent colonial settlement, and the ways in
which the indigenous history of the ocean became one of war,
division of spoils and rape of its resources. The encounters between
Europeans and Americans were disastrous for Pacific civilisations.

We felt pierced through with darksome nails as the Americans
annexed Hawai'i and American Samoa; the French, Tahiti and
New Caledonia; Easter Island became a special territory of Chile
in 1888; the Germans held Samoa until 1914; the British, New
Zealand and Australia. They variously named our dismembered
parts Polynesia, Melanesia, Micronesia and Austronesia.

Could they not hear us sorrowing for our sea?

4.

> Et mon coeur s'est levé par ce matin d'été;
> And my heart arose on this summer's morning;
> Car une belle enfant était sur le rivage,
> For a beautiful girl was on the beach,
> Laissant errer sur moi des yeux pleins de clarté,

Letting eyes full of brightness wander over me,
Et qui me souriait d'un air tender et sauvage.
She smiled at me with a tender and wild expression.[4]

GRIEVING, WE FLOATED THROUGH time and space, through the
20th century with its First World War, Second World War and
War in the Pacific and, when we awoke, we discovered that the
island nations and their human inhabitants had been subjugated. It
was the bitterest of tortures to witness the conflagrations in Korea,
Vietnam and other countries on the Pacific Rim.

Our Ocean had also become the site of nuclear bomb testing by
the very country that had first adored and loved us.

The great foodbasket that had been created to feed all was
bickered over as other world nations sought to claim rights over its
bounty. From the northern Arctic to the shelves of Antarctica, the
Great Powers were rapacious.

THEN THE 21ST CENTURY arrived and, with it, a young woman to
look upon us in 2005. As soon as we saw her our hearts leapt.

'This is one of our descendants,' we exclaimed with joy.

Thus did the artist Lisa Reihana come into our lives. We called
to her: 'Neke mai e mokopuna, i raro i a Kōpū.'

She was a filmmaker and installation artist with a fierce political
intelligence.

She stood before us and made her karanga, her ritual call. She
gave us her whakapapa, her genealogy.

'My ancestor Kupe was from Purotu,' she began. 'His mother
was from Point Venus, the same place from which Cook observed
Venus in 1769. Kupe voyaged from Ra'iatea to New Zealand but,
although almost two hundred and fifty years have gone by, the
Māori still honour you and remember you, our ancestors of Te
Moana-nui-a-Kiwa.'

She then gave greeting across the genealogical latticework to all the Pacific peoples on the wallpaper. Driven by her faith in legacy and enduring power of kinship, she placed her nose against the wallpaper in hongi.

We felt the sweet brushing of skin on our parchment as she exchanged the breath of life with us.

THUS BIDDEN, WE ROSE to discover that we would have a new purpose in the world.

Whereas Dufour and Charvet had originally created us 'to delight the imagination without taxing it' Lisa Reihana wanted to develop us as a panoramic video installation.

E hika. He aha tēnā *video installation*?

'Oh, that's an easy question,' she answered. 'I am going to make you into a moving image of the wallpaper.'

Well, she sure took us on a long ride, that one.

For six years she travelled worldwide to many countries, including Hawai'i, Australia, the UK, the Netherlands, France, the US and New Zealand. She worked with a huge diversity of contributors including performing arts students, filmmakers in costume and production, musicians, animators, technicians and actors and dancers from Pasifika and Māori communities.

Her project was on the scale of a feature film. There were many stories to tell, collaborators to communicate with, performers to include and computers to be wrestled with.

'I am giving you a new visual language,' she told us, 'and within it you will move and dance and tell your stories in an altogether different way.'

WHEN LISA WAS FINISHED we discovered that we were in a different Time and Space.

It was 2012, and we had become a two-channel panoramic work called *in Pursuit of Venus*. Our new purpose was to engage the legacies of European romance and representation in the Pacific in relation to our own sense of self. It was also to interrogate representations, gender, mythologies in our original make-up.

'I want to restore to you your tino rangatiratanga,' Lisa said. 'I've used 21st-century digital technologies to reclaim you and to re-imagine you, not through the European Gaze but through the eye of the Pacific. You have been a fabulation invented in someone else's elsewhere. Let all who look upon you marvel at your mana, the ways in which you powerfully bestride our world.'

We danced in Auckland, we sang in Amsterdam and we boogied in Toronto. We got down in Singapore and Dunedin. We danced, danced, danced.

And then we made a triumphal return in the hokinga mai where, as in *in Pursuit of Venus [infected]*, we were fêted among the iwi in Auckland in May 2015. The references of the original wallpaper have been expanded to include vignettes that concern cultural resistance and conflict. The small pictorial account of Captain Cook's death is no longer background to our narrative but foregrounded as the pivot point of Pacific–European history. The red-coated marines and blue-coated European sailors are now there as part of the evolving narrative of Oceania.

5.

> A te, sovrana augusta,
> You august sovereign,
> Indiandeniam la chioma,
> We crown you,
> A te l'Asia, a te l'Africa s'atterra
> A te l'Europa . . .
> Ora consacra e dona,
> Now let Europe consecrate
> And bestow on you this imperial crown
> Of the world![5]

The Auckland Art Gallery Toi o Tāmaki sends its greetings. We send them to Mount Aetna, the Seven Hills of Rome. To the Doge of Venice, also, greetings.

Look upon us now:

Here we are, emissaries arrived at the Tesa dell'Isolotto, Arsenale, in the city once one of the great powers of the Western world.

The kuia rangatira, Rhana Devenport, and a travelling ope of the Auckland City Art Gallery Toi o Tāmaki have escorted Lisa Reihana here to join the pantheon of international contemporary artists at the most important art event in the world, the Venice Biennale.

We lift our arms and offer you, halcyon citadel, the haka.

Great kāinga, your winged lion flew triumphant above all the capitals of Europa. You anchor at the navel of your universe just as we, in our island citadel of Tahiti, anchored at the aquamarine, gold and azure pito of ours. We pay tribute to St Theodore and the bestiary which attend him: the crocodile, phoenix, cuttlefish, octopus, swan, basilisk, hawk, centaur, dragon, cat and golden salamander. They are manaia, marakihau and taniwha of equal power to ours.

Acknowledge our mana.

FROM *IN PURSUIT OF Venus [infected]* we have come newly garbed as *Emissaries*.

We exist now in new entrées, bringing the wallpaper up to date, and thus we spiral out of the Space–Time continuum. We are still beautiful, hypnotic, haunting, floating but we are garbed in our own ihi, mana and wehi. We have divested ourselves of our original

Greco-Roman physicality and the draping of antique clothing. We stand before you as *us*.

Man, what a relief.

And we *tax* the imagination now with new photographic portraits to include Aboriginal First Australians to complete the work.

We dance before them. We challenge them.

This is our apotheosis.

From being originally a site of European imagination we have become a site of Māori, Pacific and Aboriginal strength. The ten-year-long video project has reached its final triumphant realisation in an immersive multi-channel panoramic video of seductive ravishing beauty and cinematic complexity. So does it reflect the renascence of the Pacific as all our peoples reclaim our mana, our sovereignty.

Thus do our original narratives continue to twist through Time to you, all of you who live in the Pacific today.

Our āhua, which had been made whakaāhua, has become real again.

We have become *you*. And you are *us*.

You are our grandchildren.

Mokopuna.

E MOKOPUNA, THIS IS our karakia:

Continue to reimagine our colonial legacies.

Reclaim the past in the pursuit of our present.

Engage in interrogating our diverse histories and make your speculations on the present and future.

You are all, truly, bronzed inheritors of the Pacific bounty. You are the generation of the future and you have a dual role. Not only are you inheritors of Pacific history, you must also be protectors. What must you protect? Why, the Pacific's future.

Therefore, become kaitiaki.

YOU FACE DAUNTING CHALLENGES.

The Pacific covers one third of our globe, e mokopuna, and it has become a contested space. The larger nations of the world enforce their militarist technologies, nuclear and other, deliberately coercing the smaller island groups to submit to their experimentation; already some of our citizens suffer from nuclear radiation and the ongoing genetic effects of radiation poisoning. Distant water fishing nations operate illegally, with unregulated fishing bringing all our marine ecosystems to the point of collapse; one day, we may not hear whalesong. Accidental oil spillages create sinister scenarios for our seas and waters. Seabed mining threatens to bring with it a new colonising of the sea; when that happens, the mineral infrastructure will be stripped of its goodness and the sea may die.

And, of course, climate change has brought radical alterations to our environment. The shelves of Antarctica, the well at the bottom of the world, are already breaking up and we are losing one of our world's greatest resources of water.

Sea levels are rising. How many islands will sink below the ocean?

E MOKOPUNA, ALL OF you come from a long line of ancestors stretching back to Rangiatea or to Europa or America to whom you are accountable and with whom you have an implicit contract.

That contract is to protect the ocean which is now your home, to protect your history and whakapapa, so that you may go onward and secure the future for your children's children.

We hand to you all the tokotoko, the ceremonial stick of
leadership
Go forth! Navigate a future for all of us. Haumi ē, hui ē, tāiki ē!
Let it be done.
Kia hora te marino,
May the calm be widespread,
Kia whakapapa pounamu te moana

May the ocean glisten as greenstone
Kia tere te karohirohi i mua i tou huarahi
And may the shimmer of sunlight
ever dance across your pathway.

Notes:

1 A hee mai te tua: after an ancient Arioi chant.

2 *Forêts paisibles*: after Jean-Philippe Rameau, *Les Indes Galantes,* 1736.

3 E ngā iwi ē: after Tommy Taurima, *E te iwi ē,* contemporary Māori action song.

4 *Et mon coeur s'est levé*: after Ernest Chausson, *Poème de L'amour et de la mer,* 1890 (translated by Christopher Goldsack).

5 *A te, sovrana augusta*: after Claudio Monteverdi, *L'Incoronazione di Poppea,* 1642.

Works consulted:

Witi Ihimaera: speech, opening of the exhibition in Auckland, 2 May 2015.

Lisa Reihana: *in Pursuit of Venus [infected]*, Auckland Art Gallery Toi o Tāmaki, 2015.

SEPIA
From *Aristotle's Lantern*

MARY ROKONADRAVU

TIME HAS PLACED A shock of white on her scalp. Loosened her breasts from the vice-grips of her chest. Hung bags under her eyes. For three days I have not called her Atteh. Aunt. Do you need more tea, Shanti? She gnaws her nails to the quick, the stubs of her fingers a raw lamb-chop red. It is a new habit. Her teeth are foreign to it. Her chews run her nails crooked across flesh. She takes almonds to bed. She grinds her teeth in sleep. Where do you keep soap, Shanti? Have we run out of baking powder, Shanti? Her eyes do not register offence.

Webs of cataracts trap most of the light in her world. She lights the lamps in the afternoons. Wrings her hands at the kitchen door. Look at these chickens, she says. Scratching the ground at night. It's not proper. The world is about to end soon.

How Christian her words have become. Pati had forever remained Hindu. I am about to end soon, she said for twenty-five years. Then collapsed under a banyan tree opposite Hop Kee's. The waft of fresh loaves deluged by ambulance sirens. She was dropped into a hole the Levuka Prison convicts dug. Leaving me alone on the thin, shaky crust of this world.

Pati's words were of constant erasure. We lived in Navua, she told Abraham Lazarus. On a rice farm. We made more money from ducks than rice. My son died in a rice field. Buckling under a burst appendix. I hated the floods there. Just a light sprinkle of rain and you walk knee-deep in the fields. I'm grateful for the dry streets here. Fresh fish at the market. Enough sun for the clothes. A clear telephone line. Water in the taps. Good bread.

In my eye, a thousand coconut palms in a single glance. A gaggle of geese dying of a mysterious illness. Jungle roosters the colour of fire. A half-cabin wood boat floating on a field of seagrass. Saltwater snakes the colour of zebras. My tongue limp with questions.

My words have yet to arrive. Sometimes I have imagined them to be foreign little people with foreign little hats, waiting at the door of my mouth, begging to be spoken. I need words the crisp of pears, the cold of raspberry ices, to speak my forgetting. I cannot do it in Tamil, or Fijian, or English. These are the languages of my remembering. Their words sit warm and familiar in my palate. Keen to roll out voices.

I returned on the *Amiable Josephine*, arrived at Siwati's jetty in the dark, then 45 dollars for a Yamaha engine to take me to Liverpool. I made the return voyage alone. Captain Edward L. Stockwell's pupils fastened on a star. The islands of Lomaiviti a scatter of fluffed-up pillows. The sea a black sheet stretched tight and tucked under the horizon. Eighteen hours against a wind blowing knots. Not a wink of sleep alighting on my eye in that chug.

The man who sent us away is in a pine coffin. In a lemon grove on a quiet hill. Parrots nest there. Their fledglings dark skinny. Hours from sprouting electric-blue tail feathers. Crowfoot grass will cover the oblong patch. Lichen will cover the black stone at its head. The remains of sadness from his knuckles will seep to become the tartness of lemons. I could plant a banyan tree on the oblong patch. Let its massive roots drill holes into his skull, its root hairs accumulate and knot in his sockets to confuse his eyes in death. I am straight-backed at the mahogany table, slicing boiled sweet potatoes into cubes. The man who ruptured his appendix in a rice field finally breathes no more.

His sister lives on. She wants me to leave. I feel her unease in the ferment of her hesitations. In the pauses between mouthfuls of fried bananas. In the hard tinkle of a teaspoon in a teacup. In the fast melt of butter on a hot scone. In the sweet curl of a sugary lemon rind fished from the marmalade jar. She seeks to delight me into forgetting. She tells me it is not safe to walk alone in the bay. To not bathe in the ocean at dusk. She lies quiet in her lightless bedroom. A checked cotton quilt tangled at her feet. Under her kapok pillow, in page three of a 25-year-old *Fiji Times*, a fistful of marigold seeds for the lemon grove. She stands outside my bedroom door at night. Curls her fingers to knock. Lets them fall to her side. I picture her like that. Changing her mind. Slipping away with her words.

She cannot tell whether I remember. I will not say that in those days I lay awake in the dark. Watching Ratio slip into my bedroom to take my sea urchins for a walk. Listening to his footfalls join hers in the long verandah. The crush of her skirt. The pop of buttons. The stealth of a quiet zipper. Her hair spilling like a black waterfall from the kitchen table. Afterward, she buttons a wool cardigan and drops me into Pati's marigolds for my trudge to the cows. I grab a fistful of hair while sinking into marigolds. Smell apples on my fingers while looking at blue threads in the udders of cows. Horatio's hands gentle on the flanks of a Friesian. I smell apples on cows.

She does not know that for twenty-five years I laboured to forget. A cat the colour of Japanese oranges. Three sea urchins. Frothing milk in a tin bucket. The tale of two Gilbertese who sucked the juice of raw fish eyes and almost ate a newborn.

But my pen moves far ahead here. Way, way ahead. Because that was never the beginning. The start of things seeps from a pond dyed olive with dying water plants. It is not safe to go there. You need shoes with grip. Sensible shoes. Wet green stones lace the pond. It is possible to slip. To feel the hem of your skirt stir a cloud of mud from the pond floor. To see a frog leg kick above your right eye. To die with a water hyacinth stem lodged in your throat. They are as long and soft as garden snakes. As slippery too. It is safer to skirt the stones and sit on a grassy knoll. To watch for a trickle from a rising lip. The beginning is not one. The beginning is many.

I separate the beginnings by tongue. The start is when I have not spoken English. I have not heard the sounds. The beginning is when everyone on Makare says *Opal*. My only English word for five years. I am two when I first speak it. It does not qualify as English though. For when it is spoken it does not mean a sky-coloured stone that may hang from one's ear or rest on one's breast. When it is spoken it means the white man who won a gold prize for Sea Island cotton in Paris. It means the white man who broke his violin against a Solomon labourer's back for not holding music at an ample angle to a moonlit window. It means the white man who bought Pati's mother and Pati's father for eleven pounds and two shillings on a stormy pier in Levuka.

The egg and sleek-tailed seed that are to sculpt me are still apart. Couched and alive in this man and this woman. Deaf to the whipping foam under the pier. The hundreds who with them contribute to the curve of my flared nose are scattered in the south tip of India. Some diving for oysters. Some beating coconut husks into coir. Some drying peppers on a sun-scorched ground. Countless drowned in the Palk Strait.

Opal is God in my family tree. He nails long mirrors to coconut trees and eleven San Cristobal men knife each other. He sends Pati's mother to fetch a rifle and Pati is born. He sends Pati to look for a red hen and Shanti is conceived in a guava patch. He sends Pati to fetch a gravy boat and Horatio is created roughly against a broom cupboard. He lifts his gun and eight San Cristobal men drop their pants.

This is years after the rain on the pier in Levuka has dried. Pati's mother is dead. Pati does not know how to soothe cracks in her right nipple. Pati's father watches for rain clouds so Opal's copra does not sprout mould. Shanti cries until dawn. The day Opal puts a shotgun to his own mouth, Pati's father rides a horse for the first time. Opal walks the verandah with a loaded rifle when I am born. The pigeons he intends to shoot hatch their young under the eaves. But even this is far ahead into the tale.

There is another trickle from the green pond. Another happening revealed. It is possible to see a pearl diver fill his chest with air. Sinking into the depths between Madras and Ceylon. It is possible to see the glint of a knife between his teeth. Pried oysters in a string bag around his neck. The measured let of air from his cavernous nostrils. A kick for the rise to the surface. From day's break to day's end. At night, in the captain's pouch, pried pearls from pried oysters. Rice and salted fish under the moon. I marvel at the length and breadth of his breath. Marvel at the sharks that do not shred him. For in him rests a seed that is to halfway across the world become a fraction of me.

There is a woman also. She works in a mustard field. She will fold a banana-leaf parcel of mint chutney and rice. Add a mango pickle. She will give her cat a sardine. She will walk away from her husband's house. Her five daughters will be playing under a tamarind tree. She will meet the pearl diver at the bazaar. Between the cardamom seller and the pounder of turmeric. As planned, he will have robbed the Portuguese merchant who presses orchids and paints filigrees on heron eggs for nieces in Lisbon. With his eyes, he will frisk her cotton sari for bulges and lumps. Bring nothing with you, he will have whispered a week earlier. Bring nothing with you.

When they sail for Fiji, he will have eighteen white pearls the size of gecko eggs nestling in his rectum. They will strain excrement all the way across the Indian and the Pacific. They will not find a single pearl. The pearl diver will believe the pearls swam up and lodged themselves in his spine. Years later, he will insist his family strain their faeces by his deathbed for chances he passed them on in the seeds that grew them. Pati will tell me these things after she tucks smooth coral in the spaces between my big and second toes. She will tell me these things on Makare, at home, in a dead cotton planter's house, where she still speaks the truth.

This is way before she and I are rowed to the *Catherine May*. Before she walks into Edna Stanhope's kitchen and pulls out a gilt-framed portrait of Queen Victoria from under her skirt. The she-monarch sits bejewelled in sepia in the kitchen Tom Partridge built for Eberhard Karl Muller, Esquire. She holds the world in her hand. She sits between a mound of peeled taro and a cleaned pig's head on the porcelain kitchen sink. She feels pig-blood dropping off the chopping board, inching toward her royal carpet. The she-monarch does not look amused.

Pati wipes a vermilion dot from the she-monarch's forehead and proceeds to wail. I stare at the pig's teeth. I smell ginger. In my head, I slide my fingers along the silken down of its ears. Edna Stanhope bolts the kitchen door. Runs water into a kettle. I will squeeze the juice of half a kumquat into your dhal soup, Pati says to Edna Stanhope in Fijian. I will scrub your kettle with steel wool. Pati and I have chugged the Lomaiviti waters for exactly twelve days. The number of eggs in a blue cardboard tray. One less than the ill-omened thirteen. I let a cinnamon cookie soften against the roof of my mouth. Queen Victoria is the colour of egg yolk. Her royal carpets and the round world she holds in her hand are egg yolky too. I am seven years and twelve days old. This is the last day my name is Dewane Nair.

FACEBOOK
REDUX

NIC
LOW

MICHAEL SHOWERS AND SHAVES, then snaps a few self-portraits in the mirror. He lifts his phone high, tilts his head and pouts. *Click.*

He's a substantial man, with ruddy jowls, a small, pleasant mouth and cheerful eyes. At sixty-seven his head is a gleaming dome. Most of his male friends are doing that ridiculous neo-comb-over thing: a few last pathetic hairs brushed down over one eye, emo-style. He prefers total baldness — chemo-style. *Click.*

Michael stands back and takes a coy full-length shot, half-turned to hide his cock. He's in good shape these days. He used to have to watch his weight, with all the dinner parties and long lunches, the breakfasts of salmon hollandaise eaten in bed with Margot. *Click.*

His smile is captured mid-collapse. He deletes the shot. These days he mostly steams a few vegetables. He really has lost a lot of weight. He thinks of it as a small, positive side-effect of his wife's death.

IN THE KITCHEN THERE'S no sign of Sophie. It's half seven, and she has classes at eight. While Michael waits for coffee, morning images from friends blink up in his retina overlay. He's intrigued, and mildly annoyed, that the system keeps choosing sequences from women his age. There's more from a Bernadette. Her dyed black hair is glossy and tousled, and she holds one hand across her breasts. She looks wonderful at seventy, though the effect hasn't been the same since her mastectomy.

These days, he thinks, we're all a bit maimed.

There's a knock at the front door. Michael blinks. Odd — nothing registers in his overlay. He hears Sophie's bedroom door open, then the shower. He carries his coffee down the hall and opens the door.

He can't see anyone there; just a jogger across the street, kids ambling off to school, two gaunt shanty-dwellers having their morning bucket-bath on the footpath. Each of them appears in his overlay as a faint swarm of data, visible, available.

Morning!

It's Sophie's friend Eloise, standing on the bottom step. He stares. She's wearing an emerald headscarf that surrounds her face like a cowl. Is Sophie ready? she asks.

Surprise makes Michael abrupt. No, he says. What's with the scarf?

I've taken the vow. Sophie didn't tell you?

No. Come in.

He stands aside and sips his coffee to hide his distaste. He sees more kids wearing the scarves every day. To him, their cloistered faces look like they have something to hide. He wonders what her parents think. It was one of the few things he and Margot had argued about. He agreed with the papers: privacy led to unrest. Nonsense, Margot had said. They've got every right to disappear.

So you're just — disconnected? Michael asks Eloise at the kitchen table. He finds it unnerving, talking to someone with zero data presence. It's like sitting across from a small black hole.

We can still access everything, Eloise says. We're just not sending anything out.

And what brought this on? Is it a religious thing?

No, it was History of Privacy. You should hear the lectures.

People used to just give it up, for free. There was this thing called Facebook, where you—

Facebook. The word comes to him out of a dream.

You mean the website? he says.

Yeah. Have you heard of it?

I used to use it.

Eloise sits forward with a kind of excited repulsion. Really? You were one of them? So did you just give away your — everything?

That's a personal question, he says. He's joking, but she blushes anyway.

Sophie bangs into the kitchen, hair damp from the shower. Are you hassling Lou?

She's hassling me, Michael says. About my time on Facebook.

Sophie looks dismayed. You were on *Facebook*?

I was. Your mother, too. We . . .

Michael trails off. He's suddenly wide awake. He had completely forgotten: Margot was on Facebook.

Two years on, his natural memory of Margot is as frayed as old rope. He has a wealth of digital captures, but he's exhausting them too. There was one he used to loop, of Margot singing in the shower. He went about his day with the hiss of water and her sweet, off-key high notes ghosting down the hall. Over time it had become background noise: a radio left on in another room.

But Margot was on Facebook. She would have posted videos and photos, decades ago. It's like he's discovered a forgotten chamber of his mind. The thought is exquisite.

Michael realises Sophie has asked him a question. Sorry? he says.

You do own your data, don't you?

Absolutely not, he says. Everything's out in the open. Why lock yourself away?

Eloise smiles at Sophie. PP, she murmurs. Sophie looks embarrassed.

What's that? Michael says.

You're PP, Eloise says. Post Privacy. We call it Publicly Promiscuous.
He laughs. The wall clock chimes eight.

Merde, Sophie says. We're late.

They're halfway down the hall when the thought strikes him.

Hey, girls, he calls. If I'm PP, what are you?

PPP, Eloise says. She flashes a small gold ring over her shoulder.
Post Post Privacy. We're saving our data for someone special.

MICHAEL HAS NO APPOINTMENTS in the morning. He calls his
secretary. With your permission, he says, I'd like to engage in a little
senile leisure time.

He sits at the desk in his study and thinks about Facebook. His
retina and cortex are hardwired, like everyone else on his income,
and the results come up in his overlay. There's a wealth of historical
analysis and old news items. Then he finds what he's looking for. In
a grey zone of southern Russia's deep web, buried in the sediment
of an archival server, is a copy of the Facebook data. A fossilised
social network.

He's not expecting much when his system attempts to connect,
but a moment later, there it is: the homepage. It's surprisingly
familiar, right down to the precise shade of blue. At the top is a
link: *Recover your profile.*

Not bloody likely, he says aloud. It's been forty-odd years since he
was on here. But he follows the link, skips the privacy statement and
fills in a form. His overlay shows ancient code routines waking from
sleep on the host server. Obsolete analytics grasping at new filaments
of data. There's another procedure too, shimmering just below the
intelligible horizon, that his own system does not recognise.

While he waits, Michael crosses to the window. Another main-
land family is building a tarpaulin shanty on the nature strip. The
young father waves; he's not too badly burned. Michael would
have been about that age when social media took over his life.
Twenty-three? Twenty-three and full of love, and full of himself.

He remembers Margot teasing him about wasting his life self-promoting on Facebook. So much so that he deleted the thing . . . Shit. They both did. It felt like a spiritual breakthrough at the time. They deleted their profiles, went to Thailand, got married, got on with their lives, and now she's dead.

Michael leaves the room. He's in the kitchen, trying to summon enthusiasm for work, when it blinks up in his overlay. *Profile reactivated. Welcome back.*

Michael's profile picture stares at him across the decades. His head is shaved, cocked to one side, lit with an insolent grin. It's eerily similar to the picture he snapped this morning. He runs a hand over the wearied flesh of his face. What skin — what a pup!

Beneath his photo is a random-seeming list of things he'd claimed to like. Cormac McCarthy. Someone called Seamus Heaney. *The Wire*. It seems so archaic — that you would tell a system what you liked, rather than trusting it to tell you. There is an invitation to something called a Permablitzkrieg, and one to a Climate Action Rally, back when they thought they stood a chance. He didn't want to think about it then, and he doesn't want to think about it now. He scrolls down.

His heart lurches. There's something from Margot.

It's a photo, too small to properly make out, but she looks to be pulling a face. Below, it says: *This content has been removed by the user.*

Michael clicks through to her profile. That same line is repeated, time and again. He clicks through messages, events and comments, drumming his fingers in irritation. The same fuzzy avatar makes the same taunting declaration. He begins to feel like Margot removed herself just to spite him.

He scrolls through photos, hoping to glimpse her in other people's shots, and before long he's distracted. Long-dead friends beam their vitality through the years. They're in and out of clubs, crammed in the back of cars, camped among valleys of tangled bush. He lingers over a shot of himself diving off the side of a boat at dawn. He is reaching down through the bright and liquid air, an instant before the surface is broken. He can't find a single person crying, or angry. Everyone seems brand new.

Halfway down the page, Michael finds a sequence from a woman with an expressive, intelligent mouth and smoky eyes. It only takes a second to remember who she is.

June-Mee! he says aloud.

Michael clicks through to her profile. There's a new entry at the top of the page, exactly the same as his own.

Profile reactivated. Welcome back.

Michael gradually becomes conscious of a rattling from the air conditioner on the wall. He stretches over and gives it a whack that makes his hand sting. He can't believe he's found someone else on the network.

He loses an hour trawling through old photos. She's lazing on a beach in Greece, hiking in the Yellow Mountains out past Shanghai. The images stir something in him. Curiosity, and nostalgia.

They'd met at a party. He'd walked into the crowded bathroom and she was reclined in the bathtub, laughing among the ice and beer, reciting some speech she was studying. Their eyes had met.

Free at last, she cried. Free at last!

On a whim, he sends her a message.

Later, he is propped in bed reading, still carefully on his own side of the bed, when a reply comes through.

Michael, what a surprise! Are you well?

He gives a wriggle of delight and kicks off the sheets. The chatter in his overlay is immediate and positive: eighty-eight per cent of his friends are intrigued. Sophie, studying in her room, sends a *WTF.* She turns up her music, and it seeps through their shared wall.

MICHAEL STARTS EACH DAY searching for traces of Margot, and ends up chatting with June-Mee. He finds her quick and funny. It seems she's the only other living person on Facebook, and he likes the irony: from a billion people down to two. She hints at a simple, affluent life. They both live in the leafy suburbs of Tasmania's Greater Melbourne, and he gets the feeling she's recently divorced. He doesn't ask for details. He mentions Margot's death and Sophie's presence, in passing. They talk as if they're still twenty-one.

June-Mee recalls a night when they took ecstasy in his bedroom, then cried with laughter through a dinner with scandalised friends. She had a boyfriend who lived interstate. He recalls the sexual tension of their nights out, a gaunt stranger in a club asking if they were lovers. They weren't — but if he's honest, he wishes they had been.

MICHAEL WAKES A FEW days later with a good restlessness in him. He catches Sophie at the breakfast table. Her hair is getting long, and she's taken to wearing it pulled across her face. She ignores his questions about school. She won't be drawn on the History of Privacy. Finally, he stops trying to sidle up to the conversation.

I discovered an old friend on Facebook, he says.

I know, she says. It's creepy. Don't you think it's weird how she just found you?

I found her. June-Mee is a lovely woman. She makes me feel—

Just don't, she says. It's private.

It's not private, he says, amused. I want to share it with you.

Sophie stares into her coffee mug. You've already shared it with anyone who'll listen.

It's worth sharing.

You think brushing your teeth is worth sharing. Eloise says you make your life cheap by just giving it away.

That's ridiculous, he says. What does it cost you to be open about your life?

It costs — something.

Rubbish. It costs to be private. Fine if you're loaded like Eloise's parents. They can afford to let her turn off her—

He catches himself.

Sorry, he says. Look, do you think this is disrespectful to your mother? To have dinner with June-Mee?

Maybe, Sophie says. Yes. And to you. Couldn't you just do something for yourself?

You mean, do something private? he says.

Yes.

Turn everything off?

Would you?

Well, Michael says. I guess.

MICHAEL SHOWERS AND SHAVES, and slips into his old dinner jacket. He lifts his phone. *Click.*

The jacket is far too big. More than that, it reminds him overwhelmingly of Margot. The feeling of buttoning it up in the mirror, the tang of aftershave, the anticipation of good food: he is dragged so sharply back to their shared life that he is forced to leave the jacket on the bed.

On the way into town his overlay briefly takes over the driving. The doors lock and the car cuts west, through the vast shadowed slums of New Brunswick to a boutique overlooking the city's western firebreak. The staff have a simple but expensive blazer picked out when he arrives, precisely to his taste and cut. He knows he doesn't need to check it in the mirror.

Outside the restaurant Michael stops to turn off his phone. It's a symbolic act, because most of the hardware is carried under his skin. But he mutes it all, and one by one the chattering streams of data that have accompanied his adult life fade away. His overlay is gone. The streetscape and the passing crowds flatten into surface and light.

There is a man beside the restaurant door, hand out, begging. The faint swarm of data around him winks out, and Michael finds himself staring at the man's face: two bloodshot blue eyes, without lids, gazing back at him from a mask of flesh so badly burned it wears no recognisable human expression. Air sucks and blows from two small holes. Michael fumbles a note into the man's hand, and pushes open the restaurant door.

There are two women sitting by themselves, both with their backs to him. As he approaches the first, he sees straight away that she is too young. Her hair spills long and dark down her back. He passes the table and fixes his attention on the next woman, sitting alone with a book and a glass of wine. His pulse quickens.

A voice calls to him from behind. Michael?

He turns. It is June-Mee sitting at the first table, after all. She rises in greeting and a shock goes through him. She is twenty-three or twenty-four. Thirty at most. Her skin, beneath the lightest dusting of makeup, is flawless. When she smiles, he sees the same strong teeth that bit his bottom lip when they kissed on his doorstep, that one and only time.

Michael, she says again. It's me. June-Mee.

Hello, he says. You look — lovely.

She searches his face, affectionate and curious. How are you? she says.

I'm good, he says. I'm great. And you?

They dive into conversation. Michael talks and laughs, but he's on autopilot. His mind grasps for clarification. He turns to his overlay and the datasphere and his friends, but they're gone. Soup comes, he eats it, the waiter removes the bowls. He tastes none of it. Is this her daughter? Has she had surgery? It can't be her, and yet it is, unmistakably, the woman he knew some forty years ago. The way she talks, excited and playful and sharp, and her ready laugh, even the way her elbows tuck to her sides when she walks to the bathroom: it's her.

When she returns he fumbles towards the question. So, what have you been doing for the last forty years? How come you look so — good?

You remember I went to France? June-Mee says. I started a

fashion label, skirts made from vintage men's suits. Like the one I wore to . . .

The conversation swings back to the past and they're off again, reminiscing and laughing. The next time he tries, she turns the conversation to him. He finds himself talking about Sophie.

She insisted I meet you in private, he says. I was going to turn up in a green headscarf.

He talks about his fears, his hopes. It floods out of him. June-Mee asks perceptive questions, and follows his answers, even when he wanders into the dull maze of his professional life. She laughs at his tales of how he avoided the horrors of the '30s, and reaches across to cuff him when he grows cheeky with wine. He avoids talking about Margot.

After the dessert plates are cleared, and the two of them are standing out in the street, wrapped in their coats with the taste of coffee on their lips, while Michael is summoning the courage to ask her, once and for all, what's going on, he realises he can't handle this by himself.

He's desperate for clarification. But it's more than that: he has to share this feeling. It means nothing if he keeps it to himself. A maimed beggar cannot be his only witness. Michael switches everything on, and as the real world comes swarming in, June-Mee kisses him on the mouth.

Goodbye, Michael.

Her lips are soft and yet firm. As different from his own clumsy lips as can be. He can't believe how good it feels. It's been decades since he's had a kiss like this. June-Mee doesn't have to reach up like Margot did. She simply presses into him, her body lithe against the swell of his belly. As the moment — its image, its imprint, its strange reality — flows outwards through the datasphere, he feels joy blooming inside him, ruthless and swift.

Goodbye, Michael.

She bites his bottom lip, and is gone.

MICHAEL SHOWERS, LONG AND vague beneath the scalding water. He doesn't bother shaving. A hangover beats on his skull. He raises his phone and snaps off the morning's shots. *Click.*

It's all there in his face. Guilt hangs in the shadows under his eyes. But there's more: the conflicted intimation of a smile. He needs coffee. Sophie will already be at school. He makes his way slowly down the hall in just his towel.

Sophie is waiting for him in the kitchen. The first thing he sees is the emerald headscarf pulled low over her brow. He scans her data in a panic. Total blackout. She looks furious.

Are you going to pay? she says.

What? What are you doing wearing—

You haven't even looked at it, have you? Here.

She blinks, and his overlay fills with Cyrillic characters. He dimly remembers seeing it when he woke.

What's that?

That's the bill, she says.

For what?

You went on a date with a twenty-four-year-old woman from your past, she says.

I don't understand, he says.

No shit. Did she know exactly what you liked?

Michael nods.

Did she have an unbelievable memory?

I guess.

She was pretty much perfect, right?

Well—

And you don't own your own data?

I told you, Michael says. Of course not.

See, that's how they do it! After you shared your disgusting little moment with the world, I looked it up.

Michael sits at the table. The towel rides up around his thighs. He tugs it down. You're going to have to spell this out, he says.

You've let them log everything you've ever done, she says. They know what you've watched and bought and clicked. They even know what porn you like — they use that too. It's in the fine print when you reactivate your Facebook account. You're liable for premium services.

She's not real? he says feebly.

She's a *premium service*, dad. They used to send emails from Natalya in Russia, wanting to meet for a good time. This is just the latest version of the scam. Wait, what's the woman's name again?

June-Mee, he says. June-Mee Kim.

Sophie blinks, accessing her own data. Hang on, she says. Yes, here. Did you even check outside Facebook? Jesus, she died twenty-five years ago.

She sees his expression, and the righteousness fades from her face.

Dad, she says. I know you've been lonely. But so do they; they know how you're feeling better than you do. It's total manipulation.

They've built this — woman — out of everything I've ever said and done?

Pretty much.

Michael is quiet for a long time. And you've taken the vow? he says.

Sophie places her hand on the table, and he sees the small gold ring. She tilts her chin defiantly. Yes, she says. Eloise came over last night.

He tries her data stream one more time. Nothing. His own daughter is beyond him now, encrypted to hell. He thinks of Margot — their life, their shared history — and how she is beyond him too.

Then he thinks of June-Mee, and the taste of her lips, and how June-Mee is right here.

Michael looks at the bill. He can afford it.

WHALE BONE CITY

From *Praiseworthy*

ALEXIS WRIGHT

1

Since he, sometimes been called big time, named Aboriginal Sovereignty, young hope dream and all of that emotionally charged asset language of the modern day, say he bin finished up one time for all times from the Cause Man Steel family like rubbish dump sort of dead discarded thing on the face of the earth by disappearing into the mighty ancestral shark infested ocean around here. And what say this same boy — one time, caused his people to gulp in the throat, feel badness in the head for a long time *for where so yo go*, by really abbreviating his life span into a complete zero, millivolt, flashgun millisecond, micro scale thing — full stop milliwatt, and whereforth, his eighteen years ended up like some shit piece of holy smoke in the imagination, from him being snuffed out into nothing by suicide wishing for himself. To get to the point, as dead as a doormat somewhere in that old spirit dust haze hanging around over the sea, and you know what this kind of thing resulted in? Well! Fool people, it resulted in a proper dead fella the people henceforth say for the northern provincial Aboriginal township of Praiseworthy — right! And in the shock of the terribleness, there was no scrap of fuss.

Nothing made out of some personal genius thinking by Aboriginal Sovereignty. Well! So all right, maybe he thought God got room for him in his camp in Heaven.

Say though bro, it was not like that, and that dust lady must have taken him . . .

And he became precipitation, like virga . . .

Might be true! Might be anything. Anyhow he killed himself dead.

What happened to the lungs of country then?

Was the country's law heralding a message to we from out of the windpipe of storms blowing up over the sea?

Useless brains, what was the cultural comfort in losing Aboriginal Sovereignty then?

Marginalized spacey people can you say something about this?

Go on. Have your pick of stories from any empty wide-open field in the brain. There were what? What you say? Empty tin cans. Heinz baked bean tins and all that rolling in the ocean. Could have been something like that.

Search around in the dirt. Scrape sand aside with your foot. See if you can find Aboriginal Sovereignty's killer there. Someone might have murdered him.

He took a journey to the Dreamtime.

Look! Did any useless brain cells fall out over the matter?

Why fuss? Huh!

2
No fuss.

All the surly dust, widespread in the atmosphere, had lain over
the country of perfect youth suicide nights in Praiseworthy.
The haze rises in the afternoons, settling the dust far out to sea,
while beneath, treading lightly through the water, another child
of Praiseworthy was leaving the butterfly country, that enormous
brownish-red, white and olive winged tipped Lepidoptera eternally
unfolding its wings for flight. Aboriginal Sovereignty had left, like
those other little children who had already gone over previous weeks
and months. Elders frowned, were pretty overwhelmed, turned
their backs, and were left philosophising in whisperings and what
have you, about how children were being led astray from culture,
influenced by the white hand that was a local esoteric shorthand
word meaning government help.

So! What happened to Aboriginal Sovereignty? You could ask the
question in a thousand different ways. All the why. Why? Why?
Was anything gone for all times? Nah! They don't talk to me.
Immemorial sacredness violated? *Nope!* Heaven collapsed? Didn't
see it myself personally. What ends, ends. Who knows? Was there
a sharp dip in the humanness, of the modern sine qua non in this
region of the anthropocene?

The answer? Blanket no. Couldn't see it myself.

Of course you could not see it. Fools! Nothing was blessed! No
promises fulfilled. There were no mass performances of trumpets
blaring *te deums*, or drums rolling Handel's royal fireworks with
wind ensemble, nor anything else magnifying any significance of

God's will filling up the void where these children walked.

3

Ancestral stories abound this country, they move, dance around in their own time.

And out of this normality, air and salt was blown this way and that across the wings of pure white birds flying like angels above heaving seas, out there in the direction of where Aboriginal Sovereignty went. Further out, amidst the tempest of cyclones gnashing each other, fish fly out from the ocean. All was astir out there.

It is a wild morning wind that flies around Praiseworthy from these seas. At this time of year the atmospheric shimmering rustled and bustled with so many stories of colliding twigs, dead leaves, cigarette butts of the dreamers, pieces of puppy dog-ripped-up foam mattresses, a thousand winds-shredded plastic shopping bags, tin cans rolling, loose corrugated sheets of iron carrying some clinging ants on a magic ride through space, and the red dust — all dancing across the horizon. This was a tiring wind. You would have turned your back to it, put speed into your step to be out of it, hastened in doors, shut the house, windows closed, because this wind spreads more than rubbish. It's a lonely sound that gets in your ears, and it makes you feel isolated in its din of whistling, banging and slamming houses, rattling windows, making the roof creak, as its gale force brings the ancestors home. Again! Yes again, the old people of the past crowding around outside, swishing around the streets looking for something, trying to rip the town apart with things flying everywhere, while looking around at what in the hell was going on inside the heads of these people of Praiseworthy.

You even start to hear small startling voices get real smart in your ear by dropping a line here, or sinking a line there from old country stories — fishing in the sea of Praiseworthy modernity, trying to hook ancient linage in the people of this place. They remind you of what it feels like trawling for fish hiding in flotillas composed of millions of empty beer cans, but nothing would reach the suffocating stories reminding you about me and me about you, while somewhere else in the wind-consumed town, an old granny cloth moth lady who lies in her bed on the ceiling while pretending to die makes her presence felt in the little wind gusts that blow into her house through cracks under the door, in tiny holes in the ceiling, for that morning's plebiscite, to see which children were gone.

Then, all of sudden dead set in the deafening blustering and buffeting howls through town, everybody saw her ring-eyed wings staring down from the ceiling, and heard her voice screeching as though it was coming though tinny loud speakers that could be heard above the sound of the TV blasting in the lounge room. The old woman who was nearly dead, was going on and on about this recent suicide. Why wasn't the moth quiet? Why was she repeating for what seemed like hours, *Why he been gotta die that Aboriginal Sovereignty?* But he was not even frightened of dying you heard yourself speaking back to her, sort of trying to reassure the fallen moth who was dying on a foam mattress on the floor, and you say that she should only be thinking about herself now and not be getting bothered about the worry of politics or anything else about the humanity of Praiseworthy, even though you feel pretty silly realising that you were only speaking to yourself.

But there was nothing on Earth that was going to becalm her, not now with the rush of Praiseworthy people spilling over one another to get inside her mind, and telling the old moth, *Shh! Up! Be quiet.* But the wind kept pulling at her voice, and it was frightening. You could hear her all around town frightening people, especially the children screaming at the moth's ring-eyed wings staring at them.

We done it. All blaming themselves for Aboriginal Sovereignty committing suicide. *Why he been picked out?* And straight from a clear conscience the truth you say like other Praiseworthy people would say, *We did not know anything about it.*

Must of been something, that old woman amplifier broadcast crossed hundreds of kilometres of sand and bush to reach every bit of humanity she could find. *Must have been dragging him out to sea.* Her hostile big mouth made you ashamed. *You real gammon type people you are. And you thought, what is she blaming me for, I had nothing to do with Aboriginal Sovereignty's death.*

This wind makes you feel like you are going mad, and you start to wonder why that old cloak moth woman was cruel, and why was she blaming the whole town for something when that boy had made up his own mind, and had decided to take his own life for his own reasons, and which were his own private business. You like the lightness of being an individual like white people, to be in a personal space where you can no longer feel the totality of culture, or feel any of its depth of connectedness, or of being reminded how you are related to the total country, but it was no good thinking you wanted to be something else while some old lady who should have been busy dying herself was still screaming at you to listen to all this business about suicides which you know nothing about anyway because it was not related to the new individual you — it was the government's job you say, so you feel like telling her to go to hell. She goes on and says: *You got to tell me why this fella got to die. Why he got to been give up his life for, and you gammon people.* She was so full of scorn, and reckoned, *You been think about heaven been open up and grab Aboriginal Sovereignty for God? You are wrong about that one, and I cannot hear you people crying for that boy, or children crying. Something wrong about this place.* Then after hours of this howling, the wind always stops. Dead too, the moth. Conscience, when it finally comes, it goes.

Ah! Tell them country, how the little children were not frightened of dying, of killing themselves. Were they frightened of the world, or the future, everybody wants to know? Kids dream. Dreaming so much. Dreams were becoming legends now. Beneath all of that, gone to some place where they got to go, and becoming spirit children. When country speaks, memory is telling you the story of what happens, its voice low, putting all those sad stories back into your thoughts.

4

Something small enough did happen though in the middle of the night when Aboriginal Sovereignty had walked off into the sea, and finally in one last deep breath — puff, he disappeared into the dust. None of this would have happened if only the country was being read properly, like those old people read country across the land, yes, yes, yes, this and that, like reading a newspaper. The map of culture slept, while country's censer wafted its whirling red haze further out to sea, even while spinning back on itself time and again that night, to see if Aboriginal Sovereignty was still coming through the glassy flat sea.

All through the noisy night, hordes of insects screamed in the spear grass and monsoon thickets that flecked the coast, and if you looked from the reddened skies to what caused the squawking among the seagulls — thousands storming around in the darkness above the sea, and listened to where all those mongrel community dogs were racing around through the haze and barking uncontrollably at each other, you might have heard the news about Aboriginal Sovereignty killing himself. But wait a minute! The people of Praiseworthy were asleep after having been rocked into their nightly slumber while thinking that they were saints, and you probably would have believed this too, if you were hearing hours of hymn singers carrying on, on a nightly basis. Everyone had a choir singing in their head, in their backyard, and from others singing to God out in the streets until their voices grew too weary to continue, and then, the singing went on anywhere else where a loudspeaker could be plugged into an electricity socket, and a power board connected to leads for amplifiers and microphones. Well! Everyone woke up in fright and you could hear the yelling from a bunch of angry and not very pleasant people cursing the dogs, *What! What! What is all this? Stop! Stop your friggen barking, you useless pack of worthless other people's mongrel dogs.*

If you had heard the miracle of a volley like that, then you might have been a single fish jumping over the top of the Arafura Sea's silver trevally leaping in a ray of moonlight squeezing through a crack of dust clouds. Seen how the fish were leaping in and out of the sea to see up into the back beach of red darkness, able to peer further into a patch of mangroves, and seen snake's heads on the tip of each wing of the *Attacus wardi* floating through the air as giant brownish Atlas moths were awakened to the enormity of time about two in the morning, which was their hour anyhow, and were now fluttering about clumsily and slowly, and being blown about in breezy pockets among parched dust-coated vines in the sleeping monsoonal jungle. If you had been the trevally that jumped highest into that night before splashing back into the sea, you would have seen that there was one human being in this preoccupied, hymn-singing town of Praiseworthy who had actually witnessed the suicidal departure of Aboriginal Sovereignty.

5

Way over in the shadows of mangrove copses where the mud was full of scurrying hermit crabs, and mangrove butterflies, the blue tigers, orange wanderers, black and white crows, copper jewels that had been flittering about for blossoms all day and were now with wings folded asleep in their stories high up on the branches or trunks of trees, or had flown off to congregate on the walls of damp caves, and an odd sacred old saltwater crocodile hundreds of years old was murmuring, asleep in the mud — its spirit more invisible than visible; if you looked just in that one spot where the spirit of place might lie, before the whole suicide thing happened that might have been preventable, you might have noticed the witness. Shh! Look now, where those brownish-looking emperor moths were flying about over there. *Syntherata melvilla,* laying their eggs on a mangrove leaf. There he goes. Some fat little Ninja assassin kid sneaking about among the mangroves, who was silly enough to think he was so far out there from reality that he was invisible. The kid thought he was an assassin, who believed he had terminator powers to make people die. Why did he not wish to be an Australian politician, or a senator for the Praiseworthy's vision, instead of being a killer?

Thought was one thing, but if you saw what was happening in the mangroves you would have noticed other things about the assassinator. But then, who knows? You would have had to feel the power of country, know how you can get tugged into the stories it was creating, but hey! Who except the traditional owner wanted to weep from knowing that much about country now? Maybe you would rather just wish to deal with the facts, not about how the Ninja was hidden in the old skeletal city of bones, a sacred place spreading across the mangrove landscape that had originated from a pod of whales — maybe hundreds of them, who knows — who had once beached and died among the mangroves. That was one hell of a long time ago, of a time when these whales had been tossed across the world like peanuts by mighty waves in seemingly never-ending multiple cyclonic episodes. These big mammals were rendered powerless, and had been thrown around the skies like sticks. Then one big and frightening lightning ancestor grabbed them, and decided by whacking these creatures onto the sands of Praiseworthy to die amidst a congestion of plenty of other stories for this part of the world, she would give this big story about caring for the country to this mob, who in return, raised this assassin.

This gift by the ancestor was why Praiseworthy people believed that the whale bone city was the biggest incident that happened on Earth to them, and that this ancient architectural marvel of all times, built in the creation period of time immemorial, was continually being moulded by the ancestors working with the waves crashing into the mangroves to cover and uncover the whales' grave. There was a great consensus in Praiseworthy's thinking people about how to create a tourist venture of the sacred skeleton city, to tell the other billions of people on the planet about this beautiful thing, of those ancestors still caring for the bone architecture with sand and rain blown in gale-force winds throughout summer to continually polish the bleached bones of thousands of years ago, which was long before the Australian government ever came along with its big dreams and ideas for creating a place like Praiseworthy as an asylum, a madhouse for the traditional owners, and ripping the life out of the country.

Who knows what those old spirit whales thought about becoming a tourist venture, who you might have thought were rolling about in their graves about having an assassin sheltering in their bones. Well! This was where you would have just seen in the stillness of the haze through flickering moonlight, among thick dark clouds of mosquitos and sandflies hordes, the outline of that fat little boy. The Ninja killer was busily slapping himself all over his body while trying to kill as many of the unrelenting insects as he could that were either stinging him or sucking out his blood. It was as if even these insects were trying to get this kid off the beach, teaching him properly for once, as though they were his actual parents, to get home to bed.

Yes for sure he was the witness, Aboriginal Sovereignty Steel's younger brother Tomahawk — A1 student with more brains than he knew what to do with, who was now prowling around with the stray pussycats hunting for crabs. The boy too clean for the feel of ancestral mud to be on his skin, covered in mosquito bites and sandfly welts from head to toe. If anyone had known that he had secretly code-named himself Ninja Assassin — the smartest kid in the school who was never a spot of trouble — no way, no one would have believed it. But trouble itself had sprouted all over the place, like grass seed after rain, in that kid loitering around in the dark.

Tomahawk continued to stare out to sea, would not leave his desire. Could not. The boy was obsessed, and acting as though he had lost all control over himself, but Tomahawk knew that he had to be deadly sure this time, had to stand quite still, to remain undetected, to keep willing his brother to keep going. Why are you taking your time? You have to do it. You have to. Goodness, that Tomahawk keep wishing his brother to go further out to sea just so that his own dreams would become a reality, but the boy dared not think ahead of himself, not yet. He needed to resist the sensation of anticipating, of how he foresaw a phenomenal personal chain of events unfolding to reach its dizzy heights in his own lifetime. No! He had to resist thinking about his own ambitious plan to leave Praiseworthy for good — something that could not happen soon enough, and now for heaven's sake, it was taking Aboriginal Sovereignty hours to end his life.

So this was the truth of the anxiety that was befuddling in this little boy's brain, of what lurked in the shadows. Tears of outrage gathered and rolled down Tomahawk's tortured face, now fed up from having to endure the indignity and injustice of standing around all night on behalf of his brother, and because of Aboriginal Sovereignty taking his time — again, he was being covered by a rouge-coloured cloud of insects hording and massing for fresh child flesh.

Tomahawk became convinced that his brother was being totally selfish by taking his time to die, and making him wait. He watched his older brother moving even more slowly in the shallow water of a high tide that stretched forever over the mudflats, and Tomahawk was convinced that even he could move faster than that. Yet it was true. Aboriginal Sovereignty was taking his time — perhaps weighing up the future, and he was not just disappearing in a puff like he should so as not to be continually inconveniencing everyone, but was instead, just inching himself further and deeper out to sea like a moron, Tomahawk thought, and again as far as he was concerned, it felt just like a number of other aborted attempts of Aboriginal Sovereignty trying to take his own life where he had been forced to stand around like this, wasting time to keep watch, and now it was happening all over again, this having to just stand there willing him on, having to over and over watch him die.

The little scholar boy fretted that he still needed to do his homework for the night and the way things were going, he was never going to get it done, so he was growing even more impatient even though everything seemed to be going according to plan, though unbearably slow, and while being constantly bitten. Then what became worse, after finally reconciling himself to how he could rush off his homework in the morning before school anyhow because it was nothing — he was that smart — Tomahawk's own journey started to sneakily flick through his mind. These were the images of seeing himself living like a rich prince mind you in his new home — the flashiest place in Australia, Parliament House. Best place to live. Yes, he was fully convinced that he was going to live in the big white building in Canberra, as soon as he was adopted by the government, whom he already knew from watching the news and current affairs on the TV, going on and on for months about how Aboriginal people did not know how to care for their children, that only the government loved Aboriginal children, and wanted to save them from their paedophiliac parents.

Tomahawk had to pinch himself from daydreaming about his plans for future happiness, when the Minister for Aboriginal Affairs would become his mother. But Tomahawk had to stop thinking about the golden-hair mother swivelling around in her office chair in the sky, because Aboriginal Sovereignty's askew suicide was beginning to overwhelm his own belief in himself. There was too much happening, and he started questioning himself — if the government would really adopt him; whether his older brother's self-doubt was being projected onto him; and he spiralled downhill.

What if, Tomahawk reasoned, his power to make things happen would not come true, and what if he had missed a step in the synchronisation of his plan? What if Aboriginal Sovereignty was just trying to stuff everything up for him and was playing games with him? And Tomahawk started itching to just run off from the mosquitoes and sandflies, get down to the beach and rush straight through the sea, and get the whole suicide thing over and done with by drowning Aboriginal Sovereignty himself. He knew he could do it, even though he was half the size of his older brother. But nothing like the facts of who was physically stronger mattered right then, because Tomahawk believed in the strength of his own mind even if it felt a bit dubious at the moment, and his confidence was starting to feel a bit wobbly. Yet why worry? Tomahawk knew enough about the sea in his eight years of life to know that he could run through the water after his brother and, if it occurred to him, even try to save him if he wanted to, but wait a minute, he realised this was not what a proper Ninja with a self-preservation plan would do.

He knew precisely what a real assassin would do, because he had already studied a lot of internet games about how to knock out an enemy on his brand new Apple Mac Pro, and his new MacBook Air, and his new iPad, all gifts from the government for being a spy boy, which was not what his teachers had told him about winning a donated prize for his essays about the failings of Aboriginal parents. They said he was lying when he said he really did have a hotline to the Minister of Aboriginal Affairs so that he could tell her about paedophiles the government was looking for to prove Aboriginal children were not safe with their parents. Well! It was the apparent truth of the moment screaming across the country's TVs. Tomahawk pointed to his brother's dark form, now waist-deep in water, and thought the future would be easier if someone could just go *click, click, click* on a newer iPad to speed up reality, and then kind of go *pow!* And see streaks of laser lightning spitting across the water like on the computer screen.

Why couldn't the dream just go as planned for once without Aboriginal Sovereignty stuffing everything up, Tomahawk kept repeating to himself, *for God's sake stop mucking around and hurry up you gutless idiot, take the journey, you know you are going to die anyway if you go to jail, because the government is after you for being one of those paedophile people they are going to stop to save us children. That was why the police arrested you for marrying your underage girlfriend. Just get it over and done with. Go out to her. It is pretty easy. I have seen even little kids get it over and done with faster than you.* It was true. Tomahawk had seen the other children from Praiseworthy commit suicide too, from where he was standing now. Well! For sure people thought it was a trend, but Tomahawk always stayed and watched them walk out to sea, and he had never left until he was sure they were not coming back.

The slap, slap of squatting insects continued, and Tomahawk felt the dampness covering his skin, running down his stomach and back, from his shoulders and down his arms, and his legs, from the mixture of his own perspiration and blood from mosquitoes and sandflies that he had now killed. This was the sticky blood on his hands. Yet he remained unmovable. No, he would not be stolen from this place he argued. He was going to become the richest child in the country, as rich as the government when he was living at Parliament House. Grieve for his brother? Sorrow for losing Aboriginal Sovereignty? Not Ninja. He was Aboriginal Ninja. Neat. Complete. The teachers warned about untidiness, of something only half done, and said he was the model of the class.

So Tomahawk! Not a muscle stirred, and he knew he would have to be even tidier in the future, where he never had to watch something like this for hours again, and now at the threshold, he no longer felt mosquito proboscis puncturing his skin and feasting on his blood, because a real assassin would not feel pain. A proper Ninja kid held the line, not like lesser kids who gave up and believed they were going on a journey to paradise and everything would be okay, when it was never going to be okay for him. Tomahawk had made a game out of their belief of leaving to be in the Dreamtime, to see who was weaker, to see who gave up.

AB-SO HAD TO DIE. Could anyone risk this ordeal again, of creating more lies to make his brother want to kill himself for nothing. Not really. Killing your brother was not an easy thing to do, not with everything that had to go according to plan for Tomahawk's own life to begin.

Yuki Kihara, *Roman Catholic Church, Apia*, 2013

NAFANUA UNLEASHES

From *The Adventures of Vela*

ALBERT WENDT

(1)   **Introduction**
At evening   after the last pilgrims had melted
into the diving light   Auva'a and I would
sit in the Temple and let Her filter
through the sieves of our selves
Sometimes the old priest interpreted Her messages
Other times She whispered to me as She flowed

So much to record   She said   my centuries as atua
never to be plain girl   wife
or to know the kiss of decay
Tired of Atuahood but too corrupt to relinquish
It   arguing indispensibility
and anarchy if I abdicated

What have the centuries of power meant?
To you   Vela   flatterer most flatulent
I'll unleash my flatulence that we

may savour all the ingredients
in the stench — badwind locked in
can blast open the mana-gluttonous moa

(2)   **Origins**
I was the prophesied tail of a genealogy:
my father   Saveasi'uleo   was my uncle
Tilafaiga   my mother   was his brother's daughter
No incest taboos for atua   only mortals
must keep blood apart or degenerate insanely
(Guilt has not been my inheritance)

My father was part-beast   (eel to
be exact)   but no mark of it on me
though in my childhood my scrupulous mother
inspected me for its signs and barred
me from playing with animals
(She should have peered inside me!)

Sonless my father ignored my gender and fed me
on the 'manly' arts of war
He was an exacting feeder
My teachers   all men   he selected each day
from the new swarms of the Dead
(His kingdom   don't forget   was Pulotu)

And in Pulotu there was no shortage
of any variety of man   and all   being spirit
could be killed and rekilled to rise again —
whole armies   tribes   nations   worlds
of them to do with as I pleased
in the killing arts

The Way of the Weapons is the ideal life
preached by father   so blind Tiʻalele
of Fualuga taught me the swift
way of the tiʻa   Masters Fau and Ogafau
trained me in the philosophy of spear and club
until I was the deadliest weapon of the Way

(but without penis   that weapon that defines a man)
practising my civilised craft from sunrise
to orgiastic sunset on the recycled Dead
the ideal warrior with balls
and liver   as they say   utterly true
to the enlightened Way

(Is it that we feed rapaciously on death
when we can't love or know the gift of birth?
In being immortal value life less —
forgetting others die?   Is Atuahood
the supreme vice that corrupts supremely
because we can't self-destruct?)

From champion warrior I understudied
the Commanders of Pulotu's Armies —
victims of their own wars now devising
strategies to reverse those defeats
With endless supplies of spirits we refought
those battles and won them (never mind the cost!)

From the Commanders I learned the details
of every battle   anywhere   ever fought
To prove my ultimate worth they organised
new wars and led the enemy against me
Every time I won they reduced my forces

but I outmanoeuvred them all

because I had a sight they didn't have:
I could read the future and their rooted
dread of death that stopped them from
risking all in the deadly game
Until even my father dared not challenge me
'You're the ideal atua and warrior now'   he said

Poor Dad he couldn't live down
his tail of the beast though he was
the most feared atua of all
By ideal man he'd turned me into
a soulless beast   an atua without gender
or guilt   an eater of darkness like him

And for a ravenous stretch of my youth
I devoured the darkness like the tanifa
that fearless gob of eternal hunger
(Auva'a will give you the official gospels
on which my worship is now rooted —
soul-food-for-the-swooning-believer!)

(3)   **Conquest and Queendom**
Auva'a said   You mustn't believe everything She says
She loves to exaggerate — who doesn't —
goodness and immortality can be boring
and we   in decrepit old age   confess to
imagined misspent youths riddled with juicy
sins and guilt!   She wasn't the monster

She professes   How could She have been?   She was
the most civilised knower of the future and

every crevice of human behaviour   My ancestors
— wise and sensitive taulaaitu — wouldn't
have established our religion around Her if
She'd been the raging beast She's professing!

Remember taulaaitu make atua through
dedicated proselytising and conquest
My aiga made Her who She is now
(She's never refuted that!)   Without us
She would've remained mere local atua
insignificant   destined to fade into oblivion

Admittedly She loved to kill and conquer
(and was superb at it) but of what use
is that without informed stateswomanship
and cunning — use others to war with
and you receive the glory and honour.
That art She learned from the first Auva'a

True She arrived at Taliifiti Falealupo from
Pulotu with Her four magic clubs
and it was an anonymous couple   Matuna
and Matuna   who found Her asleep and helped Her
recruit Her army of aitu She disguised
as dragonflies   se   and lelefua

True She slaughtered our enemies
who'd enslaved our district but She
didn't know the full potential of Her mana
and accidentally killed Matuna and Matuna
and loyal squads of Her own forces
It was Auva'a Leo'o   my illustrious

ancestor who   after She appointed High Taulaaitu
taught Her She was both Destroyer
and Creator — to conquer sanely so as
to have subjects (even Her followers) to rule over
It was he who   through clever publicity
spread Her fame throughout Samoa

and made every hungry ali'i warrior
scurry to Her for help to grow into power
First the local warlords came with
their petty quarrels and ambitions
Auva'a offered Her protection at the price
of becoming Her subjects

Those who refused Tupa'i   General of Her
Armies   whipped into submission while She
enjoyed the watching   (It was unbecoming
of an atua to participate in
petty quarrels   they persuaded Her
So she marvelled at Her general's undeniable ability)

Then the ali'i of ali'i   the Tama'aiga
came and beseeched Her   through Her taulaaitu
to reconquer titles they'd lost to tougher rivals
(including brothers):   Auva'a and Tupa'i agreed but at
the price of the Tafa'ifa   our country's highest titles
being returned and bestowed on Nafanua

Tuiatua   a miserable braggart   begged Her help
and Tupa'i and our armies fought
his enemies and gave him the victory
Tuia'ana Tamaalelagi asked the same
and was victorious (with Tupa'i's aid)

So did Malietoa and Aiga Tunumafono

Until Nafanua (and our religion) held all
the Tafa'ifa Titles — the first in history
Now there was unity in Her person
and wars were outlawed (as Auva'a
and Tupa'i had planned for)
She was hailed Diviner and Uniter

(4) **Ailalolagi**
To Her subjects   Her devoted taulaaitu
projected a noble   gracious and loving atua
with all the undeniable virtues of a Mother
But behind that front we had to cover up
Her enormous misdeeds to do with
Her appetites and preferences

In Her youth — the first hundred years or so — She
was   to put it crudely   insatiable even
by the licentious standards of atua   (atua
of course are excused from incest   animalism
sadism   masochism   fetishism and all vices
we consider inhumanly deviant)

Toothless hypocrite!   Nafanua interjected
unexpectedly   You schizoid guilt-ridden
humans want us atua to play out all
your secret yearnings and cravings!
True   replied Auva'a   but you   my dear
overindulged our sins and vices

Really wallowed in your meaty excesses
You were an Eater-of-the-World like

Mulialofa   Vela's special friend   and we've
never blamed you — after all your
brainless eel-tailed father raised you totally
as male with not one but four hefty clubs

Consequently   You were four times
more greedy than other atua
four times more a World-Eater than Mulialofa
chasing four times more women than even
Tuialamu of the Endless Penis (but alas
you're cockless!)

Up you with a spear   She swore   I'm going to bed   (Auva'a chuckled as She
rushed into the inner chamber)   You're
just a dirty oldman wormripe for
death and hooked on shit-stench
pissings-on   obscene whispers and raw dog testicles

You love having your excesses recorded!   he called
Poor shrivelled taulaaitu   you can't raise
it any more   She replied   Power   most demanding of
aphrodisiacs   has buggered you to slackness
Ungrateful girl   he muttered   tears like dew
drops in his cataractous eyes

You must never fall in love with Her   he warned me
His was a hopeless love as deep as
his aiga's history and Her taulaaitu
before him   with power as their fatal aphrodisiac
And without Her   they would lose that
They could not exist without each other

NOTES

TUSIATA AVIA is a poet, children's book writer and performer of Samoan/ Palagi descent. Her latest books include *Wild Dogs Under My Skirt* (VUP, 2004), *Bloodclot* (VUP, 2009) and *Fale Aitu/Spirit House* (VUP, 2016), longlisted for the Ockham New Zealand Book Awards 2016. In 2016 she also released *The New Adventures of Nafanua* (IPSI). She has written a radio drama, *You Say Hawaii* (2002), and her acclaimed solo show 'Wild Dogs Under My Skirt' premiered at the 2002 Dunedin Festival. She has also published two books for children: *Mele and the FoFo* and *The Song* (Learning Media, 2002). Tusiata has an MA from the International Institute of Modern Letters, Victoria University of Wellington. She received the MacMillan Brown Centre for Pacific Studies Artist in Residency 2005, the Fulbright-Creative New Zealand Pacific Writer's Residency 2005, the Ursula Bethell Trust Writer in Residency 2010 and the Janet Frame Literary Trust Award 2013. She teaches Creative Writing at the Manukau Institute of Technology.

SERIE BARFORD was born in Aotearoa New Zealand to a migrant German-Samoan mother and a Palagi father. She lives in West Auckland and has published three collections of poetry, as well as *Entangled Islands* (Anahera Press, 2015), a collection that combines poetry with prose. Serie's work has appeared in many literary journals and anthologies, in print and online, most recently in *Essential New Zealand Poems, Whispers and Vanities: Samoan Indigenous Knowledge and Religion, Cordite Poetry Review, Jacket2, Best New Zealand Poems*, the *School Journal* and the Phantom Poetry Project. Serie performs poetry at public events, and was awarded the Seresin Landfall Residency in 2011. Some of Serie's short stories for children and adults have played on Radio New Zealand.

CASSANDRA BARNETT is a writer and art theorist raised in Auckland but with roots in the Waikato (Raukawa ki Wharepūhunga). She writes ficto-poetry, ficto-criticism and scholarly essays about contemporary art from Aotearoa and beyond, exploring questions of indigeneity, belonging, whakapapa, diaspora, cultural multiplicity and the endless flux of identity. In keeping with this flux, Cassandra's work weaves together Māori cosmologies, fictive practices, and molecular, rhizomatic and decolonising Western philosophies. She holds an MA (Continental Philosophy, Warwick) and a PhD (Media, Film and Television, Auckland), and is a Lecturer in the School of Art at Massey University, Wellington.

Note:

'Pitter Patter, Papatūānuku: Monologues of 3 Gods', a kind of ficto-criticism, is written from the points of view of three gods speaking from Pukeonaki (Mount Taranaki), Te Tai-o-Rēhua (Tasman Sea), Taranaki, Ohakea (Manawatu), and Te Tau Ihu-o-Te Waka, Wairau, Waiautoa, Manirauhea and Okuku (South Island). Barnett writes:

I was compelled, after viewing artist Alex Monteith's perception-splintering multi-channel video artworks (which feature roving sheep, surfers, jeeps, planes and helicopters), to ask the question: How might Papatūānuku, Tangaroa, Ranginui *look back* and *speak back* to us contemporary humans/posthumans through these ancient environments? If they ground us, what grounds them?

To voice such Māori atua tapu *in English* smacked of neo-colonialism. Seeking some form of restriction to shift the power relations in the text, I have adopted a literary constraint of using only the (approximate) consonant sounds of te reo Māori. The only Māori words included are proper nouns (and bird names!). The constraint is loose, the approximation of an impossibility: to speak Māori without speaking Māori, to hear Papatūānuku's voice in an English medium.

I have pieced my narrative together where possible from Ngāti Raukawa stories of the ancient environments of the text: stories of Tainui waka; a Raukawa (as well as Ngāi Tahu) telling of the creation story, in which Papatūānuku is intimate with Tangaroa the sea before she (more famously) couples with Ranginui to produce the atua of te taiao, the natural world, and ultimately all the generations down to us – a love triangle to mirror that of Taranaki, Tongariro and Pīhanga.

Because relationships are never simple binaries, multiple perspectives have been taken, points of view coiled within points of view – artist, protagonists, landscapes, viewers, writer, Māori, Pākehā, Raukawa, Taranaki, tupuna and atua. It is so impossible for me to inhabit one single position or whakapapa . . . beyond the bare fact that we are all descended from Papatūānuku.

GINA COLE is of Fijian, Scottish and Welsh descent. She lives in Tāmaki Makaurau, Aotearoa. She is a lawyer and writer of short fiction and poetry. Her story 'Glacier' was published in *takahē 70* in 2010 and her creative non-fiction piece 'Na Noqu Bubu' was published in *SPAN 64: Kaumatua, Journal of the South Pacific Association for Commonwealth Language and Literary Studies* in 2011. In 2013 she completed a Masters of Creative Writing at the University of Auckland. She won the Alternative Bindings Auckland Pride Festival creative writing competition in 2014 for her poem 'Airport Aubade', which was published in *Express* magazine. In 2015 her story 'Black Ice' was published in *JAAM 33*. Her debut book of short stories, *Black Ice Matter*, was published in September 2016 with Huia Publishers.

SIA FIGIEL is a tandem parent to two sons. She is also a diabetes advocate, an artist, a performance-poet and a writer. Sia's poetry won the 1994 Polynesian Literary Competition. Her first novel, *where we once belonged*, won the 1997 Commonwealth Writers' Prize for fiction for the South East Asia/South Pacific Region. She has also written three other novels, *The Girl in the Moon Circle*, *They Who Do Not Grieve* and *Freelove*, and a collection of prose-poetry, *To a Young Artist in Contemplation*. Sia's work has been translated into Spanish, Danish, German, Portuguese, Catalan, French and Turkish. She has held writers' residencies in Europe, the United States and the Pacific, and has travelled extensively as a representative of Samoan and Pacific literature. Sia has performed her work at universities, high schools, halfway houses, bars, women's prisons, streets, theatres and under trees.

DAVID GEARY is from the Taranaki iwi and Ngāti Pākehā. His writing for theatre has earned both the Bruce Mason and Adam Foundation awards.

His plays include *Lovelock's Dream Run*, *Pack of Girls* and *The Learner's Stand*. David also works in film and television, and currently teaches at Capilano University in Vancouver, Canada, in the documentary and indigenous film programs. Geary's book of interlinked short stories, *A Man of the People*, was published by Victoria University Press in 2003. His short story 'Gary Manawatu [1964-2008]: Death of a Fence-post Modernist' appears in *The Penguin Book of Contemporary New Zealand Short Stories* (2009). An occasional poet, David writes haiku on Twitter: @gearsgeary.

ANAHERA GILDEA (Ngāti Raukawa-ki-te-Tonga, Ngāi-Te-Rangi, Ngāti Toa Rangatira, Te Āti Awa, Kāi Tahu) is a writer and 'artivist'. Her first book *Poroporoākī: Weaving the Via Dolorosa* was published by Seraph Press in 2016. She holds a Bachelor of Arts in Art Theory, Graduate Diplomas in Psychology, Teaching and Performing Arts, and a Masters Degree in Creative Writing from Victoria University. Her poems and short stories have been published in a variety of journals and she has won both the *takahē* Short Story Competition and the Huia Best Novel Extract in English. She has worked as a drama teacher, a visual artist, a florist, a stilt walker and a journalist. She currently lives and works in Wellington with her partner and 12-year-old son, and is completing her first novel.

DÉWÉ GORODÉ is a leading political and literary figure of Kanaky/ New Caledonia. The longest standing government minister since 1999 (holding numerous portfolios, including Culture and Women's Affairs), this ex-teacher of French language and literature published several collections of poetry and short stories before writing *L'épave*, the first Kanak novel. From an early age, Déwé's father inspired a highly eclectic love of literature: 'My father used to tell us stories in Paicî: jèmââ or oral histories; fairytales like *Tom Thumb* and stories from Victor Hugo's *Les Misérables*.' Among the first contingent of Kanak university students, Déwé began to write seriously as an undergraduate literature student in post-May 1968 France. Entering politics on her return as a founding member of Kanak independence party Palika, she was jailed several times for her activism. Untiring in her deep attachment to her cultural roots yet always open to otherness, Gorodé's life and literary oeuvre speak of her country's journey towards emancipation.

PATRICIA GRACE is one of New Zealand's most prominent and celebrated Māori fiction authors and a figurehead of modern New Zealand literature. She garnered initial acclaim in the 1970s with her collection of short stories entitled *Waiariki* (1975) — the first published book by a Māori woman in New Zealand. She has published six novels and seven short story collections, as well as a number of books for children and a work of non-fiction. She won the New Zealand Book Award for Fiction for *Potiki* in 1987, and was longlisted for the Man Booker Prize in 2001 with *Dogside Story*, which also won the 2001 Kiriyama Pacific Rim Fiction Prize. Her children's story *The Kuia and the Spider* won the New Zealand Picture Book of the Year in 1982. Her latest novel, *Chappy*, was a finalist in the Ockham New Zealand Awards for fiction and winner of Ngā Kupu Ora Award 2016. Patricia received the Prime Minister's Award for Literary Achievement in 2006 and was the recipient of the Neustadt International Prize for Literature, sponsored by the University of Oklahoma, in 2008. She was a recipient of the Distinguished Companion of the New Zealand Order of Merit (DCNZM) in 2007. She has received Honorary Doctorates for Literature from Victoria University of Wellington in 1989 and the World Indigenous Nations University in 2016.

SHANE HANSEN is an artist, designer, husband and Dad. Born in New Zealand in the 1970s, he is of Māori (Tainui, Ngāti Mahanga, Ngāti Hine), Chinese, Danish and Scottish descent. Shane is the benefactor of a life lived long and well in Aotearoa. His work uses bold colours, Māori motifs, optimism and clarity inspired by his multi-cultural heritage and pop-art, strong graphics and profound appreciation of the landscapes that surround him. He was selected to create Māori designs for Rugby World Cup 2011 and commissioned to create a bike to be presented to HRH Prince George in 2014. His work includes projects for BMW NZ, Air New Zealand, Te Wānanga o Aotearoa and the New Zealand Olympic Committee. shanehansen.co.nz

Note: 'I Am Mixed Media' represents Shane's mixed heritage. The gold 'good fortune' symbols are a 'mixed heritage' symbol combining Chinese & Māori elements.

JIONE HAVEA is a Methodist pastor from Tonga who is Research Fellow in Religious Studies at Trinity Methodist Theological College (Aotearoa New Zealand), and Honorary Research Fellow with the Public and Contextual Theology Research Centre of Charles Sturt University (Australia) and with the University of Divinity (Australia). Havea is the author of *Elusions of Control: Biblical Law on the Words Of Women* (Society of Biblical Literature) and editor of, among others, *Out of Place: Doing Theology on the Crosscultural Brink* (Routledge), *Indigenous Australia and the Unfinished Business of Theology* (Palgrave), *Postcolonial Voices from Downunder: Indigenous matters, Confronting readings* (Pickwick, forthcoming) and *Sea of Readings: The Bible in the South Pacific* (SBL, forthcoming).

WITI IHIMAERA was the first Māori to publish both a book of short stories and a novel, and since then he has published many notable novels and collections of short stories; he began a parallel career as an anthologist in 1984 and *Black Marks on the White Page* is the eleventh initiated by him to chart the continuing development of Māori and Pasifika writing in New Zealand and the Pacific. Ihimaera's last book of fiction was *White Lies* (2013), which won the Ngā Kupu Ora Aotearoa Māori Book Award for Fiction, and his memoir *Māori Boy* (2015) won the non-fiction category of the Ockham New Zealand Book Awards. His next book, *Sleeps Standing*, about the Battle of Orakau, will be published in 2017. Four of his works have been adapted to the screen: *Whale Rider*, *Nights in the Gardens of Spain*, *White Lies* and *Bulibasha*. He has recently revised his play *All Our Sons* for production in Auckland in 2018 and is currently working on *Native Son*, the second volume of his memoir.

ROBERT JAHNKE (Ngāi Taharora, Te Whānau a Iritekura, Te Whānau a Rakairoa o Ngāti Porou) was born in Waipiro Bay and lives in Palmerston North. His practice straddles design, illustration, animation and sculpture. His work possesses a creative vitality, often with a political edge, and focuses on differing perceptions of reality according to historical facts and circumstance. Jahnke's practice questions and challenges the established Eurocentric narration of New Zealand's history, promoting and championing the Māori experience within his considered contemporary metaphor. A leading Māori academic and a pioneer in contemporary Māori art, Jahnke is the former Head of the School of Māori Art, Knowledge and Education at Massey University in Palmerston North. He is currently the Professor of Māori Visual Arts for the Toioho ki Apiti Māori Visual Arts programme in Whiti o Rehua, the School of Art. Major public works include window and door designs for the Museum of New Zealand Te Papa Tongarewa, wall reliefs for the High Court Building and Bowen House in Wellington; a pou for the ASB Waterfront Theatre in Auckland and a stainless feather arch for the Square in Palmerston North.

KELLY JOSEPH (Ngāti Maniapoto) is a writer and artist currently living in Westland with her family. She has previously had stories published in *Huia Short Stories 5*, *7*, *8* and *10* and in *Hue* and *Cry*, *takahē* and *JAAM*, and broadcast on National Radio. She has been runner-up twice in the Best Short Story in English section of the Pikihuia Awards. In 2009 Kelly spent eight weeks on Kapiti Island as the Tau mai e Kapiti Māori Writer in Residence. She has an MA in creative writing from Victoria University and a Master of Fine Arts from the Rhode Island School of

Design, USA. *White Elephant* is dedicated to her daughters, Opal and Ursula, small muses who love stories and see magic everywhere.

BRYAN KAMAOLI KUWADA is a Hawaiian-language translator and PhD candidate in English at the University of Hawaiʻi at Mānoa, focusing on translation theory. He is also part of the blogging collective Ke Kaʻupu Hehi ʻAle, which writes about Hawaiian and Pacific issues at hehiale. wordpress.com.

YUKI KIHARA (Shigeyuki Kihara) is of Samoan and Japanese descent. Her photograph, entitled 'Roman Catholic Church, Apia' (2015), is part of a photographic series entitled 'Where do we come from? What are we? Where are we going?' (2015) featuring the artist in the guise of a 'Salome' — a Samoan woman dressed in a Victorian mourning dress — viewing various historical sites of her postcolonial homeland in the Island of Upolu, Independent State of Samoa. In this photograph, we see Salome reflecting upon the history of Christianity first introduced to Samoa by LMS missionaries in 1836. The photograph was taken in January 2015 when the construction of the church was halted due to the lack of financial support. The construction site, however, exposes the interior structures of the church which resonates with Renaissance and byzantine architecture often not associated with the picturesque image of 'paradise' in Samoa.

NIC LOW is a writer of European and Ngāi Tahu descent with a love of satire and apocalypse. His first book is *Arms Race* (Text Publishing, 2014), a collection of mischievous, polemical stories about technology and tino rangatiratanga, Facebook and drone warfare, that was shortlisted for the Queensland Literary Awards and the Readings Prize, and was a *Listener* and *Australian Book Review* book of the year. He's just spent 18 months in the Southern Alps researching his second book, a history and philosophy of Māori in the mountains told through walking journeys.

TINA MAKERETI writes essays, novels and short fiction. 'Black Milk', inspired by Fiona Pardington's 'A Beautiful Hesitation' exhibition, won the 2016 Commonwealth Short Story Prize for the Pacific Region. Her novel *Where the Rēkohu Bone Sings* (Vintage, 2014) was longlisted for the Dublin Literary Award 2016 and won the 2014 Ngā Kupu Ora Aotearoa Māori Book Award for Fiction, also won by her short story collection, *Once Upon a Time in Aotearoa* (Huia Publishers) in 2011. In 2009 she was the recipient of the Royal Society of New Zealand Manhire Prize for Creative Science Writing (non-fiction), and in the same year received the Pikihuia Award for Best Short Story Written in English. Makereti teaches creative writing at Massey University. She is of Ngāti Tūwharetoa, Te Āti Awa, Ngāti Rangatahi, Pākehā, and according to family stories, Moriori descent. www.tinamakereti.com

SELINA TUSITALA MARSH is a Pasifika poet-scholar of Samoan, Tuvaluan, English and French descent. As the 2016 Commonwealth Poet, Selina recently returned from Westminster Abbey where she performed her commissioned poem 'Unity' for the Queen. Her award-winning poetry collection *Fast Talking PI* (Auckland University Press, 2009) won the New Zealand Book Jesse Mackay Best First Book Award and its titular poem took on cult status in schools and community groups. Her second poetry collection, *Dark Sparring*, was published in 2013 (Auckland University Press) to critical acclaim. Selina is a Senior Lecturer in the English Department at the University of Auckland and teaches New Zealand and Pacific Literature, convenes its largest undergraduate course in Creative Writing, and supervises poets in the Masters of Creative Writing Programme. The sequence of poems in this anthology will appear in her third collection, *Tightrope*, in 2017.

COURTNEY SINA MEREDITH is a poet, playwright, fiction writer and musician. Her play *Rushing Dolls* (2010) won Best Female Playwright and Runner-Up for Best Play in the Adam New Zealand Play Awards and was published by Playmarket in 2012. She launched her first book of poetry, *Brown Girls in Bright Red Lipstick* (Beatnik, 2012), at the 2012 Frankfurt Book Fair, and has since published a short story collection, *Tail of the Taniwha* (Beatnik, 2016) to critical acclaim. She was selected for the prestigious International Writing Program Fall Residency at the University of Iowa and she was also the Writer in Residence for the Island Institute in Sitka, Alaska, in 2016.

KELLY ANA MOREY (Ngāti Kurī, Te Rarawa, Te Aupōuri) is an award-winning writer of both fiction and non-fiction. Morey writes: 'The stories I have told for cash, my friends . . . 'Poor Man's Orange' is an old story; it was highly commended in the Open Category of the now sadly defunct BNZ Katherine Mansfield Short Story Awards in 2012 and has been published . . . somewhere . . . maybe even twice. The orchard, the juicing shed and the eclipse are true, the rest just grew up around it.'

PAULA MORRIS (Ngāti Wai, Ngāti Whātua) is the author of the story collection *Forbidden Cities* (2008); the essay 'On Coming Home' (2015); and seven novels, including *Rangatira* (Penguin, 2011), fiction winner at both the 2012 New Zealand Post Book Awards and Ngā Kupu Ora Māori Book Awards. She teaches creative writing at the University of Auckland, and is the founder of the Academy of New Zealand Literature (www.anzliterature.com).

ANYA NGAWHARE lives in the Bay of Plenty, where she spends most of her time chasing after her three-year-old niece and her growing collection of costly, oddball animals. When she was nineteen, her strong-willed parents forced her to pursue her dream of becoming an author. She completed her NZIBS Creative Writing Diploma one day before finding out she had been selected for the 2012 Te Papa Tupu Programme, and in 2015 she received a highly commended award in the novel extract category of the Pikihuia Awards. She has been published in *Huia Short Stories 11* and *Stories on the Four Winds*, both from Huia Publishers.

JAMES ORMSBY is a recognised national artist, with over 20 years of Visual Art practice in New Zealand and overseas, including 20 solo shows and over 80 group exhibitions. He has received two major Creative NZ Grants for practice-based research at the University of Oxford, and resulting exhibitions in London, Melbourne and Auckland. Drawing is his passion; he describes it as his first language in an era when artists are increasingly experimenting with new technology. He carries out a huge amount of historical research and questions the significance of the visual symbols his ancestors chose to depict. Ormsby lives and works from his family home in the Bay of Plenty.

CERISSE PALALAGI is of Niuean (Tuapa) and Māori (Ngati Pikiao) descent. Born in 1977, Cerisse lives in Brisbane, Australia. She works predominantly in the mediums of printmaking, painting and photography. Palalagi's interests are diverse, often contemplating the interconnected mix of Poly-slang, youth culture and identity. Palalagi's work is characterised by an impressive mastery of a wide array of print- and mark-making processes, such as silkscreen print, painting, drawing and photography. Her art merges hiapo practices with contemporary printing and portraiture. The works respond to Palalagi's experience of current social trends and developments in Pacific cultures and community. 'The patterns I use are a reflection of my identity. I like the juxtaposition of cultural symbols and people in my portraits. They are usually of people in my family, including myself. This is my way of celebrating my culture and ancestry, showing people that our culture, arts and language are not dead.'

FIONA PARDINGTON is of Scottish (Clan Cameron of Erracht) and Māori (Kāi Tahu, Kāti Māmoe, Ngāti Kahungunu) descent. Her work is held in major public collections in Aotearoa New Zealand and abroad, including Musée du Quai Branly, Paris and the National Gallery of Canada, Ottawa. Pardington has exhibited widely throughout Australasia and beyond, including the 17th Biennale of Sydney (2010) and the Ukraine Biennale (2012), and is looking forward to launching her latest project, *Nabokov's Blues: The Charmed Circle 2017*, at the inaugural Honolulu Biennial curated by Fumio Nanjo, March (2017). She has been awarded a Doctor of Fine Arts by the University of Auckland and has received many fellowships, residencies, awards and grants including the Moet & Chandon Fellowship, France (1991-92), the Frances Hodgkins Fellow (1996 and 1997), the Ngai Tahu residency at Otago Polytechnic (2006) and both a Quai Branly Laureate award; La Residence de Photoquai and the Arts Foundation Laureate Award (2011). She is represented by Starkwhite, Auckland.

MICHAEL PULELOA, PhD, was born on Majuro in the Marshall Islands and raised on Moloka'i and O'ahu in Hawai'i. He is currently an English teacher at Kamehameha Schools in Kapālama. His most recent publications appear in *Huihui: Rhetorics and Aesthetics of the Pacific* and *Hawai'i Review* 79. His story 'The Laynetters' is in the 'Guahan and Hawai'i: Literature and Social Movements' issue of *XCP: Cross Cultural Poetics*. His story 'Flight:1880' is in the early stages of becoming an animated short film.

RAYLENE RAMSAY is a world-renowned specialist of French Pacific literature. Ramsay and Walker-Morrison, who have both lived and worked in New Caledonia, have produced a multi-media literary history of the country (*Nights of Story-telling: A Cultural History of Kanaky-New Caledonia/La nuit des contes*, University of Hawaii Press, 2011) and translated Gorodé's poetry (*Sharing as Custom Provides*, Pandanus, 2005) and novel (*The Wreck*, Little Island, 2011).

ROSANNA RAYMOND aka Sistar S'pacific, is an innovator of the contemporary Pasifika art scene as a long-standing member of the art collective the Pacific Sisters, and founding member of the SaVAge K'lub. Raymond has achieved international renown for her performances, installations, body adornment, and spoken word. A published writer and poet, her works are held by museums and private collectors throughout the UK, USA, Canada, Australia and New Zealand. A dynamic artist, her work is consistent in its celebration of Mana Moana and the engagements it invokes and evokes; whether between museum collections and contemporary Pacific art or museums and urban spaces.

LISA REIHANA (Ngāpuhi and Ngātihine Ngāitū) has contributed powerfully to the development of time-based art in Aotearoa New Zealand. Spanning film, video, photography, installation, performance, design, costume and sculptural form, Reihana's art making is driven by a strong sense of community, which informs her collaborative working method. Through technically advanced and poetically nuanced works, her practice offers an astute disruption of the colonial impulse. Reihana's commissions include a new single-channel video *Tai Whetuki — House of Death* for Auckland Arts Festival 2015, a major public art project for the Victoria Park Tunnel, 2010; *Rangimarie Last Dance* for Q Theatre, 2011; *Mai i te aroha, ko te aroha* — the ceremonial female entrance to Museum of New Zealand Te Papa Tongarewa's marae, 2008. Reihana's work has featured in many significant international exhibitions including, most recently, *Suspended Histories*, Museum van Loon, Amsterdam (2013); *ImagineNATIVE* Film + Media Arts Festival, Toronto (2014). In 2017 she is New Zealand's artist at the prestigious Venice Biennale with *Emissaries*, her panoramic video expanded from *in Pursuit of Venus* and *in Pursuit of Venus [infected]* and augmented with a series of new photographic works. Curated by Rhana Devenport, *Emissaries* is a moving image interpretation of the neo-classical French scenic wallpaper *Les Sauvages de la Mer Pacifique*. Witi Ihimaera was invited to create a fictional work for the accompanying book to the exhibition, and 'Whakapapa of a Wallpaper' is the first draft of his story. It is reprinted here with the kind permission of the artist, Rhana Devenport and the Auckland City Art Gallery. Reihana was made an Arts Laureate by the New Zealand Arts Foundation in 2014.

VICTOR RODGER is a writer of Samoan and Scottish descent. His first play, *Sons*, debuted to critical acclaim in 1995. His most successful play, *Black Faggot*, has toured throughout New Zealand and Australia and had a successful season at the Edinburgh Fringe Festival in 2014. He is currently developing *Black Faggot* for film. A former writer for *Shortland Street*, this year he co-wrote the TV series *This is Piki* with Briar Grace Smith. 'Like Shinderella' was written while he was the Robert Burns Fellow 2016 at the University of Otago.

MARY ROKONADRAVU is a Fijian writer of mixed heritage. English is her third language. She won the 2015 Commonwealth Short Story Prize for the Pacific Region for her story 'Famished Eels', which is part of this anthology. Mary works in the areas of culture, heritage and arts in Fiji and the Pacific.

PATI SOLOMONA TYRELL is an interdisciplinary visual artist with a strong focus on performance. Utilising lens-based media, he creates visual outcomes that are centred around ideas of urban Pacific queer identity. He has shown work at Fresh Gallery Otara, PAH Homestead and most recently at the Pingyao International Photography Festival in China. Tyrell is a co-founder of the arts collective FAFSWAG. Currently he is a third year student enrolled in the Bachelor of Creative Arts at Manukau Institute of Technology, Otara. Pati is originally from Kirikiriroa, Waikato but is now based in Maungarei, Tāmaki Makaurau.

DEBORAH WALKER-MORRISON is Associate Professor of French at the University of Auckland, Aotearoa New Zealand. Of mixed European and Māori descent, her iwi affiliations are to the Raakai Paaka and Pahauwera hapu of Ngāti Kahungunu. Her interests include the translation of French-Pacific literature and sub-titling of Māori cinema. Walker-Morrison has produced and directed (with husband Neil Morrison) a documentary, narrated by Witi Ihimaera: *Déwé Gorodé, Writing The Country/Écrire le pays*, 2015.

MAUALAIVAO ALBERT WENDT is regarded internationally as one of Samoa's, New Zealand's, and the Pacific's most influential novelists and poets. His novels include *Leaves of the Banyan Tree*, *Ola*, *The Mango's Kiss*, *The Adventures of Vela* and *Breaking Connections*. His books of poetry include *Inside Us the Dead*, *Shaman of Visions*, *The Book of the Black Star*, and *From Manoa to a Ponsonby Garden*. He lives with his partner Reina Whaitiri in Ponsonby, Auckland, and continues to write and paint full-time.

ALEXIS WRIGHT is an activist and writer from the Waanyi nation of the Gulf of Carpentaria. Her debut novel, *Plains of Promise* (UQP Black Australian Writers), was published in 1997 and was nominated for several major literary awards, including the Commonwealth Prize. Her second novel, *Carpentaria* (Giramondo Publishing, 2006), won the Australian Literature Society Gold Medal, the Miles Franklin Literary Award in 2007, the 2007 Fiction Book Award in the Queensland Premier's Literary Awards, and the Victorian Premier's Prize for Fiction. Her latest novel, *Praiseworthy*, will be published in 2017.

CREDITS

'After the Tsunami', Serie Barford, first published in *Writing the Pacific: an anthology*, the Pacific Writing Forum, 2007, edited by Jen Webb and Kavita Nandan

'Black Ice', Gina Cole, first published in *Black Ice Matter*, Huia Publishers, 2016

Extract from *Freelove*, Sia Figiel, first published by Loihi Press, 2016

'Tribe My Nation', Déwé Gorodé, first published in *The Wreck*, Little Island Press, 2011, translated by Deborah Walker-Morrison and Raylene Ramsay

'The Vanua is Fo'ohake', Jione Havea, first published in *Writing the Pacific: an anthology*, the Pacific Writing Forum, 2007, edited by Jen Webb and Kavita Nandan

'my father dream new zealand', Witi Ihimaera, first published in an earlier version as 'when the door opens', *New Zealand Listener*, 17 December 2015

'White Elephant', Kelly Joseph, first published in *takahē 74*, Summer 2011

'Rush' and 'Facebook Redux', Nic Low, first published in *Arms Race*, Text Publishing, 2014

'Black Milk', Tina Makereti, first published in *Granta*, 2016

'Pouliuli: A Story of Darkness in 13 Lines', Selina Tusitala Marsh, poems are formed from *Pouliuli*, Albert Wendt, University of Hawaii Press, 1977

'The Coconut King', Courtney Sina Meredith, first published in *Tail of the Taniwha*, Beatnik Publishing, 2017

Versions of 'Great Long Story', Paula Morris, have appeared in *Ora Nui*, Anton Blank Ltd, 2012 and *Gutter*, Freight Press, 2011

'King of Bones and Hazy Homes' (extract from 'Average Kids and Bigots'), Anya Ngawhare, first published in *Huia Short Stories 11: Contemporary Māori Fiction*, Huia Publishers, 2015

Uncanny Tui/Kakahu, Fiona Pardington, from the collection of the Whanganui Museum, courtesy of the artist and Starkwhite

'Like Shinderella', Victor Rodger, first published as 'Skip to the End' in *Landfall 231*, Autumn 2016

'Sepia', Mary Rokonadravu, first published in *Writing the Pacific: an anthology*, the Pacific Writing Forum, 2007, edited by Jen Webb and Kavita Nandan

'Famished Eels', Mary Rokonadravu, first published in *Granta*, 2015

'Whale Bone City', Alexis Wright, first published in *Carpentaria*, Giramondo Publishing, 2006

'Nafanua Unleashes', Albert Wendt, first published in *The Adventures of Vela*, Huia Publishers, 2009

ACKNOWLEDGEMENTS

The editors wish to thank all the incredible writers and artists who contributed to this anthology. You are the new Oceania.

Many thanks also to Harriet Allan, Abby Aitcheson and the team at Penguin Random House New Zealand for enthusiastic support and meticulous publishing. Thank you to the International Institute of Modern Letters for providing office space for an editorial meeting — it is key that creative writing schools in Aotearoa continue to seek new ways to support Māori and Pasifika writing. Gratitude to the Commonwealth Foundation for the Commonwealth Short Story Prize, which continues to give our writers the opportunity to write on a world stage. Ngā mihi nui to all our colleagues and friends who have offered support and advice. The Auckland City Art Gallery and Trustees gave permission for 'Whakapapa of a Wallpaper' and the Lisa Reihana image that goes with the story, coincident with Reihana's appearance at the Venice Biennale, 2017.

Our thanks also to Rhana Devenport, Rose Dunn, Anita Heiss, Christine Jeffery, Cath Koa, Brandy Nālani McDougall, Craig Santos Perez, Deborah Walker-Morrison and all who submitted work.

WITI WISHES TO THANK: Jane Smiler, Jessica Ihimaera-Pritchard, Olivia Ihimaera-Dawkins and the mokopuna for always keeping me real. A special mihi to Tina Makereti — you done good.

TINA WISHES TO THANK: Witi Ihimaera, for issuing the invitation; Lawrence Patchett, for always listening, and Kōtuku Underwood and Aquila Underwood — the future.